SLOW BURN

A DRIVEN NOVEL

K. Bromberg

A SIGNET ECLIPSE BOOK

SIGNET ECLIPSE
Published by the Penguin Group
Penguin Group (USA) LLC, 375 Hudson Street,
New York, New York 10014

USA | Canada | UK | Ireland | Australia | New Zealand | India | South Africa | China
penguin.com
A Penguin Random House Company

First published by Signet Eclipse, an imprint of New American Library,
a division of Penguin Group (USA) LLC

First Printing, March 2015

ISBN 978-0-451-47392-9

Printed in the United States of America
10   9   8   7   6   5   4   3   2   1

Chapter 1

My sensations are dulled by the alcohol. And I am *so* okay with that. Okay that I've had enough to drink so that for the first time in six months, the ache that hits me with the memories isn't as sharp.

I look around and try to focus on everything—the abundant flowers, the welcome chill from the ocean breeze, the pair of high heels abandoned in the corner—but all I can think about is how beautiful and happy Rylee was tonight. And my mind keeps recalling what my sister, Lexi, looked like on her wedding day. The words she said to me, her laugh ringing out above the guests as Danny made his toast to her, the smile on her face as the future stretched ahead of them.

Stop it, Had. Don't ruin a perfect night. You deserve to celebrate your best friend's wedding without feeling guilty.

But I can't stop thinking about that other wedding, although the details are starting to fade in my mind. And I so badly want to remember every little detail about her. I need to be able to tell my niece, Madelyn, about how her mom loved to stand in the rain because she wanted to catch it on her tongue, how she ate pizza backward because the crust was her favorite part, how she loved to face the opposite way on the swings so we could give each other high fives. There are so many things I fear I'll forget.

And so many other memories from the past year that I wish I could.

"We'll be back in the morning, miss, to pick up the tables and chairs and the lot."

The caterer's voice pulls me from my melancholy thoughts—thoughts that don't belong after the sheer beauty of today's wedding. I turn to look at him, words choking in my throat.

"Not a problem." Becks's voice startles me. I didn't realize he was out here on the deck, but I'm so glad he answers because, between the alcohol and the memories, I'm in no shape to respond coherently. "The housekeeper, Grace, will be here at ten to let you in."

I finish the rest of my drink as the caterer thanks Becks. Then I turn around on unsteady legs to face him as he steps out of the night's shadows into the light of the full moon. And it must be a mixture of the heady emotions of the day and my lack of sobriety, but my breath catches when I meet his eyes.

It's just Becks, boy-next-door handsome as usual . . . dirty blond hair spiked up at the ends, aqua blue eyes so light the night makes them seem transparent . . . so why in the hell are parts of my body suddenly on alert?

I dart my tongue out to my tingling lips as he leans a broad shoulder against the post of the trellis and stares at me, head angled to the side, shirt unbuttoned at the collar, and bow tie hanging loosely around his neck. I hear the ice in his glass clink as he shifts to set it on the table beside him, but his eyes hold steadfast to mine.

"You okay?" That slow, even drawl of his breaks the silence. I nod my head, still not trusting my voice, still trying to figure out why all of a sudden there is this tension between us—this electric energy—that has never been there before. Sure we've flirted harmlessly since we met through our best friends, Rylee and Colton, but this is different. And I can't quite put my finger on what's changed, not sure if I even want to.

Maybe it's the fact that right now, face shaded with darkness, he looks a little dangerous, a little mysterious, a lot more the bad-boy type I usually fall for. He's always struck me as more of a good guy, a down-home country type. But somehow the mixture of moonlight and night shadows brings out another side of him I've never envisioned; he looks edgier, more the wilder type I waste my time on, get my heart broken by, have a hard time resisting. That has to be why I'm feeling a sudden attraction.

So if I know the reason, why is my drunk mind still wondering what he'd taste like? What his hands would feel like as they run up my inner thighs? How the slow, even tone of his voice would sound as he loses control?

The silence sparks between us, only interrupted by the distant roll of ocean waves. I draw in a breath and shake my head again. "I'm okay," I say, and laugh, trying to avoid the questions I don't want to answer. "Just drunk and enjoying the feeling."

"*Feeling* is most definitely a good thing," he says, straightening up his tall, athletic frame and taking a step toward me, "but, City, I think it's best if I get you to bed before it starts to not be a good feeling."

I smile softly at his use of the term of endearment. He gave me the nickname City the first night we met in Las Vegas, back before my life had been torn apart by Lexi's death. It feels like a lifetime ago when in reality it has only been a year since the unexpected overnight trip with Rylee and Colton to the city of sin where the two of us flirted, first acknowledged the attraction we felt but have never acted on. . . . I close my eyes and remember the carefree feeling I had that night. I'd called him *Country* to tease him about that laid back demeanor of his, so opposite from everything I usually find appealing. And yet as he sat there in the Las

Vegas nightclub, the club's lights flashing over his face while he called me *City* in return, I caught myself wondering just what Beckett Daniels would kiss like.

The question floats through my mind again. *Forget about it, Montgomery,* I tell myself as I go to place my hand on the railing at my back and miss by a mile, causing him to chuckle, low and soft.

Chills light a path over my skin, and I can't help the giggle that falls from my lips as my mind wanders to other things I'd rather be feeling right now. Other distractions I could use to shake the bittersweet emotions weighing me down.

Christ on a crutch! Why didn't I think of it earlier? Going to bed — especially someone else's — is most definitely a good idea.

That'll fix it. Always has, these past six months. I'll just go grab my keys and my cell, call Dylan or Pete and let them know I'm on my way over. I'll let whoever is the first to answer know that I'm feeling a little *sexually festive* tonight. I'll use one of them to try to forget; feel a little less, by feeling a whole lot more.

"Something funny?"

I cover my mouth with my hand but can't stop myself from snickering. "Just feeling a little festive, is all." And the giggle returns as I think of Lex and how she used to say that women are not sluts, just sexually festive. And tonight? God, tonight I just want to be that. I don't want to think. I don't want to care. I just want to escape a bit from my thoughts.

"Festive, huh?" he asks, eyes appraising me and full mouth tugging up at one corner.

"Yep!" I nod my head. "Time for this girl to carry this party to another location, Country." I start to walk — well, stumble. *Shit!* How the hell am I going to drive? I keep walking, hand running across the wall to help steady myself.

"Nice try, Haddie. Did you forget that the limo brought you here? I have to drive you home."

Crap! I try not to falter. "Well, I guess I'm taking your car, then," I say as I keep walking away from him.

"That's funny, but, uh, you're in no shape to drive." His voice calls out to me, and the amusement in it pisses me off. "You're not going anywhere, festivities or not."

"Like hell I am." I toss over my shoulder and keep walking toward the house. Just leave me alone, I yell in my head. Don't go all alpha on me now when all I want from you is slow and steady because I'm way too drunk and way too needy to see in him what I'm attracted to.

"Try me." The arrogance in his voice sets me off. Pushes me to be bitchy and defiant so that I don't make a huge mistake I don't want to make. Do want to make. Fuck if I can think clearly enough to know what I want, but I do know that Beckett's one of those guys you settle down with . . . and no way in hell do I want to settle down.

Ever.

The hurt comes flooding back, the memories riding shotgun right alongside them. I stop to steady my legs and remind myself not to repeat the mistakes my sister made.

I can hear him behind me, know he's waiting for me to respond. "Neither of us is in any state to drive tonight. *Festivities* are over." I hear his shoes step on something that crunches just behind me, and I squeeze my eyes shut to fight off the whirlwind of shit in my head. "C'mon, Montgomery. It was a perfect day, but I'm taking you to bed."

I snort a laugh because even though his comment is innocent in nature since we both told Rylee we'd stay the night to oversee all of the postreception cleanup, Becks just hit the nail on the head. To bed is exactly where I want him to take me right now, *his in particular*. Wait! No, I don't want that. Goddamn alcohol is making me wishy-washy. I hate wishy-washy.

He says my name again, and something in the way he says it causes my feet to falter. We stand there, my back to him, in a silent standoff. I don't move, don't turn around to face him, because I just want to run. Rewind time and get *me* back again. The carefree, careless me who has been drowning in grief these past few months.

His hand closes over my biceps, and I don't know why I'm so angry at him, but I am. I don't want to be touched gently. I don't want to be coddled. I just want to leave so I can escape the memories today dredged up from deep within me, reopening the wounds I don't think will ever heal.

I turn around, trying to shrug out of his grasp, but the movement makes me wobble on my heels. "Whoa!" I hear him say as one of my ankles gives out and I fall into him. His back is pressed against the wall, and I land solidly against him.

It's not as if I haven't been in this position with him tonight already. We danced so many times earlier during the reception, so why is it that this time, when my breasts rub against the firmness of his chest, the fight leaves me? The need fills me? I don't even want to think about it, but it's all I can focus on when our bodies touch from chest to thigh. It's all my mind can grasp, because when I look up at him from beneath my lashes, my eyes catch sight of that magnificent mouth of his.

Maybe it's the alcohol. Maybe it's the sentimental aftermath of watching two people who really belong together get married. Maybe it's because I felt closer to Lexi today than I have in a long while. I don't know. What I do know is that I don't give a fuck about mistakes or consequences. *I just need to feel*. Need to lose myself. And shit, it's just Becks after all.

I don't meet his eyes. Don't want to know whether he wants this, because I do. I lean forward and press my lips to his, not giving him any time to react because damn if his lips aren't the perfect combination of firm and soft. His body tenses as mine softens into him, and I slide my hands up his chest at the same time my tongue slips between his lips. I moan softly at the warmth of his mouth, the taste of the rum on his tongue, the feel of his breath catching. His strong palms slide slowly up my bare arms as we sink further into the kiss, when all of a sudden his fingers dig into my shoulders and he's pushing me away. A shocked gasp falls from both of our mouths when our connection is broken.

"Haddie." His voice is pained as he says my name, a contradictory plea and curse at the same time.

And my mind may be a little fuzzy and my body coiled so tight from his kiss, but that break in his voice tells me he more than enjoyed it. That he wants me just as badly as I want him.

I force myself to look up, meet the clouded shock in his eyes. "What? Don't you want me, Becks?"

I feel his fingers tense on my shoulders, hear a strained chuckle deep in his throat. "Oh, there's a whole lot of want here," he says before closing his eyes momentarily. He works a swallow in his throat and then pushes me away. "I'm just trying to play it safe, Had."

His rejection stings—the alcohol softening the blow—but I feel the hesitancy in his fingers before he removes them from my shoulders. And with desire coursing through me, lust fueling its fire, I use my need to forget as the match to light the flame.

I step into him, slide my hands up his crisp white shirt, and meet his eyes. "C'mon, how much safer can we be? I'm with you, aren't I? You're not going to hurt me . . . are you, Becks?" I may have drunk a lot tonight, but I know desire when I see it, and damn if it doesn't look sexy on Becks.

His jaw clenches, head tilts ever so slightly to the side, and his body tenses as he stares at me through the moonlit night.

"Isn't it normal for the best man and the maid of honor to hook up, anyway?"

"Haddie." My name is a drawn-out sigh, and I can hear his frustration laced with desire. I can feel the heat of his breath hit my lips.

The way he says my name causes the fire within me to rage because now I know the answer to my question: how he sounds when he loses control. And if he thought he was going to push me away after hearing that, he's got another think coming.

"No one wants to play it safe tonight. . . . Live a little," I tell him, reaching out and running a fingernail up the hollow of his neck where his shirt is unbuttoned. I lean in closer and whisper, "Please, help me live a little."

"Oh, I believe you live a whole lot." He chuckles with a subtle shake of his head, but those blue eyes of his remain locked on mine, a war of unexpressed emotions between us. "That's what I love about you."

My need to have him escalates with his nonchalance. And fuck, *this is frustrating*. Can't a girl just get laid here? I'm not used to having to convince guys to get what I want, so why in the hell is this so difficult?

"I didn't say shit about love, Country." I say the words playfully but taste his rejection on my lips. "I don't need strings. I just need you to make me feel . . . help me lose myself for a bit."

He leans his head forward so that we are eye to eye, his hands coming up to frame my face so that I can see the concern and unwanted desire dancing in them. "I didn't know you wanted to be lost."

"We all need to lose ourselves sometimes, don't we?" My question hangs in the still of the night as his eyes search mine for answers I won't give.

He shakes his head, and I can tell he's trying to convince himself to step away. "I don't want to complicate things," he says with a clenched jaw as he lowers his hands slowly from my face and stands back. Physically distancing himself to emphasize his words, but they contradict the look in his eyes.

"No complications. I told you, Becks," I say, trying to keep the desperation I suddenly feel from my voice, "no strings, just sex. A little release after this incredible day. C'mon, what guy would pass up that chance?"

He groans. "A guy who's trying *really hard* to do the right thing here and play it safe." He steps forward, and I think I've gotten to him. He places an arm around my shoulder and starts steering me into the house. "C'mon, *festive Haddie*, I'm gonna help you to your room."

"You're a buzz kill, Becks," I whine like a petulant child, nearly stomping my four-inch heels.

"And you're a lot drunk like me," he says into the crown of my head, followed by a chaste kiss. "Hell, if I don't want you, Had ... hell, if I don't doubt that sex with you would be incredible, but fuck, I don't want to do anything we'd regret in the morning because we're drunk. Don't want there to be awkwardness every time we hang out together. And goddamm it if you're not making it hard to do the respectable thing and walk away." The heat of his breath on my scalp sends chills down my spine.

"Aha!" I shout out, feeling like my feet are a bit more steady, now that I know he's not really rejecting me, but being the *good guy* I pegged him to be. "You do want me!"

He stops immediately and looks down at me as if I'm crazy, brow furrowed, eyes wide. He starts to say something and then stops and shakes his head, before sighing and starting to move again. I turn into his body so that I can look up at him as he steers us through the house to our respective rooms. I take in his strong jaw and tanned skin and wonder what he would taste like as I run my tongue up the line of his neck. The ache of sensations that at this point I can only imagine spiral through me, make me even more determined than ever to prove to Becks that I need this, need him, tonight, and that we can do this without complications.

Shit, every man needs a push now and again. . . . Guess I'd better start pushing.

He stops walking and raises his eyebrows with a lift of his chin toward the open door to my room. *It's now or never, Had.* I press against him, the hum of my desire igniting instantly. "Please, Becks?" I lower the pitch of my voice even though it's just the two of us. "All of the romance and nostalgia of tonight didn't get to you? Didn't make you need the comfort of a woman? Want to hear her moan, bury yourself in her, feel her heat?"

My God, my own damn words are turning me on. My attempt at seducing Becks is making my own need undeniable. I lean up and bring my lips to his ear. "Comfort me, Becks."

"You're making it so damn hard to be good." He says it like a curse, and when I step back, his body instinctively moves forward. His reaction causes a part of the old me to spark to life, and I grab onto it. I hold it tight as I push the sappy, needy, emotional Haddie away. And I welcome the forward, balls-to-the-wall attitude that's been drowned by my grief.

And God, it feels good, slipping back into her shoes, even if for just a bit.

"Hard. Hm," I hum deep in my throat, "now, there's a good word."

I step backward into the room, my eyes still trained on him as he stands in the doorframe, hands gripping the sides. I know I've won him over, know it'll just take my next move to get what I've been working toward. What I desperately need.

And as I stare at him so handsomely framed in the doorway, I wonder fleetingly what it is about this moment that has made me feel normal again. Allowed me to shed the guilt that's burdened me and taken my carefree attitude with it. I push the civil war of thoughts that's been a constant refrain as of late from my head. I don't allow myself to think any more about it, because all I want to do is feel.

With our eyes locked, I pull down the zipper of my dress. "Hey, Becks?" His eyes widen at the coy tone to my voice. The dress falls and pools around my feet. "Fuck playing it safe."

Chapter 2

Beckett stares at me for a beat—jaw clenched, eyes locked on mine, body tense—before his restraint crumbles. As buzzed as I am, I notice that as he walks toward me his eyes never leave my face. They don't wander to take in what I'm handing over to him—my body, the lace hugging my curves, and all of its temptation. They stay steadfast on mine, desire brimming and disbelief warring inside them.

But when he reaches me—when his hands flash out to pull my body into his, one hand on the nape of my neck, the other pressed against my back—my thoughts are lost as my need surges. His lips find mine in a frenzy of lust. Lips mesh, tongues lick, teeth nip.

Desire unfurls and breaks its way through the haze of alcohol. His hands map the lines of my body, fingers dipping beneath the lace of my bra to tempt and touch but not to take, not just yet. Soft moans turn into urgent murmurs of *hurry*, *quickly*, *I want*, and *I need*.

I'm desperate to feel the heat of his chest against mine, skin to skin—the initial connection that will sate the frenzy until I can expose the rest of his flesh. His lips and tongue continue their pleasurable assault on my lips, distracting me thoroughly from the task at hand, getting him naked.

I can't help but giggle as I drag my mouth from his to draw in the air he's knocked out of me, and to get my fingers to unfasten instead of grip his shirt. I laugh again as I try to concentrate on the little buttons that don't want to slip through the tiny holes.

His chuckle is deep and strained, and I can feel its vibrations against my fingers. "Let me," he says, my eyes flicking up to his, but not before I catch the amused smirk curling up the corner of his mouth. His hands close over mine and tug apart the shirt. The sound of buttons hitting and scattering over the hardwood floor is the only other noise filling the room besides our labored breaths.

His eyes darken and cloud, and then his lips are on mine. I run my hands up the toned plane of his chest while he pulls his arms from his shirt. My nails scrape and his breath hisses as he brings a hand up to fist in my hair and pull my chin up so that he can work his mouth along the line of my jaw and across the curve of my neck.

"Sweet Haddie," he murmurs as his hand finds my breast and yanks down the cup of my bra, his callused palms replacing the softness of the lace. I gasp out loud as his mouth slides in its tempestuous descent. "Sweet, sweet Haddie . . . I wonder if your pussy tastes just as sweet as your kiss . . . as your skin . . . as right here."

The heat of his mouth replaces the caress of his fingers on my breast, and I'm swamped by the sensation of it. Of him. My head falls back, and my words tumble out. "What are you waiting for?"

That chuckle of his hums against my breast before he tilts his head back and looks up at me under lust-laden eyelids. "Demanding, are we?" His eyes dance with humor before the dare flickers through them. *Try me*, they say.

And a part of me wants to. A part of me wants to push him to see just how much control he's willing to give me. Is he going to do what I say, or will he do what he wants?

Challenge accepted.

"Then taste me, Becks. I want to feel your mouth on me, your tongue in me. I want you to taste me on your lips as I'm still coming and while you're fucking me."

He sucks harder on my nipple; a tortured groan escapes his lips as he rises to his full height and stares at me. "Fucking hell, Had," he says before his lips brand mine, his mouth possessing, taking, claiming as if I were his. "Are you trying to tell me how to fuck you?"

I feel the heat of his breath on my lips, see the taunt in his smirk and the raise of a brow, but I can't think of the witty comeback I know is there. His hands slide down my torso and grip my bare waist, causing my breath to stutter as he yanks my body into his. His impressive hard-on presses against my lower belly, causing the ache simmering there to intensify.

Becks leans in close, his lips grazing my ear in a move that causes chills to chase over my skin. "Rest assured, Haddie, I know how to fuck you. I know how to make you come." His teeth tug on my earlobe to reinforce his words. "I know how to make this hot-as-fuck body of yours tremble, tense, and beg for more . . . so lie back, and let me taste you."

And just when I think my body can't coil any tighter from desire, from the explicitness of his words and the taste of his tongue on mine, he picks me up at the waist and throws me back on the bed. I giggle as I hit the mattress, the air escaping from my lungs, and before I can take a breath, Beckett's on me. I try to wriggle away—try to flip over as we both laugh in our alcohol-infused state—but I'm no match for him.

"Sweet Haddie," he taunts as his arms pin my wrists to the bed on either side of my head. He leans down and teases my lips, tracing my bottom one with his tongue before slipping it into my mouth, his erection pressing exactly where I want it to be. I wriggle my hips; patience is so not my virtue. He pulls away and sits on his knees, between my thighs. My eyes scrape down the defined lines of his torso—a torso that I've seen so many times before—but tonight, with him sitting in front of me like this, holy hell, do I realize I've never taken the time to appreciate just how hot he really is.

I work a swallow down my throat as he angles his head to the side and stares at me for a beat. I'm so entranced by the unsated need pooling moisture between my thighs that when I feel his fingers trail up the outside of my panties, I gasp. "The question is," he asks with an arch of his brow as he leans down, "how many times can I make you come?"

And with those words, his hands press my thighs down, and his mouth closes over the fabric covering my clit. The warm heat of his mouth causes me to grip the comforter beneath me. The seduction of his words already has me craving his touch, and now the silk barrier between his tongue and my flesh drives me insane. Giving me and not giving me what I want all at the same time.

"Becks" is all I can manage as I throw my head back, close my eyes, and allow myself to absorb the pleasure. Fingertips trail up the inside of my thighs, and I can feel the cool air on my heated flesh as he uses a finger to pull my thong to the side. And when his mouth makes contact this time, I cry out as the liquid heat flows through me, my arms and legs tensing.

"God, you taste good," he says, his voice hitting my ears as I'm being pulled under a tidal wave of sensation. His tongue continues to lick while I feel his fingers spread my flesh apart so he can slide inside me. He moves them so subtly, but whatever he's doing has me moaning instantly when they find the spot that sets my nerve endings ablaze.

He continues his tantalizing barrage on my senses, rubbing and laving with just the right amount of friction to cause the wave of sensation to rise up and crash all around me in a flurry of breath-stealing ripples. His name falls from my lips, over and over, as I ride out my climax, his mouth still buried between my thighs, licking his way into me until the sensation is almost too much to bear.

My eyes are shut tight, the room spinning from the heady rush of desire, and I feel him slide his way up my body. Then his mouth is on mine again, tongue delving between my parted lips. "Can you taste how sweet you are? Can you taste what I just did to you?"

My response is an incoherent moan as he moves his knees to either side of my hips. He brings his hands up to cradle my head and control the depth and angle of his kiss, holding nothing back until I am left breathless from the intensity when he pulls away and looks in my eyes.

"That's one . . . ," he teases, his voice trailing off as I reach out to his waist. He sits with such a delicious weight on my lower belly and I start to undo his trousers. My body may still be pulsing from my orgasm but I want more.

Becks hisses as my hands slide between his boxer briefs and his heated skin, gripping onto his erection and pulling it free. I slide my hand up and down, my thumb rubbing the drop of moisture at the tip around his length. He angles his head up to the ceiling and emits a groan of satisfaction that leaves my core tingling for more.

"One, huh?" I tease, trying to keep this playful because fuck if his mouth alone isn't worth coming back for seconds. I take his length in my palm and slide back down him, enjoying watching his abs tense. "Please, tell me you'll keep your promises because I need to come more than once," I tell him, delighted at how he's pushed away my thoughts from earlier. "And, Becks, you've had more to drink than me, so please tell me you won't suffer from a case of whiskey dick right now."

His head snaps forward, and his eyes hold mine, that chuckle falling from his mouth again. He shakes his head as he closes his hand over mine on his cock and says, "Demanding, are we? Is that not hard enough for you?"

I fight my smirk, because if he's going to throw out promises, he sure as fuck had better keep them. "It's hard all right, but I just wanted to make sure it stays that way."

"I believe you're insulting me," he says, running our joined hands up and down again, eyes closing momentarily from the sensation.

"It's not an insult if it's true."

He continues to stare at me, and within a beat, he's off the bed. I push myself up on my elbows, trying to see what in the hell he's doing. *Please, tell me he didn't get offended by that comment.* If he did, he can just keep on walking, regardless of his magical tongue. I don't need a man who gets his feelings hurt by a little teasing.

But then again, his tongue is *pretty* fantast-orgasmic.

A small part of me sighs in relief when Beckett stands still with his back to me and doesn't walk to the door. The other part of me frets that if he stays, he just might be the completely unexpected but perfect combination of naughty and nice that has the ability to make me go back on the promises I made to myself. Promises about what I will or won't do in the long term. *No strings, Haddie.* No ties, I remind myself.

And then any rational thinking I've been doing is vaporized when Becks drops his pants and turns around. I know his eyes are on me, but mine are focused on him and his condom-covered erection. The alcohol has most definitely not affected him. I tear my eyes away from the impressive sight and take in the whole package as he walks toward the bed in a predatory, purposeful manner. His eyes are filled with a combination of amusement and lust, and his body signals that I'm his for the taking: shoulders broad, gait confident, and smirk goading me to tell him otherwise.

He reaches the edge of the bed and, without comment, grabs my calves and pulls me toward him so that his hips are nestled perfectly between my thighs, which are hanging off the bed in his hands. He reaches down to slowly slide off my thong and then steps back to pull it over my heeled feet and tosses it carelessly over his shoulder. I am more than turned on by watching his eyes take in every inch of my body, completely unashamed as he watches his fingers play over my sex and run their way up and down my seam. His breath stutters, his nostrils flare, and his lips fall lax as his eyes observe his finger slide slowly in and then back out.

We both gasp, me from the sensation and him from the sight. His fingers rub and slide in a slow, even rhythm that has my already sensitized flesh on high alert. A moan falls from my lips as my body starts to heat up and Beckett's eyes flash up to meet mine. His tongue darts out and licks his lower lip as his fingers withdraw, but keep me open as he lines himself up with my entrance.

His eyes hold mine when he slowly enters me, every thick inch of him, filling, stretching, engaging every single nerve within me. He seats himself fully root to tip; his jaw clenches in restraint, and his eyes darken with desire as it takes everything I have not to roll mine into the back of my head at the sublime feeling. I want to watch him. Want to stare into those eyes and take in his incredible body as he works mine into a fever pitch.

I clench my muscles around him, silently telling him I'm ready for what's to come when he surprises me by leaning over and kissing me. A slow, hypnotizing dance of tongues as his cock presses even farther into me until I don't think I can take it anymore. My body surrenders, and just when my head starts to fill with so many thoughts of how this unexpected action is tying the strings we're not supposed to have, he leans back, face inches from mine, and smirks. "Is that hard enough for you?"

I focus on that arrogant grin instead of the thoughts in my head, and release a soft groan when he withdraws a fraction as he stands up. He holds still, eyes locked on mine and he pulls out ever so slowly until just the tip of him is inside of me. "Well, is it?"

God, yes, it is. God, yes, I want him pounding into me,

driving me to the oblivion just beyond the horizon. I open my legs wider and reach my hands up to squeeze my own breasts. My muscles tighten around him in response to the moment, to the anticipation, in reaction to him withholding what I want the most.

"Fuck me, Becks." It's all I can say, because before his name is out of my mouth, he rears back and thrusts into me, my body rippling with a shock wave of pleasure. His hands grip into the flesh of my thighs as he begins again, each drive in and sensation-inducing withdraw out, allowing me to climb the ladder at a maddening pace.

My pulse pounds and my breath chases after it, on an endless race toward the finish line. My senses feel drugged, overwhelmed, scored with his possession of my body. My muscles tense and chills dance across my flesh, despite the sweat misting it as he drives into me harder and harder. My hands snake down my torso to part myself and allow my fingers to add that little extra friction to push me over the precipice.

I bring my eyes up to his to watch his reaction—to see if he's one of those assholes who think only he's allowed to bring me to climax—and I see his eyes dart down and focus on me pleasuring myself. His fingers dig deeper, his hips pound harder, and the muscles in his shoulders grow tenser.

I cry out as the dynamite detonates within me. An explosion of liquid heat paralyzes my body—legs tense, arms stiff, breath held—as I succumb to my orgasm. And even though my body feels like it's so overloaded I can't possibly take any more, Becks keeps going, keeps raking his head over my walls that are sated with such a pleasurable pain I'm not sure if I want him to stop or keep going to see how much farther he can take me.

"Becks." His name is a broken cry on my lips as my body begins to shake from the force of my climax. He slows down some but adds a grind of his hips as he thrusts into me.

"Hold on, hold on," he moans out before rearing back

and driving into me a few more times. A groan falls from his lips as his head drops back and his hands hold my hips still. I can feel his dick pulse inside of me as he claims his own release, his body rocking subtly as he rides out the feeling. I lay my head back and close my eyes, allowing him a few moments to come down from his high.

I feel him shift, and then I cry out in surprise when his five o'clock shadow scrapes over my abdomen as he kisses his way up the midline of my chest. He stops beneath my jaw for a moment, as he collects his breath before murmuring, "That's two."

"That was most definitely two," I tell him as the deep timbre of his laugh is muffled against my skin. I stop my hands from reaching out and running up and over his back as his weight rests comfortably on me. A touch like that is too much, too intimate when I'm just trying to keep it casual.

We remain like this for a moment, unspoken words replaced by our labored breathing, when all of a sudden Becks starts to move. I assume he is going to slip out of me and go wash up, put an end to our unexpected nightcap, so I'm surprised when he kisses his way back down my neck. He stops and takes one nipple in his mouth while his hand palms the other, both lips and fingers manipulating my tightened buds until I'm writhing again.

He slips out of me and I sigh with audible satisfaction. His mouth starts the slow descent down to the apex of my thighs, and I whip my head up to look at him.

Again?

Holy fuck, he's trying to kill me.

He kisses the top of my sex and looks up at me with a salacious look in his eyes. "I've read a woman comes harder the second or third time," he says. "Be sure to let me know."

He kisses my skin again and chuckles. "Oh, yeah, here comes three."

Chapter 3

My eyelids are closed but it's still so damn bright from the sunlight streaming into the room. I squeeze my eyes tighter to try to block it out, trying to clear the haze from my thoughts. I struggle to remember details from last night. How is it possible that I drank enough I can't remember, but my head isn't pounding like a damn tom drum?

I decide to snuggle farther into the down comforter, not wanting to wake up just yet. Wanting to forgo the headache that will inevitably hit me at full force the minute my body acknowledges it's awake. But the fog starts to dissipate, and my thoughts replay the perfection of yesterday and what an incredible day it was. Smiles and laughter and love. Dancing and drinking and ... oh fuck.

... fuck playing it safe ...

... here comes three ...

The words flicker through my mind and now I'm completely alert and cringe from the sun when my eyes flash open. I blink against the harsh light, and when I can focus, I'm staring straight at Becks. *Oh shit!*

His head is angled to the side on his pillow, the lines of his face relaxed and his hair sticking up every which way. There's a five o'clock shadow where I'm used to seeing his clean-shaven skin, and I vaguely recall the feel of it grazing against my abdomen. My eyes admiringly trace the line of his throat down his chest to that sexy-as-hell infinity zone, which disappears beneath the sheet right where I want to look the most. The sight of him undressed is even more overpowering now that I am completely sober.

I admire the view momentarily and wonder if I pull the sheets a little tighter around me, will they slip far enough off of him to grant me the view I want? I start to slowly draw them toward me when last night comes flooding back to me in full high-definition color.

Whispered words and moaned sighs. The heady combination of playful teasing, unfettered need, and insatiable desire. His adept hands and skillful mouth creating an ache so intense, I felt as if my body was on fire.

I remember how he gave me exactly what I wanted—to feel physically so that I could be numb to emotion. How when I looked into his eyes, I pleaded with him to bring me to the brink, push me into that oblivion of sensation. And when he finally entered me, he was a considerate yet demanding lover who left me breathless, sated, and confused.

My thighs tense, and my core clenches as I recall all of the sensations he evoked in me. I lay my head back down on the pillow and close my eyes to try to push away the desire that's already burning anew.

It was a onetime thing.

Sex without strings.

Exactly how I wanted it.

So why is my mind focusing on what he murmured into the silent room as I lay curled up against him when he thought I'd drifted off to sleep? His sighed words were laced with frustrated confusion. *"Goddamn strings."*

The alcohol-blurred details continue to play behind my closed eyelids like a slide show, and all I keep thinking is: What the fuck was I thinking? But I know I wasn't really thinking at all. I was so busy trying to mask my grief that I selfishly never considered the harm I might do to him in the end.

Fuck. Damn. Shit.

I also can't help but think what a truly good guy he is. This is all my fault—even though my mind is floating with fuzzy bits of our time together, I can still piece together the fact that Becks tried to do the right thing. He tried to put me to bed, let me sleep it off, prevent me from getting behind the wheel.

This is on me. Completely on me. Why couldn't I have followed through with my plan to leave and go screw around with someone who wouldn't have given a shit if I left in the morning without another word? Why last night of all nights did I need to feel something just a little bit more? Was I afraid that the dam I'd built around my heartache might break and maybe, just maybe, I wanted someone around who I knew would take care of me if it did?

And so I used him.

Used a good man who didn't deserve to be used. Guilt eats at me until I force myself to open my eyes again and face Becks. I take in his handsome face and all-American good looks. He's the quintessential good guy—most definitely not my stereotypical go-to tattooed bad boy. I study him for a minute, my eyes drifting back down to where the sheet rests low on his hips . . . because he may not be my type but that doesn't mean I can't admire his hotter-than-hell physique. Soon my mind wanders back to the feel of his muscles bunching beneath my fingers, and I can't help but wonder if I could ever get used to him. To this.

I am so used to thriving on the wild, volatile but fun-as-fuck drama-filled relationships—*well, if you can really call them relationships*—with the rebels in my past.

I can't help my hushed chuckle when the thought hits me: Who would've thought that Ry would have spent the night—shit, married—the reckless bad boy, while I spent it with the Southern gentleman? Talk about switching places. Something was most definitely screwy with the world.

When I look up, I startle as I meet Becks's blue eyes. We stare at each other for a moment as we struggle with the awkwardness and figure out where to go from here. He looks at me from beneath half-closed eyelids and says, "Morning." He yawns softly but never takes his eyes from mine as if he's waiting to gauge my reaction before saying anything else.

"Good morning," I murmur back, my fingers tracing idle lines on the sheet. A slow, sluggish smile turns up one corner of his mouth, and my heart stutters in my chest.

And panic starts closing in on my throat.

I don't want to feel the warmth that just spread throughout my body at that lazy, boyish grin of his. I don't want to feel the contentment I feel right now. And most of all, I don't want to see that look in his eyes that tells me this could be so much more if I let it.

That's what Lexi did.

And look where that left her and Danny. *And Maddie*.

I shake myself from my thoughts and try to swallow the lump of anxiety taking hold. I avert my eyes quickly as I calm my overactive imagination and stop freaking the fuck out. I remind myself that I took my batteries out of my biological clock and put them in my vibrator for a reason.

I can do this. I may not remember all of last night, but I recall telling him that it would be sex without strings. He understood up front what this was. No matter what the fuck last night was, it was just a physical connection between two willing adults. So why am I afraid to look up from my fidgeting fingers and meet his eyes?

"Hey?" The rasp of his voice, laced with concern, pulls at me until I can't stand it anymore. I look up to his eyes. "What are you thinking . . . ?" His voice trails off as I find mine.

I gather the sheet around my chest, "Becks," I say his name with a shy smile on my face, "this is okay." I shake my head for emphasis. "We may have been drunk last night, but, one, I'm never too drunk to not remember and enjoy . . . and boy, did I enjoy." I can't resist adding that last part because, casual or not, the man's got some moves. Number three was definitely more earth shifting than number two. And hell if four wasn't pretty damn good too. My comment causes the lazy smile on his face to spread into a sheepish grin, which instantly has me wanting to melt into him. And I can't. It's not an option, regardless of how much my insides are warmed by the thoughts I refuse to welcome.

"We agreed no strings. No complications," I say, shrugging my shoulders to let him know that I'm more than okay with this. Something flickers in his eyes, and I can't quite get a read on it, so I continue. "I'm not the typical, clingy female that—"

"You're anything but typical," he murmurs sleepily.

I just stare at him for a beat before I tell myself to get my point across before I say something stupid. "Thanks, but all I was trying to say is that I'm not the type of girl to turn into a psycho stalker after a night of casual sex."

"Coming *four times* is not exactly casual sex," he teases with a playful smirk, which has me laughing nervously.

"Becks, I just don't want this to be awkward. . . ." I shake my head, needing to say this to remove the guilt from my conscience. "I'm sorry that I pushed you last night . . . I didn't mean for . . ." I sigh out loud as the thoughts I want to convey aren't forming into the words I need.

"No one pushes me to do anything. Especially sex."

His eyes search mine like he wants to say something else but he doesn't. So I continue blurting out the first thing that comes to mind. "Thank you for taking care of me." I cringe and avert my eyes immediately, embarrassed but glad I said it.

He continues staring at me for a moment with his quiet

intensity, before nodding his head subtly and shifting to sit up. "Well, I'm glad we got that straight," he says, swinging his legs over the edge of the bed so that his back is facing me. He scrubs a hand through his bed head, leaving it sticking up all over the place, before rising slowly. "No strings," he repeats, standing up completely naked before walking toward the bathroom. I swear he mumbles something about a lasso, but I'm too busy looking at the view to care.

I may want no strings, but that doesn't mean I can't appreciate one last lingering glance of that fine ass of his before he closes the bathroom door.

I smile smugly, understanding why Colton says Becks is the best pit crew chief in the business. He sure as hell kept my motor revving with perfection last night.

I roll over on my back and stare at the ceiling as the toilet flushes, and then the shower starts. I hear the muted sounds of the ocean outside and stare at the shadows playing across the ceiling. I exhale as my thoughts turn to last night, my mind recalling and my skin remembering all too well his touch, his taste, his scent.

And then I start giggling. Wave after wave of laughter rolls through me as I realize that this is the first time in a long time I've woken up without the constant grief from Lexi's death heavy on my thoughts and smothering my spirit.

I wipe the smudges from under my eyes, asking myself why today I finally feel like I can get through this: the grief, the loneliness of Lexi being gone.

And even though my mind keeps wandering to the fine-as-fuck man occupying the shower, I push those thoughts away, push him away. There is no possible way I could suddenly feel all of this because of him, and how he treated me last night or how he made me feel.

It was just the physical release that did this to me. It had to be.

Whatever. Who cares about the why, right? Because I'll take the four orgasms he gave me and do my walk of shame with an enthusiastic bounce in my step.

"So, how do you like running your own business? You keeping busy?"

Becks's question pulls me from my thoughts as the world outside flies by the passenger side window. I shift in my seat so I can study his profile. God sure as hell didn't skimp in the looks department on him. So why am I all of a sudden just noticing it?

"It's pretty cool working for myself." I shrug, glad he's keeping this casual and trying to avoid any awkwardness. "I have a couple events coming up with that company Scandalous that bought some of the older nightclubs around town to revamp them. They hired me to do the promotion for the reopenings, and if they like how things turn out, they'll retain me as their premier promotion company."

"So, you'll have a high-profile client that will attract other clients. Nice," he says, drawing out the last word and absently nodding his head.

"I haven't clinched the deal yet. This chick doesn't count her chickens."

He snorts out a laugh. "Well, you should start counting because we both know it'll be a success just because it's *you*."

A part of me is pleased he thinks so favorably of me, even after last night. He flicks on the blinker and glances over at me, before looking back to the highway in front of him.

"So what's your story?"

I furrow my brows as I stare at him, thinking the question odd since we've known each other more than a year, but then I realize in all that time, aside from superficial questions, Becks and I have never spoken about our pasts, how we got where we are. And then it bugs me because I can't figure out why he's asking me. I mean this is supposed to be casual, so we shouldn't weigh it down with any history.

"Becks," I sigh out his name. "Look, I appreciate you trying to make this situation so it's not awkward, but we don't have to do the whole 'twenty questions about your past' thing."

He chuckles low and shakes his head like he's trying to process what I just said. "You must have dated some real winners in your past. First of all," he says, looking over to me and then back to the road as I try to not appear irritated by his comment. "I'm not asking you because I feel obligated. I find you intriguing and am curious about what got you here to this point, so humor me. . . ."

"And second?" I ask, a little taken aback by his interest.

"Second? Hm. Second, I don't have a clue what I was going to say because those sexy legs of yours distracted me." He laughs, and how can I be anything but flattered? "But I assure you it was damn good."

"Smooth," I tease, enjoying the ease between us.

"Oh, there's still a whole helluva lot of rough." He smirks and reaches over to pat my knee. "So humor me?"

I sigh loudly, not getting the point of this exercise since there isn't a future between us. "Grew up in Long Beach. Pretty normal childhood. One sister, Lexi," I say as if he didn't already know and glance over at him to see if he noticed the waver in my voice, but he's looking at the road ahead of us. "Was okay in school, nothing stellar. My mom got sick my junior year and—"

"Sick?"

"Breast cancer," I tell him as I watch the shock flicker across his face that more than one person in my immediate family has been afflicted with the devastation of this disease. "She was in and out of treatment, surgeries, whatnot well into my senior year but I managed to get into UCLA." I smile at the memory of how torn I was because Lexi went to

Arizona for school. How I'd wanted to follow her and fulfill our goals of getting an apartment and living on our own together, but I wasn't accepted there. "I walked into the dorm freshman year and there was this brown-haired girl with curious eyes and a shy smile sitting opposite of me."

"Rylee."

"Yep. My parents left after I'd unpacked, and Ry and I have been inseparable ever since. We went through the freshman fifteen together, boyfriends, heartbreaks, so much during those four years and everything life threw at us after. I graduated with a degree in PR and got lucky right off the bat with an internship at a company called PRX. Worked my way up from gofer to managing my own events. I loved my job there and was able to build a decent reputation after proving that the cute little blonde was more than just a decoration."

"That's an understatement if I've ever heard one." The words on my tongue falter at his oddly satisfying compliment. "So, why leave and start HaLex, then?"

The smile tugs at the corners of my mouth while my heart aches with the sadness of the truth. "Because Lexi and I always wanted to do something together.... Even when we were little, we'd pretend to have a business where we scheduled our Barbies for photo shoots or had our Cabbage Patch Kids doing commercials." I laugh at the memories that flicker through my mind. "So, we decided with her business degree and my established connections we'd try it. What did we have to lose? I had a few clients offer to give me some smaller jobs, so I quit PRX . . . and two months later, Lex was diagnosed."

"Had . . ."

I shrug, try to act like it's no big deal when in fact it was my whole world tumbling down. "Yeah, well . . . now . . ." I let the thought drift off, unsure exactly what else there is to tell of my heartbreak. I clear my throat of the emotion, and the car falls into silence.

"Your mom is okay now?"

The shards of heartbreak spike anew. "She was in remission for four years and then it relapsed. The second time was bad." Chills chase one another over my skin. "Double mastectomy, endless chemo and radiation . . . just bad."

He reaches out and holds my hand in his, a silent show of support that's unexpectedly welcome when I'm so used to shunning it. I appreciate his avoidance of the word *sorry*, the most overused word on the face of the earth when someone becomes ill or dies. The quiet falls again, both of us lost in our thoughts.

After a bit Becks brushes his thumb back and forth over the top of my hand, and while it's a simple, nonverbal acknowledgment of my grief, it's also a subtle reminder of the damn good sex we had last night. My body reacts without thought, that ache between my thighs reawakening unexpectedly. I steal a glance over at him, but his attention is focused completely on the road ahead of us.

Does he feel it too?

Ah crap. *Lock it down, Montgomery.* No need to be thinking with your crotch when this was a onetime deal. It's not a budding flower, for God's sake. Think snapdragon. Think Venus flytrap. Think shutting it down to prevent his dick from dominating your thoughts.

"Last night . . ." It's all he says, his voice trailing off as he glances behind him to change lanes.

Dick dominance gone.

Hello, awkwardness.

No need to cool the ache of desire between my thighs now because that sure as hell was the jolt I needed to pull my thoughts and body from the edge of desire.

I feign that I need to scratch my other arm, an excuse to pull my hand from his and break our connection.

His sigh tells me he sees right through my bluff, so I stare at him, waiting for him to look my way again. I need him to see the expression on my face that says I'm totally cool with what happened. But he doesn't look at me—not even a glance—so that I can figure out what it is he's getting at.

"Was it about Lexi? I mean, you've got to talk to someone eventually or else—"

"Nope," I'm quick to respond, a knee-jerk reaction. I'm not doing this right now. Don't want to; don't need to. *Please, don't ruin my feel-good mood, Becks.* "Sometimes don't you just want to have a little fun without complications? You know how it goes, Becks. Shit, vibrators are cool and fun, but nothing gives more satisfaction than the mighty tongue."

He barks out a laugh, and I know I've chased the question away for now. "I don't know from your perspective, but from mine, tongues are most definitely welcome." He glances over at me with a suggestive look before shaking his head and laughing again.

"What?" I ask, raising my eyebrows. "You know it's true." I'm about to make another smart-ass remark, but I stop when I realize we've just pulled into my driveway.

I grab my overnight bag from between my feet on the floor and reach for the door handle when his voice stops me. "Are you going to be okay?"

His question can be taken several ways. Am I going to ever be okay with Lexi's death? Am I going to be okay with Rylee gone? Am I going to be okay no longer having the two people I relied on the most in my life every day?

I opt for the question I'm comfortable answering. "Okay? You mean living on my own? It's not like Ry's really been staying here for a while anyway. . . . Now it's just official." I say the words calmly, but a bittersweet feeling comes over me at the thought that my best friend will never be my roomie again. Talk about a year of changes. Shit. It's time for the whirlwind to calm some so I can catch up to everything. "It'll be nice to live on my own for a bit. To be able to walk around naked when I want . . . stuff like that." I flash him a smile as I open the door and start to scoot out of the SUV with my overnight bag in one hand.

I feel like I should say something else—some parting wisdom, but nothing comes to mind. I begin to stand up when I realize my phone is still in the center console and reach back in for it. Becks grabs my wrist and startles me. My eyes flash up to meet his, and I can see the sincerity in them, the kindness, the honesty, and I'm unable to look away, no matter how much I want to. I can see so many things in his eyes, and I don't want him to say any of them, so I try to pull my hand back, but he just holds tight.

"You know you can call me if you ever need me, right? For anything," he says in that slow, even cadence of his that pulls at so many things deep within me, and I can't think of a witty retort to lighten the mood.

"Okay. Thanks." It's all I can manage. With our eyes locked on each other's, I reach down and fumble for my phone before exiting the car. I shut the door and exhale a sigh of relief, as I turn my back and head toward my house.

Chapter 4

'm not sure how I'm feeling as I step inside and lean my back against the door—listening for Becks to pull out of the driveway—but once I'm inside, I take a breath for the first time in what feels like forever.

What the fuck is wrong with you, Montgomery? It was just sex. Just mind-blowing, multiple-orgasm-inducing sex. So get over it. Get over your thoughts of him. Move on.

My head wants to, but hell if my body does.

I drop my bag on the floor and toss my keys and phone in the basket on the table in the foyer and head toward the kitchen. I hit the button on the voice mail and tune out the telemarketer's message as I open the fridge and look for a Diet Coke. The machine beeps, and Maddie's voice fills the empty kitchen.

"Hi, Auntie. I hope your fancy wedding was loads of fun. I bet it was better than all of the Sour Patch Kids in the world put together. Can't wait to see you tomorrow. I have the whole day planned out for us."

I automatically smile at the sound of her voice, and my love for her swells like always. I can only imagine what her plans for us are this time. Last week it was mud pies and Barbies, with pretend tea served by Strawberry Shortcake.

The doorbell rings, and my heart immediately skips a beat at the thought it might be Becks. Maybe I left something in his car.

And why in the hell is my pulse thundering?

Crap. We really just need a little time apart so that we can let everything from last night settle and fade away. So I can let the taste and scent and sound of him dissipate from my memory.

I grab the handle and pull the door open, prepared for Becks, and am completely thrown for a loop by who stands there.

"What the hell are you doing here?"

"Nice to see you too." It's that same gravelly voice that used to turn me inside out. Those gray eyes that can be cold as steel or soft as silk from one second to the next. That muscled torso that my fingers and mouth memorized every incredible inch of. The sight of him invokes images of wild, against-the-wall, rip-your-clothes-off sex, and at the same time, schizophrenic emotions and volatile tempers surge through my mind.

And yet his pull on me is still there, still as magnetic as ever. This is the man I once upon a time thought could be *the one*, could be worth the fight, until he disappeared just as quickly as he appeared.

Just like he does every time.

"What do you want, Dante?" I huff out a breath and put my hands on my hips.

"What, no kiss? No hug? That's all the welcome I get?" He shoves his hands into the pockets of his worn jeans, his biceps bulging, and he leans a shoulder against the doorjamb. I try not to look twice at the new ink peaking up from under the collar of his shirt, but I find myself wondering what he chose this time. My eyes rise from his neck to his face when he runs his free hand up and over his goatee. Between the smirk on his lips, and the look in his eyes, I swear he does it on purpose to evoke thoughts of how exactly that patch of hair can tease and tempt me when positioned between my thighs.

I take hold of my thoughts and am able to recall the hurt he inflicted on me, which still scars me deep inside. "You're lucky that your welcome doesn't include a swift kick in the nuts." I fold my arms across my chest and raise an eyebrow at him.

He laughs, that arrogant smirk strengthening the intensity that always etches his face. "Ah, there's my girl, spirited as fuck, just how I like you."

"I'm not your girl. You lost the chance to call me that when you walked away without a word." I absently look over his shoulder at the neighbor kid running down the sidewalk, before looking back at him.

"You afraid lover boy's going to come back and get pissed I'm standing here?"

"Lover boy?"

He lifts his chin. "Yeah. That your boyfriend who dropped you off? You switching things up, Had? Going from the reckless to the refined?"

I laugh. Beckett refined? That's not exactly the first word that comes to mind, but I guess in Dante's view, Becks's lack of tattoos makes him just that.

"He's just a friend, and besides, what he is or isn't is none of your damn business."

"You're always my business."

I snort in response. Does he actually think that he can show up on my doorstep after disappearing over a year ago and that I'd welcome him with open arms? "C'mon, babe, are you really going to bust my balls? Besides, you know how much I like it when you're rough with me," he teases, trying to get to me in that way that always seemed to work before.

But I've been here, done this, and don't plan on having a repeat performance. Heartbreak is not my thing.

"What do you want?"

He shrugs sheepishly. "I'm back in town."

"Good for you. What for? Chasing the dream fail or something?"

He laughs with a shake of his head, his dimples deepening. "Babe, I'm always chasing something. . . ."

"Yeah, but chasing tail and chasing dreams are two entirely different things."

He takes a step toward me, and I take one back, leery of him getting too close, the proven weakness in my armored heart. "I wasn't that bad," he says softly. "We were good together."

I bat away his hand when he reaches out to touch my arm. "Yeah, and the good was only about twenty percent of the time," I tell him. "I seem to remember the other eighty percent a whole helluva lot more."

"But that twenty percent? I've got fond memories of that twenty percent." He grins at me, trying to get me to remember the damn good sex we used to have. I figure I'll beat him to the punch.

"I don't." I lie without batting an eyelash since he's the king of telling untruths.

He stares at me for a moment before taking another step toward me. I tell myself not to be affected, and then of course his cologne hits me, causing memories to surge to the forefront of my mind. "It seems you've gotten all hard on me, babe."

And I can't help it: My mind immediately flashes to last night. The word *hard* makes me think of the look on Becks's face when he wanted to prove just how hard he was. I shake my head and exhale in exasperation, thinking about how different Becks and this man in front of me are.

But both dangerous.

He tilts his head down, smile still in place, and looks into my eyes. "Ahhh, she's giving in. You know you can never stay mad at me. Resistance is futile, babe."

And I'm so pissed because he's right. I never can. Of

course, I respect myself and all that shit, and would never allow myself to go back down that path with him again, but I swear to God, Dante can make me bend my rules like no one else can. I fight the smile that threatens to curl up one corner of my mouth, knowing it's basically useless to even try. "Dante . . ." My voice trails off, my internal war waging within me, as I try to figure out what he wants this time. "Why are you here?"

His smoldering smirk surges to a megawatt smile because he knows he's got me now. "I need a place to crash for a bit." His eyes darken with an unexpected solemnity that throws me, but with him, you never know what's the truth and what's a game.

"And you see a vacancy sign on my porch or something?"

He blows out an audible breath. Used to taking without asking, he doesn't like having to explain anything. "C'mon, babe, I know Ry moved out." I raise my eyebrows, causing him to pause and explain. "It's not like speculations over her wedding details weren't the buzz all over *TMZ* last night or anything." He rolls his eyes and flashes that smile at me again, but I stand my ground, arms crossed, impatient. "I just need a couple of days, a week or two at the most, so that I can straighten some shit out."

There is something about the way he says it—something about the stress lining his face—that has me angling my head and looking past his tough exterior and wondering what he's really doing in town. "So, you came here? You think you're charming enough that I'm just going to forget all of the shit from before?"

"You suck." I almost laugh at the grade school response coming from this big, bad rebel.

"No, actually I don't." I shrug, looking down at his crotch and then up to his eyes. "Sorry, but small objects like yours are a choking hazard."

A half smile plays at one corner of his mouth. We stare

at each other silently for a moment before he begs. "Please, Haddie?" His plea does me in, and I'm ready to consent, but he continues before I can reply. "You know me. Know my story. Thought you might take pity on me when so many others would turn me away."

We stare at each other for a few moments as I try to decipher what he means. Because yes, I do know his story: only child raised by his mom, dad nonexistent, so what's changed now? Does this have to do with his mom? His job? What? Frankly, it's none of my damn business, but between the look in his eyes and the desperation in his voice, I begin to feel sorry about my initial desire to kick him in the nuts.

Hell, it's still an option, but I'll make sure he's okay first. I shake my head in resignation and close my eyes for a moment, mentally chastising myself for the disorder and chaos I know I'm inviting into my life.

"No funny stuff, Dante. I mean it."

He holds his hand up. "Scout's honor," he promises with a victorious smirk.

"Yeah, that's what I'm afraid of," I tell him, knowing full well the Boy Scouts kicked him out for inciting mutiny when he was in grade school.

He flashes a devil-may-care grin and steps over the threshold.

And so it begins, I think as he walks past me and into my house.

Chapter 5

I roll my truck to a stop, glad to finally be here and thankful traffic was nonexistent. I turn off the ignition, and say a silent thank-you to Howard Stern for allowing me to push the fucking thoughts out of my head, all the ones I'm not supposed to be thinking.

As I climb out of the truck and look at the trees around me, I take in the one place where I've always been able to clear my head, forget my worries, and just chill. So why, when I should be walking up the porch, cracking a cold one, and sitting by the pool, are my thoughts still stuck on her?

Haddie.

Sweet fucking Haddie, and that look on her face as I pulled her to the edge of the bed last night and stared at her: blond hair fanned out beneath her, cheeks red, lips parted, and pussy so goddamn wet and tasting like Heaven. Why do I keep remembering that look in her eyes—taunting, innocent, and weary—and wondering what put it there? Am I right to assume she wanted to feel to forget?

I shake my head and whistle at Rex to jump out of the truck before I slam the door. Her words run through my head over and over now that Howard Stern's voice is no longer filling my ears. *We said no strings.* But there was no fucking *we* about it. She said no strings. She made it clear over and over that we were a one-night stand. *No strings, my ass.* I feel like she threw a goddamn lasso around me and pulled it tight.

No strings, yeah . . . but rope? She didn't say a fucking thing about any rope.

I knew I should have done more to resist her advances last night, knew that one goddamn taste wouldn't be enough. Shit, that's why I've kept her at arm's length this past year and a half. Haddie being sexy was a given, but getting tangled with her in the sheets was something I didn't want to risk since she was Rylee's best friend. And best friends dating best friends usually always turns ugly.

So I tried to play it safe. Lot of good that did me since I fell off the cliff last night and don't even think I want to be rescued from the rope I'm dangling from.

I reach up and adjust my ball cap, and then I grab my bag out of the bed of the truck. This is the problem with pussy: When you want it you can't get it, and when you don't want it, you get it and then you can't get it out of your fucking head.

And fuck if I can erase sweet goddamn Haddie's from owning my thoughts.

"Hey, asshole?"

The voice shocks me from my thoughts. I snap my head up and look toward the porch. "What the fuck are you doing here, Walker?"

"Glad to see you too, dude," my brother says as he leans over to get a sloppy kiss from Rex. He laughs and ruffles his fur before looking back up at me.

I look around to make sure I didn't miss seeing my brother's truck on the way in, but nope, it's not here. "I didn't know you were going to be up here." I pull my bag over my shoulder and start walking toward the old ranch house.

"Yeah, well, it was last minute. Aubrey had a bachelorette party in Vegas." He shrugs as he lifts the beer in his hand to his lips. "I figured I'd head out here for a couple of days while she was gone. Recharge. Relax. Become one with nature," he says with a raise of his eyebrows as he repeats the motto our mom used to say when she hauled us off to this old house in Ojai. It has been in her family for years. We used to roll our eyes at the motto as kids, but understand it as adults.

"My truck's behind the barn. I was letting Raul use it," he explains, causing me to look over toward the barn to see if the caretaker is there to wave a greeting to, but he's nowhere in sight. "What's your excuse for coming up?"

"I was looking for some time. *Alone,*" I say as I climb the steps.

"Oh, poor baby," he teases. "Is my big brother sad that his bromance has been interrupted by a little wedding?"

"Fuck off," I tell him, even though I already know he's not going to. He never does, when it comes to how close Colton and I are. "I just needed some R and R. I drank too much last night . . . thought I'd come up for the weekend and recover. *By myself.* Leave it to my dumb-ass little brother to ruin my plans."

He slaps my back and laughs. "Good thing he did, because he stocked the fridge with ice-cold beer."

"Seriously?" *Sweet.* Saves me the trip into town to get more.

"Seriously. Dontcha love me now?" he says as he heads toward the kitchen while I head toward the bedroom to drop off my stuff.

"I'd love you even more if you grabbed me one. Or two or three," I yell down the hallway to him.

Pulling the brim of my hat down, I sink down in the chair a bit more. The sun feels good on my skin and the ice-cold beer sliding down my throat feels even better. Walker keeps yakking on and on like a woman, and I tune him out. He definitely got our mother's talk-about-fucking-nothing-ad-nauseam gene.

I close my eyes, and my thoughts wander back toward last night. And then they drift to how fucking great the sex was. How great Haddie was. I feel like a chick thinking about it again, about her again, but shit, the sex was incredible. Not to mention that it's such a damn turn-on when a woman is confident and not afraid to speak her mind in the sack.

"What's your deal, dude?"

"Huh?" I glance at Walker.

"Who is she?" he asks with a smirk.

"Who is who?" I aim for classic avoidance. Walker doesn't need to know zip about Haddie because it was just a one-night stand. And if he thinks any differently—Mr. I love to be in a relationship—he'll run blabbing to Mom, and then she'll start in on me about grandbabies. And of course, then I'll get the phone call from Dad telling me she's driving him crazy with all of this baby nonsense, but can I hurry it up some so that he can have some peace and quiet? Shit, I'm okay with having kids someday, just not now.

I've still got oats to sow, places to see, and people to do before I take a chance and bareback.

"Becks . . . you're sitting over there with your eyes closed, a stupid-ass smirk on your face, and you're adjusting your dick every five fucking seconds." He raises his eyebrows at me. "So either you're remembering getting lucky—and it seems like it was a damn good lucky—or else you're having some kind of pornographic wet daydream, and if that's the case, you're a sick fuck since you're doing it while I'm sitting right here."

I stare at him and see amusement in my pestering little brother's eyes. "Shut up." It's not a very good comeback, but it's all I've got, because he caught me red-handed.

"Ha! I knew it!" he says, turning in his lounge chair to

face me. "What poor woman was subjected to your lack of skill last night?"

And so his screwing with me begins. I love my brother to death, but he needs some new fucking comebacks. I swear to God he hangs out too much with his girlfriend, Aubrey, because he couldn't be sporting more estrogen if he were wearing some lipstick and heels.

I start to respond to his dim-witted comment when I hear a cell phone ring. I drop my head to the side and stare at him. Yep. Way too fucking much estrogen. "Please, tell me that is not your ringtone?" I beg of my brother as a Katy Perry song plays on.

He looks at me like I'm crazy. "Dude, my cell is right here," he says, holding it up for proof. "That's yours."

What the . . . ? I rise from the chair and head toward the sliding-glass doors, where I set my phone on the counter inside. Katy keeps singing about California girls and melting Popsicles, and I swear to God, this has to be one of Colton's fucking pranks. A final parting gift before he left for his honeymoon. The last time he did this my ringtone was "I Touch Myself," and it went off in the middle of a pit crew meeting. He's such an asshole sometimes.

I reach for my black iPhone, the screen announcing Rylee's name. He had better not have fucked with my contacts too.

"Hello?" I answer the phone cautiously.

"Becks? Why do you have Haddie's phone?" Rylee's voice comes through loud and clear, and all of a sudden, it hits me. Haddie picked up the wrong phone this morning when I dropped her off. But what female has a plain black cell phone case? Haddie's anything but plain. "Becks, you there?"

This is fucking stellar. I might as well post on social media that I had sex with Haddie because me answering her cell phone did just as well. For fuck's sake. Deflection is my only choice. "I'm here. . . . Shouldn't you be doing something else on the first day of your honeymoon instead of calling me?"

"We're delayed at the airport," she says at the same time I hear a flight number being called in the background.

I laugh. "Like that's gonna stop Colton from getting busy—"

"Are you with Haddie?" she says, cutting me off, and I can hear the curiosity in her voice. I don't want to deal with this, especially because Walker is standing in the doorway, hanging onto my every word.

"No. I don't know where she—"

"Then why do you have her cell phone?" She lets the question linger, and I struggle with an explanation that she'll believe. "Did you two—"

"Give me the phone." It's Colton's voice, and now I know I'm screwed. I hear shuffling and then, "Becks?"

"Hello, Mr. Rings-with-strings, you old married fucker."

He laughs. "Dude, at least I'm getting some on a more than regular basis. You're just jealous. If you decided to lower your standards and get some too, you'd be a much happier. . . . Oh shit . . ." And I swear I can hear the light switch on in his head. "You slept with Haddie, didn't you?"

"Don't be ridiculous," I tell him, grimacing momentarily. "Nothing happened."

"Aha, you so did!" He shouts out with a mocking laugh. "Nothing happened, my ass. . . . Besides the only time you take a chick's cell phone is if you're escaping in the dark before she wakes up, or if you're so flustered from figuring out whether to kiss her good night . . . er . . . good morning"—he chuckles again—"that you grab it accidentally."

"Whatever. They were both on your kitchen counter. I must have grabbed the wrong one." What he doesn't know won't kill him.

"Yeah, right, and I'm the goddamn Easter bunny."

"Well, you do like tail." I offer.

He chuckles again "Yeah, just one. I'm reformed now," he says, before falling silent for a moment.

"In that respect, yes . . . but every other part of your life? You're still a crazy fucker." I walk over to the refrigerator, pull out an IPA, and twist the lid off. "Seriously, nothing happened." When he just grunts in disbelief, I continue talking before he starts thinking too much about it and asks more questions I'll have to dodge. "So, why are you calling?"

"Ah, the subtle change of topic . . . like that doesn't scream *I fucked her*." He laughs.

"I'm hanging up now," I threaten, knowing this can go on and on with him.

"Sweet Jesus, dude, *relax*. Don't be such a little bitch. I was actually dialing you while Ry was calling Haddie to ask a favor."

"Anything." No details needed. It's Colton, after all. My brother from another mother.

"I just got a call from Firestone. The shipment of tires is two days early—"

"That's a first. . . . What the hell happened? Is Armageddon coming or what?" I laugh. Our semitruck full of sponsorship tires is usually two weeks late and always forces us to trim some time off of our testing.

And time on the track is like gold.

"No shit. I said something similar to Ry."

"Ha. Yeah, I'm sure that's what you were moaning to her."

"Whatever, dude. You're just jealous." He laughs and then stops. "Or maybe not. Maybe you were busy moaning yourself, huh, Daniels?

"Fuck off. I told you that—"

"Yeah, yeah, yeah . . . keep on thinking I'm buying it and I'll keep believing you. Not."

"What do you need?" I exhale out in a frustrated breath.

"Don't think I'm not noticing the change of topic here, but our flight just got called, so I've gotta go. . . . Look, I know you said you might go up to the farmhouse for a couple of days . . ."

"I'm there right now."

He sighs. "The trucker is on a tight timeline, needs to turn the truck, and get back before that storm hits the Midwest. . . . Man, I hate to ask . . ."

"No, you don't."

He laughs deep and loud, and there's the sound of movement on the other end of the phone. "You're right. I don't . . ."

"You suck for asking when I just got here and am on my fifth or sixth *cerveza*, but yeah, I'll drive back to town in the morning and open up shop for the delivery."

"Thanks, brother. I owe you."

"That's the understatement of the year."

"Hm. Maybe you already were paid in kind." He laughs. "I did warn you Ry had a hot friend. I guess you decided to dip your thermometer in and take her temperature."

"You're a sick fuck!"

"You wouldn't want me any other way."

"True. But nothing happened." I hear the flight called in the background as he snorts a response to my denial. "Fly safe."

"Later. And thanks."

I hang up the phone and immediately dial my own cell, part of me hoping she picks up the phone, and the other part of me hoping she misses the call.

I have one more ring before my voice mail picks up when she answers.

" 'Lo?"

The male voice throws me for a loop. I pull the phone away from my ear and look at the screen to make sure I dialed the correct number. Yep. Sure as shit did.

Who the fuck is answering my phone? Did I lose it at the wedding instead?

" 'Lo?" he says again, irritated. He's irritated? He's answering my fucking phone.

"Who the hell are you?"

"What's it to you?"

His arrogance fuels my temper. "Because it's my goddamn phone you're answering."

"What?" Now it's his turn to be confused as fuck. "Hey, babe?" he says, his mouth pulled away from the receiver, but I can still hear it clear as day. And I can hear Haddie's voice answering him.

Babe? Did I actually hear that right? Did I miss something?

"Some guy is calling and says you have his phone...."

I hear shuffling and garbled words. "Hello?" Her breathless voice fills the line, and even though I'm not really sure what in the hell is going on, my balls tighten at the sound of her sexy-ass voice.

"You have my phone." I'm not trying to be a dick, but I can't help it. Less than ten hours ago, we were having sex, and now she has some guy answering my phone? I guess when she says no strings, she really means no strings. "When can you take time out of your *busy* schedule to meet up so we can switch?" I can't hide the sarcasm in my voice.

Seems like sweet Haddie isn't so fucking sweet.

She's silent for a beat. "Becks?"

"Yup." At least she remembers my name. Fucking ridiculous. "When can we meet up?"

"Becks, are you okay?" There's a concern that I don't want to hear in her voice, but by now I've moved from shocked to bitter. Fucking women. "Oh. Oh," she says as she realizes why I'm pissed. "It's not what you think. Dante's—"

"How about tomorrow? What time can you meet tomorrow, *babe*?" Did I really just say that? What the hell am I jealous for? No fucking strings, right? So then why do I feel like I'm tangled in a goddamn cobweb?

"Oh...." I hear the hurt in her voice. And now I'm pissed

that I'm acting how I'm acting. It was a night of incredible sex. *Get over it, dude.* Grab your balls back and suck it up.

Then I hear her sigh. And fuck if that sound doesn't bring back memories of burying myself in her last night, over and over into the early morning.

"Um, I can't," she says, and I can hear the television in the background fading as she moves around. "I have a commitment tomorrow, and then an event all night."

I bet you have a commitment. I shake my head. "Where's the event?"

"Downtown. I can meet up with you in the afternoon before I have to be there if you want."

"Fuck," I say, since I was hoping to head back to the ranch after I met with the trucker. "Yeah, okay . . . I'll figure out how to make it."

"Becks?"

I hate the searching tone in her voice. If this really was a onetime thing, then why are we both acting like fucking teenagers?

And they say sex doesn't complicate things.

"Yeah?" I respond, but I'm getting impatient. I want to hang up, get my phone back, and take a break while Ry and Colton are on their honeymoon so that we can skip this awkward stage where both of us are overanalyzing what the other is thinking.

She sighs again. "I just . . . last night . . ."

And then I hear his voice again. *"Babe, I'm gonna hop in the shower."*

". . . was a mistake," I finish for her. Great sex but huge mistake. You don't fuck friends. Lesson learned.

"No, it wasn't. I thought that—"

"Apparently it was." I shift and move toward my bedroom just in case Walker is listening. "We may have agreed to no strings, Had, but fuck if we didn't fray the edges some."

" 'Fray'?"

"Yeah." I take a deep breath.

"What the hell does that mean, Becks? We both went into it knowing what was there."

"Yep, we sure did." Mayday, Mayday, this conversation is going downhill fast.

"Then what's the problem?"

"We blurred the lines," I say, "and now we need to clear them up."

"You sound pissed."

"Nope, I'm just fucking peachy. I'll call you when I'm in town tomorrow."

"Becks, wait! I don't unders—"

"Your rules. I sure hope they're clear to you. Good night."

When I hang up the phone, a mixture of anger and relief sits unsettled in my gut. Whatever. Bygones. I toss the phone on the counter and take a long pull on my beer.

"'Peachy'?" I cringe at the sound of Walker's voice. The eavesdropping little fucker. "Who was that?"

"Shut the fuck up, dude." I toss my bottle cap at him. "None of your business."

Chapter 6

Just fucking peachy?

If there's supposed to be no strings—which was my own rule, for God's sake—then why am I standing here staring at Becks' phone, upset at his nonchalance about last night?

Shit, he has every right to be an asshole to me. I groan at the irony that today of all days Dante would show up and then answer my damn phone.

Beckett's damn phone.

I rest a hip against the kitchen counter, and as much as I tell my head not to go there, I can't help the thoughts and images playing in a loop from last night. I remember looking up at him as his arms flexed on either side of my body, filling me, challenging me, satisfying me.

I groan again, trying to shake both the ache from my core and the disquiet, knowing Becks is pissed off. I clench my jaw and shake my head. I shouldn't care that he's upset, shouldn't give a flying fuck that he was snide with me. Whatever. This is exactly what I feared was going to happen. Weirdness between us.

I shake my head in frustration. Can't a girl get a guy to give her a little dick without thinking that he deserves more?

I sigh out loud, the snarkiness starting to abate and the

guilt starting to walk over the well-worn welcome mat laid out for today.

Dante laughs at something he's watching on the TV in the other room, and I immediately roll my eyes.

Fuck.

I can't imagine what Becks is thinking right now. I glance down at his phone in my hand and can see how I made the mistake of grabbing the wrong one. I look over to the kitchen counter, where my jeweled phone case rests. The one I took off yesterday so that I could slip my phone into my bra under my dress undetected.

My internal debate over whether to call him back and explain Dante's presence is almost decided, finger ready to dial, when Dante himself asks the question I'm trying to figure out myself.

"Who was that?"

I look over to him leaning against the doorframe into the kitchen. Hands shoved into his pockets, pushing them to ride low on his hips, a hint of the toned and inked abs beneath showing. He smirks when he sees my eyes dart down to the span of skin. Confidence is something he most definitely doesn't lack.

"Good question," I murmur mostly to myself as I try to figure out the answer as well as why I have so many unsettled feelings.

Dante snorts out in amusement. "Babe, you have his fucking phone, so it's kind of obvious he is somebody."

What exactly he is to me though, is the damn question. I pull my head from the land of orgasms and what-ifs and tell myself I must be too damn close to my period if I'm this wishy-washy over sex that's just supposed to be sex.

Head straight, libido on lock down, Montgomery. I look back and focus on Dante—a hot but royal pain in my ass— trying to dig for information and, by the look in his eyes, possibly wanting something more. Dante may see a vacancy sign flashing above my head, but he'd better think again because I've grown from the mesmerized girl he once dated. I might have once thrived on the reckless nature of who we were together—living on the edge, sharp words followed by hotter than hell makeup sex. Explosive emotions calmed momentarily for the coveted few days of peace before the cycle started all over again.

I break our connection and glance away; my mind immediately moves back to Becks and the hint of things I don't deserve. I push all thoughts away and toss the phone on the counter, the thud of it echoing into the emptiness I feel inside of me. "Nah, he's nothing. Just a mistake."

"I do believe you used those same words to describe me once," he says, suggestion in his tone as he makes his way across the kitchen.

"Ha. Exactly. And look where that got me." I know that look in his eyes, know exactly what that predatory purpose in his walk means, and I grip the edge of the counter, uncertain what I'm holding on for.

I suck in an anticipatory breath as he steps in front of me and places his hands on the counter between my hips and my own hands resting there. "Care for me to show you just how good of a mistake I can be again?" The tenor of his voice washes over me. The pure maleness he exudes tugs momentarily, tempting me to use him as a means to quiet the riot of confusion I'm feeling over Becks.

Use one to forget the other. Yeah, that's real classy. What is my problem?

I smirk at him, but my eyes fire off a warning to back off. And who the hell am I kidding? Issuing a warning to Dante is like throwing down the gauntlet. And fuck if I didn't just hear him toss his on the tile floor in acceptance.

"Dream on." I force out the comment, trying to hide the slight waver in my voice—my only tell that I'm affected by his proximity, by that magnetic draw of his that seems to always be a losing battle for me to fight.

Our eyes lock, with amusement dancing in his as he

makes that slow lean into my body. My hands are immediately on his chest, pushing him away, trying to protect myself from everything I usually want. From the temptation I don't need, but holy fuck, I could use to eradicate those little tentacles of need burrowing beneath the surface in regards to Becks. That need to snuggle into him this morning, make lazy love under the heat of the sun's rays coming through the window, and the instant swarm of butterflies that fluttered in my stomach when I thought he had come back to the house.

Dante chuckles low and soft, the sound vibrating against my palms pressed against the firmness of his chest that I used to know and use handily like a road map. He knows what he does to me, knows that he's pegged every number of mine from sixty-nine on down.

"Dante . . ." My voice trails off as he grabs my hands from his chest and presses them to the counter with his on top of them, holding me there. I glance down, warning bells going off, and when I look up, I don't even have a chance to speak before his mouth captures mine.

My resistance is fleeting. I'm not sure if it's the confusion, the need, the what-the-fuck-ever but within seconds his tongue has pressed between my lips. I don't respond at first, don't react, but when his tongue connects with mine, it rekindles everything to life. Parts Becks sparked to life last night.

No strings.

I push the thought away and move my body into him. And when I start to respond, Dante takes control. He groans deep in his throat and presses the hard length of his body into mine, hips pinning me to the counter. One hand fists in my hair, and the other presses against my lower back. I accept the domination of the kiss, the command of his touch, a part of me enjoying the current that zings through me. The one that knows just how wild of a ride Dante can be—good, bad, pleasurable, and painful.

And I want to welcome it. The taste of his kiss, the complete chaos he'll unleash in my life because I'll be so busy focusing on the scattered mess that I won't even notice I'm wading through the broken parts of myself that Lexi's death left behind.

That Becks began to help piece back together last night.

Becks.

Last night.

What in the hell am I doing? I struggle to pull myself from the drug of Dante and the ever-apparent need to lose myself. I press my hands on his shoulders, attempting to pull back from his mouth, but his hand holds firm on my neck. My body tells me it wants this: My heart and head tell me to get my shit together and have some damn dignity. That being festive is fine, but there's no need to be a twenty-four-hour Mardis Gras.

"No," I murmur against his lips, knowing that the longer I drink him in, the harder it is going to be to walk away. "No!" I say again with a defiant shove against his chest.

He steps back from me, eyes wide and nostrils flaring. His shoulders move with the force of his panted breaths. I can see anger stemming from my rejection vibrating just beneath the surface, and for a moment, I think it's going to escape but he reins it in.

My lips tingle from his kiss, but I know this is no good. Would be no good. I push off the counter decisively. "I've got stuff to do."

"What the fuck, Had?" There's an annoyed exasperation in his voice, but I couldn't care less.

I keep walking out of the kitchen that now feels so small from his presence. "You want a place to stay? Don't touch me again."

His laugh—empty and hollow—follows me out of the kitchen. And there's something about the sound of it that tugs at me, causes me to stop after I turn the corner to the hallway. I lean my shoulder against the wall momentarily when I realize why it bugs me so much.

It's the emptiness and hollowness that resonate the loudest.

His laugh echoes what mine has sounded like for the past six months. A false pretense—sounding fine when I'm anything but. I stand there in indecision. The compassionate part of me feels like I need to go back and see what's wrong, ask what has stolen the warmth from him. I should make sure he's okay because I sure as fuck know that I'm not. And then the find-another-doorstep-to-cry-on part of me says I need to run like the fucking wind the other way, high heels and all.

Wouldn't it be nice if the other way led to Becks?

What the fuck? Jesus, Haddie, get a grip.

I sigh and shake my head as I start moving down the hallway toward my bedroom. My head is all over the place, and the all too familiar burn of threatening tears is there.

Again.

I enter my room and flick on some music. Something, anything to concentrate on other than the quick flash of desire downstairs and the slow burn from the man whose telephone I accidentally grabbed.

The problem is that when you purposely want to forget someone, you remember them the most. Lexi. Dante. Becks. All three ride the wave of thoughts crashing around in my head.

It hurts too damn much to think about Lexi. I'll have the whole goddamn day tomorrow to struggle with her memory, fight the tears, soak in the only part of her I have left, so I push her as best as I can from my head.

The door to the backyard slams shut, and my thoughts are drawn to Dante. *Delectable Dante.* Damn if there isn't just a main line from that man's mouth straight to my crotch. But alongside that is the wrecking ball on a direct path to my heart. So good but so damn bad.

The night we met should have been an indication of our volatility when he mistook me for the wrong girl outside a club. Spun me around and knocked me breathless with his kiss long before he realized I wasn't who he thought I was. I'll never forget the look on his face when he realized it, eyes wide with shock and jaw slack. But then that lazy, arrogant smirk grew as we gave each other the once-over, and the look on his face mixed with the fuck-if-I-care attitude emanating off of him . . . I was lost to lust and not long after falling in love.

We were a predictable disaster: a mixture of spontaneity, recklessness, and youthful, carefree nature. The problem is, with Dante love was never easy. Our relationship came with tempers, constant unpredictability, and the attitude that attracted me eventually turned me off when the fuck-if-I-care was directed my way. He sabotaged us with his disregard for every staple that is needed for a successful relationship. And yet I loved him despite the emotional chaos he unleashed in my heart.

But love isn't always enough. Especially when the one you love up and leaves without another word and disappears for months.

Hell yes, I loved Dante, but he taught me that when it comes to men, there are only three moods to be had: fuck you, fuck off, and fuck me. Thank goodness the *fuck me* part was pretty damn good or else the positive memories would be few and far between.

Fuck Dante.

Fuck Beckett.

I snort out a laugh because that's exactly the problem — my body wants to do just that. And now, of course, I'm thinking of fucking, so my mind can't help but wander to Becks and his adept demonstration last night. I adjust my hips as a sweet ache settles there at the memory of his hands on me, mouth on mine, cock buried in me. And the way he looked at me while waking up, the iota of hurt in his voice earlier on the phone.

I groan and throw an arm over my eyes as I try to block out the image of him, tan skin against white sheets, hard muscle against soft bedding. It's useless. I don't want any strings. None. So why the hell do I feel like he's already woven them through my thoughts, binding us together somehow?

He's a keeper. No doubt there. Too bad I'm looking for the disposable version. A Mr. Right Now. But the man won't leave my mind. I lick my lips, taste Dante there but find myself wishing it was Becks.

This is so not fucking cool. My head had better start giving my body a damn road map and directions on how to get to the same place, and that place is nowhere connected to Beckett Daniels.

My onetime lap around the track with Becks is over.

Fuck.

Time to grab the wheel with both hands again and get control.

Chapter 7

I pushed myself too damn hard this morning. Ran too far at too accelerated a pace, and now my muscles are screaming with fatigue. But I was able to run out the emotion, put it at bay so that I can get through the initial sucker punch to the gut when I walk into the house.

The California sun is warm, beating through my windshield as I shift my sore muscles and stand from the car. I look down the street for a moment, take in the trees lining it and the dogs barking. The sounds of moms calling to their children and life being lived. I try to focus on that, try to block out the thoughts of elevated white blood cell counts and tumor markers. I force myself to remember Lex so brave and strong, saying, "Fuck cancer." Her fighting like hell to beat, then to prolong, then to steal a few more moments, a few more breaths.

My fingers grip tightly to the top of the car door. Tears burn my eyes, and memories flicker to the unwelcome thoughts I wish I didn't have. Ones I wish no one would ever have. Ragged gasps and morphine drips. Hushed promises and silent pleas for more time, for less pain. For a miracle.

The memories are still so raw, her touch still so tangible

after just six months but so vague at the same time. Holding her hand, watching her slip away, telling her I loved her, promising her Maddie will grow up with her spirit a constant reminder. That it would be my mission in life for her daughter to know her, remember her, live a full life for her. Saying good-bye to her one final time as peace settled over her.

I suck in a deep breath, drowning in the grief when I should be dealing with it, moving on. But every time I come here, it hits me with such force. Walking into her house, seeing the touches of her personality when she's gone forever.

And then I hear the squeal from the front door—the patter of little feet and cries of excitement—and it all eases some when I look down into my sister's eyes mimicked in her daughter.

I catch the running bundle of love and life in my arms and squeeze her to me. Breathing her in, in that quick second I get before she starts in on me with the barrage of questions and smiles full of love.

"Whoa!" I nuzzle my nose into her hair and just breathe her in for another moment as she starts wiggling to get down.

"Auntie! I'm so glad you're here," she says, the words tumbling out in a burst of excitement as I set her down on the ground. Her hand finds mine immediately, brown eyes fringed with long lashes look up to me, and her heart-shaped mouth spreads in a grin. She begins tugging on my hand toward the front door and her love, her happiness, her ability to thrive are contagious, even if only momentarily.

We clear the foyer, Maddie's incessant chatter sounding sweet, heartwarming, and overwhelming all at once. Hand in mine, she pulls me into the family room, never breaking stride in making her requests for the day.

"Daddy! She's here! She's here!"

I hear Danny's chuckle before I see him, my eyes slowly taking in the wall across from me, where pictures clutter the area. My heart squeezes at the images, the memories, the lack of new ones, and I force myself to look away and over to my brother-in-law.

I meet Danny's gaze, the soft smile on his lips, the love for his daughter evident on his face, but when his eyes meet mine, the devastation is there, a reflection of the constant sadness. "Hey, Danny, how's it going?" I say the words, the simple greeting, but what I'm really asking, what my eyes are saying, is *How are you holding up?*

"Good. I'm good," he says as I start the count of how many times he's going to use that word in the next five minutes. My gauge of how crippling his grief is today. "Good," he reaffirms with a nod of his head as Maddie releases my hand and jumps up and down in excitement.

"Good," I say softly, my own anguish weighing heavy on me. Emotions war within, not understanding how he can live day to day in this house full of her and at the same time feeling like I'd never be able to live anywhere else.

He breaks eye contact and looks over at Maddie, who is bouncing with excitement. "So what are you two going to do today?" he asks, enthusiasm forced but sincere.

Maddie looks up at me with sparkling eyes and begging for me to tell her since I usually keep our plans for our special days secret. "Hmm," I tease her. "I'm thinking a movie, then maybe some ice cream, then the bookstore for Fancy Nancy story time."

The look on her face makes my heart clench as she squeals with excitement. "Really?" Her voice is so high-pitched—full of emotion—that I cringe at the sound. "Story time?"

And the smile comes easily because her love of books is so my sister that I find a tinge of happiness in the fact that she is so much like her. "Yep . . . but I need to talk to your daddy for a minute, so why don't you run upstairs and get your sweater in case it's cold in the theater, okay?"

Her smile widens and then just as quickly falls, her head

angling as she stares at me. "You're not going to leave me too, are you?"

I have to fight back with every single thing within me to not break down from the pang that just debilitated me from her comment. I hear the choked sob from Danny, turning his back so that Maddie can't see him fall apart. I steel myself, knowing I need to reassure her without my face reflecting my own heartache.

I squat down on my haunches so that I'm at her eye level, that bottom lip of hers quivering as she tries to be strong. "Oh, sweetheart," I tell her, my voice breaking. I reach out to smooth my hand over her hair and cheek. "Your daddy and I aren't going anywhere. I promise you. We're Haddie Maddie," I say, calling us the nickname that Lexi used to have for me when we were kids. The same name she chose to name her baby girl in tribute to me. "We've got hearts to break and high heels to wear, right?"

She angles her head and stares at me with her big chocolate brown eyes and chin quivering as she fights back the tears, trying to figure out if I'm telling the truth or not. I hold out my pinkie finger. "Promise."

A soft smile curls up the corner of her lips as her pinkie grips onto mine. "Haddie Maddie promise," she whispers, her smile growing wider. "Hearts and heels."

"Always. Okay, then." She looks at me one last time and then rushes down the hall.

I turn around once she's gone to meet Danny's tear-filled eyes. There is nothing I can say to him that I haven't said before, nothing that can ease the ache in his soul, so I just shake my head and swallow through the tears in my throat. I'm gazing at a picture of Lexi and newborn Maddie when he speaks from behind me.

"You know," he says, his voice soft and uneven, "when Lex was sick . . . when she was going through chemo and losing her hair . . . it used to drive me crazy." He shakes his head as he remembers, and I'm trying hard to follow his train of thought—give him time to get it out—but I know Maddie will be here soon. I don't want her to hear him talking about Lex with sadness. She's had way too much in her short life already.

"I used to tease her that she was shedding hair like a dog. Tried to make a joke about it. Strands of it would be stuck in the couch, balled up on my shirts when they came out of the drier...the seats in the car....It was just *everywhere*...." He laughs with a quiet sadness and then falls silent. I turn to face him, listening but not wanting to hear it, not wanting to remember how upset she'd get when hair would fall out clumps at a time.

He sighs, his shoulders shaking as he reins it in. "God, Had...I missed her so much the other day. Her scent's fading from her clothes in the closet....I...I was losing it, needing to feel connected to her." He runs a hand through his hair and presses his fingers beneath his glasses to wipe his eyes. "And I remembered her hair being everywhere....I was like a lunatic, searching all over this goddamn house for some of her hair. Any of it. A single strand." He looks up and meets my eyes, disbelief warring with sorrow. "I couldn't find any, Had."

I breathe in a slow, measured breath, trying to control the emotional floodgates from breaking. And even if they did, I think I'm all out of tears. I've cried enough in the past six months that it shouldn't be possible for me to shed more.

"For Christ's sake, I was scraping the lint trap in the dryer to find some." He shakes his head, tosses his glasses on the couch, and scrubs his hands over his face. The muscle in his jaw tics as I watch him struggle not to break down. "I feel like I'm going crazy here."

I take a step toward him, a single tear dripping down my cheek, and pain in my heart. He holds his hands up to stop me, knowing damn well if I hug him, we'll both be blubbering messes in a matter of seconds. "You should have called me. You don't—"

"And say what, Had?" A sliver of a laugh escapes, but I can hear borderline hysteria in it. "I know you're dying just as much without her as I am. I can't call you every time I have a bad day . . . bring you down."

The things I want to say are in my head, but I have a hard time getting them out. They choke in my throat, words cutting like razor blades. "Lexi wanted you to keep living, Danny. She wanted you to find someone eventually and move on." My voice is soft, but I know he heard me because his body stills and his head snaps up, his eyes flash with anger.

"Never," he says with conviction. "She was my forever, Haddie. You know that. My everything . . . I—I can't even imagine anyone else." He looks down for a minute before meeting my eyes again with absolute clarity. "No one will ever be able to fill this hole in my heart. Ever."

Maddie's footsteps shuffle on the floor behind me. Danny's face and posture transform immediately, a facade of normalcy for his daughter, but the smile on his lips never reaches his eyes.

And as he holds her tight—pulling her into his chest as if he's afraid he's going to lose her too—my *no strings* affirmation is solidified.

I turn around to face the wall of pictures, unable to contain the anger burgeoning inside of me. Mad at Lex, mad at me, mad at fricking everyone.

My mind wanders to the inconclusive BRCA test result sitting on my counter at home and about how the DNA test's lack of an answer—whether I'm carrying or not carrying the breast cancer gene—is more unsettling than settling. I need to make an appointment for a blood redraw—but the unknown is oddly more comforting than the known to me.

Fuck this. Fuck Lex for leaving me. Just fuck everything.

I suck in a breath and try to calm myself down, get a grip, and rein it all in. But it's so incredibly hard. And when I turn around and see Maddie standing there, bouncing up and down on her toes, my anger dissipates because I know I can't control the why or the when, but I can most definitely control the here and now.

"You ready to go have some fun, pretty girl?"

"Yes!" she says, and then pecks Danny on the cheek one more time before bounding out the door.

"Have fun," he says with a tight smile.

"Always," I say softly. "Hearts and heels." I nod at him and then turn to go buckle Maddie in the car.

We head off on our once-a-week adventure, singing silly songs and chatting on the way to the movie theater, and I can't help but glance in the rearview mirror at her more often than not.

I think of everything I need to tell her about her mommy. I remember sisterly secrets that no one knows to this day, but how I can't wait to tell her when the time's right or when she's old enough. I worry whether I'll be able to make her mom come to life enough with my words, with experiences, with laughter and love so that she feels her like I do. Like she's still here. I then realize of course I will. I have no choice.

I'm all she has now.

Chapter 8

I look down at the picture on my iPad and laugh. Maddie has texted me a picture of Danny with barrettes and clips in his hair. At least our time together today left her in a good mood. And with a smile.

My own widens as I think of what a resilient little girl she is and the fun we had this afternoon. And I try to take the little bits of peace I found spending time with her and apply it toward fulfilling another promise I made to Lex. Making the company we were going to start together become a reality.

And not only a reality, but the best damn promotional company out there.

I'm running through details in my mind as I unbuckle my seat belt. I need my phone like I need to breathe right now. It has everything in it—my to-dos, names of the VIPs to commit to memory, the schedule of events—everything. And I need *everything* to make sure I pull off this first of three events for a huge potential client without any glitches.

I blow out a breath in exasperation, check the clock again to make sure time's not standing still as I sit here waiting in the parking lot where Becks's text indicated to meet him. But who am I kidding? It's not that I'm pissed at the timing but more unsure what it's going to be like between us. Awkward? Normal?

It's a bitch when you can't see the strings, but they're still tying you up in their invisible web. But the bigger question is, what is wrong with me? Why do I care so much?

I'm trying to ignore the questions that are whirling in my mind on an endless reel when I look up just in time to see his SUV pull into the parking lot. "Well, hal-e-fucking-lu-jah," I mutter, annoyed at myself for the thrill racing through me because I get to see Becks again.

And that in itself is a huge problem. But it's a problem I don't have time to delve into any deeper if I plan on being ready for the event and the setup on time.

He pulls up beside me and my stomach flip-flops when I look over at him through our car windows. His head is angled down, looking at something in his lap, wraparound sunglasses covering his eyes, and I study the line of his profile as I wait for him to look over at me. Finally, he finishes whatever he's concentrating on in his lap and glances my way before getting out.

My heart quickens as I exit my car, and fuck me sideways because I don't want it to quicken. And I don't want that sudden ache between my thighs.

I walk to the back of our cars just as he does. And of course his presence—the sight of him, the scent of his cologne, that easy way he moves—has every one of my senses on high alert. He leans his shoulder against the back of his car, arms folded across his chest and my cell phone fisted in his hand. His eyes are hidden behind his tinted lenses, but I can feel them scrape their way over my body, despite his impassive expression.

He purses his lips as we stand in a silent standoff, each of us trying to figure out how the other is going to react. And the problem is, I'm supposed to be unaffected by him, but hell if my eyes don't keep wandering to that mouth of his, thinking of the incredible things it is capable of doing.

Suck it up, Had. It was a one-off thing. Time to be a big girl and lock and load the chastity belt.

"Hey, there."

"Haddie." He nods his head at me and says nothing further. This behavior is so unlike the Becks I know that I'm at a loss trying to figure out how to play this. I'm sure he has questions about Dante answering the phone, but in all reality, it's none of his damn business. If it makes anyone look bad, then it's me, and frankly that might be for the best in order for him to knock this shit off.

Whatever.

I hold his phone out to him, and he takes it, his fingers grazing over mine—that cataclysmic current shocking up my arm at his touch. I pull back immediately and curse myself for it because it's impossible for him not to notice my reaction. And my curse is also for being affected once again by the one person I don't want to be affected by. More than that, though, is the fact that Becks has refolded his arms across his chest and has still not given me back my phone. Or shown the slightest reaction to our connection. What the hell?

"Are you pissed at me?"

He looks at me a moment longer, head angled to the side. "Nope," he says as he pushes off the car and stands to full height. "I just have to keep repeating them in my head."

What? I'm lost here. "Repeating what in your head?"

"My rules." One side of his lips curl up, a smarmy smirk playing over his mouth. I want to tell him to take his sunglasses off so I can look in his eyes, so I can see that easy-go-lucky Becks I know, not this arrogant, closed-off guy standing in front of me. I shake my head because I've never seen this side of him, and, well, it's kind of hot.

Damn it! Just what I don't need to be thinking right now. Don't need to be seeing right now: Becks in this light.

"Your rules?"

"Yep," he reaffirms with a measured nod, and just keeps

looking at me. I'm about to ask him what exactly those rules are when he continues. "Rule number one: Don't sleep with friends. . . . It just seems to complicate things."

I can see him fighting the full-blown smirk on his face, and the quip is off my tongue before I can stop it. "Well, it seems you already broke that rule, Country." I fight the urge to step into him. Hating the potent mixture of need, attraction, irritation, and irrefutable lust that's vibrating within me.

And then he gives me that flippant, smart-ass quirk of his brows above his hidden eyes. "Yep, and look where that got me."

"Well, it's not like we're exactly friends." What the hell is that supposed to mean, Haddie? My God, I'm losing it. Fricking losing it.

"We're not friends?" The mocking tone in how he makes the statement pisses me off, pushes my buttons as I glance down to my phone still in his hand. He takes a step closer to me. I retreat one step, but my back bumps against the back of his vehicle. He takes another, the space between us receding. With the angle of the sun, I can just barely make out his eyes through his lenses, and they meet mine with an amused curiosity.

I swallow down the sudden lump in my throat from his nearness, my pulse erratic and the words that are always on a constant flow from my brain to my mouth a faltered jumble on my tongue. What the hell does Becks have on me? It's like some stupid hold I can't crawl out from under.

He raises his eyebrows again in a gesture denoting he's waiting, and in a move that is so unlike the sure-footed woman I am, I force words out that don't make any sense. "No, not friends . . . we're kind of like family."

Becks throws his head back and laughs loud and free, an almost palpable release of tension, before he lowers his head back down to look at me. He shakes his head back and forth, bemusement on his face. "City . . . that's a whole lot of fucked-up after what we did the other night, but strangely, I follow your logic."

And for the first time, I see the Becks I know come through. The boyish smirk that tells me I got to him. That my comment knocked the attitude back and relaxed him some. "So, rules, huh?"

Now that Becks is back in slow-and-easy mode, I feel a little bit more stability beneath my feet. He throws me when he shifts gears and goes all alpha on me. Definitely hot but at the same time confusing as fuck.

He just gives me a measured nod again and glances down at my hand held out for my cell phone before disregarding it and looking back at me with his lips pursed in a lopsided smirk. He's not giving in until I keep talking. And that's fine. I can talk until the fricking cows come home, but he's making it difficult the way he keeps getting closer and closer, the space between us dwindling, the air around us feeling as if it's becoming scarce.

Fuck a duck. Get a grip, Had. Chastity belt, chastity belt, I repeat to myself, trying to infuse some of my own humor into the situation to calm the nerves I never get but that are suddenly running rampant.

"It's okay. I get it," I say with a nod, and I'm not quite sure if I'm talking to myself about why I'm suddenly on edge or to Becks about the need for rules. I breathe out a sigh, readjusting my thought process off of him. Onto him. And damn if my dirty mind doesn't conjure up images of me on him. *Riding him.* Jesus, I need to get my head back into this thing—out of the gutter. I try to shake those thoughts. My head clears, but my thighs clench as his tongue darts out to wet his lower lip, completely oblivious to my thoughts.

"Mm-hmm," he murmurs, letting me struggle with my response. He reaches out, and I think he's going to give me my phone and put me out of the unfamiliar tongue-tied misery I'm in, but no such luck.

His finger grazes my cheek as he pulls a strand of hair off my face. My breath hitches and my pulse races, but I bat his hand away, his touch on my skin giving me just the wake-up call I need. "I have rules of my own, you know. . . ." I mean to sound like a petulant child, but the words come out in a breathy exhale.

That knowing smirk of his grows even wider. Irks me more than it should, because I shouldn't care. I don't care. But my libido sure as hell does.

"You do, do you?"

Mr. I-always-talk-a-lot is now being stingy with words? I can beat him at this game, no problem. "Yep."

"*Yep?* That's all you're going to give me?" He chuckles as he takes the final step to close the distance, reaching up to raise his sunglasses to the top of his head. His aqua eyes blink from the sun for a moment before finding mine at the same time my breasts brush against the firmness of his chest.

And damn. What was I going to say? I can't remember because I feel his breath feather over my lips, and a chill breaks out over my skin despite the warm weather. "*Yep?*" he taunts again, drawing the word out in a long breath, and for a minute, I'm relieved to know that he is just as affected as I am.

"Mm-hmm." It's all I can manage, desire increasing with each passing second.

"And they are?" he prompts as he leans in closer, our connection even stronger now.

"Lots of them," I say in a whoosh of air, my mind not comprehending my lack of wit because everything I am concentrating on seems to be centered around the apex of my thighs. Ache. Need. Desire.

He does that closemouthed laugh again. "I dare you to name one right now." His breath feathers over my lips, the warmth of it a tantalizing taunt to my unsated need. I know he asked me a question, but hell if my synapses are firing efficiently right now. Thoughts of that mouth of his on me, tasting me, obliterate all coherent thoughts. He leans in closer, my breath unsteady now and my eyes drifting closed in anticipation of his kiss.

A kiss I don't want.

Do want.

Just give it to me, Becks.

"Do you want something, Had?" he murmurs, his lips so close, I can feel their movement as he talks.

Every nerve in my body is attuned to him: his body pressed against mine, his scent, his energy. I give my second "Mm-hmm" in a matter of minutes and mentally chastise myself, tell myself to quit being so pathetic. Guys have always been a dime a dozen to me . . . so why does Becks seem like that million-dollar check I can't wait to cash?

"Gonna have to do better than that in order to get what you want." His taunting tone calls to me, breaks through my mental haze, and ignites the desire that's already smoldering.

"No strings," I whisper, hoping that now that I've said it, I can get a taste of him—get what I want—but the minute I say it, the heat of his body is gone. My eyes flash open, lips fall apart. *What the . . . ?*

"Nice try, City, but I'm already well aware of that rule," Becks says as he lowers his sunglasses back down over his eyes with one hand while the other places my phone in my hand. He takes a few steps away from me, smirk still owning his mouth, but I can see his arousal as crystal clear as the sky above me. And hell if he hasn't flipped me on like a fucking switch and is leaving me high and dry without giving me the electricity needed to light me up.

I go to say his name, mouth opening and closing a few times before I just give up and shut it.

We stare at each other a moment longer, my sexual frustration obvious and his point made with a victorious grin before he nods at me. "Good luck with your client tonight," he says, and then disappears around the driver's side of the car. I step over to the back of my car as I hear his engine rev before he pulls forward through the open spot in front of him and leaves.

And I stand there for a moment longer, my body amped up on adrenaline and my desire for him a mixture of necessity and damnation.

Well played, Daniels. Well played.

Hell, if strings aren't looking pretty damn appealing right now. I want to tie him up, get my fill of him, and then leave him bound up with need like he just did to me.

Chapter 9

I let the hot water sluice down my back as I soap up and clean the ocean's salt from my skin. The wave sets were pretty damn impressive this morning. Nothing like the ones I learned from at the beaches up in Santa Cruz, but decent nonetheless. Add to that the forty minutes I put into running on the beach's waterline after surfing, and I'm a happy man.

Well, I'd be helluva lot happier if I were standing here with Haddie, soaping up that ridiculous body of hers. Sliding sudsy hands over her smooth skin and perfect curves, and then sliding something else inside her until we're both panting, spent, and needing to soap back up again.

Goddamn.

The onslaught of thoughts and desires that the memory of that body invokes has me hard as a rock with no relief in sight.

Not if I can have anything to do about it.

Her body might be the holy frickin' grail of perfection but something in her eyes said what's inside doesn't jibe. The confidence she exudes—that she used to own like her golden tanned skin—is tinged with something now. Whether it's sadness or grief...who the fuck knows? But the glimpses are there when that wall she lives behind slips every once in a while. And when it slips, so do the connections she's made to everyone around her.

Well, everyone but Rylee, and that's to be expected, them being best friends and all. Just like Colton and me.

And hell if I don't miss that asshole. Happy for him that he found happiness with Ry after all of the shit that's happened to him, but damn if I don't miss his sarcastic mouth and annoying micromanagement at work.

I pull myself from my thoughts when I realize my dick is still flying full staff in my hand from thinking about Haddie. Then why in the hell has my mind veered to Colton?

Dude, that's fucked-up. I laugh out loud into the shower stall, knowing I must be stressed over all the preparations at work for the upcoming race season if I'm about to ease the ache from Haddie and my mind shifts gears halfway through to Colton.

Thoughts back to where they should be, on sweet, sweet Haddie, I roll my head back as my hand begins to stroke, adding only a small measure of the pleasure that Haddie gave me that night—when I resisted, tried to do the right thing to prevent what could be a fiasco of catastrophic proportions if our one night together went sideways.

Sideways. Hm, now that's an option when it comes to bending that sweet-ass body of hers.

I close my eyes and recall the purr from deep in her throat that she emitted right before she came, how her fingers tightened on my body, fingernails digging in when she let go.

I can feel my body tensing, my orgasm gearing up to release some of the rampant need that seeing Haddie the other day made resurface. It's lingered persistently, like a ghost, always reminding me of every damn thing about her.

And then Rex starts barking like a damn maniac.

At first I force myself to block him out, focus on the task at hand, but then realize that someone is at the door. *Are you fucking serious?* I stand there midstroke as I try to decide whether I should finish or should just chalk it up as a sign that I need to wait because I'll have the real thing soon enough.

Optimistic thinking at its finest. Even though the woman I'm after has proven more complex than a goddamn Rubik's Cube.

Fuck. Waiting it is, then. I turn off the shower just as the doorbell rings again. I can barely hear it above Rex's howling and tail thumping against the wall by the front door. It's wagging, so it must be someone he knows at least.

"Just a minute!" I yell as I rub the towel over my head momentarily before wrapping it around my waist. I make my way to the door, mentally telling my dick to downgrade its status, although all thoughts of Haddie and the boner I just had completely vanish when I see the smile on the other end of the peephole.

"Shit," I sigh as I reach out to grab the door handle. I make a quick check that I'm not pitching a tent beneath my towel, and my own smile widens without preamble. The door swings open, and she gives me a once-over, up and down with a smart shake of her head. Before I can even say hello, she's barreling into the house right past me.

"It's ten a.m., and your lazy butt is just getting in the shower? Is that how I raised you, Beckett Dixon?" She breezes in, and I know she's serious because she's using my middle name. I hold back a laugh because I can see her bloodhound nose trying to scent if I'm here alone or have had any females in the house as of late.

"Hi, Mom." I roll my eyes, one hand holding my towel up at my side, and my smile growing wider as I watch her set the bags in her hand on the counter before meandering around the family room. Her seemingly aimless stroll to the couch is actually a fishing expedition to see if there is an errant *Cosmopolitan* magazine on the table or a pair of pink flip-flops randomly left about—a surefire sign in her eyes that I'm settling down, ready to marry and give her grandbabies.

Ha. That's about as likely as me giving up racing.

"You can tell your lady friend who was in the shower with you to come on out now," she says loudly as she walks past the hallway to my bedroom, her hand down at her side, petting an exuberant Rex all the while. "I won't judge, I promise."

"Mom," I laugh with a shake of my head and exasperation in my voice, "there is no one in my bedroom."

"What about your shower? You were in the shower, right?" The expectancy in her voice makes me sad I've disappointed her because at heart who wants to let his parents down, but seriously, marriage and a baby? At this juncture in my life, it's something I most definitely want, but it's a blip on my radar for the near future.

I run a hand through my still soaked hair. The woman is relentless in her pursuit for a grandchild. Early retirement from her teaching job has been good to her but has also left her bored and pining for someone to coddle and rock and sing the ABCs with.

She walks past me and now that I know my towel is secure, I grab her and wrap my arms around her. "Hi, Momma. Good to see you."

She slinks her arms around me and pulls me in close. "Hi, baby. You're getting me all wet!" She pushes me away as quickly as she pulls me near. To her it's been hard enough to let us go, so she tries to prevent the emotions that are clogging her voice from spilling over as if I don't see it each and every time.

"Well, that's what happens when you waltz on in when I'm in the shower, now, isn't it?" I quirk an eyebrow up at her, a smart-ass smirk on my face.

"Oh shush!" She shoos me away but doesn't move as love fills her eyes.

God, I love this woman. Class, grace, and comfort all rolled into one. I study her as she does me and notice the lines a little deeper around her mouth, her cheeks a little fuller, and her eyes sparkling with happiness. She may be a constant proverbial thorn in my side, but I'd drop anything on a dime for her if she needed me.

I readjust my grip on my towel, and she swats at my arm. "Relax. It's not like I haven't seen your goods before. I did wipe that rear end of yours, you know."

"Yeah, like thirty years ago," I correct her as she turns her back on me and gives one more glance around to make sure I'm not lying to her about having company.

Her appraisal gives me a second to slide a glance at the clock, knowing this little visit is going to make me even later for work than my run already did. I mentally scan my calendar and figure I can take my scheduled conference call with Firestone on the drive in.

"So tell me," she says as she walks over to the counter and pulls out plastic containers of sugar and chocolate chip cookies, various other packages of food, and then last a tinfoil-covered dish, which has my stomach growling because it looks like my favorite of hers, lasagna. "Why is my handsome son not shacking up with some hot, little thing?"

"Ha. I'm the handsome son. Then where does that leave Walker?" I'll take any chance I can to throw a dig at him, even when he's not around. Brotherly love and all.

"Now, Becks, don't be mean to Walk. He's just as handsome as you, just in a different way," she scolds as she places the container into the refrigerator.

"Is that lasagna?" My mind shifts to what's more important, food. I'll put up with the ration of shit she gives me any day if she's going to fill my fridge and bring me home-cooked goodness.

I'm all for being self-sufficient, but cooking is for the birds. Plus I suck at it.

"Yes, it is," she answers, not really hearing my question before she continues. "Walker says you came up to the ranch all hot and bothered by someone. Why aren't you busy with her this morning?"

Fuckin' Walker and his big fat mouth. I should have known better.

"Hmm?" she says when I don't answer. And the way she says it, like she has absolutely no interest, and as always, I play along and act like I don't notice her blatant intrusion into my privacy.

"Mom, you know Walker. He's such a chi—" I cut myself off before I can say the word *chick*, knowing I'll get scolded for it.

"Beckett," she scolds, "do not use *that word* around me. You should know better by now. That's a word men in bars use, and frankly, yes, you're a man, but one, you are not in a bar, and two, you are educated and should know women are not meek little birds that chirp." I roll my eyes, her back facing me, as I hear the reprimand for what feels like the hundredth time in my life. "Quit rolling your eyes. Now, tell me all about her. Does she by chance have a pair of pink flip-flops?"

"Jesus, Mother! You and your pink flip-flops!" I bark.

"Don't ever doubt me. I told you I had a dream, and your wife was wearing a pink pair of them. . . ."

"You're incorrigible."

"And you're handsome. Now, quit trying to distract me, and tell me all about her!"

I stop myself from sighing out loud before thoughts of Haddie cloud my head, and my frustration with whatever it is we have comes tumbling out of my mouth.

"That good, huh?" she says in response to my exhale and continued silence, the smile on her face so wide, I swear her cheeks are going to crack.

I stare at her, the correction on my tongue, but I stop myself. I'm a goddamn grown man—in a towel, no less— and my mother is here scolding, probing, hoping I'm sleeping with someone. And yet I can't find it in me to let her down and tell her there is no one on my immediate radar.

Talk about twisting my balls . . . and not by any means in a pleasurable way.

There's so much wrong with this picture, I don't even know where to begin. My mother wanting to discuss my sex life? Talk about getting the heebie-jeebies.

"There's a possibility there," I tell her, hoping the response is enough for now. "How are you doing?" Time to change the subject, get her talking about dad and their aches and pains and their newest plans for travel.

I walk up behind her and place a kiss on the top of her head, the open container of cookies calling to me. I grab one, settle down on the barstool, and prepare for the rest of my conversation with her.

No one ever rushes Trisha Daniels.

No one.

Not even her elder son, who's going to be so damn late to work, it's not even funny.

Lucky for me I'm in good with the boss.

Chapter 10

I tap my pencil to the beat coming through my speakers, notes strewn around my desk, and my mind focused on nothing in front of me. Instead, my thoughts keep wandering to Ry's text: **Just because I'm on my honeymoon, doesn't mean I've forgotten to remind you to make your appointment.**

"Get off my case," I mutter, hating that she's remembered and loving that she's remembered all in the same breath. I glance up at the calendar on the wall beside me and laugh at the five doctor's appointments I've written on there and then X'd out when I suddenly had to cancel because—*I don't know*—the sky was blue that day.

I'm being such a chicken about it, but denial is my strongest truth now. I've dropped my pencil, and my hand is unconsciously rubbing soft counterclockwise circles around my breast through my clothes. Not pushing firmly, though, because I'm too scared to find what I know is lurking there beneath all the tissue. The same cancerous parasites that took my mom's breasts and stole my sister's life.

That I know deep down will shorten mine as well.

I shake my head and blow out a breath and pound my fist against the desk. I know I need to find out the truth, get the test results, but at the same time, *I watched Lex die.* I watched the cancer take every single part of her, day by day, piece by piece until there was nothing left of her but pain and promises. Tears and denials. Then finally resignation and devastation.

I know the road, know the pain, know it's no use. . . . Even if they find it in time, it might not matter. She wasn't responsive to any treatments. We're cut from the same cloth, so neither would I be. I try to tell myself I'd rather live without the fear, knowing that what helps define me as a woman also may have death knocking at my door.

Anger fires within me—at Lex, at myself, at everything— because I'm scared to death. To know the truth. Not to know the truth. I realize I'm being ridiculous. I know the right thing to do is to find out, take the blood test and catch it early if I have it, to give myself a fighting chance . . . but, man, Lex thought the same thing and look what happened to her.

Six months and she was gone.

"Fuck." I sigh and run a hand through my hair before I pick up the phone and dial the number I now know by heart. I make the appointment and promise not to cancel this time. I've just finished writing the details on my calendar—a slight weight lifted from my shoulders so another one can fill its place—when my cell rings.

I groan when I see Cal's name, my contact at Scandalous. The event went very well this past weekend, good turnout, lots of chatter in the press about his new club, a few more celebrities confirmed for the next event this weekend, but . . . it's Cal. He's never happy. I put on my fuck-you smile when I answer the phone as my own personal tribute to his douchery.

"Cal! How are—"

"I need Saturday to be bigger than last weekend." His voice comes through loud and clear, words clipped, impatience emanating through the line.

And hello to you too, douche bag.

I bite my tongue, wanting to tell the wanna-be-rico-suave where to go, but I can't. This is a huge account if I can land it. Their constant events can equate to a continual revenue stream and the possibility of more clients. I force the sweetness I'd rather choke on to lace my voice. "Okay." I draw the word out pleasantly. "What exactly wasn't to your liking, Cal? What other suggestions might you have?"

"Honey, I'm paying you, right? The suggestions should be yours."

I roll my shoulders, not in the mood, but know that if I get the gig, I will no longer have to deal with him. Since he only deals in *new talent*, as he calls me, I'd move onto a retainer with a different company representative and away from him. The thought makes toning down the quip on my tongue that much more palatable.

"Point made." I let the silence stay on the line for a moment so I can check my notes and give myself a second to try to figure out what to say to make him happy and not put him on the defensive. "With last weekend's event, I brought in three additional sponsors and an additional four VIP celebrity attendees. The attendance was thirty percent higher than what you had anticipated, and the club was all over social media sites. So, in other words, I'm not sure how much more overachieving you expect out of HaLex . . . but I think we surpassed the mark you set handily. And while, yes, you are paying me, Cal, if I don't know what extra something you're looking for, I won't be able to provide it." I take in a deep breath and realize what I've just said. The door I've opened for him to step through with his chauvinistic bullshit.

He chuckles low and soft, and the hair stands up on the back of my neck at the slippery sound. And from the laugh alone, I know he is going to walk right over the threshold. "Oh, Ms. Montgomery, *something extra* is always welcome on my end if you're really wanting to secure an account as handsome as Scandalous would be for you."

And that's a big fuck-off-and-die-I'm-not-sleeping-with-you in my book.

My skin crawls at the suggestion in his tone, and pride has the words spewing off the tip of my tongue, but dignity has me biting them before I can make a monumental mistake. Speak my mind—give him attitude—and I risk losing this account. I hang tight to the knowledge that I will not have to deal with Cal after the end of the month. "I think it's best we stick to the contract. I'll figure something out for the event. No worries."

There is silence on the other end of the line, and I'm not sure if I should be amused or pissed that he's taken aback by the fact that I've completely ignored his unwanted and completely unwarranted advance.

"Well, good, then," I continue, not letting him gain his bearings so he can prove to be the supercilious prick I know is hiding beneath the surface. "Unless you have something else for me, I'd best be going. I need to put in some added time to get you that something *extra* for Saturday's event."

I hang up the phone before he can speak and ruin my perfect exit. I drop the phone, the clatter of it against my desk filling the silence of the room, and drop my head into my hands. I sit there for a moment, hoping the buzzing in my ears will dissipate, but it just continues to rage incessantly until it becomes almost white noise.

My shoulders are tight, my body amped up with a Molotov cocktail of emotions just waiting to explode when lit by the right match. My mind leaps to Becks, and I curse myself for that damn ache he's created, which isn't going away no matter how many times BOB and I have reacquainted ourselves since Sunday.

It's just not the same.

Not even close.

I groan out in frustration—memories of that one night together flickering through my mind as I hear Dante's motorcycle pull up in the driveway. I really don't need to be around him right now—primed alpha male oozing sex appeal and willingness for a quick romp in the bed.

Or on the kitchen counter.

God, yes, I know sleeping with him would be a huge mistake—huge—but damn he might be the perfect flint to spark this sexually frustrated woman's fire. But no matter how much I know he'd be incredible in bed and pleasure me sufficiently, I'm not crossing that line.

I just can't.

Not just for my sake or the satisfaction of my sex drive, but because when I think of sex and what I'm craving, I think of Becks. I see him standing between the V of my thighs, that sexy-as-fuck smile on his lips and how he lifts his head up in rapture just as he sinks into me. Yet the fact that I can't stop thinking of him—of these things—means I just might do something stupid and use Dante to sate my simmering lust.

And that would solve nothing but prove how fucked-up my logic is.

I can't use one man's hand to scratch another man's itch. Well, I could, but that would involve both of them being in the same bed with me, and that's a whole different can of worms.

The chuckle comes on the heels of the mental image. The exhausted laughter at my ridiculously immature thoughts of two men and their cans of worms tells me I need to leave the house. I need to get out and get some fresh air and make my raging hormones simmer down. Grab hold with both hands and get a grip.

It takes me a second as I look out the window to the front yard to figure out what I need. And it is most definitely not the sight of Dante pulling off his shirt and wiping his hands on it after he adjusts something on his bike. Bare skin, defined muscles, etched ink.

I shove the chair back.

Time to go.

*   *   *

"See? Just what the doctor ordered, Maddie Haddie."

Maddie giggles loudly as she takes another lick of the melting massive ice-cream cone in her hands. "Yes, Haddie Maddie," she says reversing our names like Lexi used to do. "This is the best idea ever!"

"It is," I agree, holding my own cone up to hers and tapping it in a toast. There's nothing like time with Maddie to relieve any stress I may have. Clear my thoughts and make me forget about easy mannered country boys I have no business thinking about. I'm glad she was home when I called Danny to see if I could take her out for some ice cream. It made her smile, and it made me forget all the crap of my day.

She continues to chatter incessantly, filling me in on the minutiae of her elementary school life, and I love how the simplest things bring her joy. It forces me to realize how even though she's been through so much, she's persevered, and she is a bright and thriving, little soul.

Our spot on the grassy hill in the park overlooks a huge farmers' market to the right of us, and off in the distance to the left is the beach. I reach in my purse to grab a napkin for her when my eye catches sight of the dandelion hiding nearby.

My breath catches momentarily. I know it's there just because it's a weed, but I can't help but think it's a sign from Lexi and a nod to our childhood fixation on them and their potential to make wishes come true.

I pull the weed, careful not to disturb its seeds and hold it out in front of me. Maddie tilts her head to the side and looks at me, curious what I'm doing. "Your momma and I used to love to make wishes on dandelions when we were little girls."

"Really?" she asks on that edge of being too old so that it's silly but at the same time thrilled to learn something new about her mom.

"Yep. We even had a phase where we'd pick them all and

make potions with the seeds to try to make our wishes stronger. Then we'd let them dry from whatever we put on them, make a wish, and blow them into the wind." I smile softly, the memory so bittersweet.

"Like what kind of potions?" She scoots closer to me now, the fascination to know more causing her eyes to widen.

"Hm ... anything we could sneak from the house so Nana wouldn't notice: perfume, glitter, salt, a little bit of everything all mixed together." I laugh now. "Your poppy would get so mad because we'd leave them drying all over the place, and then yell at him not to move them and disturb the wishes on them. He even started calling us the dandelion duo for a while."

"The dandelion duo?" She smiles as she looks at me, and I nod toward the weed in my hand. "Did your wishes ever come true?" The awe in her voice tugs at everything inside of me.

"All the time." I reach over with my free hand and run it over her cheek. "In fact, the one your mom wished the hardest for happened."

"It did? What was it?"

I smile, tears burning the back of my eyes. "It was you," I whisper. Maddie's eyes lock on mine, the grin spreading on her face, but the sorrow glistening in her eyes. I put my arm around her and pull her in close to my side. We sit there quietly for a moment while I figure out how to make her a part of this, a way to feel close to her mom. "Do you want to be part of the dandelion duo?"

Startled, she bounces her head up, huge brown eyes staring at me full of hope. "Can I? What do I need to do?"

"Well, you need to make a wish, and the way a dandelion sister makes a wish is by saying, 'I wish I may, I wish I might, have this wish I wish tonight' ... and then you close your eyes, make your wish, and blow as hard as you can on the seeds so they take flight."

"That's all I have to do?"

"Yep. Would you like to become one now?"

"Yes!"

I hold the dandelion out for her to take in her hand. She looks over at me and I nod for her to go ahead. "I wish I may, I wish I might, have this wish I wish tonight. . . ." She squeezes her eyes and falls silent for a moment as she makes her wish before blowing all of the seeds into the air.

"Look," I tell her so she opens her eyes and watches. "One day one of those seeds carrying your wish is going to come back and bring you your wish, okay?" She nods her head before resting it in the crook of my arm as we watch the last of the seeds disappear. Memories flash through my mind, so faded by time but there nonetheless, and I feel a soft contentment at being able to share this with Maddie. "See, now anytime you see a dandelion, you'll know it's a sign from your mom since now you're officially part of the dandelion duo."

We sit there a while longer before gathering our stuff. We walk toward the parking lot and decide to stroll through the farmers' market on the way to the car. Of course, Maddie's eyes stop on every booth, and we pause numerous times to ooh and ahh at the random items on display.

We are busy discussing why she doesn't need the huge bag of kettle corn she's eyeing since she still has smudges of chocolate ice cream on her face from her snack moments before when I freeze at the sound of the slow, familiar cadence behind me. I know it can't possibly be him, but it's not like I can resist looking because before my brain even tells my mind to stay focused forward, I'm already turning my head.

At the same moment that my eyes lock on the owner of the voice, his eyes find mine. And all of my resolve, every damn bogus, bullshit lie I've told myself about not wanting more with Beckett comes tumbling down around me when our eyes meet.

I feel that instantaneous spark—that firing of desire in my core—when a slow, lopsided smirk spreads on his lips. My vanity has me immediately cringing at my cutoff denim shorts and oversized shirt hanging off of my shoulder. My hair piled high on top of my head in a messily fashionable ponytail compensates for my complete lack of makeup.

Or so I tell myself.

We hold each other's gaze for a moment, while we both try to figure out what the other's eyes are saying. And then my chance to infer any meaning there is knocked clear to the wayside when I notice an arm looped through Becks's. I follow the arm up to take in the woman at his side. She says something to him, and he looks at me a moment longer before turning to see what she's pointing to.

I can't tear my eyes away from them. I don't want to acknowledge the pang of jealousy that starts gnawing through me at the sight of him with another woman. And not just any woman, but a woman who's the complete opposite of me. Dark and exotic compared to my blond hair and dime-a-dozen cow brown eyes.

Maddie tugs on my hand and breaks my trance. And as I'm pulled back to the here and now, as I blindly buy the popcorn for her because my mind is so rattled by seeing Becks with someone else, I find myself dismayed by the fact that for the first time ever, I feel completely insecure.

What the hell is he doing to me?

I silently chastise myself, tell myself to pull on my big-girl thong and own it like a stripper does her pole, but I think I'm a little stunned at the realization that my ever-confident self has pulled a disappearing act. And even now I'm at a loss because I suddenly notice that the guy who handed me the kettle corn is staring at me like I've lost it until I realize I've paid and am blocking the next customer in line.

Fuck.

I let Maddie lead as she pulls my hand while I attempt to

come to grips with this foreign feeling of inadequacy inside me. I laugh. Mad thinks I'm laughing at her excitement over the popcorn, but in all honesty, I'm dumbfounded that of all men to make me feel this way, it's Becks.

Wanting more of him is most definitely a possibility . . . but it's the what comes after that's not in the cards for me.

And while I sit at a picnic table shoveling popcorn in my mouth without thinking, it hits me. This is how he must have felt when he called the house and Dante answered his phone. No wonder he was a prick to me.

But Dante is no one, and she . . . she obviously is someone to him.

It's not like I care or anything.

Before I can finish lying to myself, I look up from the bag of popcorn, and he's right in front of me. Or rather his abdomen is, and that in itself causes my breath to hitch as I recall the feel of my fingers over the defined muscles beneath his T-shirt. I have to angle my head up to meet his shadowed eyes under the brim of his baseball cap.

"Dante."

The name falls out before I can even process my thoughts properly and get a handle on what I'm about to say. And of course I really mean that I understand why Becks was angry at me—I want to explain Dante's presence properly—but my brain is scrambled with whatever jacked-up hold he seems to have on my coherency.

Becks's brow furrows immediately in response, and before he can voice the question I can see on his tongue, Maddie makes her presence known.

"What do you call a bad popcorn joke?" her high-pitched voice asks to my right.

His eyes narrow at me momentarily before darting over to Maddie. To the little girl I should be answering, but my eyes are fixated on Becks's face and the range of expressions that are playing over his features: confusion, interest, amusement. His smile spreads wide and genuine on his face as he steps toward her and lowers himself onto his haunches so that he's about eye level.

"Hm," he says, and then purses his lips in thought. "I think I have an answer but I'm not supposed to talk to strangers . . . so I'm sorry but you're a stranger." He just keeps his eyes focused on her as she erupts into a fit of deep giggles from her belly.

She angles her head and rolls her eyes at him, the laughter still bubbling up as she forgets all about the popcorn and falls under Becks's charm. "I'm Maddie," she says.

"Ah . . . you wouldn't be half of that fabulous duo Haddie Maddie would you?" he asks, and my heart immediately swells, watching him engage with her—and at the knowledge that he remembers who she is from overhearing my past conversations with Rylee, knows how much she means to me. And then of course, I don't want my heart to swell because how can it swell if I don't like him in *that way*? Maddie's giggle pulls me from my overanalysis, which seems to be the norm as of late around him.

"Yes," she says.

"Oh, well, in that case, I do know you," he says, holding his hand out to her. "I'm Becks. Your aunt Haddie's friend."

Friend. Hm. I mull the word over in my mind, wanting to like the sound of it but at the same time wanting to reject it immediately. Lover of hot monkey sex with strings tying me to the headboard sounds so much better.

Maddie's voice pulls me back again as she shakes his hand. "So, what's the answer?"

"What do you call a bad popcorn joke?" Becks repeats as he stands up and grabs a handful of popcorn from our bag on the table in front of him. "I'd call it *corny*." He chuckles as Maddie's jaw falls open momentarily in shock that he guessed the answer correctly. Then she grins ear to ear.

Question answered, Becks turns his body toward mine, and I find myself standing without thinking, like he has some kind of magnetic pull on me I can't resist. He angles his head to the side and just stares at me for a moment. "Hey."

"Hi," I say, my body thrumming instantly from his attention. Nipples tight, pulse racing, body flushed.

"Dante?" he asks, and I immediately cringe that he remembered my greeting to him. "Am I missing something here?"

I sigh and shake my head. "Yeah. I just wanted to explain who answered your phone the other day. Dante is—"

"Not my business." His matter-of-fact tone stops me momentarily, but I want him to know the truth.

"He's someone from my past. He needed a place to stay," I tell him, but he just quirks his eyebrows at me. I glance over to see Maddie watching our exchange with amused curiosity, popcorn in hand for the show.

"You can say ex, Had. No strings, *remember*?"

I swear to God if I never hear that term again, I'll be a happy woman. He taunts me with it every chance he gets, a verbal assault on my conscience. A way to let me know that . . . what? If I wanted strings, then maybe he might too? I mean that's just not plausible.

"Becks, it's important for you to know that I didn't hop from being with you to being with someone else. Nothing is going on between Dante and me."

"Just like nothing is going on between you and me, right?" he asks, suggestion in his tone and the question hanging in the sexually charged air between us. I avert my eyes as I sigh, my gaze dragging down his T-shirt and board shorts to flip-flops as I try to find my footing in this world, which is continually tilting beneath me.

And shit, I hate earthquakes.

"Becks . . ." My voice trails off, and I'm not sure what to say because he's right. There is most definitely something here between us. Something that I don't want but can't seem to stop thinking about. Maybe we should just hook up one more time, flush this need from my system once and for all.

I start to think it's a brilliant idea. I'm already mentally undressing him when his name is called out over the hum of the market's activity. "Becks?"

And I'm instantly bristling at the accented voice calling to him. He stares at me a moment longer, his tongue darting out to wet his bottom lip while his eyes dare me to question him. "One second," he calls out to Ms. Exotic, holding a finger up to her before turning his attention back to me, challenge back in his gaze. It's almost as if he's taunting me, wanting me to ask him to stay, to explain who or what she is to him.

As desperately as I want to know, I settle for smiling subtly and shaking my head in response. When I shift my gaze, I meet Ms. Exotic's eyes, and she smiles genuinely at me, making me hate her on the spot. Can't she be some superficial catty bitch so that I have reason not to like her? And I hate that I hate her for it, but she has no clue who I am. Or how expertly Becks has handled my body.

And now holds my emotions.

Maybe it's her presence that has me immediately wanting Becks all that much more. Makes me wish that easy smile he's giving her was directed at me instead of the one that always seems to taunt me. The one that says you know you want this—want more of whatever this is—so why are you fighting it?

"Haddie?" His voice fortifies my obstinacy, but the gentle probing in it tugs on my resolve.

I glance over to Maddie for a split second before looking back to him. "Yeah?"

"You know I'm here if you need me, right?"

I roll my shoulders, not needing my scattered emotions to find a home here right now. I don't need this man I have somehow let in to start offering me more than I can readily accept. Something beyond friendship.

"Thanks," I say, hating that my voice sounds unconfident and needy. I try to find my dignity, try to find my trademark wit. "No strings, right?" My laugh sounds weak; my thoughts are inconsistent.

He steps in closer, reaching out to run a hand up and down my arm. I know the gesture is one of comfort, but my senses go haywire from his touch. "Run all you want, Haddie," he murmurs, his deep cadence a strong sound against the white noise around us, "but you're going to find yourself all tangled up in those dangling ends you refuse to tie to something. . . . Who's going to rescue you then?"

His words scar my psyche, telling me truths I don't want to know but already believe to be true. Want to be true. Because if I'm all tied up in my own web of protection, then when the inevitable happens, I can't hurt anyone else.

"I don't need to be rescued, Becks."

He steps back and shakes his head, sorrow in his eyes as he searches mine, trying to see past the impenetrable guard I've put in place. "That's where you're wrong, City. Everyone deserves to be rescued at some point."

He holds my gaze for a moment longer before nodding his head at me, ruffling Maddie's hair, making her giggle, and walking away. I watch his strong shoulders and broad back until the crowd around us swallows him up. I don't let myself wonder if she kisses his cheek when he reaches her, if he laces his fingers with hers, or if she puts her arm around him.

I don't.

Because he's a forever.

And I can only focus on todays.

Chapter 11

Exhausted, I top off my glass of wine, walk out into the backyard, and sit down on the chaise longue. I sink into the warm summer air, face up to the fading sun, and close my eyes. Then I let the emotions that have been warring inside me during the past week wash over me. I keep my eyes closed but lift my wine to my lips and drink the tart liquid as the tears well behind my lids.

I think of my sweet Maddie girl and how she cried and clung onto my neck earlier when I dropped her off at home. I think of the what-ifs and never-gonna-bes for her, and I'm filled with such melancholy that it's easier to just sit here in the warm summer night with the light dwindling and the sound of kids playing beyond the fence than to go inside and face the silence.

Because in the silence, doubts creep in, memories come, and need swelters.

So instead, I sit and enjoy the sounds of life around me beyond my fenced in backyard and think what a metaphorically sad description that is of me and my heart. The wine goes down too easy, and with the comfortable warmth sliding over my skin, I slowly drift off, succumbing to the grueling aspects of my week.

I jolt awake when my wineglass is taken from my hand. I'm immediately startled, but when I snap my groggy eyes open, Dante is sitting on the side of my chair and has placed my empty glass on the table beside me. His gray eyes hold mine, and he appears both concerned and amused at my midevening nap in the backyard.

"Hey," he says softly, his hand moving to the side of my face. My body freezes at the graze of his callused fingertips against the line of my jaw, but my heart races. I tell myself that my pulse is pounding because of being startled awake, but the simmer in my lower belly puts my cards on the table.

I rub my lips together, stalling for time to figure out what I'm thinking, what to say, but just end up staring at Dante, trying to get a read on the look in his eyes. "Hey, you okay?" I finally manage to ask.

I watch the muscle in his jaw tic and feel the tensing of his fingers, and then just as soon as I see something flicker in his eyes, it's gone. "Yeah, I'm just not used to seeing you so sad." He angles his head to the side for a moment. "You're not my firecracker that I'm used to."

I take in his hair curling over the collar of his T-shirt, and the goatee on his handsome face. When he rubs his thumb absently over my bottom lip, I sit up immediately, despite his hand still resting on the crook of my neck. The air between us shifts suddenly, and I need to put this back into comfortable territory for me.

"I watched Lex die. That kind of changes you, you know?" And I know he knows, know that he held his grandfather's hand as he passed on from cancer too, but that was over fifteen years ago. My sister's death feels like it happened yesterday.

He nods his head in understanding as his free hand moves from the cushion to the bare skin of my thigh, his eyes never leaving mine. Warning bells go off in my head, but I can't figure out what is louder: the alarm or the desire.

I work to swallow as his thumb rubs concentric circles up my inner thigh to the hem of my shorts.

"What are you doing, Dante?" My voice is barely audible, my warning lost in the exhale of breath that comes with it. I know I told him no sex, to not even go there . . . but at the same time, I'm so needy right now, so desperate to forget again.

The problem is, this time it's not Lex I'm trying to forget. It's Becks.

And the flickering thoughts of forevers and tomorrows that I most definitely don't want. Will not allow myself to have.

"You know Lexi wouldn't want you to stop living. She'd hate that you have." He begins to lean in, and I feel my eyes narrowing and my breath hitching as he gets closer.

"Dante . . ."

I know I should stop him, know I should push him away, but the minute his lips touch mine and his taste hits my tongue, I feel alive again. And I push all of the objections from my head—the ones that scream a warning about the devastation I know he can have on my heart once he gets ahold of it—and let myself fall under his spell. I want to lose myself, and the headiness I feel from his touch, his body, and his dominance doesn't allow me to think.

Make me numb, Dante.

Right now, I just want to be taken. Transported away from my thoughts and my questions and my insecurities. And I try to lose myself in the physicality of it all to convince myself that I want this—to be pushed to the brink so hard and fast so that I can forget everything I don't want and remind myself that this is enough for me. Will be enough for me. That this is the way I choose to live my life.

Sex with someone who wants nothing more. Someone who will be out of my life just as quickly as he came into it.

That's safe. That's what I can accept.

"No, no, no!" I stop Dante by pressing my hands against

his very firm and tempting chest, forcing him back so that his lips tear from mine. I can't do it. Can't lose myself in Dante when Becks is the one I really want.

Dante stares at me, jaw clenched in frustration, eyes telling me he wants me. "Yes, you do," he murmurs. "I can help you forget, Haddie. Make you feel alive."

My body and heart have two different mind-sets, but I keep him at arm's length as I try to calm myself down. He angles his head, his eyes holding mine until they glance down to where his fingers begin to untie the laced ribbon crisscrossing the cleavage portion of my shirt.

. . . but you're going to find yourself all tangled up in those dangling ends you refuse to tie . . .

Becks's words hit my ears again. Pull me back from the brink of making a huge mistake. Make me think of him when all I was trying to do was use Dante to forget about him.

"No!" I tell him with more determination.

Dante leans forward against my palms, his fingers untying one more lace. "C'mon, babe, you want me as much as I want you."

I keep my hands up in defense as my heart and head win over the control of my body. I give one final shove against him and turn so that my legs fall over the opposite side of the lounger from where he is sitting, his hands still on my body. I shrug out of his touch and shove myself up out of the chair and start walking toward the house.

"Such a fucking tease."

I hear his snide comment from behind me, and I falter in my footsteps, fingers on the handle of the sliding-glass door. "Make sure you taste your words, Dante, before you spit them back out."

I start to tug on the door, anger firing in my veins at him, at me, at who the hell knows? "Now you're just playing hard to get, babe. You know how hard that makes me," he says, his voice close behind me, "and I do know you like it nice and hard."

And Dante's words should turn me on, but they don't. They make me cringe, make me think of Becks—and how much more tempting the comment was from him instead. Jesus Christ. Why won't he leave my thoughts?

"Touch me again and you'll have to find a new place to stay," I say with my back to him as I walk into the house.

"Is that a threat or a promise?" he asks with a chuckle.

"It's a fact," I shout back to him as I enter my bedroom and slam my door shut. And I just stand there. My hands fisted and my mind humming with confusion. Hell yes, I'm mad at Dante, but I think I'm mad at myself more than anything.

When did I become this woman who uses men to forget other men? I mean how fucked-up is that? Not that it's right, but using sex—being a little festive—to help forget the grief of Lexi's death is one thing, but to use it to forget another man? That's taking it a bit too far even for my own standards.

I begin to walk to the bathroom and then turn abruptly and pick up my cell phone. I just need to hear her voice. That's it. A little something to help me get a grip on my reality and remind me of that woman I used to be. Sassy and spunky. Not this whiny shadow of myself that I don't even like.

I can't seem to find and hold on to myself anymore.

Except for when I hear her voice.

Or that one night with Becks.

Gah! I dial my voice mail and fast-forward past the new messages I don't want to listen to right now. There's only one saved message I want to hear, and I don't care how many times I replay it, my chest still constricts at the sound of her voice.

I listen to her ramble, her voice breathy from the exertion of speaking as she neared the end. She wanders in her message, inconsistency in her thoughts, but at my favorite part, my fingers clutch onto the phone. "Remember, Had.

Time is precious. Waste it wisely." She pauses while her breath rattles in her chest, the slight wheeze coming through the line that still squeezes my heart and brings those days flooding back. "I love you. To the moon and back's not far enough, Had. I'll always love you."

The sob catches in my throat, and the chills race over my skin as I listen to my sister's breaths while she fumbles to end the call. I drop to the bed, needing her in so many ways. She was my rock. The serious one so that I could be the funny, flippant one. I let a few tears fall before I wipe them away hastily, mad at myself for being sad at that lasting gift she left me in that voice mail.

The knock on my door startles me. I don't want to talk to Dante right now. I just want to be left alone and fall into a dreamless slumber. I ignore the summons and crawl farther up onto my bed and pull the blankets up around me.

"Haddie, c'mon. . . . Look, I'm sorry. I didn't mean to . . ." I hear him sigh on the other side of the door and what I can assume is his forehead hitting the wood. "Who am I kidding? Of course I meant to. It's you, isn't it? But I apologize. I shouldn't have. It's just being here brings it all back, and you're just so fucking sexy . . . I just . . . Please, babe, talk to me . . ."

As much as it's a slight shock to hear the never-wrong Dante Teller apologizing, the words do nothing to me. Nothing for me. They don't pull me from the sadness that wraps around me like a blanket. I squeeze my eyes shut and throw one arm over my face in a fruitless attempt to protect myself from everything I don't want to feel right now.

"Had . . ." His voice trails off while I sit with the covers pressed to my mouth and I wait him out, wanting to be alone. Needing to be alone. After a minute or so, I hear him sigh and then the sound of his feet padding down the hall-way in retreat.

I suck in a breath of air as my body shudders with the violent sobs that I prevent myself from crying. And after a bit, I calm down some to realize night has descended and find myself staring at the ceiling in my darkened room. Time passes, and I really want to talk to Rylee right now. I need the even-keeled and sound advice of my closest friend to tell me that I'm being stupid. That I should take my own damn advice: live a little. That life begins at the end of my comfort zone.

I pick up the phone and dial, not sure if I'm looking to find where my comfort zone exactly is.

My mind-set wavers from wanting to needing. From being angry to being resigned. It doesn't really matter what I feel, though, because when his voice fills the line, I feel completely alone in this room right now but at the same time not so isolated anymore.

"Hello?"

I struggle to find the right words to explain why I'm calling. Except I can't find anything beyond the jumbled garble that fills my head, so I revert back to my new standby, sarcasm. "So you're a constant rule breaker now, are you?" And I'm not sure where my anger comes from. I shouldn't direct it at him, but I do. Unabashedly.

I hear shifting on the other end of the phone, and then the sound of a television fades as he moves away from it. Wait. Why is he moving away from the TV? Is *she* there with him right now?

"Had? You want to help me here?"

My emotions are in such a tumult that I don't even realize that I'd planned on taking this conversation here until it's too late. "Your rule number one: You don't sleep with friends. Is she a friend, too?"

And I can't believe I just said that out loud. I don't think he can either because the line is silent as he processes my comment. "Is *Dante* a *friend*?" There is an edge to his voice this time when he speaks, exasperation mixed with irritation that has me chewing the inside of my cheek as I try to figure out what to say next.

How can I say he's just a friend when I was going to use him an hour ago to get over the man I'm speaking with? "We weren't talking about him." I force the issue, not wanting to delve into the potluck of problems I have sitting on the table.

"Then we're not talking about her. Besides, what's it to you Haddie? I'm giving you exactly what you asked for, right? One night, no strings. So why do you care what Deena is to me?"

Ah, Ms. Exotic has a name. Deena? I hate the name Deena. Well, not really but I do now. I immediately imagine his voice moaning it, and I instantly feel sick to my stomach.

"You don't get to keep me at arm's length but then call dibs when it's convenient for you," he continues when I'm silent, lost in my thoughts.

"I've never done that!" A blatant lie but if I'm reaching, then I might as well stretch as far as I can.

"Bullshit, Montgomery. Dante or whatever the fuck his name is may mollycoddle you, stroke you when you need it but leave you alone otherwise, but I'm not like that. I'm not him. You can't fuck with people's emotions and expect them to want to be there for you, either." He sighs out in frustration while I'm taken slightly aback by the bite to his tone.

"Who the hell mentioned emotions? Emotions weren't included in my rules," I say childishly.

"You want to talk about rules, Haddie? You want to know my rule number two? I don't play games."

"Hmpf." It's a disbelieving sound followed by a roll of my eyes he can't see.

"Yeah. That's one way to put it. Is there something else you called for besides trying to stick your nose in where it doesn't belong?"

I open my mouth and then shut it, unsure how calling him because I just needed to hear his voice has devolved so quickly into this. Into me scrambling for words I can't find to fix shit that doesn't need fixing.

Because I don't want this. Don't want him.

"Well, then, if you want to actually talk instead of pull this ridiculous bullshit, I'm here for you . . . but, Had . . . ? Whatever this is here . . . this passive-aggressive crap? I don't do too well with that. We had our one night. You made it quite clear you didn't want anything more than that, so you don't get to call me up and question what I might or might not be doing with anybody else. You want no strings? Then cut the ties . . . but frankly, I don't think you know what the fuck you want. So until you figure your shit out, I think it's best that we say good night before we make a bad situation even worse."

"Wait!" Desperation rings in my voice in the single word. And I hate myself for sounding like this, but I'm so lonely, so scared, and just want the comfort I know he can bring me right now.

I wait for the sound of the dial tone to assault my ears. Wait for the incessant beep that reaffirms why I have barbed wire wrapped around my heart—painful but necessary. But there is nothing for a few moments until I hear the phone scrape against the stubble on his face.

And I wait . . . my throat burning with the tears I want to shed but am so sick of. The ones that no longer bring me comfort.

"I'm here, Haddie. I'm not going anywhere, okay?" The timbre of his voice carries his concern and sympathy to me through the line.

The incoherent sound I make is all I can offer to thank him for not hanging up on me. For not giving up on me.

"Talk to me. What's going on?" he asks gently as if he's afraid if he pushes too hard I'll run away and hide. Just like I want to. How he has me pegged so well, I don't know.

"I'm sorry." My words are barely audible. I don't even recognize my own voice, can't come to grips with how this man I don't want to let in has gotten under my skin.

Losing Lexi was one thing I couldn't stop, but losing myself is something I never expected. And there's something about Becks—his easygoing nature, his personality, his kindness—that has me reaching over my iron walls and wanting to connect. Wanting to reach for that shadow of myself that is floating away just beyond my reach.

The balloon without a string at the top of your ceiling. There. Present. But never within reach.

Until it deflates. Falls lifeless.

"Don't be sorry, Had. Never be sorry for needing me."

I don't need you. The words are almost off my tongue. But the gentleness in his tone causes the pain to burn brighter.

"You want to talk about it?"

You have no idea. I want to explain this all to you. How I want you, how I'm scared, how if I give you the whys, I know you'll give me the get-over-it speech, and that's the one thing I'm sick of hearing. The "Lex is dead, Haddie. She'd want you to keep living, keep dreaming, keep going. Live for her. Get over it."

And I'm not sure what's worse to me. Him telling me that and ruining this perfect image I'm holding close of him or letting him in, allowing whatever this is to run its course and then devastate him like Lex's death did Danny.

I hear the jingle of a dog's tags in the background, and for some reason, the sound makes me smile. So I seize on to the idea of Becks having a fur person to keep him company at night, my mind trying to distract me from the vulnerability that is seeping from my every fiber.

"No." The word is a soft exhale on my lips.

"Are you okay? Do you need me to come over?"

Yes.

"No," I lie, unable to take that next step in admitting how much I want that right now. Having Becks here would be like admitting there is a chink in my armored heart. And the only problem is that I've let him in—past the steel walls—but he can never know. If he knows, if he lets me into his heart, into his life, then I open him up to feeling how I feel.

"What do you need from me?"

And my heart squeezes at his words. Not what *can* I do for you but what do you *need* from me? Where is the arrogance when I need it? Can't he be an asshole so that I can cling to that, grab onto that to help me push him farther away?

Protect him and isolate me?

"Nothing . . . I just . . ." I can't finish my thoughts because I want to tell him everything I need from him. Why I want him but won't let myself risk the chance of hurting him. At my own fear of taking a stupid blood test. So many things but all I can do is live day to day, moment to moment.

But isn't that part of the problem? If I'm adhering to that theory, then I should be living it up. If tomorrow is unknown, I should be living with reckless abandon, throwing caution to the wind. Driving with the top down. But I'm not.

Because I'm scared.

I close my eyes as a silent tear slides down my cheek, and I try to shove my fear away, but I get a sense that I don't even need to speak because Becks just knows.

"I'm here, okay?"

I nod my head as if he can see it and sit there for a few seconds before realizing it. " 'Kay."

"So, uh, we never finished the other day."

I let the silence hang, unsure of what he's talking about and at the same time wondering if I have enough in me to care and knowing damn well that I do.

"I was born in Texas. Moved at age six to the Santa Cruz area for who knows what reason. . . . Hmm. I feel lame doing this, but it's only fair, right? Let's see, it's just my little brother, Walker, and me."

I smile at the comment, love that he's giving me his turn to tell his history. "Mm-hmm," I murmur so that he knows I'm listening and encouraging him to talk more.

"When I was twelve, I think, my dad got transferred down to Santa Monica.... He was a big wig at the bank he worked at, and their corporate headquarters was down here, so we moved. I was so mad at him for making me leave my friends and my football team that I packed a bag and ran away." He laughs at the memory, and the sound of it lifts the veil of grief some. "I made sure I had my Nintendo Gameboy and some snacks and sat on the green electric transformer box that was just out of view of our front door for a while, pondering where to go. And then of course, my mom knew my biggest weakness—chocolate chip cookies—so she baked some and called all the kids in the neighborhood to eat them on our front lawn. She made sure she yelled loud enough to every kid within earshot about them.... I couldn't take it, so I came home after a whole hour and a half of running away."

"So we moved down here. Played football and baseball and wrestled in high school. Was a decent student. Became friends with a kid in high school named Smitty. His dad worked on a local race team. One day he asked if I wanted to go, and I had no interest really, but shit, two hours at the track and I was hooked. But it wasn't the driving that was the draw. Hell yeah, there was an adrenaline rush, the pull of the speed, but it was the organization of the crew, the calculations of the gas and timing.... All of the mechanics of it mesmerized me." He sighs as I hang on his every word, wanting to ask so many questions about that first time and about so many other things, but my acknowledgments remain soft murmurs and sounds.

"I asked if I could help, became a regular at the track and learned everything I could. I stayed out of the way initially, but then as I grew confident, I made suggestions, filled in when a crew member couldn't make it. Then one day when I was about eighteen, I saw this cocky son of a bitch named Colton take the wheel of a car out at Fontana. Heard he was some Hollywood actor's son, so I stayed to watch him wreck because the ones who think they're better than everyone else always do. He looked about my age, but shit, he surprised the hell out of me because he had some real talent. I introduced myself to him, he came out a few days later and tested the car, and, as they say, the rest is history."

I can hear the dog's tag rattle again, and I want to ask Becks about their friendship, his love life, what his parents are like . . . but I snuggle into the silence, grateful for the comfort I find in him opening up and the lack of questions he aims in my direction.

It's weird that he understands just what I need and yet I haven't asked for a single thing from him. The thought settles into the recesses of my mind, and I wonder what exactly that means and how it fits into whatever this is here that I'm fighting so ridiculously hard.

He continues talking aimlessly about Rex, the mutt he rescued from the animal shelter, and his brother and their family house in Ojai. All safe topics. All great info but not what I want to know the most: Who is Deena? What is she to him?

And then I'm mad that I care. Furious actually, so I let him ramble. Not wanting to give in to my catty side again and make him regret staying on the line and talking.

Silence falls back across the line after a bit. "Hey, Had?"

"Hm?"

"As you can tell by my rambling, I'm kind of lonely tonight. Would you mind hanging on the phone with me until I fall asleep? You don't have to talk or anything. . . . It's just nice to know you're there."

I know damn well he's not lonely, know he's lying to take some of the embarrassment off me, and hell if it doesn't make me want him that much more. A soft smile is on my lips, the salt on my cheeks stiff as my muscles move, his kindness weakening my resolve. "Sure."

And I can feel it happen. That part of my heart starts to tremor with the first beginnings of a hairline fracture as he chips away at it with his hammer consisting of patience and understanding.

Minutes pass with just the even rhythm of his breathing and the thumping tail of a dog against what sounds like his mattress. I sink farther into my bed, into the silent comfort of his presence on the other end, and let it wrap around me.

"Thank you." The murmured words are on constant rotation in my head, but I'm not sure if they ever make it out of my mouth. And if they do, Becks never acknowledges them.

Chapter 12

The sounds of the club ring out in a continuous thump of bass and beat. A little too loud, a lot too trendy, and way too superficial for my taste. Give me a dark corner, a draft beer, and some short skirts paired with pairs of boots, and I'm in Heaven.

Then again, a man has no right complaining about the ample display of bare flesh making the rounds in front of me. But damn, just like that first night we met in Las Vegas, I can't help the one sight my eyes keep drifting to.

The one person they keep getting lost on.

This is beginning to be a serious problem.

Now that I've tasted the temptation of Haddie—taken her scent, her sounds, and her addictive flavor to compare others against—hell if that one time hasn't been seared into my goddamn memory.

And damn.

Just damn.

Then there's that look in her eyes. The one that screams she needs someone to help her see through the grief, to prove to her that opening up doesn't mean she has to close the fuck down.

And hell if I'm not a sucker for long-legged blondes with smart mouths who need a shoulder to cry on. Who the fuck am I kidding? The only crying I want her doing is my name while she comes. But that would make me an insensitive fucker, and I'm anything but. Hell yes, I may be thinking it, but, c'mon, it's Haddie.

I'd be a stupid bastard not to want her again. Or a blind one.

My groan as I watch her work her clients on the floor—laughing, connecting, entertaining—is smothered by the music of the club, and it's clear as day that there's just something about her that pulls me in and makes me care. Like "sitting on the other end of a silent phone line for two hours just to make sure that she's okay" type of thing.

I've sure as hell never done something like that before. She sounded so lost, so much like a little girl. How in the hell could I hang up when she so clearly needed me?

And as I watch her across the club from me, she most definitely does not look like a little girl. The way she moves is beyond enticing. The sway of her hips and the flip of her hair over her shoulder. I take in her shapely legs and the low cut V of her top hugging those perfect tits of hers. Lips glossed, smoky eyes, and body screaming to be sexed.

As much as my dick is begging for a second—huh, I guess I should say a fifth—time to make her come and find its way between those supple, tanned thighs of hers, all I want to do is be close enough to see her eyes. To make sure she's okay.

I take a long drink of my Merit and Coke, my head nodding to the beat, my eyes tracking her.

"Dude, if you want to fuck her that much, then go get her. Talk to her. Take what you want."

If looks could kill, Walker would be in a body bag about

now. "First of all, that's no way to talk about a lady," I warn my brother, shifting in my seat to face him, let him know to shut his goddamn mouth and not to talk about Had like that.

"Yeah, but I have a feeling the things you want to do to her fall in the 'the lady on the street but a freak in the sheets' type of category, so then in all reality, we really aren't talking about the 'lady' aspect now, are we?"

I glare at him, my call to the coroner on speed dial right now. Hell yes, he's right, but, uh, no one gets to talk about Haddie that way.

And why is that? Why do I care so much when she doesn't?

I call bullshit. She cares. She doesn't want to, but she does.

I guess that's why I dragged Walker here, anyway. I mean, fuck, I can see the struggle, hear trepidation in her voice, feel the fear emanating off her. . . . The question is, why?

So I watch her move through the club. Head thrown back as she laughs. Hand placed on a male patron's biceps, which has me gritting my teeth. Skirt inching up as she bends over to grab the shot glass from the table in front of her and downs the liquor like a pro. Impressive. Too bad my thoughts drift to where else those lips of hers can go down.

"Oooohhhh," Walker says, synapses firing and his eyes widening with understanding as I look back at him, "so I was under the impression you dragged me along tonight because you wanted to spend time with me. Well, that and because your *broom* is on his honeymoon."

"Broom?" I laugh, trying to figure out what in the hell random thing my little brother is talking about.

"Yeah, bromance. Married. Groom." He shrugs with a shit eating grin on his face. *"Broom."*

I laugh again. Can't help it. He's such a little shit, but dude's funny as hell. Plus I know he's sometimes jealous of my friendship with Colton—how close we are—so I allow him a few digs now and again just cuz he's my little brother. "Where do you come up with this shit?"

"It's what happens when you're born second." He takes a swig from his bottle of beer. "Mom used up all the errant genes with you, and so I got all of the vetted ones. The smart ones who didn't go multiplying at first sight, dazed by the big fat prize, you know?"

Is he really serious? He must be drunk already, and we're only an hour into our night. I just blink and shake my head as I try to process the fact that he most definitely was dropped on his head as a child. Had to be. Mom must have had an accident one day—dropped Walker—then just brushed him off and kept on going, not knowing the damage done beneath the surface.

"Order another drink, Becks, and it will all make sense," he teases me. I roll my eyes at him and then look back out to the club beyond us, eyes searching to make sure she's okay. I catch sight of her sparkly top, the lights playing off her movements and reflecting against her pale hair. My dick stirs in reflex to the sight of her. Can't help it.

When I know she's fine, I look back toward my little brother and raise my eyebrows at him, wanting to see what pieces he fills in because I sure as hell am not going to offer up the information he wants freely.

Walker points to me and then back to the vicinity of Haddie and then back to me. "So . . . uh . . . that's Haddie? You two . . . uh . . . ?" He raises his eyebrows at me but doesn't ask if we've had sex. "Yeah?"

"Yeah, what?" I'm not giving any details here. He may be my little bro, but dude's gonna have to work for the info since he'll most likely go straight to Aubrey, who in turn will go straight to my mom. And I really don't need her breathing down my neck right now about marriage and babies.

And those damn pink flip-flops.

"Dude, I'm a lot confused."

I reach over and cuff him on the shoulder. "Like that's a

news flash." I flinch back as he fakes a punch to my biceps in a move between us as tried and true as time.

"Well, you show up at the cabin with fucking stars in your eyes. Deena shows up out of the blue a few days later.... I kinda just figured you were having some regression pussy—"

I almost spit my drink out—find it very hard not to—so I cough out in choked laughter instead. "Regression pussy? What the hell, Walk ...?" The coughing strikes me again, my eyes watering and my throat burning. "What in the hell are you talking about?"

He just continues looking at me, amusement in his eyes and a smirk on his face. He shrugs. "Well your birthday is coming up. You keep saying you're feeling like an old fucker, so I figured that you were double-dipping into the past by starting shit with Deena again. Regressing some so that you could feel like you did back in the day, a young buck and shit. But now we're here tonight, and you're watching that hottie over there like you want to hit it like you're a baseball bat, and so now I'm curious."

"I swear there is no way we came from the same mother." I shake my head at him, even though I should be used to his roundabout randomness. "And first of all, buck? Stallion would be more like it."

"You wish," He snorts. "So? You banging Deena and now moving on to her," he says, lifting his chin in Haddie's direction, "or what? Cuz, dude, that's so unlike you."

Irritation flickers. "There was no banging Deena." When he just rolls his eyes in disbelief, I continue. "Been there, done that, and honestly, I know you always had a crush on her, but she's not that great."

Now it's his turn to choke on his drink. And for some reason, I find an odd amusement in watching him cough. "She's like a fifteen on a scale of one to ten."

"Yeah, on the hot factor, she's definitely a fifteen, but the things I know now versus the things I knew back then ...

man." I shake my head, recalling how perfect I thought Deena was. How I thought she was the shit in bed, yet now with age and more experience, I realize how naive we really were. I think of how one night with Haddie blew the fifty-odd times with Deena out of the water.

"Maybe Dee's learned more since college too."

"Quite possibly." I mull over thoughts of her and young love, but none of them sticks in my mind. It was all fumbling hands and false fronts of confidence as we explored and experimented. Then I think back to a few days ago when Deena showed up out of the blue, just passing through town. I was more than down with rekindling things for one night . . . and then we ran into Haddie.

Fucking Haddie. With her doe-shaped eyes and quivering chin asking me questions without any words. So stubborn she refuses to admit she needs someone when she's hurting. And then she called me and unloaded on me about friends and strings and hell if I was going to sit there and take her shit without saying something in return.

Until she made that one little sound. That hiccup that told me everything. How much she feared and needed and wanted and didn't want to be alone.

"Dude, like I said . . . you want to hit it, it seems like she's quite the flirtatious one."

It takes everything I have not to snap back at him. How dare he judge her when she's out there doing her job? And I realize that's exactly what he wants. He wants me to react, to call me to the table so that he knows where I stand, and hell if I'm going to walk right into that open fucking door.

"First off, Walker, it's a wonder Aubrey doesn't kick you out to the curb with that mind-set. Secondly, don't you know sometimes slow and steady wins the race? I sit back, bide my time, and reel her in, and then once I have her hooked, I can figure out just what it is that she wants."

"This ain't the tortoise and the hare, bro." He shakes his head at me as if he's ashamed and takes a sip of his beer.

"True." I nod and motion for another round to the waitress as she walks by. My mind vaguely recalls Haddie's words to me the night we first met in Vegas, something similar to what I just said about slow and steady wins the race, and I think how well she pegged me way back then. "But at least the tortoise stays hard and has one hell of a shelf life."

"Jesus fucking Christ! You really need to work on not being so goddamn dorky if you think you're going to catch the likes of that hotter-than-hell woman."

Little does he know I already have. Little does he know the woman owns more than just my thoughts right now.

The drinks come more slowly, the night wears on, but I can see Haddie getting a little less stable on her feet. Fuck. I know she needs tonight to go well. This is event two of three for her, and if she wants this client in the bag, then she needs to be on top of her game. Is she still upset so she's drinking to bury it and put on a brave face?

It bugs me that I care so much. It pisses me off that Walker is watching me like a goddamn hawk, trying to figure out why I'm so wrapped up in a possible piece of ass that he doesn't even know I've had yet.

Thank God she hasn't ventured to our side of the club—doesn't even know that we are here—because for some reason I think that if she did, she might be drinking more. Her need not to need me would fuel that desire of hers to escape by downing another shot.

And speaking of shots, I watch her toss back another and cringe. Yeah, she's stretched them out, but hell if they're not taking their toll and beginning to cloud her judgment. Fuck. Why do I care? I run a hand through my hair to shake off my own displeasure with myself. I mean, seriously . . . why am I here? Why the hell did I drag Walker out here to watch Haddie work the floor like some overprotective brother?

Or some lovesick idiot?

Shit. Maybe I should call Deena. Maybe I should revisit those thighs to remind me why Haddie is just too much goddamn work right now since her head's all over the place.

And then I see him. The asshole to her right—slick-backed hair, one too many drinks under his belt and his hand placed perfectly on her ass. I'm out of my chair in a flash, but before I can even take five damn steps, her hand is fisted in his shirt, and something is said before she shoves him backward.

"Well, there's that," I mutter under my breath, more than pleased to see that Haddie can take care of herself. And for some reason that little show of hers makes me want her that much more. It shows me that despite being perfectly capable of handling assholes like him, she still has that vulnerable side to her that I get to see, that needs me.

And hell if I don't like that an awful lot. The mixture of feisty and vulnerable is a total turn-on. When I turn around and sit back down, Walker's studying my every movement, ready to pounce on me with a comment about what a little bitch I'm being, watching some chick—letting her drag me around by the balls.

But hell, he has no clue about the power of Haddie's voodoo pussy.

I choke on my drink. Did I really just call Haddie my *voodoo*? Oh my fucking God. I'm turning into Colton. My heart races momentarily as I recall his explanation for why he fell so hard and fast for Rylee. Then I consider the fact that the term just rolled into my thoughts and correlated with her name without a second thought.

There's no fucking way. She can't—I can't—I mean, shit, we had sex one time. A lot of sex in that one time, but hell if I'm going to let a woman grab me by the balls and own me after one night of sex.

Incredible, mind-blowing, ball-tightening, toe-curling sex, but sex nonetheless.

Damn.

I shake my head, trying to push the thought away. Blame it on the alcohol. Immediately I order a round of shots for Walker and me. I need something to clear my head—or numb it—of the ludicrous thoughts that keep circling. Of voodoo pussies that most definitely have no right as of yet to lay any kind of claim on me.

The shots come, the music drums out an annoying electronic vibe—who the hell can dance to this techno crap, anyway?—and my brother keeps me entertained as he starts a rating system of the women who approach us.

"C'mon, she was a left nutter," he says as I simply sigh and down the rest of my drink.

I stand, needing to stretch some. "Walk, I agree that the one before was most definitely fugly, but I'm sure she had some kind of awesome bedroom skills that would knock your socks off...." I look toward where she disappeared and then back to him. "But that last one? I'm sorry, but I wouldn't be giving my left nut to sleep with her. Too much empty space up top," I tell him, as my thoughts shift back to the one woman I would give both of my nuts to have beneath me right now.

"Dude, if I wasn't happy with Aubrey, the empty space I'm worried about is between her thighs and not in her head. I mean . . ."

Walker's words are drowned out by the noise of the club because I'm on the move without any further thought. The slick-haired bastard is back, and his hands are on her. He has her positioned perfectly against a wall where she can't escape, and all I can see is fucking red as I move across the crowded space between us.

I don't even pay attention to whether she's fighting him off. Can't tell if she's kissing him back when his mouth takes hers because all I can think about is that she's mine. And I don't even flinch this time as the thought crosses my mind because somewhere in that space of time I've determined that I don't care how fucking long it takes to prove otherwise, but Haddie Montgomery is not going to walk away from me again without a fight.

I immediately know I'm going to regret that personal decree, but I don't have time to argue with myself because I see her head trying to twist from side to side, her hands shove against Slick's chest, and I see her knee lift up.

But I have him by the shoulders, and I'm pulling him backward before she gets the chance to even connect. I move on instinct, alcohol fueling my irrationality, and I really don't give a crap. I'm blinded with anger and disgust, and I shove Slick back up against a wall, the strobe lights making everything seem like it's happening in slow motion.

"What the fuck?" I shout at the guy, forearm against his chest, other hand gripped firmly in his shirt so that the buttons are popping off. "The lady said no."

And the goddamn asshole just laughs at me. He has the gall to smirk and chuckle without even coming off like I've scared him at all. "Fuck you. I don't believe *more* is her saying no, asshole."

His words shock me somewhat sober. What? Was Haddie wanting this asshole to kiss her?

It's my name I hear now. Haddie yelling my name over and over breaks through the rush of white noise that's filling my ears. Her hands on my biceps, holding my cocked arm from propelling forward and into his nose.

And I'm so confused. From him. With her. My mind undergoes a sudden assault—dredging up every one of the five senses of mine that she has marked somehow with her presence—and so I react in the only way that makes sense to my alcohol-influenced mind.

Slick is forgotten in a second. I hear him gasp in a breath, but it's drowned out by the one that Haddie sucks in as I turn from him and face her. Without even thinking, I have her lifted up and tossed over my shoulder.

I don't think about her ass hanging out beneath her tiny skirt for the world to see. I don't care about the event she's supposed to be managing because frankly it's well under way, and it seems to me like she's caring a little too much about the patrons for my liking. I couldn't care less about her fists pounding on my back, demanding that I put her down or the looks from half-drunk clubgoers that tell me I'm crazy. I don't care about any of it.

None of it.

Because all I can focus on is the thought of her hands on him and how I want them to be on me instead.

I readjust the grip of my arms over her hips, her fight growing stronger as I wait for the crowd to disperse so that I can walk through without her kicking somebody. The music is so loud, I can't really hear the curse words I know she's calling me right now, or maybe I choose not to because I sure as hell hear Walker say, "So much for slow and steady, huh?" as I walk past him.

I just raise my eyebrows and keep moving out the side exit of the club, where a bouncer approaches me and then steps back when I say, "She's gonna throw up. Watch out."

And that just makes Haddie struggle more, fists pound harder, and me laugh louder. When I clear the exit, I keep on walking though. Down the sidewalk, the whole two blocks to my conveniently and centrally located condo.

I hear her say *Bastard* and *Put me down* and *How dare you?* I get puzzled looks from passersby, and I am actually quite shocked that not a single one of them tries to stop me to make sure she's all right and that I'm not some random psycho kidnapping her. Either the crazy-ass grin on my face tells them all is okay or that I am a lunatic and to back the fuck off. Regardless, I'm so busy trying to concentrate on not dropping her squirrely body that I don't have a moment to think about this narrative on our society as I normally would.

Of course, by the time I walk up the front steps to my building, Haddie's skirt has inched up so handily that my arm is touching bare flesh, meaning my only line of sight is toned legs and four-inch heels.

I work a swallow down my throat as I wait for the elevator. I debate taking the stairs—think it might be best to work off some of this pent-up lust, which makes me want to take her up against the elevator wall right now—but I know that she's going to put up a damn good fight—already has—and I'm going to need my strength to make sure she hears me this time around.

Because I'm not letting her go until she hears what I need to say.

And I need to say a whole helluva lot.

Chapter 13

I can't focus on much. But the few things I take in between my rage and my incessant pounding on his back is Becks being the ever-consummate gentleman as he carries me down the streets of Los Angeles.

Over his shoulder like a sack of potatoes.

All the while saying, "Good evening," to people like he's on a goddamn Sunday stroll.

I'm seething. Fucking bastard.

I'm tired—my head feels like it weighs fifty pounds as I try to lift it up again to work out where we are—and I'm about to succumb to the exhaustion and sag over him from the mixture of too many shots and expending too much energy when all of a sudden, I'm being thrown through the air.

I'm shocked into what I'd like to think is semisobriety—but really is probably far from it—when I land with a loud *oof* on the softness of a couch beneath me. But soft or not, the impact of my weary muscles against the cushions is jarring. The moment I hit it, though—the minute my mind catches up with my body—I'm scrambling to get up, to get in his face and ask him how dare he treat me like this.

Before I'm even standing, Becks is on me: knees straddling my hips, hands pinning my wrists on either side of my head. And God, I'm so fucking pissed at him, I want to knee him in the crotch, and at the same time, I want him to lean in closer so that I can devour that sexy-as-sin mouth of his, which is so temptingly close to mine.

I know I've had a lot to drink—the alcohol must be making me want him as desperately as I do—because as angry as I am at him right now, all I want is for him to release one of my hands so I can fist it at the base of his neck and force his mouth down to mine. I want to steal a taste of the man who's been owning my thoughts.

Did he really think I didn't see him sitting in the club across the dance floor? It was like an electric current buzzing through the room the minute my body became aware of his presence. A lightning strike to my libido. And yet he kept his distance.

The. Whole. Time.

It unnerved me.

Me, the girl who's always on her game. I knew Cal was there observing how I ran things, but fuck, having Becks there was ten times worse. I tried to tell myself he was there with his friend—that it was merely a coincidence he was at the same club as the Scandalous event—but I don't put that much stock in fate.

As the night wore on, I could feel his eyes on me the whole time. I knew he was watching and waiting, but for what? He had farmers'-market-what's-her-name, didn't he? And then I was hurt thinking about it—also confused—all the while trying to paint a damn smile on my face and make sure everyone was having a good time. Pretend to focus my mind on them when it was always fixated on him.

And with each shot I slung back, the nerves got a little less powerful, and the anger grew a little more. How dare he make me like him? How dare he make me like the idea he was sitting over there just to make sure that I was okay? And how do I know that's why he was there? Because that's just the type of guy he is. Fuck, I don't want that. It's just not a possibility.

And that made me even angrier.

So another shot down, a smooth line delivered by a decent-looking guy to my alcohol fuzzed mind, and I was so game to be a little festive. To lose myself in him and forget Becks. And then by the time I realized I was progressing from wanting to use sex to forget the grief of losing Lexi to wanting to forget the ache of not allowing myself a chance with Becks, it was too late.

I was kissing the guy except the problem was even with the shots and the high of kissing a different person, the thrill was nonexistent. He wasn't what I wanted. And then what I wanted was there, all alpha and arrogance and sex on a stick. As Becks pulled him away from me, I was pissed at being caught, at what it looked like, at *what he thought of me now*. I turned the embarrassment into anger, and a lot of fucking good that did me.

Now the man I don't want to want is tempting me in so many ways, it's comical.

And arousing as all get out.

"Let. Me. Go." I pant out the words as I struggle against him.

"Uh-uh." He grunts with exertion as I buck beneath him, trying to escape. And of course, I can feel him thick and heavy against my lower belly, and that sets off warning bells to my staunch resolve not to have him, not to want him.

And a slow burn of liquid heat starts to spread from my core through my body, the ache coiling like a loaded spring waiting for its chance to spiral out of control.

"Goddamn it, Montgomery. Calm the fuck down, and I'll let you go . . . but you're not leaving until we talk."

"Fuck. Off." The words are out of my mouth before I can filter them. I don't really mean them but damn if he's not riling me up something fierce.

He laughs at me. Fricking chuckles at my assertion, and

that irks me even more. I hold my head still and look up at him, the shadows and the muted light from the hall playing over the angles of his face. He leans in closer, his mouth a mere whisper from mine, causing my breath to emit a betraying hitch, and says, "You'd like that, wouldn't you? For me to walk away without asking you a single question." I furrow my brow as his slow, even cadence hits my ears. He licks his lips, and I swear to God, my nipples tighten at the sight alone and the memory of that tongue of his.

"Fuck you." I grit the words out as I writhe beneath him, struggling within the confines of his thighs, my hips grinding up against his. My thoughts scatter momentarily when I feel him hardening against me. Damn if my desire isn't surging through my body like the blood in my veins.

He emits a sliver of a laugh—the sound of a man on the edge of losing control—before he continues. "Oh, believe me, I'd love to do just that right now, *to fuck you*, but I prefer my women to be willing participants in the act . . . and you, sweet Haddie, are nowhere near compliant."

Compliant, my ass. He thinks that he can throw me over his shoulder and force me to go wherever the hell we are, and I'm going to be a willing participant? Is he fucking crazy? Obviously. And he's . . . he's . . . My thoughts are lost as he lowers his mouth to mine.

I part my mouth on reflex. My tongue and lips are so thirsty for a taste of him that I arch my neck in a nonverbal begging motion. I'm stunned momentarily, but it's a split second before I feed my craving.

And take.

I let his tongue lick against mine—absorb the warmth, the comfort, the desire, all mixed into one heady combination that has a moan in the back of my throat before his lips even begin moving against mine. His hands tighten their grip on my wrists as his mouth takes without asking, as it brands and claims and owns every inch of mine.

I fist my hands—a useless attempt to halt the freight

train of desire hurtling out of control within me. But it's too late . . . especially when I can taste the mint mixed with rum on his breath and smell the earthy scent of his cologne, the fragrance of his shampoo—because all I want is more of the man I've told myself I can't have.

Before the kiss even ends, I'm telling myself this—the taste of Beckett Daniels on my tongue and the comforting feeling of his weight on top of me—is enough, but I know it's not. I try to convince myself that it's the alcohol screaming in my mind to beg for more, to ask him to drive me to that mind-numbing place I know he can help me find, but just as I'm about to blurt the words out, Becks tears his mouth from mine.

And his weight lifts from my body.

"Goddamn it!" I hear him bark out the curse beside me as I'm busy trying to assess what the hell just happened. How we went from the club to the couch to nothing in such a short period of time. "I need a minute."

I scramble up from the couch, and I stare at the broad lines of his back as he walks away from me, both hands shoving through his hair as he confuses me even more when he mutters something else about the click and how it's fucking ridiculous. "Haddie . . ." My name is a groan on his lips, but when he falls silent, I can't figure out what in the hell he wants right now.

I'm so primed with need, so invigorated by his kiss and amped up with anger, that my body reacts on instinct. I want him—no, need him—to quiet the constant sadness that hasn't been silent since the last time we were together. And hell yes, I know I want to use him right now. Need him to use me right now. Because if I know it's mutual, I won't feel bad when I have to walk away because I can't commit to anything more than this with him.

Or anyone.

I step into him, cup him through his jeans, and bring my lips to his. He tries to resist me at first, tries to talk, but I can feel the pulse of his dick through the fabric as it hardens. His breath hitches and his body tenses with the demands made by my greedy hands. But when our mouths meet again, a vicious meeting of lips and unspoken needs, he relents. He kisses me back with just as much aggression. We bruise and nip and take from each other. Our actions scream anger, carnality, pure need, but he doesn't touch me, hands flat against the wall beside him.

I tear my lips from his, as his refusal to touch me—a blatant denial of what I want—challenges me, urges me to push a little harder, seduce a little more. I'm a woman used to getting what I want, and what I want is him. I decide to change tactics and press my lips to the underside of his jaw, lacing openmouthed kisses up the line of his neck. His skin is warm. the slight taste of salt and pure Becks hits my tongue and enrages the heat he seems to control within me.

He remains stiff—both in posture and in my hand—as he wavers on whether to give into the primal need that continually reverberates between us or to resist this temptation for whatever reasons he seems to have. And I don't care what the reasons are, nor do I want to think about how impressive his restraint is, because all I want to do is satisfy the ache in my core.

"Haddie, we can't . . . my rules . . . We shouldn't—"

"Sh-shh!" My finger is on his lips stopping him. "I know . . . but we've broken all the rules so far. Why stop now?" I look at his lips and then back up to his eyes before leaning in closer, my teeth tugging on his earlobe in a move that earns a hiss from him to help reinforce the words I murmur in his ear. "Please, Becks. I want to feel you."

"Damn you, Had. I'm trying to do the right thing here." His hands start to move now, his head angling back, and I fear it's so that he can pull away from me, so I curl my fingers in his hair to hold him still.

I wait for him to look into my eyes so he can see how badly I want this. How badly I need this. "You can respect

me all you want later. Right now, though, I'm all about doing what's wrong." I see a flicker of unfettered need in his
gaze and know he wants me. Know that he's riding that ra-
zor-thin line of restraint. Time to tip the scales. "I want you
to make me feel owned."

His eyes widen, his teeth clench, and I know I've gotten
him with my forward demands. My body tenses in reaction
at his silent acknowledgment.

We stare at each other in a suspended state of acceptance of the hard and fast that is about to happen. I feel like
everything raging inside me is reflected perfectly in his eyes
and in that telling hitch of his breath.

And between one heartbeat and the next Becks's mouth
is suddenly on mine, where it belongs. One hand fists in the
sequined shirt on my back and presses my body against his
while the other cups my ass through my skirt, fingers knead-
ing into the flesh there. He nips my bottom lip, soothing it
with a tender lick of his tongue before taking ownership of
the kiss once again.

There's something about the way he kisses that makes
me hope he never stops. Soft and firm. Demanding yet giving. Teasing but desperate. I get lost in it. Get lost to him. I
can't think. His tantalizing assault on my mouth doesn't allow me to. I'm ready and willing, my body his for the taking,
and he's done nothing more than kiss me.

That single thought breaks through the haze of desire
clouding my mind and causes little flutters in my stomach
and tingles in my toes at the anticipation of what's to come.

I want to urge him to hurry, to rip my clothes off and
take me right here, right now, but something tells me that I
might have gotten away with ordering Beckett Daniels
around one time, but one time is all I'm going to get.

Becks just might be that rebel at heart that I go for after
all. Sweet, ever-loving fuck yes!

My hands find the hem of his shirt and snake their way
beneath the fabric so I can score my fingernails against the

hardened slab of muscle. I feel his torso flinch in reaction, as I use touch to entice him, to connect with him, to tease him. I map my hands along his flank and then up the strong lines of his back.

His hands inch under my skirt so that his fingers can tempt my bare flesh. Chills race across my skin from his incendiary touch despite the surge of heat intensifying with each passing second. I lift my leg and wrap it around his hip so the apex of my thighs rubs perfectly against his denim-clad erection.

The moan falls from my lips without thought. My hands act on reflex to pull his shirt over his head while our mouths break contact for the first time so that it can pass over his face, and then our lips crash back together as if we need each other's air to breathe.

My hands roam freely now. So many places to discover, so many nerves to tease into a frenzy. And I know it's work-ing—the combination of kissing and touching—because slow-and-steady Becks begins to move faster, dominance evident in his touch, but he's anything but steady. Cupping my face, taking the leisurely trip from the curve of my ass up the line of my spine to fist my length of hair, demanding more of me from our kiss before easing back some and then starting the process all over again.

I'm left breathless by his thoroughness—no man has ever kissed me this completely—and I'm ready to scream for him to lay me back on the couch or table or floor and press into my wetness. Drive me to the edge so that I can score his back and yell out his name.

"Becks..." His name is a pant on my lips, my call to him that foreplay is overrated because right now I don't care about lighting the fuse or the leftover collateral damage.

I'm in the moment—the here and now—and all I care about is the detonation, the need for release.

I allow my hands to leave his skin for a moment, crossing them in front of me as I pull my shirt over my head, tossing it to the side without a second thought. And hell if the groan that Becks emits from the back of his throat when he realizes that there's nothing else beneath my top—no bra, nothing—isn't sexy as hell and spurns my need brighter.

I back away from him, ready to take this erotic dance to the next step. I stay facing him and retreat to the couch until the backs of my legs hit the edge. He follows, eyes locked on mine before momentarily running up and down my naked chest, miniskirt, and high heels. My lips are numb from his kisses and my sex is damp and humming with anticipatory need.

And he just stands there, fists clenched, body tense, staring at me as if the thoughts in his head are working way too hard when it's the other head on his body that I want working hard in me right now.

"Fuck me, Becks." I have no shame in admitting that I want him. No embarrassment in confessing my needs. But a trace of unease tickles the base of my spine when he stands there and looks at me, head angled to the side, eyes probing through the darkened room into mine.

He glances up to the ceiling momentarily as if he's gathering his strength to push me away. Panic fires anew because his words from moments ago hit me. *I'm not letting you go until we talk.* I know that he's going to start asking questions I don't want to answer. But why now? Why in the middle of what was about to become some incredible nail-scratches-down-his-back and teeth-marks-left-in-my-shoulder type of sex?

Because he wants *more*.

The thought dawns on me. Well, at first it dawns on me, and then it turns into a wrecking ball of panic bearing down on me. I know Becks isn't that manipulative, know that he grabbed me from making a mistake with that guy from the club because he's a good guy, but hell if the mixture of alcohol and his possible rejection isn't feeding my irrationality right now.

He rolls his shoulders and spits out a slew of curses as he turns from me and stalks away for the second time tonight.

My temper ignites into an inferno of rage fueled by warring pride and desire with a touch of disbelief. "What?" I yell, the sound of my heels filling the frigid silence as I stomp after him. He starts to walk one way and then stops and paces back the other way, shaking his head, shoulders tense. I walk the few feet to where my shirt lies discarded and tug it over my head as if it's a layer of armor to protect me from what I fear will come next. "You haul me from the club, kiss me like you want to fuck me, and then what? Change your mind?" There's fire in my veins and ice in my voice.

"Yeah, imagine that," he huffs, sarcasm rich in his tone, as he puts his hands on his neck. He lets his head hang momentarily as the silence grows stifling. "Christ, Haddie, I know all you want is a quick romp and to walk the fuck out the door with an 'I hope this won't be awkward next time we see each other.'"

I stare, face impassive at him and his dead-on assessment before he continues. "But one of has to step back to prevent the disaster this is heading toward since you sure as fuck are determined to give nothing of yourself."

"Nothing of myself?" My voice escalates with each word as my temper flashes hot again. Does he have any clue how hard it is for me to hold back right now? How much I think about him? How I want to take the leap, not look at tomorrow and see what the future holds?

But I can't.

I can't until I know for sure. Until I know that I have tomorrows to offer him.

"I'm giving you everything I can right now, Beckett." My voice is soft but resolute, and I can practically see my words drift across the space between us and slam into him full force.

"I call bullshit," he swears as he continues toward the

wall of windows. He shoves his hands in his pockets and stares out at the world beyond us. A striking solitary silhouette. And all I want to do is walk up behind him, wrap my arms around his waist, and let him in. Tell him I want more so that I can share this pain, the fear, with someone so that I'm not alone anymore, but that would make him feel obligated to stay when things go to shit—and that's not fair to him, either.

How can I ask so much of him when I feel like I'm a ticking time bomb myself?

I force myself to look away from everything about him that calls to me. I make myself take a moment to glance around the room so that I don't have to look at him or acknowledge the comment he's thrown at me. So that I don't focus on how the confliction he's feeling is so palpable that I can feel it roll off him and collide into me. Because right now if I acknowledge it, if I accept it, then I might take that step forward and tell him I want those strings tied to him with knots and pretty little bows covering them.

The whole package.

The Danny and the Maddie.

I squeeze my eyes shut and pull myself from a momentary panic attack that threatens at the thought of what I'm never going to allow myself to have. I tell myself to shut down, to disengage so that I can't feel.

I open my eyes when I hear movement to see Becks walking back toward the entryway. He stops and turns to face me, an apology etched on his handsome face. "I promised myself that I wouldn't break my rules again regardless of how damn tempting you are. Haddie . . . *we either are or we aren't.*" He shrugs, his eyes begging me to make the right decision. "So you tell me, what the fuck is this, Haddie?"

Panic claws its stifling fingers around my throat as he asks me to make a decision I can't make. Either answer hurts one of us, hurts him or breaks me. So I try to play dumb, hope he thinks I've had enough alcohol to pull it off.

"What the fuck is what? Seems to me you wanted me, and now you don't. What else is there to figure out?"

And I know I've failed miserably because he's on the move again, crossing the few feet until he stands at the front door. He pounds his fist against the wood—the boom reverberates around the room—before turning and leaning his back against the door, thumbs stuck in his pockets, one foot propped behind him and his eyes assessing every inch of me.

"That's how you want to play this? Turn this into you pretending that I don't want you. That I'm rejecting you? Haddie, everything about you makes me want to beg to take you ... to fuck you into oblivion so thoroughly that you forget your own name because you're so goddamn busy moaning mine." He rolls his head back on his shoulders, staring at the ceiling for a moment while my body recovers from the visceral reaction to his words, my panties now damp from their dark promise. He's offering everything I want. "Hell, I'm all for casual sex, Had—been there, done that—but this, *us*, it's too goddamn complicated to be anywhere near the realm of casual. So make me the bad guy if you have to—*blame me*—but really, this is on you until you answer the question: Are we or aren't we?"

Images flash through my mind. Memories we could make together if I answer the question truthfully. If I let him in ... allow myself to feel with one hundred percent of my heart rather than the bits and pieces I dole out when I'm not cautious.

Then the images switch from hope and happiness to darkness and grief: Lexi's casket, tears falling like rain, and my heart cinched like a vice. My body may be screaming yes to the thought of so much more with Becks, but my head and heart argue no.

They say disengage.

And I'm a hot mess. A cornucopia of fucked-up and conflicting thoughts that pushes me toward the irresistible man before me and pulls me back all at the same time. I try to rationalize, to tell myself that my heart is in the right place. That the fight I'm about to instigate to push him away is justified. To save him from the train wreck I can't control.

Please, forgive me. I throw the thought out into the silence of the room and hope that somehow the universe delivers it to his mind, allows him to understand sometime in the future that I'm doing this to save him in the long run.

"It doesn't have to be this way. Complicated. You're the one rushing in to save the day when I was far from the damsel in distress." If I wanted him to look at me, this was obviously the right thing to say because his eyes snap to mine and anger sparks in them.

I see that muscle in his jaw pulse from his gritted teeth as he tries to contain his emotions. As he tries to rationalize my lie and hide the hurt I see flash in his eyes. "If he's what you want, feel free." He shifts off the door. "You know the way back to the club."

His eyes taunt me, dare me, say, *Try me.* And hell yes, I want to walk toward him—but not to leave. Every part of me tells me to answer the question honestly—say, *we are*—and that right there is exactly why I have to walk out the door and back to the club.

Except I'm not thinking too clearly. I still have that last shot humming through my blood and the taste of Becks's kiss on my lips. Just enough of both to make me defiant, want to pick a fight with him for his caveman stunt. For pulling me away from quick and easy with club guy and bringing me here to the worth it and complicated. Two things I can't have right now. I know that I can't be tempted with wanting more even though for some reason it just feels so damn right with Becks.

And he mistakes my internal struggle for something else, for wanting someone else. "Cat got your tongue? Weighing your options because I'm sure Slick back there will treat you like a lady. Make sure the bathroom is empty at least before he brings you in there and tries to fuck you in one of the stalls." He lifts his eyebrows. *"Real classy."*

He's pushing my buttons. I recognize it, but it's just what I need to hold on to to make me leave and prevent the mistake I'm about to make. The one I want to make to sate the craving he started when he pinned me to the goddamn couch and kissed me like a man starving for more.

But it's so much easier to hold on to the anger, latch onto it and be mad at him. Use his words as my reason to hold fast to the fight. I tell my feet to move, tell my sexy-as-hell heels to put one foot in front of the other, but they stay rooted to the floor right along with my gaze.

He chuckles low and even, a sarcastic amusement woven through the sound that pisses me off. "What are you afraid of? Why is his offer so much more tempting than mine, huh? Oh, I know why," he says, sarcasm dripping from his words. "He'll walk away without any questions. But I won't, will I, Haddie? I have plenty of questions. The first one being, what *exactly* are you running from?"

My eyes flash up to meet his, and the look—the moment that passes between us—is too honest, too raw. I have to break it. I can't let him see the truths that even I'm trying to hide from. How I feel and what I need to fix me—the answer being *him*—because I'm not going to allow it to happen.

I can feel it. I can know it. But he can't.

My mind flashes back momentarily to the night of the wedding. Of how I asked him—gave him no other option, really—to take me to bed. Did I know then that unzipping my dress and inviting him between my legs would lead to this? Me wanting something more? Me standing in the middle of his apartment, wanting to take the next step but unable to because of the fears that are holding me hostage?

So just tell him the truth, Had. The thought flickers through my mind.

Fuck. Damn. Shit. I just can't.

"I'm not running from anything." My voice is steady

when I speak, and I hope he can't hear the waver of uncertainty on the last word.

I don't know what I expected in response, but it wasn't a smarmy smirk and a raise of his eyebrows. "You keep telling yourself that, and one of these days you might believe it. Whatever it is *he* did to you must have been quite a number for you to run like this. Every damn chance you get."

I have to hide the shock on my face from his assumption. The fact that he thinks I don't want to be with him because another man damaged me. "You don't know anything about me." I start to refute him, and then I realize it might be easier if I let him think that. Let him blame another man for my own shortcomings.

Feed the lie.

"I'm beginning to think that same thing myself," he says. The potent combination of disappointment and judgment flashing in his eyes causes my anger to fire anew. "But, uh, like I said, be my guest." He cocks his head to the side on the last words as he pats the door beside him.

"Fuck you." The words are out of my mouth before I can stop them, earning me that patronizing chuckle again.

"Well, there's always that possibility, but I haven't heard an answer to my question yet."

His unaffected nonchalance throws me when all I want from him is to tell me to choose him. Pick him. Give me the words to anchor my runaway thoughts and give them something to hold on to—weekend mornings where we fall back onto rumpled sheets to make love all day, cooking dinner together, knowing someone will pick up when I call my own house.

But he just continues to stare at me. Then it begins to piss me off as he stands there with amused eyes and the patience of a saint when all I want him to do is to tell me to quit being such a goddamn tease—a fucking coward—and either commit to him or get the fuck out of his life because I don't deserve him or his compassion.

Because all of the personal touches I'm noticing around his condo—the tattered dog toys, the Carole King CD on his shelf that reminds me of Lex, an orange ceramic giraffe on his coffee table when I love giraffes—if I know all of these personal little touches about Becks, then it makes him real. It makes the feelings for him I don't want to possess real. It makes him too genuine, too perfect, and too accessible for this girl who wants her heart to be inaccessible.

Make the decision for me, I scream in my head.

But he doesn't. He simply stands there, watching me, waiting for me to make the next move. Hoping I make the right one.

"Well, if it's that hard of a decision—if you think I'm comparable to Slick—then I'll make it for you," he says, unknowingly giving me what I want. He turns the knob and swings the door open before leaning against the doorjamb and crossing his arms across his chest.

Shock filters through me as I realize he's kicking me out. I can't believe he just did that. I refuse to let my mouth fall open like it wants to because I can't let him see any of my schizophrenic emotions, which would show him how much I care.

Rejection kicks me solidly in the gut until I feel like I can't breathe.

I glance around the room, rapidly looking for another exit because I'm pissed and I sure as fuck don't want to give him the satisfaction of walking past him on the way out. I don't like that he's got the upper hand now, especially since it appears we are several floors up and he's leaning against my only chance to escape.

Jumping off the balcony is looking pretty tempting though.

"Get away from the door." I stride a few feet toward him, my heels kicking a blue pillow that must have fallen on the floor in his abduction and subsequent trapping of me on the couch.

"Nope." A soft, lopsided smirk tugs at the corner of his mouth, amusement reaching his eyes. His hair is mussed from our struggle, and his shirt collar has been tugged askew.

How can he look like something I want to sink into when I'm so angry at him right now?

"Daniels, I don't think you have any clue how pissed off I am at you right now."

When he responds with that condescending chuckle again, I want to knock it out of his mouth. I walk toward him, his smirk in full force, and he just stares at me and shrugs. "As you can tell, I don't really care how pissed you are, City."

"Do you have any idea how important the job of mine you're jeopardizing right now is to me? How you just kidnapped me from a potentially huge opportunity?" I yell at him, my sanity ebbing with his blatant disregard for everything I've worked for.

"It looks to me like you were doing a damn good job of jeopardizing that client yourself." That cocksure smirk on his face goads me, pushes me. "Couple more shots and another tongue down your throat, and hell, Had, you might get more than a publicity job out of it." He raises his eyebrows at me, a nonverbal *Try me*, and I can't help but react at the buttons he's pushing right now. Every single one but the one I really want him to push. "At least you'd be getting paid for it, right?"

I'm unable to speak at that, the unexpected nasty side of Becks I've never seen before throwing me off balance. So I move, using my nervous energy, and take a few more steps toward him. The hallway light falls over a segment of his face, and despite the contempt in his words, I can see the desire in his eyes—as well as the fleeting confusion about what in the hell I was up to with the guy in the club.

"Get out of my way." I sneer at him as I begin to go through the door. His hand flashes out and grabs my arm before I can make it over the threshold. Our eyes lock on each other's, his fingers flexing at my wrist as he fights whatever internal battle he's waging right now.

And I really don't care. God, yes, I'm being selfish — would readily admit that to Becks if he hadn't completely clouded my thoughts — but all the same, I just need to go so that I can clear my head of all this shit. But that's impossible when he makes me want him — kissing me like I'm his last breath so that all I want to do is stay right here — before shoving me away like the sack of potatoes he carried here over his shoulder.

"That easy of a decision, huh? You sure about that?"

I snort out in disbelief. Want me, push me away, and want me again. Can this get any more confusing? But I'm not sticking around to be insulted. To be manhandled, kissed until I'm breathless, accused of wanting to sleep around, and then be told to stay. I try to pull my arm from his grip, but he holds firm.

I fight to ignore the little thrill that shoots through me and reverberates around the anger.

"Let me go, Beckett. I'd best be getting back, at least someone should benefit from my whorish ways." I grit the words out because at this point I don't even know if I'm angry because I want him and he doesn't want me anymore or if it's because he wants me and I can't give him the more he's asking for.

I want to scream, to rage, to kiss him, to fuck him, to hate him, to let him walk away and not want more. And none of those things is going to fix that ache in my heart I get when I look into his eyes and see him asking me again for an answer. For a sign of where this could take us, if we can work out our kind of complicated to make it our kind of right.

"You leave, Haddie, I'm not chasing you again. So you'd better make sure that's what you want." His voice is quiet steel. "And if you stay, I'm going to start tying some knots in those goddamn strings of yours."

His words make shivers run up my spine, make the ache in my heart throb, and send a panicked fear straight through me. Because God, yes, I want. And I don't want. Everything I'm feeling is in such extremes right now that I feel like I'm going crazy.

As I begin to tug my arm from his grip, my only thought is to escape the inexplicable hold he has over me so that I can think straight without his presence clouding things, but he tightens his grip. "Really? Gonna leave just like that, huh? Take the easy way out? I figured you for a fighter, not a coward."

And I don't know if it's the moment, his words, his proximity, or my fear but it all collides into a wrecking ball of irrationality when I turn on him. "You don't get to judge me!" The volume of my voice escalates as every part of me wants to expel my irrationalities out on him. I lunge at him, hands flying, hurt reigning, emotions overloading.

My hand connects with his solid chest with a thud, and it's nowhere near as satisfying of a feeling as I thought it would be. So I try again, and what pisses me off even more is that he stands there and takes it. He doesn't fight back, doesn't try to grab my hands to stop me. He just stands there and accepts it.

Even has the gall to laugh softly at the lack of harm I'm inflicting.

"Let me go!" I shout, fists connecting, rage increasing. "You asshole! How dare you make assumptions about me, about my job . . . call me a whore after you've sampled—"

"Then quit acting like one . . ." He grunts as I move my knee, and he blocks it efficiently, which only infuriates me further. "You want to hurt me?" He chuckles. "Go right ahead. Hurt me like you want to do to the bastard that hurt you."

His words tear into me because his assumptions are so off base, and yet my head's so messed up that I'm pissed he's talking about Lexi like that.

"You have no fucking clue what I've been through," I shout in a voice broken from my exertion, while his calm demeanor fuels my anger, my hurt, my everything. "How dare you—"

"That all you got Had?" he says, his grip like iron, his voice laced with amusement.

"I hate you!" I yell needing more of a reaction to justify my hysterics. "Let. Me. Go!"

And of course, I continue to hit him. Continue to shout obscenities about what he can do with his opinions, where he can shove his boy-next-door charm. Words fly and punch harder than my fists do. And I'm so messed up that it feels so good to hurt someone else for a change rather than being the one to take it.

I'm on the verge of hysterical—making no sense whatsoever—and I don't even care anymore because I'm so sick and tired of caring that for once I let it all go. All of the hurt and the pain and the shutting everyone out so that when he finally wraps his arms around me, I don't know what to do but struggle some more.

And he just holds on, my name a repeated murmur on his lips, the warmth of his breath against my hair as I cling to him.

But something happens in the moment—I struggle a few more times and then all of the fight leaves me.

I sag into him as large hiccupping sobs overtake my body, and my spiteful words turn into incoherent murmurings. My fists still pound against his chest, and he takes a hand and smooths it over my hair and holds my head against him, his thumb rubbing reassuringly back and forth on my cheek. He rests his chin on my head. "I'm right here, Had. I'm not going anywhere, so let it all out. C'mon ... shh ... c'mon."

And it feels so damn good to need him. It feels so nice to use someone else to help with the emotion I've barricaded for so long that I can't stop it from pouring out and running down my cheeks. It is such a relief for him to be strong while I break down in this foreign place with a man I don't want to want but can't seem to separate myself from somehow.

So Becks holds me as I fall apart. As the months of grief and fear of the unknown become a perfect storm of release. Until my body trembles and my nose runs. Until my feet ache from standing in my heels and my fingers are sore from gripping his shirt so tightly. All the while he just holds on and says nothing aside from reassuring words, telling me that it's okay. That I'm going to be okay.

Time passes.

My walls begin to crack.

I'm sure the moon moves across the night sky at my back, but I don't know for sure because my eyes are blurry from crying so damn much. I have no idea how much time has lapsed. And now that my tears abate, now that silence has descended around us like a smothering pillow, the realization of what I've just done hits me full force. Shame follows quickly on its heels. I've got a moment of desperation where I know I need to salvage my dignity, but no idea how to go about doing that. I squeeze my eyes shut, uncertain where to set my feet beneath me on this ever-shifting ground, and try to pull away from him, but he just holds me tight, not allowing me to escape.

Emotionally or physically.

"Please, let me just go home, Becks." I don't even recognize the strange whimpering voice that comes from my mouth. The sounds of a person on the brink of losing it again.

"Not gonna happen, Montgomery." He presses a kiss to the side of my head. "You're not going anywhere."

We stand there in the darkened room. At some point, he shifts us to the couch. He's seated, with my body cradled across his lap—butt between his parted thighs. I don't know how we got in this position, but I know that not once has he loosened his hold on me. It's almost as if I'm a scared jack-rabbit he's afraid will bolt the minute he releases me.

And he has good reason to think that.

I find an odd comfort in the silence for once. I'm concentrating so hard on not crying—on not thinking about tears—that I find it hard to think about anything else: Lexi, Becks, living without feeling.

Dying.

I find consolation in the rhythm of our chests resting against each other's, from the physical contact that allows me to steal his warmth and use the reassuring beat of his steady heartbeat to soothe my aching soul.

And my mind must be so exhausted from the ridiculous display that I put on at the club that at some point, I succumb. So for the second time in a week, Becks sits with me as I fall asleep.

This time I just happen to be in his arms.

Chapter 14

It's the unfamiliarity that wakes me.

My eyelids are swollen, and it takes me a minute to realize where I am. I hear the slow, even breathing against my ear, feel the light smattering of hair against my hand, and I am suddenly aware of my breasts pillowed against Becks's bare chest. I take a moment to gather my bearings, the stillness of the surroundings making every little motion and sound from him magnified in my head: the weight of his hand under my tank against my naked back and the softness of the throw he put over my shoulders but that has since fallen and is now pooled at my waist.

Embarrassment hits me first. Then an influx of dread at falling apart when I wasn't alone. The witness to the raging chaos in my psyche wasn't the neutral walls of my bedroom but rather a real person this time. Someone who experienced my roller-coaster ride from needing something to help me forget to holding me so the broken pieces of me wouldn't completely fall apart.

A part of me is relieved, but at the same time, I'm also more worried than ever. Someone finally knows that I'm not handling this all as flawlessly as I've tried to portray. It's all been a facade to cover up the turmoil within me. Rylee's seen some of my slips, but I reined them in to lessen her worry with everything she had on her plate. My parents have seen it only in bits and pieces because they lost their child too, and I can't have them worrying about the other one. Danny's been so far down the bottomless well of his grief that solace isn't something he has to offer. So I've held all of the pain deep within me for so long that tonight it must have festered up until the poison needed to escape.

And now Becks knows. He knows that perfect Haddie isn't so perfect. I'm a powder keg of emotions that any little thing might cause to ignite. I'm not as stable as my take-no-shit attitude conveys. I'm vulnerable and a mess. I'm weak and irrational. And needy. And goddamn it, I hate being needy.

But he stayed. He held me tight and didn't let my tirade deter him. As I lie here, I try to wrap my head around what that means and how I feel about it.

And I'm just not sure how I feel. So I focus on the tangible. The warmth of his body against mine. The sounds and scents and sensations of being physically close to someone again. I'm so used to that empty feeling, the one that strikes me anytime I've done that morning-after-skip-of-shame-out-the-front-door to subdue the emotions raging inside.

So I allow myself to revel in everything; since he's asleep, I'm not being watched, scrutinized, or figured out. I can just enjoy the innocent moment because I deserve to feel this, to get the chance at normalcy with him.

I've conditioned myself so well over the past year that the thought—even though it's only to myself—causes anxiety to take hold of my body. And I need some distance from the sudden ache in my chest. Becks's breath alters momentarily, but it falls back into rhythm by the time I've scooted away and sat on the coffee table a few feet from the couch. Out of habit, I wipe whatever is left of my makeup from under my eyes and then reach for the fallen blanket and wrap it around my shoulders.

I lift my eyes to take Becks in. He has a pillow folded under his neck, one arm stretched up over his head and the other resting across his bare abdomen. But it's his face that captures me. Those assessing eyes of his are closed—dark lashes fanning against tan cheeks—and I can study him for a change. Stubble dusts his usually clean-shaven face now, and with his lips pursed in sleep, the lines that usually frame them are nonexistent.

Staring at him without the constant pressure to guard against the feelings that must be transparent in my eyes, I can't help but acknowledge what a truly great guy he is. Old-school in some ways. Yet he's without the drama of the bad boys I'm usually drawn to and definitely offers more stability. He's kind and caring and patient in all things emotional when most men I've dated are out the front door the minute the first tear falls.

Even though he is the ironic best friend's husband's best friend, he is the perfect epitome of what a *forever guy* should be.

And then it hits me like a spank on my ass. A fact so staggering that I don't quite know how to process it. I rise from the edge of the table on shaky legs and walk with an unsteady heart to the windows overlooking the street below and the dark beach a few city blocks beyond. I try desperately to focus on the hustle and bustle of the city's nightlife. I contemplate how this condo isn't what I'd expect from Becks—I'd pictured porch swings and open land somewhere in the fresh air—and realize how little I really know about this man, who's slowly capturing my heart. Trying to divert my attention, I think about everything I don't know about Becks rather than the one thing I know for sure.

Chills race over my flesh, and my heart thunders. The thought staggers me momentarily, my hand pressing against the glass for figurative stability, but I know I shouldn't be surprised. What the heart wants, the heart takes . . . even when it knows its owner won't allow it.

I've fallen for him.

I let the notion wash over me, trying to figure out where to go from here when I've said love isn't an option I would allow myself. And I'm not sure how long I've been standing there when I hear a soft chuckle from the couch. It startles me because my emotions are so scattered that I can't face him just yet. I need to cover up my heart, which I'm currently wearing on my sleeve like a tattoo, before I can speak to him.

I turn around slowly, expecting him to be sitting there, waiting for me to go first in that patient way of his, but when I do he's still fast asleep. "A dream," I murmur, and I'm not sure if I'm talking about what brought on the laughter in him or the rising hope in my heart. I stare at him lying there so warm and inviting—unknowingly rocking my world—and for the first time in what feels like forever in my tumultuous life, I smile.

And my smile only grows wider as I begin to accept the feelings, acknowledge that they aren't going to go away. Just as he hasn't gone away when I've been the emotional, crazy, chaotic woman he's seen over the past week. He's stuck by my side, sat on the other end of a silent phone line so that I wouldn't be alone.

My feet, which wouldn't budge earlier, have no problem moving now, but rather than through the door away from him like I'd expected, I'm walking toward him. Somehow my mind feels calmer, but there are still heady emotions swelling up in me.

I push away the doubts that creep in. Sure, there's hypocrisy in going against the promises I've been making to myself—the ones I reaffirmed just hours ago while we screamed at each other. But I tell myself to shut up, own the stilettos I'm walking in, and take the chance.

To go for it.

My smile grows even wider because I know somewhere in Heaven, Lexi just stood up and cheered for me. And the thought alone gives me the confidence I need to continue forward and tell Becks the one thing he needs to hear.

By now I'm standing next to the couch, looking down at him. I force a swallow down my throat as I realize that my fears have been irrational. That God can't be that greedy to steal my mother's breasts, extinguish my sister's light before her time, and then want my life way too early as well.

And as I stand in this darkened condominium, where a Keurig sits askew next to a half-empty clear plastic container of sugar cookies, my realization is like a weight off of my shoulders—I want this. I want it with him.

I let the blanket slip off my shoulders and fall to the floor with a soft whisper of sound. I pull my shirt over my head and toss it beside me. My hands pull my cell from my pocket and place it on the table before finding their way to the zipper on my skirt, opening its teeth, and pushing it down until it pools around my feet.

Tears well in my eyes as I dredge up every emotion I've shoved away over the past six months, every denial of wanting more since my first time with Becks. I stand there in this strange apartment with Becks snoring softly before me. It seems silly to have this epiphany here of all places, but it also feels imperfectly perfect. I'm naked in so many ways that processing the magnitude of what I'm opening myself up to is impossible. All I know is that the silence in my head has turned into a loud buzz of thoughts that seems harsh against the raw honesty of my decision.

My mind spins in a dizzying eddy of possibilities as I sit my hip on the couch beside his waist and breathe him in momentarily. My rational side tells me to shove up from the couch and escape as fast as I can, but then every other part of me has me lean forward and press my lips to the middle of his chest.

I keep my mouth there, and the warmth of his skin and the thunder of his heart beneath my lips combined with my sudden courage are an intoxicating mixture. I begin to lace soft, gentle kisses up his sternum. His breathing changes, becomes less even with each breath he draws. I inhale the scent of his cologne at the dip beneath his Adam's apple before lifting my head and brushing a kiss against his lips. I repeat the motions with soft whispers of touch until I hear a muted moan from him as my actions slowly stir him awake.

I know the minute his mind has caught up when his lips are already kissing me before he's even awake. His muscles tense; then the arm above his head juts forward until it lands on the bare skin of my back.

"Haddie," he says in a dreamlike voice as he attempts in his sleepy state to comprehend what's going on. I just keep meeting his lips over and over until his hand on my back finds my hair and fists in it so that I'm forced to meet his startled blue eyes. He's trying to work out how I went from hating, then wanting, and then crying to now needing him.

And the smart-ass in me thinks, *Welcome to being a female*, but the moment is so much more poignant than a quip can signify. So I stay quiet, and as our eyes hold each other's, I know that this unspoken connection is so much more intimate than words could be right now.

So we sit like this, his hand in my hair, our breathing uneven, and an unasked question hanging between us that once it's answered can offer so many possibilities. Becks just continues to stare at me, the crystalline blue of his eyes holding me hostage, and I wonder what I look like in his eyes.

"I—I woke up wanting to kiss you." I fail miserably at telling him what I need to, stumbling through the words so I offer up this lame explanation for my about-face. Confusion and rejection flicker through his eyes, and I lean forward and tease his lips ever so softly with mine to buy myself another few seconds to build up the courage for what I want to say.

I pull back and look into his eyes so chock-full of concern. "I can't . . . We can't keep—"

"Sh-shh!" My finger is on his lips, stopping him instantly. *"We are,"* I whisper to him, looking at his lips and then back up to his eyes to reinforce the words I've just said. His mouth falls lax as he sucks in a breath from my unexpected answer. "I need you, Becks."

And I've never spoken more honest words in my life.

His eyes widen, the pupils overtaking the irises and his mouth smiling cautiously beneath my finger. I lean forward—praying he doesn't reject me—and slant my mouth over his again. And this time he responds. He parts his lips and allows me to slip my tongue between them and lick softly against his. It's a soft sigh of a kiss, so very different from the earlier frantic energy, but there's still an underlying desperation that I can sense . . . and I'm just not sure if it's on his part or mine.

But I choose to push the thought away. I choose to get lost in him instead. So I reach down with the hand not resting against his cheek and make quick work of the buttons on his jeans. I take a second to savor the warmth of his skin before pushing down his boxer briefs so I can take him in my hand. It takes a few uncoordinated moments of him raising his hips and helping to shove the waist of his jeans down.

No words are spoken—none are needed as we use the intimacy of our mouths to express what we feel about the chances I've just given us.

I continue to kiss him softly, gentle draws of mouth on mouth, while my hand encircles him and slides over his length. Every moan he emits as I repeat the action makes me crave another from him.

He reaches over and puts his hands at my waist, and I can feel him jolt with the awareness that I'm already naked and ready for him. And I can't deny the charge I get in knowing that I can come to him completely naked and know he's going to want me. There is something most definitely sexy and empowering in that feeling.

His hands direct me to rise up and settle over his hips so that I'm on my knees with my hand still stroking him between my parted legs. I look at him now. Run my eyes up his golden skin, the tightened disks of his nipples, to the bottom lip his teeth are biting into as he fumbles to put on the condom that he's produced from his wallet. When he's protected, his eyes meet mine just as I line him up at my entrance and lower myself onto his wide crest. I can see and feel his whole body tense at the partial sheathing—my tease to his more than ready cock—and his hands reach back up to my hips to urge me to lower myself onto him.

I don't even fight the smile when I choose to ignore the pressure at my hips and sink down at a torturously slow pace. It's absolutely killing me with a potent combination of pleasure and anticipation, so I know it has to affect him just as much, if not even more.

He hisses out when I'm over him root to tip. For a moment, I just sit there, letting the slow burn of his girth subside, before I pop my hips forward so that I slide up and down on him, earning a soft hiss of pleasure. I continue controlling the pace, the movement, and angle myself expertly so I can make sure that my inner hot spot is hit each time.

The pleasure is so strong, so intense that I'm in a state of indecision—I want to slow down, draw it out so I can enjoy every single withdrawal and subsequent settling back down onto him, and at the same time, I want to be impatient and selfish and push myself to climax as quick as I can. Find my release so that he can chase his.

He's so incredibly deep inside me—feels so fucking good—that I don't even realize my eyes are closed, face angled up to the ceiling, and hands are gripping Becks's hands, which are still holding on to my hips. The pressure begins to build, spears of white-hot heat shooting sparks up my spine, causing my breathing to quicken but my rhythm to remain even and seductively slow, despite his hands urging otherwise.

I lose myself in the feeling for a moment, letting the current of our union overwhelm me until Becks shocks my head forward when he adds a subtle grind to his hips along with my motion. I look to meet his eyes—lids half-closed as the sublime sensations begin to pull him under.

But when our gazes meet, the intimacy of the moment as we keep moving—our bodies, our thoughts, our souls connecting all at once—is so powerful that we falter for a minute. My body is damp with sweat, and goose bumps threaten, the intensity of the emotion so overwhelming, it drowns me momentarily.

His dick involuntarily pulses within me, causing a sly smirk to shadow his lips. His arrogance is unexpected and sexy as hell. I squeeze around him, and I love the groan my action garners from him. He begins to urge my hips to move again with our linked hands, and I want to keep this steady course, not rush it because damn he feels like fucking Heaven.

So I take control and move our joined hands to his chest so that I can hold them there while gaining some leverage to maneuver my hips in different angles. I lean forward and press my lips to his, slipping my tongue in between. My forward motion exposes more of his dick, from the crest just to the opening of my sex, so that when I slide horizontally, his head hits every damn nerve I possess. I moan, his mouth capturing the sounds he's coaxing from me, and with each thrust of his hips upward and my push downward, my body jolts with even more awareness, the precipice of bliss that much closer.

I tell myself to take note of everything—the slide of my chest against his, his taste on my tongue, his complete domination of every fucking sensation below my waist, the soft exhale of pleasure he makes when I take him completely inside me. All of these factors help heighten my sensations, push me up and over the edge.

The sex this time is so different from last time between

us. Whereas before it was a discovery of bodies and a proving ground of abilities, this time it is slow and mesmerizing. When my orgasm hits with a violent intensity, I'm not prepared for the breath it steals from me.

Yes, my toes curl and my back arches like normal, but I'm shaken irrevocably as the flash of vulnerability streaks through me. My body is left trembling as the intense sensations of pleasure ricochet back to my core, my heartbeat a thunderous roar in my ears, and my body starving for the air my brain can't seem to tell my lungs to suck in.

My name falls in a strained exclamation from Becks's mouth as his hands hold my hips still. He grows iron hard within me, making my body sing with the added pressure, and then he's lost to his own onslaught of sensations. His body tenses as his hips thrust fervently and his neck arches upward, his fingers digging harder into my skin as a guttural moan fills the silence around us.

I lay my head against his chest and listen to his heart, which I've helped send into its current rapid beat, my own feeling like it's quickening too but for a different reason. I close my eyes as Becks presses a kiss to the top of my head, his fingertips trailing lazy lines up my spine and then back down in a way that gives me goose bumps. We sit there for a few moments, coming down from our orgasmic hazes. He begins to soften so that he slips out of me, and I move so he can clean up, but instead he just wraps his arms around me and holds me against his chest.

"We are," he murmurs, repeating the words back to me before emitting a satisfied moan. "We are."

My breath hitches with his comment, my own response tangled in the confusion in my head. This feels so right with him at the same time that I'm worried I'm only going to cause us pain. But I push the worry from my head because everything will be okay. It has to be.

" 'Night, City."

" 'Night."

I squeeze my eyes shut, both satisfied and scared by the man who's at fault for breaking the first link in the chain I wrapped around my guarded heart. Whereas I used to use sex to quiet my thoughts, this time it's had the opposite effect.

My thoughts are screaming so loud now that they can't be ignored.

The transition between sleep and waking is gentle. I'm in that dreamlike haze where my mind is drifting softly, trying to fall back under the pull of slumber so that I can return to sitting with Lex by the pool, where we were talking. Where we were laughing and I felt closer to her than I had in forever. Every single thing I feared I had forgotten about her—the pitch to her laugh, the line of her posture, the ease of her smile—was there, allowing me to grasp it back and hold on to it a little longer.

I'm not startled or surprised by the fact that I'm pressed up against Becks's naked body or in his bed. I vaguely remember the feel of his arms carrying me in here from the couch. I note the rise and fall of his chest beneath my hand where it lies over his heart. I'm oddly the most at peace with myself that I have been in a long time, and I snuggle into the feeling as well as into Becks.

My thoughts tumble aimlessly as I will myself to go back to sleep to steal a few more hours ensconced in this feeling of relaxed contentment. But I'm at an awkward angle, my breasts smashed uncomfortably up against Becks's firm torso. I begin to shift at the same time he turns in his sleep and find myself emitting a muffled cry as he lowers his arm and pinches a part of my breast.

It's a split second of time. I'm sure thinking about it later I won't even be able to process how fast the awareness hits me. The pain is quick and fleeting, and when I move in reflex to pull away from where my breast is pinched between the mattress and his back, I become conscious of the fact that I feel something there.

I sit up immediately, my mind fully alert but my subconscious telling me I'm crazy, all while my rational mind runs through a series of thoughts that are far from welcome. My breaths come out in sharp rasps. I tell myself it's because I've moved so quickly, but I know the truth: The fear has taken hold.

I tell myself I was half asleep, my skin really was pinched, and that there's nothing there to cause pain. No tumor, no cancer, nothing like Lex.

Next I take a calming breath, my fingers already moving toward my left breast. But whereas my routine checks are usually timid and gentle—more afraid of what I'll find than not knowing what is there—I find myself pressing as hard as I can, being overly thorough. I become frantic in my movements as my mind starts running a million miles an hour. I keep moving in circles with the pads of my three fingers, but as memories and fear and disbelief start to collide, there is no rhyme or reason to my actions. I pull at the tissue, pressing my fingers together on both sides of the stretched skin, causing myself pain as I try to feel any trace of something.

Sitting in Becks's bed with a stream of moonlight falling over it, I manage to work myself into a frenzy when I should be snuggled up against the handsome man fast asleep beside me—living, feeling, loving. I don't know how much time passes because I'm so worried, so panicked that a mist of sweat coats my skin, and at some point, I must have started to cry because I taste salt from the tears that leaked out and reached my lips. My hands are trembling, and my mind is chastising me for not being able to re-create the same sensation that I felt moments ago.

Was it just moments ago? All I can think about is the possible parasite beneath my breast that threatens to take the life from me. I just about give up, my breast sore and reddened from my probing and prodding, my nerves so damn frayed that connecting one thought to another is nearly impossible. I glance at the clock and realize I've been at this for a half an hour. I haven't found anything yet . . . no lump, no bump, no dimple. I'm just making myself hysterical.

Calm down, Had. You're jumping to conclusions. It was nothing. You were asleep and you were thinking of Lex and it was just a pinch.

Quietly I sigh, glancing over at Becks to make sure he's still asleep. I've already lost it once tonight with him, so this is the last thing I need him to see. He's a patient man, but I think he just might give me the balcony exit if I lose it again.

As my shoulders sag, I tell myself one more time. I'll examine myself one more time and then be done with it for the early-morning hours. I raise my hand and go through the motions, a slight sense of ease settling over me, when I just about stop and *I feel it.*

I freeze.

My fingers stop moving, the tissue still pinched between them. My eyes widen. My shaky inhale of breath fills the silence of the room.

My body stops, but my mind races as my whole world comes crashing down around me. I raise a trembling hand to stifle the choked sob that never comes. My eyes blur as I shake my head back and forth in shock, images of Lexi colliding against one another in my mind.

Time passes as I sit paralyzed with fear, numb with disbelief, and void of emotion.

Becks shifts in bed, and the movement jolts me to the here and now. I tell myself the lump is tiny, could be fibrous tissue, for all I know, but I don't believe my own lies. I know it's something more because I've made it a point to know my breasts in and out over the past year. I try to hold on, but I feel like my thoughts are slipping away from me as a false, eerie calm begins to settle over my body.

My hands shake and my mind tries to process but just keeps coming up empty. I won't allow it to go where my biggest fears lies, so I focus instead on right now. On the man beside me. On how I just opened up my heart, invited him in, and told him we are, and then look what happened.

I rise from the bed without thinking of collateral damage or the fallout. Of Becks lying in bed asleep and what to say to him because there is nothing I can say but sorry—and sorry doesn't cut shit right now. Sorry doesn't ease the overwhelming sense of disbelief that has struck me. The overused word doesn't ease the sting of loss, of watching your loved one die, or of leaving someone so they don't have to go through it and suffer with you.

I keep my eyes averted from him as I pull my clothes on and dress quietly on autopilot, focusing on zippers and buttons, habitual actions. I have to physically think to do each thing, perform each routine movement because when I don't, I find that I just stand there and stare out the window to the world outside.

Carrying on like everything is fine when it's clearly not.

Once I'm fully dressed, shoes in my hand so I don't wake him up with their sound on the floor, my feet are still rooted in place. My chest physically hurts, and my head is pounding. My eyes burn, and my heart feels like it's being twisted, acid eating holes through the muscle at a menacing pace.

I glance over to Becks and stare at him through the light of the night from beyond the windows. There are so many things I want to say to him, but all I keep thinking is how I jinxed everything. Tonight I went against everything I had promised myself, and look how fate came with a cruel backhand to put me in my proper place.

I should be used to it. Expect it. Right when everything was okay with Rylee and Colton from their hospital stints— just when my closest friend in the whole world was looking toward happily ever after, my sister was staring down a loaded shotgun.

These memories flicker and then flood me—accompanying her to mammograms, then her double mastectomy, brushing her hair as clumps fell out, her fighting the fight and exhausting all resources—until I feel like I'm suffocating, reaffirming the fact that I can't do this to Becks. A raw sadness marries with the grief I carry, and I tell him the empty words that I hate more than any others. "I'm sorry."

The words feel like a noose closing over my neck.

I turn from the room and pad in my bare feet out to the family room, where I realize I don't have my purse or my keys. I spot his wallet on the coffee table where he left it open when he pulled the condom out earlier and add injury to insult when I pull on the twenty-dollar bill partially exposed from it. I hate doing this, but I don't have any other option. Just another reason for him to hate me even more. For him to validate his earlier accusation that I'm a coward.

Because if I didn't acknowledge it before, doing this makes it pretty clear as fucking day that I am.

But I don't know what else to do right now. I'll pay him back. I look over my shoulder through the open doorway to where he sleeps peacefully, and then I walk to the front door and slip out to the streets below to hail a cab.

The guilt is heavy and oppressive, dropping through my soul and occupying my thoughts just as handily as the fear sitting in its worn recliner, where the feeling has made itself comfortable over the past six months. All I keep thinking is, he doesn't deserve this.

Hell, neither do I.

Chapter 15

The room is cold, and the worn pad on the hospital's gurney beneath me is anything but comfortable. Hell, if it were a mattress from the Ritz, I wouldn't think it's comfortable because I swear to God these cold, clinical walls of the outpatient procedure room suction every ounce of life from me with each passing moment.

The valium I've taken slowly kicks in as the nurse makes casual comments here and there, nothing I need to answer—just innocent conversation to fill the silence and pass time. She hums softly to herself now as she lays instruments on the tray beside me with a sterile clink. I can hear my phone buzzing in my purse, which is sitting under the chair across the room, and I swallow over the lump in my throat, hoping it's not Becks. Again.

It's amazing how many times someone can try to contact you in a seventy-two-hour period.

His first round of texts started at seven a.m. the morning I left; his messages reflected concern at first and then slowly morphed to frustrated anger the longer I ignored him. My lone response after the first hour passed was lame but honest all at the same time. *I'm sorry. I thought I could do this, but I can't* was all my text said, and it did nothing to stop the barrage of his replies. And each alert, each ding, was like adding salt to my open wound because lying to someone else is one thing, but lying to yourself is impossible.

So I've turned my anger at myself onto him, blaming him for making me want something I can't have right now. I'll let it manifest into annoyance from his persistence and then irritation so I can pass the phone without wanting to pick it up to see if he has or hasn't texted.

And I'm not even sure which one of those I want more: to be ignored or to be pursued.

The hum of the phone vibrating pulls me from my thoughts, and I giggle. I know it's inappropriate for the situation, but the soft edges the valium gives me makes me feel warm and fuzzy that he's calling me again. But I don't want to giggle. I want to be angry with him for continuing to call and text me. I'm selfish, damn it. Can't he see that? I snuck out in the middle of the night without so much as a *See you later, Charlie Brown. . . .* The giggles take over again at the thought of Snoopy and Charlie.

A momentary peace settles over me, and I definitely want some more of this shit they gave me. It's more than just the valium, but whatever they put in that shot to relax me some . . . it's nice. Like riding-on-a-cloud nice. Like "sinking into the mattress with Becks's weight on top of me" nice.

Stop it. My voice is loud in my head, chastising me for the temptation of what I can't have, what I refuse to let myself have. And it's more than just his mighty fine dick. I snort out the laugh this time, which causes the nurse to look over at me and ask me if I'm having a good time by myself on the gurney. I just nod my head like a little kid and think, *Well, it's true.*

And then the thought of him and his mighty fine dick rushes in with a surge of guilt like a buzz kill on my inappropriately giddy high. I wish he'd just be so angry at me that he stops calling and texting. It would make this all so much easier on me. Because if he's mad, then it makes it easier to justify being a bitch to him like I'm being by ignoring him.

I thought that after he woke and realized I wasn't going to answer his calls, he'd get the hint. I was proven wrong when the pounding on my front door commenced five texts later. Luckily, Dante was gone, or else I have a feeling I wouldn't have been able to pretend I was not home. But fuck, wouldn't that have been kind of hot if they'd fought over me? I giggle again as images flicker of bad boy versus good guy, and I think Orgasm-Inducing Becks just might be able to take Delectable Dante.

My eyes drift closed momentarily as the wonderful world of pharmaceuticals allows me to remember sex with Becks in 3-D fashion. Thank God, my nurse and my doctor are females because now I'm horny and have an easy-access hospital gown on.

Horny Haddie in the procedures room for all available hot male doctors, STAT.

I laugh at the thought, the drugs pulling me under their haze until my phone chirps, and pulls me from loopyville.

Oh, Beckster boy. He deserves an explanation. Thank God, Rylee is still out of range of cell service, or I'm sure he'd have called her. But what exactly is there to say to him? It's not like I can give him a blow job as a parting gift, *The Price Is Right* style. "Next item up for bid is a blow job by Horny Haddie. Will Beckett Daniels come on down?" This time I slap my hand over my mouth because I laugh so hard and my head is so dizzy that I know the nurse must think I'm bat-shit crazy.

Well, she would be partially right because I kind of am. Especially now. Specifically for walking away from him, the quintessential good guy.

It's not like I can answer my phone right now and say, *Thanks for the quick fuck that was, like, porn star good and the shoulder to cry on like Oprah's.* It's a little more than three days later, and I've already had my tit smashed flat as a pancake, then lubed up with gel and pushed around with the ultrasound. I mean, at least if I'm gonna get felt up, the technician could pinch my nipples or something, give me a cheap thrill. I snort again and can't stop laughing because that was pretty funny. Even drugged I know that.

Oh. Maybe I can get them to give some of this shit to my mom, who's wearing grooves in the hallway outside so that she can relax a bit because she's telling me everything is going to be fine, but she played with her charm on her damn necklace when she said it. That means she's lying.

Girls, Rover dug a hole under the fence and ran away, but I'm sure he found a nice new home to take him in and love him. Played with her necklace as Lex and I cried buckets of tears.

Haddie and Lexi, I'm sick. It's nothing major, just something the doctors call cancer, but I'll be completely fine. Playing with her necklace the whole time. Two relapses, twenty-three total rounds of chemotherapy, fifteen sessions of radiation, and a chestful of scars that make Frankenstein's monster's stitches look like scratches.

Haddie, Lexi's going to beat this cancer, and we'll all laugh about it later. Playing with her damn necklace. But she played with it at Lex's funeral too. That meant she was hoping it was a lie, and well, fuck, it wasn't.

Same necklace but different charm over time.

And I got the necklace act today. The bad track record of that stupid chain makes me want to rip it off and chuck it as far as I can so that I never have to see it again. Especially around me.

Wait. Maybe I need the necklace when I talk to Becks. Maybe he'll catch on if I play with it when I tell him thanks for the good time, the two hours you allowed me to be a *we are*, before fate stepped in and put me in my place. Reminded me why I'd made promises to myself about not getting involved with anyone.

The door whooshes open and pulls me from my thoughts.

"You ready, Haddie?" Dr. Blakely walks in with a relaxed smile on her face, and I want to tell her it's okay to be worried because I sure as fuck am.

"Hearts and heels." I exhale, thinking of Maddie girl. I want to ask the doctor something but I don't remember what . . . oh, about giving me some of this on the take-out menu plan so I can have some of the special sauce when I need it to feel better.

A strained smile is on my lips as she snaps on her rubber gloves. "Did that valium help take the edge off?" she asks, causing me to snort out a sarcastic laugh as I nod.

How exactly does one little pill—one I actually had to ask for to stop the churning in my stomach and the anxiety controlling my nerves—really take the edge off? Because cutting into your boob is a walk in the park, right?

My mind screams with a sarcastic retort, but I just nod my head and mumble, "A bit."

"No need to worry," she says, her smile still tight as I giggle again, my head feeling like a dandelion seed floating in the breeze. "Can you feel that?" she asks, ignoring my laugh. I can see her shoulders move as she does whatever with her hands, but I don't feel a damn thing.

Why the fuck didn't they give me this shit when Lex died? I like this not-feeling thing. Maybe if I take enough, I can numb my heart and be immune to everything that happens.

"Like we talked about, I'll make a half-moon-shaped incision, remove the mass that we saw and marked from the scans, and send it to pathology. I'll stitch you up, and you'll be as good as new," she explains as she spreads the butadiene over my left breast and then covers it with a surgical drape.

Good as new? Okay. Whatever you say, Doc, because at this point I'm not real happy with you for slicing into my perfect tits. Full D, pink nipples, perfectly shaped, and perky as fuck. Never had any complaints yet. I usually get the bone-o-meter to be straight up when I show these babies, and now she's going to fuck them up.

Let's begin the patchwork quilt, shall we?

"Relax. It's probably nothing." Her smile is reassuring now.

I close my eyes and try not to read into her smile, but I want to snort and tell her good as new with some X-marks-the-spot stitches and possibly cancer, but that's nothing big at all. Just a walk in the park.

I exhale when I begin to feel the pressure and try to return to the happy thoughts I couldn't stop thinking moments ago. But this is suddenly way too fucking real, and I'm scared to death. I force my breathing to slow down, and I can feel my armpits sticky with sweat.

She passes something off to the nurse waiting at her side, and the nurse leaves the room. Dr. Blakely turns to me and explains something about the pathologist checking to see if there are clear margins. Of course, my mind starts fretting that the only way one can have clear margins is if it's measured against something that's not clear, something cancerous.

Time passes, and since I'm still under the veil of valium, I don't know how long we wait.

The phone buzzes in the room and scares the crap out of me, my valium obviously making me not as courageous when sliced apart with a scalpel. Dr. Blakely speaks to the pathologist and says she has to clear a bit more.

I fix my eyes on hers, looking for any kind of sign of what the pathologist has said, but she busies herself, preparing to rebiopsy my breast. I want to tell her to look in my eyes and tell me the truth. This is my life she's cutting into, and don't I at least deserve an inkling of what is going on?

But my mouth stays shut, my hands remain fisted, and my heart feels like it's lost its beat.

The same song and dance continues one more time, her

hands steady and sure while my whole soul is shaken to the core. But this time she has gotten a clean margin.

All in all, the procedure is quick, and I really don't feel a thing except for the hum of my nerves zinging through me from my adrenaline high. I feel the tug on the incision as she closes it up and then watch her hands move although I can't feel the steri strips being applied. I thank her, sigh in frustration when she won't answer when I ask if whatever she biopsied looked cancerous. She just smiles the tight smile that I want to knock off her face again and tells me that pathology might have a preliminary report within the next couple days, but she wants to wait for the full workup. I can't really focus on the terms she uses as the rest of the drugs and their calming effects ride out their stay in my body.

My mom comes in, and I think I smile at her, but I'm not sure because I'm so busy watching her talk to the doctor, glancing at me intermittently, with her fingers tugging on her damn necklace the whole time.

At some point the medicine must knock me out cold because the next thing I remember is waking up in my parents' house. In Lex's and my old bedroom, surrounded by memories of her in so many ways. Happy ones and sad ones. I feign sleep when I hear the door to the room open, not wanting to talk just yet about the cacophony of thoughts cluttering my head. I hear my parents murmuring their thoughts and fears in the hallway, and it takes everything I have not to cover my ears and rock like a child to shut them out.

And I wish I could act like a child. I wish I could throw a tantrum and fight and rage and not care what people think or understand the consequences.

But I'm not.

And I do.

And fuck if I want to get a firsthand reminder of just how devastating life can be.

Chapter 16

The jerk of Rylee's head up from the vegetables she's chopping to meet my gaze is almost comical. God, I'm glad she's home. I didn't realize how much I'd missed her. How much I needed to look at her and not see fear mixed with pity looking back at me like I did at my parents' house.

I meet her gaze—my closest friend—and feel the pointed sword of guilt pressing against my throat as I carry on like everything was perfectly fine while she was away on her honeymoon. Like the doctor didn't call and say she was ordering more extensive pathology tests on the mass she'd removed before making any conclusive decisions. Or how she was skirting around using the word *diagnosis* . . . because diagnosis is the word they use when they tell you it's cancer. I've never lied to Rylee, and yet here I am, the smile I have fraudulently plastered on my face feeling more and more natural as I fall under the comfort of our easy rapport.

And I feel like I'm two inches tall, strong-arming the bucket brimming with indecision from tipping over to the point where I tell her everything.

But I don't. She's gone through so much in the last few years, and I don't want to worry her unnecessarily. Plus, it's the first time I've seen her since she got home from her honeymoon, and I've missed her like crazy. I want to hear all about how sickeningly happy she is because I know her happiness will ease the weight of the unknown that I carry with me as a constant right now. The goddamn cloud trying to block out my sun.

Add to that I have the little issue of having to explain why my only question in our first conversation since she's returned was if Becks was going to attend the little "we're home" barbecue she was throwing. I wish I could kick myself in the ass for the knee-jerk reaction that's resulted in my preoccupation to avoid Rylee's assessing eyes. I've been so diligent, changing the subject anytime it circles back around to me that I realize I've missed out on hearing the details of their honeymoon highlights.

And of course my mind is so scattered that she catches me off guard. By fault of my distraction, I accidentally acknowledge that Becks and I did in fact have sex on their wedding night and then maybe, possibly one other time. It's a muttered point given under the duress of a knife-wielding best friend, who's chopping vegetables and waving said knife at me while she talks—but she hears my admission nonetheless.

"So you look nice and tan and overly sexed," I say over the rim of my glass of wine.

"Whoa! Hold it, sister!" she demands, waving the weapon in her hand in my direction. "You think you can hit me with all of this . . ." She's so flustered by my confession that she can't find the words to continue, so she keeps jabbing the air with her knife toward me until I start laughing. "It's not funny! I haven't seen you in weeks—"

"I know. It's so great to see you so relaxed. So give me all the details . . . 'sex on a secluded beach' type of details—"

"Don't you dare change the topic. Sit," she orders as she takes a sip of her merlot and stares me down until I oblige. "First, you tell me that you guys hooked up on our wedding night, which I thought a possibility when Becks had your phone . . . but then you did it *again* . . . AND you snuck out before he woke up?"

I bite my bottom lip and nod my head subtly, guilt still slicing through me like a razor blade at my cowardice—the only part I feared admitting to Ry because even I know it was wrong. Not just the leaving but the subsequent refusal to speak to him other than my inadequate text telling him I was wrong in thinking I could have any type of relationship with him.

No further explanation. Nothing. I was just trying to make it easier all around for him and for me. For the changes I fear are knocking on my welcome mat that are far from welcome.

The sad fact is even I didn't believe my own lies this time.

"Why?" She finally sets the knife down and wipes her hands off on the dish towel before placing them on the kitchen counter to brace herself. Violet eyes meet mine, and fuck if I don't love and hate this new self-assurance that Colton has brought out in my oldest friend. I really would prefer her not to have it focused on me right at this moment though.

I sigh as I break my gaze from hers. "Because I'm trying to get my shit together."

She laughs out low and rich, and despite my thoughts, the sound brings a smile to my lips.

"What?"

"I do believe that getting someone's shit together led to my current state," she teases as she holds up her hand where her wedding ring reflects the light and sends a blizzard of prisms against the walls of the kitchen. I laugh with her now that I finally get what she's saying and the irony in my own comment. How I once told Colton when they first started dating that he needed to get his shit together and only then would he be worthy of my friend.

"So . . . six months from now should I be expecting one of these on your finger?"

I cough on my sip of wine. "Are you certifiably crazy, Ry? After everything . . ." I stop myself from confessing all of the emotions I've hidden. Everything I've tried to keep inside since Lex's death so that I could be a good friend for Rylee, so that I could help her plan her wedding without the oppressive weight of grief being a downer. And I know she knew what I was doing, the distraction techniques, the false fronts—all of it—but she let me think I was fooling her because she knew that was what I needed at the time. She knew that was what was best for me. And now I fear that she's done being patient, and she's going to tell me exactly what I need to hear. Except I'm not ready—and although there are things she doesn't even know the whole truth about, I know she'll be correct in her assessment nonetheless. "I haven't even spoken to him since."

"He didn't call you?" Bemusement laces her question.

"Of course he did. Countless times. I just chose not to answer."

She chuckles with condescension. "How very mature of you."

And now she's pulling the gloves off to force me to deal with my own shit. Take no prisoners and all that. I definitely need another bottle of wine here. I reach for it without a second thought, as the soft tug of my stitches hitting my clothes with the movement makes its presence known—the ever-constant reminder of my secret, my fear, my possible future. *Tell her.* My mind screams the thought, knowing I could use her strength, but my heart can't bring her down, make her worry unnecessarily when I've never seen her this happy.

I'll tell her the minute I know something. I make the promise to myself to justify lying to my best friend, but it does nothing to ease the guilt.

She angles her head to the side, and at first I fear she's caught my grimace or my sudden silence. Her gaze dares me to look away, taunts me to try to hide everything swimming in my eyes.

And I cave with eyes averted and focus on my fingers playing idly with the stem of my wineglass. "Well, you know, while you were gone, I came up with a new motto," I say in a lame attempt at diversion ". . . 'less stress, more sex.'"

"New motto, huh?" she says, rolling her eyes, "because I thought your motto was "Whenever I don't want to deal with Lexi's death, I go have meaningless sex to not think about it.' *Slut glut*, I believe is my term for it." She raises her eyebrows at me as she finishes throwing her cards on the table so I'm forced to show my hand.

And hell if her words don't sting just as smartly as Becks's did the other night during our argument. The difference is Becks is a guy and like any male will say things to beat his chest and assert his testosterone whereas Ry's not competing for me. She's just being observant—truthful—and I hate like hell that she's right as rain.

Shame fills me, but I hold her gaze in silence for a few more moments. I can tell she already feels guilty for calling me on the carpet, but I love her even more for not backing down, for telling me what I need to hear. "Talk to me, Had. Please talk to me."

"*Slut glut?* Really?" I ask, although I deserve the shrug of the shoulders she gives me, which says, *If the shoe fits . . .* And hell, it does fit, but at least it's a really cute pair of four-inch peep-toe stilettos that scream, *Come fuck me*. I keep the thought to myself, knowing Ry won't appreciate my humor if I say that aloud.

I sigh in resignation before glancing down to watch my finger run around the rim of my glass while I figure out what to say. "The first time . . . your wedding night, I kind of didn't play fair. Seduced him when he was trying to keep his distance. . . . Then we agreed to sex without strings." I fall silent as I think about everything that I've already gone over a million times before, and whether I would change it—keep the zipper up and let him walk to his room alone.

I don't think I would. And that in itself scares me.

"And the second . . . ," she prompts, but I just sit there in silence, unable to lift my eyes to meet hers, so she continues. "Look, I love you. You're the sister I never had, so I'm going to say it, and you tell me when I veer off course." I nod my head, close my eyes, and take in a deep breath as I prepare for her psychoanalysis, which I'm sure will be much more real than I actually want to hear but probably need to nonetheless.

"I watched you watch Lex die and know how much you suffered, Haddie. How much you still suffer. I saw you hold Danny while he fell apart and then try to fill in what's missing for Maddie as best as you could. I saw you internalize it, refuse to deal with it. I watched my best friend lose herself with the worry and the fear and the grief. And that's more than understandable." I hear her sniffle, and I feel relieved that she is emotional right now because it's taking everything I have to hold my tears back. I grit my teeth, and I'm sure she thinks it's because I'm angry at her, but it's because I'm trying to prevent the confession about the biopsy on my lips.

"I've witnessed you drag your feet to take the first gene test and then refuse to take the second one when it could ease all of this fear inside you. Fear that you have cancer too. Fear that you can't let anyone love you, fall in love with you—make a life with you—because you're going to die like Lex did, and you're going to leave him devastated just like Danny is."

It's like hearing the words aloud validate my feelings and also makes my own stubbornness sound ludicrous all at the same time. I bite my bottom lip as she sits patiently, giving me the time to absorb her on-target commentary. She's right on every level of course, but the catch is that Becks was able to coax out from its hiding place the part of me that was afraid to engage. It just didn't last long before the fear of my fated future had me wanting to hold back again.

I can't speak quite yet, so I just nod my head as I brush away the lone tear that's escaped.

"I think the reason you snuck out was because Becks scares the hell out of you." Her voice softens with compassion. "He's making you think and feel things you don't want to feel, so if you leave, then it just makes it easier for you to ignore something you both sure as hell deserve. He sees the fire in your eyes and wants to play with it ... and that? That's hard to find since most men would consider that a challenge to their manhood." Rylee reaches out with the bottle of wine and refills my glass as I finally look up to meet her eyes. I nod ever so slightly at her, letting her see the fear in my eyes and telling her she's hit the nail on the head. "Haddie, you can't close yourself off forever. A life without passion and love is like slowly freezing to death."

I exhale a shaky breath, her words like a vice squeezing my heart and an exorcist relieving the acrid fear tearing apart my soul. She has no clue how dead-on she is, how she is speaking to the parts of me drowning in fear right now — and I love her for it, but I also want to forget about it if I can. Not think about any of this for the day. Shove it away and feel normal again.

"Shit, I have passion." The comment is a knee-jerk reflex on my part, my habit of defensive deflection. I realize my mistake the minute it's out of my mouth, but she continues before I can correct myself.

"A one-night stand is not passion. It's a quick fix."

I laugh nervously, not liking the magnifying glass turned on me. "Well, see, I'm already showing growth because at least Becks wasn't just a one-night stand. He was a twofer."

She smiles and just shakes her head. "I'm feeling a nostalgic déjà vu but with roles reversed here," she says, making me laugh sincerely as I think back to a day when we discussed her and Colton's one-night stand. The one-night stand that I joked was going to be a thirty-night-stand but that never ended after all.

"God, Ry . . . I *like* Becks." It's not much but it's a start.

"He's a hard guy not to like, but he's hardly your type. . . ."

"No," I tell her, not sure if she understands what I'm saying, "I *like* Becks." I emphasize the word again in a way that causes her eyes to widen and her mouth to form the shape of an O momentarily before a satisfied smirk ghosts her lips.

And I don't quite know why I'm telling her this since I'm not going to allow anything further to happen between us. Maybe I'm giving her something since I feel so guilty about neglecting to tell her about the biopsy.

"Okay . . ." She draws the word out, prompting me to continue.

I struggle to put my thoughts into words. "He really is a great guy," I try to explain. "I mean, my head's messed-up, and I can't tell you how many times I've cried or yelled at him, and he just . . . he just stays there so I know he's there, but not in that 'he's a pushover' kind of way." Tears well in my eyes, and I hate the blatant tell of what my heart feels. "But right now . . . it just might be the 'right person but at the wrong time' kind of thing."

She takes a sip of her wine and then looks at the liquid in the glass before meeting my eyes, her mouth turned down at the edges. "Humans are drawn to each other's rough edges. Look at Colton and me." The look in her eyes reinforces the words she speaks.

"Well, screw the rough. I'm more jagged as of late." I try to defuse things with humor. Broken shards of slicing glass is more like it. Come too close and you'll get hurt by association alone.

"And yet he still called." She's relentless now.

"And I still ran." I hang my head in shame.

"Haddie, look at me." She waits patiently until I lift my eyes to meet hers. "I love you both. You're both a huge part of my life, so, of course, it would be awesome if something worked out here . . . but you have to do what's best for you. I just know that Becks is the type of guy who's patient enough to help you face your fears if you let him. . . ."

"Yeah," I say, but right now she has no clue how close I'm coming to seeing my worst fears realized. She sits patiently, expression impassive as I think, collect myself to keep from blurting everything out, knowing she's right but not ready to admit it yet. "I just can't yet. It's wrong to walk into something knowing your head is not in the right place. That's just not fair to him."

"I kind of think that's for him to decide," she says, chewing on the side of her cheek momentarily before she rises from her chair and heads to the pantry. She returns with a bag of Hershey's Kisses and throws them on the counter in front of me. "Eat some. They help."

"That's the fix for all of this? Eat Kisses?" I laugh, wishing life were just that easy: all things fixable with chocolate.

"Fix? No, but it helps . . . and I think I'm going to quote a very dear friend of mine," she says with a smirk on her face, and I know my own words are headed back at me. "Life begins at the end of your comfort zone, Had. I know you're scared, but push through it. You just might miss the opportunity to live again."

I glare at her momentarily and curse myself for giving her the ammunition to fire that comment back at me. Her grin just grows wider, and I know what will knock that sarcastic smile right off her face.

Ready.

Aim.

Fire.

"I retook the test yesterday." *And a biopsy*. The words are on the tip of my tongue, but I bite them back. I can't ruin her first day back and posthoneymoon bliss with something that might be a nothing.

The chocolate she's just unwrapped drops to the counter as her eyes widen and her mouth falls lax.

"You did?" Her eyes meet mine, and I can tell that with my admission she realizes just how much Becks has the potential to mean to me.

"I did." My voice is barely a whisper. She's on her feet in a beat and has her arms wrapped around me, squeezing me tight, no words needed. We stand like this for a few seconds.

"Well, hell, if you guys are going to finally get into the girl-on-girl thing, I get first dibs on watching, being the husband and all." The voice at the doorway behind my back has both Rylee and me laughing through the emotion clogging our throats.

"Nah," Rylee says as she releases me, a smirk on her face and love in her eyes as she looks at her husband. "I've kinda got a thing for baseball players. They've got big, hard sticks," she teases, eliciting a deep laugh from him over some inside joke I obviously don't get.

"Oh really? We're back to that now? Just remember it's not the size of the stick, sweetheart, but how you use it." His smile grows wider as he saunters into the kitchen, the epitome of how arrogance can be sexy, and he owns her attention even before he kisses her softly on the lips.

"Size matters, Donavan," I tell him, earning a scoff and a raise of his eyebrows in argument. "If it didn't, they'd be selling four-inch dildos, now, wouldn't they?"

He throws his head back in laughter as he closes the distance and kisses me on the top of my head. "Point made. Good to see you, Had."

I look up at the devastatingly handsome husband of my best friend—the ever true bad boy who's been claimed and is completely smitten with her. His board shorts ride low on his tanned, toned torso, but it's the way he's looking at his wife that is the most attractive thing about him. "Hey, Colton. Marriage looks good on you."

He smirks, his lone dimple flashing and his eyes sparkling with mirth. "My wife on me would look better, but I've gotta take what I can get, right?"

The laughter comes easier this time, the emotional burden of the moment lightened by this man, who's such a mixture of contradictions and turned out to be so much more than what I ever expected him to be for Rylee. And it was exactly what she needed.

"Should I leave?" I ask, feigning like I'm going to get up from my chair as Colton skirts around the island and grabs a beer from the refrigerator. "I know you newlyweds need your privacy and all."

A blind man couldn't miss the quick look between them, which has Rylee's cheeks flushing and my mind whirling about what they got up to somewhere without privacy on their honeymoon. And my heart swells with love for the two of them. After everything they went through, they deserve all of the happiness in the world.

The distinct sound of Colton popping off the top of his bottle interrupts the momentary awkwardness of the moment, and he flashes me another of his megawatt smiles. "I'm sure you'll get the blow-by-blow, *pun intended*," he teases, "when I leave." He laughs as he grabs a carrot from the cutting board and just shakes his head as he walks toward the patio door.

I glance over at Rylee with my eyebrows raised, silently telling her I want details when she just blushes and tries to deflect my thinking.

"What time are the guys getting here?" she calls to Colton.

He glances over to the clock on the wall. "Like, thirty minutes. Throw a couple extra in there just in case, okay?"

"Sure. I'll have the burgers ready by then."

"No worries. Thanks, hon," he says, starting to walk away as we both stare in admiration of his absolute male perfection.

The question is on my lips when I look over at Rylee, but she answers it before I can get it out. "Nope," she smirks, "it never gets old looking at him." We both laugh for a moment before the solemn silence falls over us once again. I know Ry's not going to let this go easily.

And all of a sudden, the idea strikes me that this is all a setup. That Rylee and Colton have arranged this barbecue to fix this once and for all, even though she told me Becks had other obligations today. I start to panic momentarily about being forced to see him when I realize that it can't be a setup because she didn't know about Becks until a few moments ago.

Well, unless Becks said something to Colton. I stare at her and decide, *Fuck it.* "Is this all a setup?"

"What?" Rylee's head whips up, confusion on her face until it dawns on her what I'm asking. Then she starts laughing out loud. "You're really that paranoid about seeing him that you think I'm planning a fake barbecue to set the two of you up when I didn't even know there was a two of you? Um, he is getting to you, isn't he?"

Crap. Did I really just give her an in to delve further? For fuck's sake. I sigh and glance outside to where I hear Colton whistling to Baxter, his dog, while I wait for her to continue.

"So, what now, Haddie? What's your plan? You like him, rage on him, but sneak out after sex? I mean, I don't know why the hell he's calling you because most guys would tell you to take a long walk off a short pier"—she keeps her head down, focused on the cutting board so that I can stick my tongue out at her and roll my eyes—"and your silence speaks for itself."

"It's not fair to get involved with someone when tomorrow could change everything." My thoughts flash to Danny and Maddie, then to my own unanswered biopsy results, and I just can't fathom doing that to someone else.

"Don't you think that's his decision to make? Why do you get to hold all the cards?" She finally looks up and raises her eyebrows at me.

I think of how I'd never been around someone dying

before my sister. How I would've never expected there to be so much pressure on Lex to try to soothe the aftermath before the inevitable happened. And I think of how I hope for her sake she had no clue how devastated we all were when she was gone. How heartbroken we still are. My tumbling thoughts reinforce my resolve.

"I hold the cards because it's on me, Ry. How selfish does that make me to let us have a chance at more? Love me, and oh, by the way, I'm so fucked in the head right now it took me three months to take the test that's going to tell me whether or not I'm gonna get breast cancer and die in the next five years?" I stand up abruptly and walk toward the window, my restless thoughts affecting my nerves. I know she thinks I'm being melodramatic. Hell, I know I'm being over-the-top, but my undecided fate is feeding my angst. I focus on the beach for a moment, the crash of the waves a calming sight before I finish my thoughts aloud. "I mean, that's just bullshit on my part. Selfish."

I hear the clatter of the knife on the granite behind me and then the thump of the towel as she throws it down. "Cut the crap, Montgomery. If I hear you say that you're going to die again, I'm going to strangle you and make it happen myself." I remain looking at the view and ignore her. "I've stood by for six months, watching you grieve, but you know what? I'm not going to stand by for another six months while you piss away a chance at living because you're so focused on the off chance of dying. You're being ridiculous."

"Ridiculous?" I'm so primed right now for a fight. After talking to Rylee, all of the guilt I've felt over ditching Becks without so much as a good-bye or a thank-you has been exacerbated by hearing her agree with my conscience, which I've been shoving down and ignoring. I turn around to face her.

"Yeah, Haddie, ridiculous, stupid, stubborn—you pick the adjective. You took the test, you'll get the results, and they'll be negative."

"And if they're not?" My voice sounds so shaky compared to the implacability in her tone because the results she's talking about and the ones I'm referring to are two different ones.

"If they're not, then we deal with it! Lexi lost the fight, but hell, Haddie, you're just being disrespectful if you ignore the thousands of others who didn't. You could step off the curb tomorrow and get hit by a Mack Truck. Should that stop you from living today?"

"It's not quite the same thing." I refute her just because I don't want to agree with her logic. Yeah, I know it makes me a bitch, but I hate how everything inside me right now feels like a washing machine on the spin cycle. I'm just worried that when the spinning stops, there won't be much left of anything to make sense of.

"Isn't it, though?" She just continues to stare me down, our eyes locked, her need to nurture and comfort in full force until I avert my gaze back to the patio, where Baxter is thumping his tail.

"I can't ask someone to stand by me if I know in the long run the pain it will bring them." My voice is barely a whisper as I say the one thing I haven't ever spoken aloud. "I mean, mastectomies and chemo and . . . it's just a horrible process. . . ." The words choke in my throat as she places her arms around my shoulders and hugs me from behind.

Her touch makes me want to break down and confess it all. Use her strength to be the foundation for mine, but I can't worry her unnecessarily when there is nothing to worry about yet except for my own voices in my head being pessimistic.

"I know it is. You took the test. That's a big step for you. We'll wait to see what the results say and go from there. In the meantime, you have to figure out what to do or say to Books because he doesn't deserve to be left hanging. If you like him and he likes you, I don't see what the problem is."

"I know . . . but I just can't commit to anything right now, and while using him for sex again is an incredibly appealing option, that's not fair to him either."

"Not fair to him or not fair to you?" she asks over her shoulder as she releases me and heads back to the island.

"Huh?"

"Well, it seems to me the problem is about being fair to you. You like him and you are afraid to feel more. Becks is persistent, Had. . . . How are you going to keep him at bay until you figure your shit out?"

I know she's right, know all of her points are more than valid but don't really want to admit that to her because then she'll start in on how I should just let things play out when I can't break promises I've made to myself.

I'm so sick of thinking about everything. How did this easy conversation get so heavy when all I want to do is relax with my friend and not think?

"Fuck a duck." I sigh, slinking down into my chair and lifting my face up to stare at the ceiling for a moment of clarity that doesn't seem to want to come to me.

"Speaking of fucking . . ." She draws out the last word, my head snapping up as she folds her arms across her chest and leans her hips back against the counter with a knowing smile. "We need to address that department."

The combination of wine and Rylee randomly switching topics has jostled my thoughts as I try to keep up with her thought process. When my mind finally catches up, my mouth falls lax momentarily and then spreads into a cat-ate-the-canary grin, a little shocked at the role reversal between us still and a whole lot relieved at the levity that I so desperately need.

"So . . . how is he?" She flashes her eyebrows up, and her eyes dance with suggestion.

Incredible. Incomparable.

They are the first words to flicker through my mind when I understand what she's asking but I'm able to stop the reflex reaction before the words slip off of my tongue. Thoughts and memories flicker through my mind at a rapid pace, my core reacting with that sweet ache between my thighs.

I close my eyes for a second to reminisce and feel the soft glow of wine and good friendship, the buzz easing my momentary emotional discord so that I can do what I always do best. Something I've been missing about myself. My ability to have a little fun and give Rylee a good run for her money.

"Well," I begin, fighting my own libidinous smirk, "he's definitely triple-A material."

"Oh really?"

"Mm-hmm," I hum appreciatively, "anyplace, anytime, anywhere. Hell, life's all about the amount of laughs and orgasms you can have, and damn if that man didn't up the ante." The grin feels good as it spreads on my lips.

Rylee throws her head back and laughs before shaking it at me. "There's my girl! You're lucky I didn't ask you if he fucks like he drives," she says, repeating the question I asked her after she slept with Colton for the first time. Her smile is smug as she lifts her glass to finish off her wine.

"Ha. I believe your husband is the one who drives." I relax for the first time since we started this conversation, knowing that it wasn't just Rylee's curiosity that made her change the subject. She's made her points; she isn't going to push them any harder now that she knows I actually heard them. Now she's leaving it up to me to mull them over and figure out what to do with Becks in the meantime.

And the answer is nothing until I get results. I know I'm stubborn, but I just can't bring myself to cross the imaginary line I've drawn in the sand.

I pull myself from my thoughts, returning my attention to my best friend and the grin on her face. "All I'm going to say is it's a damn good thing he works with his hands for a living," I confess with a flash of my smile, "because I'm sure as fuck a lot to handle, and this girl is most definitely not complaining when he has those hands full of me." I raise my eyebrows up at her and leave that as the only explanation she needs for now.

Chapter 17

The smile on my face feels good as I carry the empty platter into the kitchen for Rylee. I set it in the sink half-full of dishes and begin putting some of the condiments on the counter away so that they don't spoil.

I hum along to the music floating in from the deck outside, where about a dozen or so of Colton's crew members are milling around, talking or standing in the pool with beers in their hands. It's the most relaxed I've felt in forever, and I hope this is a sign that things are going to be okay. That I'm going to be okay.

I shake my head, hating the sense of battle that's always a constant in me. I want to feel hopeful, but the fear never quite goes away.

I adjust the top of my suit to make sure it covers the bandage over the incision and check myself in the reflection of the window above the sink. I nearly jump out of my skin when I see Becks's reflection there. I yelp and spin around to see him standing on the opposite side of the kitchen, in board shorts and a baseball cap, his arms folded across his bare chest. I only have a second to take in the whole, incredible package because when I meet his eyes I can't look away.

Figures, just as I was starting to feel like myself again—Ry's talk helped pull bits of myself from the dust, brushing them off to take their place again as hope tried to raise its weary head—the appearance of my biggest weakness and number one complication brings it all back in an instant. My heart falls into my stomach at the sight of him, turning my relaxing afternoon into an obstacle course of pitfalls.

Our gazes lock. Although his eyes are intense, they're shadowed by the brim of his hat, so I can't quite see if the anger I deserve is there or not. I exhale the breath I was holding as nerves slowly flicker to life under his quiet scrutiny. I glance toward the patio doorway and then back to him in a move that earns me a low, condescending chuckle from him.

"You gonna run out that door too without saying a word? Seems par for the course. Or are you going to stand here and explain just what the fuck happened?"

The bite in his tone stings but I deserve it. I work a swallow down my throat as I stand before him feeling completely vulnerable. I fiddle with the string on the hip of my bikini bottoms, which causes his eyes to flicker down momentarily before coming back up to my eyes without even stopping to take in the deep V of my cleavage.

And I know that means he's really pissed.

"Oh right, I forgot." He shakes his head, contempt in his eyes. "You'd explain, but oops, you're sorry. You thought you could, but now you can't . . . ," he says, repeating my lame excuse back to me.

Yep, I'm *seriously* fucked here. There's nothing I can say to explain why I left without telling him the truth, and that's a line I'm not crossing. "Becks . . ." His name is a sigh on my lips as I try to figure out how to respond. I obviously didn't think this whole silent-treatment thing through very well. How stupid was I not to realize I was going to have to face him, talk to him, explain my actions at some point since our best friends are married? Shit!

"Was it something I said?" He pushes off the counter and walks the few feet to stand across the island from me before he continues. "Because I do believe you begging for me to make you feel *owned* was a request. Did I not do what you asked? Did I not own you enough?" The derision in his tone matches the contempt in his eyes.

I don't even attempt to respond to that, wouldn't have an answer to give even if I could, because he not only owned my body that night—he started owning my heart too. My pulse thunders as I watch him, anticipating what his next words will be because I know regardless of what they are, I deserve them.

He twists his lips as his stare bores into me, daring me to answer him so that he can knock my excuse away. "You see, I'm just having a hard time comprehending what the hell happened because after hearing you say *we are*, I woke up in an empty apartment, which seems like your way of saying *we aren't*. Care to fill me in on what the fuck happened?"

His words reach their mark, and I shake my head as his cologne hits me from his nearness and immediately makes me think of that spot beneath his jaw that smells the strongest of it. My body wants to respond—step toward him, reach out to him—but I do neither because making that physical connection is something I can't allow myself to have.

"No, I just . . ." My words falter when he braces his hands on the counter in front of him, a slight smirk on his face that doesn't reach his eyes. I can see them clearly now, along with the tension evident in the broad lines of his shoulders.

I bring my eyes back to his. "I thought you couldn't come today?"

"Oh, I think I demonstrated that I can come just fine, City, so let's quit your avoidance game, shall we?"

"That's not what I meant—"

"I don't think you know much of anything right now."

He tilts his head to the side, no signs of the laidback guy

I've come to know. "I didn't take you for the kind of girl to sneak out without a word, refuse to answer your phone or respond to a text"—he shrugs—"but shit, it wouldn't be the first time I've misjudged someone's character."

His words sting, and his questioning of my character shifts the temper I have on simmer to boil. Hell yes, I want the man, but if he can't handle me now at my worst, then he sure as fuck doesn't deserve me at my best. And I know he has every right to feel how he feels, but I'm in self-preservation mode—my ample ingestion of wine helping fuel my irrationality—and I don't want to deal with this shit right now.

"We said no strings, right?" I bite out, leaning against the counter behind me, Bitch 101 in session: Don't question me when you don't know shit, or I'll get nasty. "Did something change that I don't know about? Last I checked, I wasn't required to give lengthy good-byes before I take my shimmy of shame back to my place after a quick fuck."

I see the hurt flash in his eyes, and it kills me but tells me so much at the same time. That brief flicker of emotion confirms that he has feelings for me, and that alone has my defenses up and panic beginning to strangle me. I may have told him that night *we are*, but that was before the lump and the possible results. He can't have feelings for me.

He just can't. I can't allow it. I need to go back to how we were when we started things—casual, simple. Temporary.

My heart races. I grip the counter to prevent him from noticing my trembling hands. But I meet his glare and match it, waiting for the ball of hurt to be hurled at me.

"A quick fuck?" He runs his hand up and cups the back of his neck before continuing. "A quick fuck doesn't make you forget your own name because you're so busy moaning mine."

His words stir the desire within me. I'm not used to this side of Becks, and as much as I like it, as much as I'm turned on by it—by him—I'm also pissed. At him. At me. At the world. This wasn't part of the game plan here. Irritation sparks anew so that now we're firing barbs at each other. And I'm not even sure we're doing anything other than purposely trying to hurt each other so that we can protect ourselves.

Or maybe that's a bunch of psychobabble bullshit that holds no relevance, and I'm trying to justify why I'm being a bitch and pushing him away.

"You're quite full of yourself, aren't you, Daniels?" It's all I've got because he's right. The question is how do I get out of this situation without hurting him any further and keeping possibility between us if the cards do fall my way in the coming weeks.

He rounds the counter so that he faces me in the small space between the island at his back and the kitchen counter at mine. His eyes glint with contempt as he observes me and judges me, and I hate the feeling. Hate recognizing the emotions I see within them when I just want to tell him to hold on. To hope against hope for me that I can call in a few weeks and explain this all to him. Explain the push and the pull between us and why I've walked away.

I just hope it won't be too late.

We continue to speak volumes without words. "You know what, Haddie? I call bullshit here. . . . What I just can't figure out is what exactly is making you lie to me, why you let me get close and then push me away."

His words cause a sliver of hope. The good man that I've always taken him for has returned. Suddenly I'm both grateful and fearful at the same time that he might be able to see through my pretense. I'm trying to improvise a game plan in my head because I know with Becks I need one or else he'll say, *Come*, and I'll say how many times.

Christ on a cracker, he unnerves me in so many ways when he's this close to me. My phone chimes with an incoming text on the counter behind him, and we both jump, startled by the sound, which shatters our accusatory silence.

Becks twists and reaches for my phone, his expression shuttering when he glances down at the screen.

"Well, I guess I have my answer. It's not that you can't with me, but that you can with him," he says with disbelief before handing me my phone and striding out of the kitchen.

As hard as it is to tear my eyes away from him, I'm at a loss as to what he's assuming until I look down on my phone. Dante. His name lights up my screen as well as the text that follows it. I stare at it understanding why Becks just left, cursing and thanking Dante all at once for his inopportune timing.

Are you coming home tonight or staying at your parents? I miss you.

Dante's words are innocent. At least I hope they are. Regardless, they're enough to make me reconsider my instinctive reaction to chase after Becks and try to make things right.

"What the hell was that all about?" Rylee's voice causes me to roll my eyes and toss my cell onto the counter without a second thought about the man who just upset the one I'm so focused on.

"You said he wasn't coming!" I tell her, anger lacing my disbelief. I pick up my glass of wine and down the rest of it, glaring at her over the rim the whole time.

"He wasn't." She shrugs, a diminutive smile at the corners of her mouth as she walks up and sits on the barstool in front of me. "But he got done early, so he decided to stop over."

I look out the patio doors to where he stands now beside Colton, beer in his hand, tension in his shoulders. And it's so much easier to focus on him than to look at Rylee because I am so sick of being stared at and scrutinized today. I'm so fed up with it that I start trying to figure out how to extricate myself from this barbecue because the fun I was having fifteen minutes ago is gone now that I know I've hurt him.

"Don't even think about leaving," she warns, years of friendship allowing her to read my mind.

"Ry . . ." I push off the counter and pull the cork out of the partially empty bottle. I pour myself some more wine because I have a feeling I'm going to need it.

"Don't Ry me," she says, leaning back and locking eyes with me. I see patience there, but I also see a friend not willing to step back. "Not gonna lie here when I tell you it's going to be awkward as hell since the last time you saw each other his dick was in you—"

I choke on my wine and start sputtering out incoherent words before just dropping my jaw open and staring at her. She struggles to keep her face serious, and I love her that much more for it.

"Well, it's true!" She asserts. "It's a Saturday afternoon barbecue, Had," she says, trying to calm the situation and defuse my need to escape. "I'm not going to say a word. Have some drinks. Hide under the bushes over there. Talk to the rest of the guys. Do something because if you don't he's going to know he affects you . . . and, well, you never know"—she shrugs—"making a guy who's interested a little bit jealous isn't always a bad thing."

"Who took my friend, and what did you do with her?" I ask her incredulously, knowing damn well the call from Dante might have already had that effect. I don't think I want to push my luck any further.

Rylee glances outside and makes a humming noise of appreciation in the back of her throat. My eyes follow her sightline to see Becks reaching up to help Colton adjust the volleyball net higher over the pool. His hat falls back, and his board shorts keep slipping lower and lower on his stretched torso. Every damn ridge and etch of muscle is on display, causing every single one of mine to clench and then sing with desire.

"Damn. He's got quite the V there when his shorts are that low," she murmurs, her head angling to the side to match mine as we watch the show he's unknowingly putting on.

"Infinity." I don't even realize I've said the word aloud until I see her glance my way in my peripheral vision, her brows furrowed.

"Infinity?"

I look back out toward Becks as he lifts his other arm, trying to get the tie of the net through a hole a few feet over his head. The sight of his shorts falling even lower makes my mouth water and my fingers itch to touch him in pure carnal lust, despite everything that's happened.

I realize after a moment of admiration and daydreaming that I haven't answered Ry's question. "Yeah," I say absently, pausing for a moment before I continue. "The V—his infinity zone—the place you could stare at on a man forever and die a happy woman."

Rylee throws her head back and laughs, a low, rich sound that makes me smile. "Well, that's a new one," she says before taking a sip and looking back out toward our own private show again. "And ain't it the truth!"

"Hey! You're a married woman now. Don't go admiring my Becks." The possessive pronoun is out of my mouth before I even think it through. I hope it goes unnoticed, but the immediate cessation of her laughter and the turn of her head tells me she caught it.

Damn. Can't a girl catch a break?

I keep my eyes focused on Becks. On him bending over and his mighty fine ass as he picks up his hat. Of the way he tilts the bottle to his lips and holds it there momentarily while Colton says something to him before he tips the bottle up higher. So many little things that make me want him, and all of them on a first-name basis with my libido.

"First of all, I might be married, but hell if a sane woman would turn her head away from the sight of that. Ironically, mine's got the ink you usually go for and vice versa, but looking at Becks sure isn't a hardship," she says, and then falls silent as the laughter outside floats into the kitchen.

And for a second, I softly exhale the breath I've been holding over my claimed possession of Becks because she's missed it.

"Oh, and, Had?" she says as she rises from her chair and starts to walk toward her company outside. "Don't think I didn't catch that little slip of the tongue." She throws the comment over her shoulder and just keeps on walking without looking back.

Chapter 18

"So, uh, you brown-bagging it or what?"

Colton is standing to my right but I keep my head turned so I can watch Haddie in the lounge chair across the deck. In her bikini, she's sexy as hell all the way down to that diamond glistening in her navel, which I never knew she had because she's never worn it. And damn, it's just ridiculously hot in so many ways.

"Brown-bagging it?"

He plops himself down across from me, the cushion making a noise from the force before he leans back and props his feet up on the table catty-corner to mine. He angles his chin up to where I was just watching Haddie. "Yeah, taking her out of the bag to get a taste of her when no one's looking and then slipping her away before someone catches sight of you."

"Seriously, dude?" I sputter, turning to stare at him. Like I should be surprised at anything that comes out of his mouth. "Did you really just say that?"

"Oh, get over yourself, Daniels. *It's cool.* You and I both know you've been sampling that dessert. We've known each other way too fucking long for you to lie to me over a piece of ass."

And as much as he's right—on all counts—something in me prefers lifting my bottle of beer to my mouth to take a swallow instead of answering the question. My eyes veer back over to her as her laughter drifts across the patio. She's partially reclined on the chaise, her body covered in what any man would consider a dick-hardening bikini—ties and scraps of fabric—that makes one wonder if there are any tan lines it's hiding.

And the answer is most definitely no.

Damn. The reality that I know that for a fact tightens my sack before I realize that Colton's fixated on me and not elsewhere like I thought.

"Well, being the picky fucker that you are, you sure as fuck raised the bar with her. . . . There's not much to pick apart there."

"Dude, just because I bitched that one time about Sandy." I shake my head and roll my eyes behind my glasses.

"That one time? Are you listening to yourself? How about every time?" he chortles. "Her voice is too annoying. She's too superficial. She was—"

"C'mon, you have to admit she was . . ." I mock shiver at the memory of her and her nasty hygiene habits.

"I have not a clue what you're talking about, you picky bastard." He's enjoying this immensely, that much I can tell, so I just blow out a breath and wash down the crow he's handing me.

"Well, I guess I should just follow in your footsteps then Mr. No-pussy-is-good-enough-to-commit-to-for-life." I repeat the words he used to use as a motto for years to him with a lift of my eyebrows and sarcasm rich in my voice.

He belts out a laugh. "You got me, dude. I've learned the error of my ways because, damn, Rylee's is most definitely enough for a lifetime." He shakes his head with a laugh as he tips the beer to his lips and takes a long swallow. "Speaking of . . ." He shifts his eyes to Haddie and then back to me. *"She good?"*

"How's married life?" I ask the question, knowing he's not going to fall for it but needing to attempt changing the topic nonetheless. Besides, how Haddie is in the sack is none of his goddamn business. A litany of curses flies through my head as I realize that my not wanting to talk about her skills is a sign in and of itself of how bad I have it for her. Colton and I have talked about everyone and everything we've done with them before.

All except for Rylee, whom he's now married to.

And now Haddie.

If that's the case, then what the fuck does that mean?

He throws his head back, the laughter drawing some looks from the crew playing volleyball in the pool and luckily distracting me from looking closer at my own revelation. "I do believe you asked about married life an hour ago. Your diversion tactics need a bit of help, brother. Nice try though. 'A' for effort and all that."

" 'A' is for asshole," I mutter. In return, he flashes me a cocky grin, which has me laughing and shaking my head. "You and your alphabet."

"Yup. My alphabet is doing just fine," he says, referring to his nickname for his wife, his smile so damn big, it's still a shock to the system to see as he looks across the patio at Rylee. "Married life is good, dude. It's Ry, you know?" he says with a shrug as if that's the only explanation he needs.

The contentment in his voice and his relaxed posture show me the truth in his words, and I can't help but smile. He deserves to be happy after everything he's gone through, from his abusive childhood to the nearly fatal crash he endured last year.

"So"—he draws out the word and tips the top of his beer toward Haddie—"what gives? You've got this slow-burn type of thing going with her or what?"

I grunt a laugh. Slow burn, my ass. More like fire in the goddamn hole.

I exhale in frustration at the multiple contradictions that are Haddie Montgomery. "Fuck if I know, dude." I lift my cap from my head and run my other hand through my hair before I put it back on and adjust it. "I appreciate a good mindfuck every now and again, but she just . . . Man, I don't know how to explain the shit she's doing to mess with my head."

He smiles at me, fighting the laughter. "Welcome to the estrogen vortex, dude, where mindfucks are the norm and understanding them is as common as a fucking unicorn in your front yard."

"Thanks." I blow the word out in frustration before glancing over once again to the cause of it. I don't get it. Where exactly does Dante fall into play in all of this? If it was the fact that she wanted to play the field, that's one thing, but if that's the case, then why not just say it? And if so, why was she jealous of what she assumed was going on with Deena?

Fuck if I can figure her out, but damn it to hell, I want to. I want to know every goddamn piece of her. She's like that first taste of something you can't have—that priceless sip of Macallan poured neat—and no matter how many times you're lucky enough to get just a splash more, it's never enough to get you drunk.

Just a buzz to keep you wanting more.

I lean forward and pull another beer from the bucket of ice in front me on the table and pop the top with the opener. I take a sip and sigh at its taste—fucking beer when all I want is that damn single-malt Scotch.

I just can't get her pegged: The woman who's come undone with me is a different person from the feisty-as-fuck one in the kitchen earlier. She's hot and cold, but damn, when she's hot, it's scorching, and when she's cold, it's arctic.

"Haddie, huh?" he says. I look over at him as he's studying her. "Could do a whole helluva lot worse."

I snort at him. "Yeah, well . . ." So many things are on the tip of my tongue. But they'd make me sound more interested than I am. Or rather than I want to let on that I am because I'm not opening that door for him to walk his sarcastic ass through.

"So what gives?"

"Apparently me."

"Fuck, dude. That's your problem right there. Quit being such a pussy. She's already got one between her legs, so why would she need another one there?"

"Are you seriously insulting my manhood?"

"Well, you're kind of being a chick right now. If you like her, take her. Shit, Daniels, what the fuck happened to you while I was on my honeymoon? Your nuts shrivel up and fall off?"

"Fuck off," I tell him softly, his words hitting the mark and leaving me wondering.

I enjoy the beer sliding down my throat, as the previous ones start to hum in my veins and relax me—taking the edge off from walking in the kitchen and seeing her in that damn bikini. Those small scraps of fabric had my dick begging and my head thinking about how much I'd have liked to set her ass up on the edge of that counter, press myself between her thighs, and fuck her into tomorrow. My irritation over her leaving without a good-bye and ignoring my texts and calls urged me to take without giving her time to argue. To prove to her just why she needs me around.

But that in itself is so fucked-up. Since when do I want to make my claim on a woman so that I can mark her as mine? Usually I'm laid-back. A chick doesn't like me? There's plenty more who do. But with Haddie, hell if I know why I'm being so pansy-ass with her. I tell myself to let it go—let her go—and I realize I don't want to.

Because she matters.

And hell if I'm going to admit that to Colton, but it's the truth.

A bottle cap hits me midchest and draws me from my thoughts. "What are you thinking about?" he asks, a taunting smirk on his face.

"Scotch," I answer, watching his smile fall as he tries to figure out what the hell I'm talking about. And I love that I knocked him off his game for a moment, the cocky fucker.

It takes a second but he laughs freely and just shakes his head. "Much better diversion tactic that time around. Mad props, dude." He sits back in his chair and falls silent for a bit as we watch a heated exchange in the volleyball game that ends in a spike and a slew of curse words at a match point lost.

"So what happened? You must have whipped your little button mushroom of a dick out and scared her off—"

"Fuck off, dude. You wouldn't know a big dick if it hit you in the face," I rib him. If the asshole's going to insult my manhood when I recall one drunken night in our younger years and a ruler that proved differently, I have to at least have a comeback.

The look on his face—shocked amusement—has me biting my tongue. "I assure you I will not be touching someone's dick—with my face or any other body part of mine—now or anytime for that matter unless it's me knocking yours into the dirt for being such a fuckwad."

"The fact that you even think you can take me is amusing."

"Wow," he says, tipping his beer up to his lips and over-exaggerating the satisfied smack of his lips. "You're a cranky fucker, aren't you? No wonder she's over there and you're over here. Have another beer, dude," he says, tossing me one from the bucket on the table, even though I'm not done with the one in my hand.

"Your answer for everything, huh?" I hold up the beer and tip it toward him. "Have another beer?"

"You're the one talking about Scotch, not me. So what gives?"

I'm torn, not wanting to talk about it but thinking it

could help. Get another guy's opinion—my best friend's opinion—and as fucked-up as Colton used to be in the fuck-'em-and-chuck-'em department, as Rylee so politely used to put it, he knows me better than anyone. He'll understand and set me straight. Pull me from the shit in my head that I keep running through over and over and over. Tell me what I need to hear.

Nut the fuck up or shut the fuck up.

I scrub my hand over my chin before shaking my head. "I don't know, man. She's spooked, and I can't figure it out. And just when I think I do, something else happens to make me change my mind about what's causing it."

"Well, first off," he says, leaning forward and placing his elbows on his knees, "most of the time you kind of want your women spooked . . . prevents them from becoming repeat offenders occupying your bed."

"That is just wrong in so many ways," I tell him but can't fight the laughter at his logic. I point to the ring on his finger. "Says the barebacking, married man, no less."

He looks over at me with a smug smirk that brings me back to the first time we talked about him barebacking— screwing without a condom because he knew Rylee was *the one*. And I have to shake my head at that memory because that conversation led to the trip to Las Vegas, where later that night I got my first introduction to one fine-as-fuck Haddie Montgomery.

"Don't be knocking the almighty voodoo, bro," he says, pulling me from memory lane, and tilts his bottle in Rylee's direction. "There's some serious fucking power there."

I laugh with him, at him, because there has to be some real magic there if it's turned the poster boy for how to be a player into a bona fide one-woman man. Her voodoo pussy most definitely had to have had some special powers to transform that fucker.

"Shit," I say, reaching forward and holding my bottle up to him, "that's worthy of a toast right there."

He shakes his head once and a lopsided smirk says it all. "Here's to nipples, because without them, tits would be fucking pointless." We clink the necks of our bottles together as the mixture of way too many damn beers and my best friend happy as fuck has me laughing so hard, I take my sunglasses off to wipe my eyes.

Heads around us turn to look at the two of us laughing together, but it's Colton. I'm used to him causing a scene wherever we go, so I don't even think twice. But this time when I look up, I lock eyes with Haddie momentarily before she shoots daggers at me and looks away.

"Fuck, that's like the arctic chill, man."

"Thanks for the play-by-play, Donavan." As if I need his commentary on Haddie right now.

"Anytime, brother, anytime. What the fuck did you do to her, anyway?"

"No clue." I shake my head and then lean back and pull the bill of my hat down over my eyes, my silent gesture that the conversation is over.

"Seriously? You think that hat covering your eyes is going to stop me? You know me better than that. C'mon, dude."

"Leave it." I snap the words at him. Then I'm pissed I'm taking my shit out on him because all I keep thinking of is the image of Haddie standing in my place the other night with nothing but heels and a skirt on, nipples hard, hair falling over her shoulders.

And I stopped her? What the fuck is wrong with me? One minute I'm telling myself I'm not letting her go without a fight, and then the next, I wake up alone, her perfume on my sheets, the scent of our sex still on my skin.

Fucking Dante. It has to be because of him. What does he have that I don't? I've never even heard her mention the name of an ex, let alone one who has this strong of a hold on her.

Goddamn estrogen vortex.

It's fucking with my head because I'm sitting here, thinking about it, when I should be shooting the shit with Colton. Instead, I'm questioning everything: my own thoughts, my own feelings, even Dante.

I keep thinking back to that night, trying to pinpoint how the hell we went from fighting to her crying to her wanting more to her being gone. And it's her falling apart that I keep going back to. It has to be everything with her sister's death coming to a head and just exploding all at once since it seems she's held it in all this time.

Sure we've known each other—hung out casually—for the past year and a half, but for a year of that time she was dealing with Lexi's illness and then the aftermath of her death. I've seen her fire ebb. Her defiance slip. And hell yes, she grabs onto it every now and again, but the balls-to-the-wall, take-no-prisoners Haddie Montgomery I met that first night in Vegas seems lost. Feistiness snuffed out. Carefree demeanor now a jumbled goddamn mess of extreme highs and lows.

But hell, even grieving and a shadow of her usual self, she's that fucking sip of Macallan sitting on a bar lined with every other alcohol known to man. Cream of the crop, top-notch class.

Motherfucking perfection.

And I can't even think about her taste. Damn woman is addictive. Heat and sweetness, with a fucking mixture of unpredictable thrown in that has just enough edge to make you question what's going to happen next and where the hell she's going to take you after that.

And it doesn't matter really because you know you're already going along for the ride, regardless of the destination. Heaven or Hell, she makes both sound desirable.

With my prolonged silence, I expect a smart-ass remark about how I must be whipped already or how the ride feels without a saddle, but Colton doesn't say anything like I'd expect. His trademark use of humor to escape any conversation that's serious in nature doesn't come. And I appreciate it, take a moment to be thankful for a friend who's known me so long he knows I need a minute to wrap my head around everything.

So I start thinking of solutions. How to fix this problem: my wanting her and her pushing me away despite the desire clear as day in her eyes. The alcohol in my blood tempts me to resolve it by walking over to Haddie right now and tossing her over my shoulder. Lock her in a goddamn room with me until she talks, tells me how either Dante or Lexi is preventing something more from happening between us.

I need to get some fucking peace of mind and clarity for the first time since she pressed her lips against mine weeks ago.

"She's had a rough go of it the past year." Colton's voice breaks our silence and probably in the nick of time because I'm about two minutes away from making a scene. My own goddamn emotions are a clusterfuck of chaos—I'm pissed at her for pushing me away, but I also want to wrap my arms around her to take that look of confusion out of her eyes and ease the anger that's just beneath the surface that's so tangible, it tinges the taste of her kiss.

"That she has," I murmur softly, not wanting to elaborate since my thoughts are already owned by it all.

"Ry's worried about her."

And fuck, why did Colton have to say that? Because if her best friend is worried, then I'm sure as hell going to be concerned. I keep my hat over my eyes, my head leaned back, and my own voice impassive. "Understandably."

Silence weighs heavy between us as he figures what to say next because I'm sure my lack of a response to his loaded question is unexpected. "You really fucking like her, don't you?"

I lift the brim of my hat up and angle my head over to the side to look at him, sure the answer is written all over my face. "Just trying to figure out what to do about it since it seems she only wants to be brown-bagging it."

He smirks at me. "Keep at it, dude. If Rylee could break me down and cause this," he says, holding up his hand where his wedding band rests, "then shit, anything is possible."

I let the slight smile tug up the corner of my mouth, knowing he's just trying to be a good friend by getting me talking, showing me what could be . . . but I'm done talking.

Man up, Daniels. I need to start acting.

Nut the fuck up or shut the fuck up.

I'm feeling good, buzz still humming and mind made up as I walk toward the house. I wave my hand toward the pool and the guys I just up and left one volley short of match point, telling them to shut the hell up because I'll be right back.

We've all had more than enough to drink by now, and it's not like I wasn't obvious when I saw Had stroll past the edge of the pool and walk inside. That damn bathing suit of hers taunted me like a green flag on race day but with a whole lot less fabric.

And a hell of a lot better prize.

I throw the towel I scrubbed through my hair onto the chair as I catch Colton's eye across the deck. He has one hand on Baxter's head and his other arm around Rylee's shoulders, but the look he gives me—the *go take what's yours* one—is followed by a lift of his chin. A silent show of moral support. I see Rylee catch his look and follow it over to me before a crooked smirk follows a shake of her head.

I walk into the house and see Haddie immediately, that perfect backside of hers on display in the skimpy black bikini as she bends over and looks in the refrigerator. I hear the rattle of jars as she moves items around, but I can't focus on anything else besides the sight of her ass and knowing just what is nestled in between those thighs.

I want her on so many other levels—in fact, I feel like I'm going a little crazy, trying to prove that point—but damn it to hell if I don't want her on this level too. Tanned, toned, and tempting.

And just this simple sight has me reaffirming my decision from earlier. *At all costs*. That's my new motto. I am going to make it so that Haddie Montgomery can't resist me. Use the sex she seems to use as a shield around her to my advantage. Reel her in and then force her to understand that whatever the hell she's running from she doesn't have to worry about with me.

The question is, how exactly am I going to do that?

I mean the sex part is a no-brainer, but I need to make sure she doesn't rabbit the minute it's over. And tying her to the bed most definitely sounds like one hell of a dick-hardening option, but in the end, it earns me no trust. So my object is to make her want, make her ask for it, confuse the hell out of her. Make her want like I want, but then refuse her just like she does me.

Because I know she desires more—I can see it in those eyes of hers. I just have to figure out what it is that's going to break down those goddamn walls but still make her feel like she's protected from whatever it is that's hurt her.

So I stare at the curve of her hips and decide to make my move. I step forward and murmur, "Excuse me," when I push the door open a little wider with one hand while my other hand rests conspicuously atop the swell of her ass. I feel her body jolt, hear the startled gasp fall from her mouth, and can't deny that surge of electric current that charges through me when we touch. It's like a fucking live-wire that causes a momentary short circuit in my thoughts as it weaves around my balls and tugs them with the god-damn strings that are already laced through my heart.

The woman makes me feel in ways I never expected. It should be me who wants to bolt, but for some reason it makes me want her even more. Everything about her draws me in, hooks me, mesmerizes me.

Goddamn it to hell. She's my voodoo.

And it's not like that fact scares me. Fuckin' A, it should when I'm content meandering through the dating field for a while longer, but shit, there's just something about Haddie that's indescribable.

The sip of Macallan that ruins you for all others.

So I figuratively grab my balls with both hands and jump in feetfirst, hoping she'll be the one to help me float because I sure as hell know she's worthy enough to drown for.

She backs out of the refrigerator, and I make sure to crowd her space. Her body rubs against mine as she stands up. And the feeling of those hard nipples against my bare chest urges every single part of me to hold her against me and claim that mouth of hers. Kiss her senseless so her lips are swollen and pink when I'm done with them.

Startled, she looks up at me with my name falling off her lips in a rush of air from her mouth. We stand like this for a split second, bodies demanding and minds warring before she hurriedly pushes away from me. She seems flustered, and I can see her trying to remember what exactly she was doing before I interrupted her. I know when she remembers because she turns back to the refrigerator and grabs the platter of Jell-O shots I'd distracted her from.

She pulls the tray out, muttering, "Excuse me." She keeps her eyes averted from mine, and it takes me a minute to steady myself, the mixture of beer and Haddie enough to make a man drunk off his ass.

I shut the door, watching her move the tray to the counter on the other side of the kitchen and start fiddling with the shots, her back toward me. I close the distance, but the words on my lips falter.

"Jell-O shots, huh?" I ask, trying to act as casual as possible, not caring whatsoever because the Macallan in front of me looks a thousand times more tempting than the childish flavors in her colored cups. "What kind?"

"Mm-hmm. Tequila sunrise, I think."

I know she knows I'm behind her. Can see her hands stop fiddling aimlessly. Her body stills, and her breath hitches. I step into her—itching to touch her in so many ways, and when I see the little cups of orange Jell-O she's focusing on, I know exactly how to go about it.

Plan of attack figured out.

My front is against her back, trapping her between me and the counter, my hands placed on either side of her hips. The heat of her body, the softness of her curves, and the scent of sun on her skin are enough to make a sane man crazy. I draw it all in—everything about her—as I feel her breath release in a shuddered exhale. It's the same goddamn sound she makes when I enter her, and hell if that doesn't make my balls tighten and my dick ache to hear it again.

Preferably on frequent repeat.

I lean my face forward so that my chin scrapes over her bare shoulder and across to the back of her neck. I press an openmouthed kiss there, just below her exposed hairline from her hair being pulled up. I hear the soft sigh begin before she catches it when she feels the warmth of my lips and lick of my tongue. A small thrill shoots through me, knowing I can affect her even after she ran.

Never underestimate the power of a kiss on the neck.

Our bodies are against each other's, my lips pressed to her nape, and I just remain still so that the heat of my breath can hit her neck. So that she can think and wonder what my next move is going to be.

We stand here in that suspended state of anticipation before I move my mouth ever so slowly to her ear. And I'm not sure if it's from my breath or just our general nearness, but my resolve to tease and taunt rather than taste and take is strengthened when I see the goose bumps dance across her skin in reaction to me.

"What is it they say you're supposed to do with tequila?" I breathe into her ear as one of my hands reaches forward to take a little cup, my elbow purposely brushing against her bare torso, and my body pressing harder into hers.

She doesn't answer, but her body vibrates from our connection. "Something like *Lick it* . . ." I let my voice trail off as I run my tongue from the edge of her shoulder up to the curve of her neck. I hear an incoherent moan from her that turns me on in all kinds of ways and feel her body sag some against mine as I taste the salt on her skin.

I hold the shot up in front of us, my languorous trail of kisses stopping right below her earlobe. *"Slam it."* I raise the shot up, angling the heel of my hand softly against her breast before bringing it to my lips, her sudden intake of air pushing it farther into me. I toss the Jell-O back, its chill sliding down my throat. I set the empty cup back onto the counter, my dick hardening as it rubs against her lower back. Her inability to speak from her stubborn desire urges me on.

My mouth is back at her ear, an ache so goddamn strong to have her, I'm testing my own fucking restraint here. "I believe the last one is *Suck it*." I feel her body stiffen at the words as she anticipates exactly what my next move will be. I pause on purpose, leaving her in that suspended state of desire, wanting her to wonder just that.

After a moment I lower my lips to take the lobe of her ear in my mouth and suck on it before scraping my teeth against it as I release it. This time she doesn't try to disguise her sound of desire as it falls from her mouth. I grip my hands on the edge of the counter to prevent myself from doing any more because I really just want to slide my hands in the front of her black bikini bottoms and make her come undone.

And not a second after the thought enters my head, my hands are on the move, lust driving their actions. One hand palms her bare midriff, the diamond stud I noticed adorning her belly button just adding fuel to my raging fire of lust, as if I needed any help. At the same time, my other hand slips beneath the soft band of her bottoms and stops just above the top of her clit.

"Becks . . ." My name is on her lips again, the only one I want to be there. She takes her hands from the counter and wraps them around my forearms. At first I think she's going to try to stop me, but when she just grips them tightly, I know she's urging me on. Asking me to take her, drive her to find ecstasy, and *fuck me*, there is nothing more attractive than a woman who knows what the hell she wants.

I don't speak, and I'd like to think I made the conscious decision that words are not needed right now, but fuck, my mind is so focused on the slick lips I'll find beneath my fingertips that I can't even think clearly. Haddie's fingernails dig into the skin on my arm as I kick her feet farther apart with my own to gain better access to her heat. I lower my hand, my fingers parting her. I slide them back up to find her clit at the top of her seam and rub my fingers over it ever so slowly and then back.

Her legs weaken beneath her, and I press my hand against her stomach harder so that she can use my body for support. I work the pads of my fingers over her gently at first and then with more fervor as her breath starts to catch and she grinds her pelvis forward and into my hand, her voice silent but her body begging for exactly what she wants. I ease up and lower my fingers to recoat them with her arousal to find her dripping wet.

And as much as my own body is reacting to the knowledge that sweet Haddie is on the verge of coming, that she wants me to bring her there, I know I have her right where I want her. Needing, wanting, desperate for more.

I find her clit again, add in the friction that's causing her to writhe and buck against me. I hear her breath hitching, feel her muscles start to tense up, and as much as it pains me, as much as causing a woman to reach orgasm is a powerful high for me that I love — it makes me hard as a fucking rock — I stop my fingers.

I hold them still, pressing on either side of her clit but do not move them. I hear her gasp of shock at the pause in sensation, the sudden loss of her orgasm, and the labor of her breathing as she wars desire against dignity to ask for what I'm going to deny her.

"It's you that I want, Haddie," I say against her ear. "Only you."

I let the thought settle within her, my fingers astride her pleasure, my body taut with the pain of restraint as we stand there motionless, chests heaving. "I'm not letting you walk away from me again. I don't care what your fears are, what your doubts are, who else you're seeing. . . ." I press a soft kiss on that addictive curve of her neck again, and it earns me a shuddered breath that is sexy and then some. "This orgasm is mine. You will not give it to anyone else, even your own hand. I want you strung so goddamn tight, you beg me to fuck you, beg me to own you."

She gasps out again, but this time it's because I withdraw my hands from her. She sags against the counter in respite, effectively breaking every connection our bodies have with each other.

I lean forward, my mouth a whisper from her ear, my breath the only part of me touching her. "And I will own you, but on my terms next time."

When I take a step back, a soft "Fuck you" falls from her mouth in an unsteady tone as I notice her knuckles turning white from gripping the counter on both sides of her.

I'm curious if she's holding on to keep herself from grabbing me and forcing me to finish her off or because she wants to slap me. Either one would be hot as hell because at least I'd know I'd gotten a reaction. And that she's pissed enough to want more.

But her hands remain clenched.

I chuckle, low and taunting, her obstinacy turning me on so much, I have to leave now before I cave under the weight of desire and my ache to take her. "I believe that's the point."

I look at her one more time before I turn to go and watch her head fall forward as she tries to rein in everything—emotionally and physically—that I just brought out in her. Good. I got to her.

I walk toward the patio doors and can't resist bringing my fingers to my lips. I slide them in my mouth momentarily to get a taste of her, of exactly what I'm craving, and have to fight the urge to stalk back and just say screw the plan and instead just take her right here, right now.

Goddamn Macallan.

So fucking addictive I'm going to need AA meetings if this shit keeps up.

Chapter 19

I lace up my shoes, desperate to get out of the house and away from waiting for the phone to ring, Dr. Blakely calling with blood test and biopsy results that I've been informed most likely will take another few days. Regardless, I stare at my phone each time I pass it.

When it does ring, it's usually Rylee checking up on me, asking why I seem out of sorts, to which I reply I'm just stressed about this Scandalous deal and the impending BRCA1 test results. That answer usually quiets her down, and she comes through with the moral support that I desperately need but for something possibly much more devastating than a gene test result.

Or it's Cal, checking in with me looking to see what rabbit I'm going to pull out of my hat to make the last event bigger and better than the first two. And despite the fact they went off without a hitch and had a larger draw than he'd ever hoped for in our initial discussions, I'm calling in all kinds of favors. Because I need this rabbit to be huge to make up for the disappearing act I pulled at the last show.

Or rather the one Becks pulled when he hauled me off like Neanderthal man. I'd told the client I'd fallen ill. I didn't feel guilty because I really didn't miss much of the event. We were nearing last call for the night, and the clients and A-listers had been taken care of flawlessly, but it did not go unnoticed by Cal that I wasn't there at closing time. At least I'm not lying since I did find the lump that night, but I don't think he buys it . . . so now I'm left to produce magic from a wand that's lost its power.

I shrug the thought off, knowing I need this run to help me do just that. I grab my phone and, out of habit, glance at the screen.

Out of habit. More like out of a sick obsession to see if the man I keep pushing away is pushing back or if he's called and I missed it. Or texted. Or smoke-signaled, for Christ's sake. God, I'm emotionally fucked-up. I push him away, leave him after incredible sex without another word, and have a fight over it? And his comeback is to work me up into a goddamn frenzy over Jell-O shots and his masterful fingertips with a crowd of friends outside. Then he leaves me one rub short of detonation with promises to keep me awake from that ache he created last night but with a dominant threat to prevent me from sating it.

Slow and steady, my ass. The man's got a side to him that I never knew existed, and now I can't stop thinking about it. And that pisses me the fuck off because I don't want to be thinking about him, can't be thinking about him.

Run.

Like I'm not used to doing that.

I need the exercise to get my head clear, to push my body beyond feeling so that I can focus on getting the final details for the Scandalous event next week taken care of. Focus on that; obsess over that.

I grab my phone and, of course, glance at the screen for the umpteenth time today before opening the front door. I swing it open and cry out in surprise when I see Becks standing there. I immediately move my hand up to my chest to try to still my raging heart.

I should really be covering my crotch though because it

feels like all the blood my heart is pumping has gone straight there. I swear the bowling ball of aching need I've felt during the last few days sitting atop the apex of my thighs just got heavier at the sight of him and his half-cocked smirk.

"Becks! What are you doing here?" I try not to sound like a breathy, needy woman, but damn if I don't sound like a bad porno when the words come out.

"Had? You okay?" Before Becks can even answer, I hear Dante's voice and the sound of his footsteps in the hall behind me.

I'm looking at Becks's eyes when Dante speaks, so there's no way I can miss the flicker of irritation that flashes through them. Hm. Things might get a tad interesting here.

"Yeah, I'm fine," I say over my shoulder, hoping he'll leave it at that and go back to whatever he was doing. But I know I've got no such luck when I hear him clear his throat behind me and notice Becks's eyes stare over my shoulder and turn to ice.

I turn so that I can see both of them, and when I see Dante, I understand why Becks is visibly bristling with disdain. Dante stands in the hallway with a white towel wrapped around his naked, dripping-wet, ripped body while he haphazardly scrubs another towel over his head. His eyes whip to mine, and I see a vague irritation and a whole lot of possessive machismo reflected there, his shoulders squared, body vibrating with testosterone.

"Oh." I quickly avert my eyes back to Becks. "Becks, this is Dante, my house guest for a short while." I don't know why I feel the need to explain. Possibly because the bowling ball he's created needs to have its holes filled with some fingers soon so that the pressure can be released, but I also find it interesting that I don't explain to Dante what exactly my relationship with Becks is.

Maybe it's because I'm still figuring that out.

Becks doesn't say anything, nor does he look away from

the visual pissing match that the guys are waging in front of me. He just nods his head in acknowledgment of Dante, and I'm too busy staring at Becks and holding my breath to look to see what Dante does. Whatever it is, though, he's not moving because after a beat Becks raises both eyebrows in a silent *Do you mind?* The silence lingers for a few more seconds—the claim being staked—before I hear Dante pad off without another word.

Becks's gaze remains trained over my shoulder for a few more moments, his jaw clenched and muscles tight. I give us both a few seconds and then step outside and shut the front door behind me so that he has no other option than to return his focus on me.

"Hey," I say, a cautious smile on my lips.

He clenches his jaw one more time so that the muscle there pulses in that sexy-as-hell way before his eyes find mine again. I watch the tension fade as his muscles relax. I can see the questions on his lips, know he wants to ask what the fuck Dante is doing here or what he was to me, but I give the man mad props because he doesn't utter a single word about him when he speaks.

"I have somewhere I need to be, and you're coming with me." His voice is steady when he speaks, the timbre of it pulling at every part of me. It's the first time I've heard it since the party, since he was telling me he wanted to own me, lick me, slam me, suck me.

Fuck. I'm already a desperate ball of need, and the man hasn't said more than a sentence to me. And the fact that I almost immediately agree to go with him, no questions asked, is even more desperate and embarrassing.

What in the hell did he do to me? No one orders me around unless his hand is fisted in my hair and he's fucking me from behind. But this . . . this reaction he's caused in me is unsettling. It has to be everything else that's going on that's making me react this way. It has to be the unknown and the waiting that makes me want to jump at the chance to go wherever he's taking me just so I can push all of that away for a bit.

"What?" I'm finally able to speak as I shove the desire away and as guilty as I feel about how I've treated him, I refuse to comply with his demand in some warped form of apology. I take a deep breath as I regain the rights Gloria Steinem fought for and cross my arms across my chest and lean against the door behind me. "*We* are not going any-where." I snort at him like he's crazy, but hell if my eyes aren't dragging up over his khaki shorts and Under Armor shirt, which offers just enough of a hint at the muscles bunching beneath it.

He steps forward and places one arm on the door beside my head and braces himself there, his head angled to look at me, a lascivious smirk ghosting that irresistible mouth of his. He laughs low and taunting. "Well, that's where you're wrong, City. *We* are most definitely taking a drive."

I start to protest when he cuts me off by placing his free hand on the curve of my neck and holding it there. I swear my body ignites with bursts of energy whenever our skin touches, the tiny explosions trailing straight to my core so that the ache intensifies and my need swelters.

"And correct me if I'm wrong here, but you've made it clear that there is no *we*, so that leaves me to make the de-cisions." He darts out his tongue to wet his lips, his eyes holding me captive from getting out the words I want to say. "Oh, sweet Haddie, you may have said no strings, but sure as hell I'm taking over the reins here."

"Bullshit." The word is off my tongue, but it is such a contradiction to the hardening of my nipples and the tin-gling between my thighs in reaction to his comment.

"Don't tempt me." He warns, but then that smirk is back. "Then again, please do because I'd give anything to throw you back over my shoulder to prove a point."

Our eyes hold, a silent exchange of wills seeing how far

we're going to take this game, and I'm all for it. Bring it on, Daniels, because let's face it: I have a vagina; therefore I win. My temper streaks through me, displacing the desire with anger, sarcasm leading the way. "SoCo, you couldn't handle me even if you tried." I raise my chin and glare at him, anything to try to gain some of my own footing back.

He works his tongue in his mouth and I swear I can't help that it conjures up the memory of where else it's worked me. "SoCo, huh?"

"Yeah. You're like drinking Southern Comfort . . . trying to act all smooth and steady, but then you sneak up on me and try to make your presence known." I say the words with a bit of a bite to them, so I'm confused when he blinks at me like he can't believe what I'm saying before throwing his head back and laughing deeply. Whatever he finds amusing in what I've said is lost on me.

"Goddamn woman," he draws out with a shake of his head before looking back at me. "I'm all for whiskey, but I prefer something a little smoother, more refined . . . like a Macallan." The smirk plays over his lips like an inside joke that I'm missing, even though I feel like I'm a part of it.

My brows furrow. "Being country and all . . ." My words fade off as he steps into me, our bodies so close that our chests just barely brush against each other's when we drag in a breath.

"Well, Had, being country and all, I was raised around and got used to wild animals." He leans in closer so that his lips are a breath from mine, and I can't help myself from lifting my chin in anticipation of his kiss, which never comes. I flash my eyes back open to find his so close to mine, I can see flecks of darker blue speckled in the aqua. "I learned that you have to learn a lot of patience to tame them."

I know I should be offended, know I should be pissed he's drawing a comparison between me and an untamed animal, but hell if I can think of a comeback other than:

"Tame them?" My words mingle with the warmth of his breath, and as we stand here on my front porch, it feels like we're the only two people in the world.

"Mm-hmm," he murmurs, and just lets the comment hang in the air between us. "But I learned a long time ago that no man should tame what is wild."

"Really?"

His fingertip trails down my bare arm, slowly, taunting, knowing exactly what he's doing to me. "Yep," he whispers so that his lips just barely brush mine. I want to groan out in frustration but grasp firmly to my dignity that's slipping oh so slowly from my clutches. "Wild keeps a man on his toes . . . causes him to always pay attention, not take a single thing for granted. When a man gets complacent, he can lose sight of what matters most."

My breath is shaky, his soft spoken words hitting deep within me. Making me want and need and hope for things I don't think I deserve, things I've told myself are not fair to ask for.

"Becks . . ." I swallow over what I tell myself is the lust lodged in my throat, but I know it's so much more than just lust between us.

He moves his head so that his lips are near my ear, causing me to remember what they said the last time they were so close. "Did you come yet, Haddie?" The change of subject shouldn't surprise me. I should have known he was going to bring us back to this, but fuck me if that question doesn't leave me weak in the knees.

"Yes. Thank you for last night. It may have been my hand, but my thoughts were on you . . . and it was mind-blowing." I lie. It's all I have at this point because if we continue this little power play charade, I'm going to be in a puddle at his feet in mere minutes. And hell no, I didn't get myself off, didn't want to ease that ache he'd ordered me not to assuage because there is something so goddamn hot about doing what you're told when it comes to sex.

I hear his breath catch in surprise, his fingers pressing into my arm where they trail along my skin, and his face pulls back so he can look in my eyes. It's my turn to give him that smug look, that "Who has the upper hand now?" challenge in the raise of my eyebrows. His eyes search mine, and I know before long he'll know I'm lying, so I reiterate my thoughts from moments ago. My lips curl up, and my head angles to the side. "I have a pussy. I win," I taunt him. And I think a small part of me wants him to call my bluff, right here, right now, and drag him upstairs to prove otherwise.

But he doesn't. He just meets me stare for stare, smirk for smirk, challenge for challenge. "While you may have a point, I think you're wrong. You may have the pussy, Haddie, but I'm most definitely the one who will win it."

"Pretty sure of yourself, aren't you?" And hell if the confidence isn't sexy on him.

"Hm. You may have said no strings, but you most definitely didn't say anything about rope."

Damn. "You want to tie me up, then? I never took you for that type, Becks." I try to deflect him with my comment, but hell if the words don't have me wanting him even more.

He laughs low and suggestive. "I might be. I might not be. What type I am doesn't matter because what does is the fact that ropes or no ropes, I plan on making you weak, making you hoarse, leaving you breathless. Baby, I can dominate with the best of them. The question here is, how bad do you want it?"

Desperately.

And the volley of power resumes. The dark promise of his words leaves me wanting to relinquish the upper hand because it's no fun being at the top if there's no one underneath you.

He leans in and uses his mouth to silence my thoughts. Our mouths meet in a soft whisper of a kiss before his tongue touches the seam of my lips, asking for access. I deny him, fists clenched in restraint, libido protesting my resistance, but I know if I let him kiss me, let him own my every reaction like he so mind-blowingly can, I'll come undone here on the porch in a matter of seconds, my desire so tangible, I feel like it's rolling off me in waves.

I think he's going to be angry at my refusal. I can feel his fingers tense when I hold steadfast. That strained laugh of his surprises me yet again when he leans back, his eyes dancing with victory. "I call your bluff, Haddie Montgomery. You didn't come, and I'm going to have so much fun proving it."

And hell if he didn't just gain the upper hand, but thank God, he did because I don't mind being the low man on his totem pole, either.

Chapter 20

The sun is strong above, the ground uneven beneath my feet, and I steal a glance at Becks wandering slowly beside me. I'm still trying to process how I ended up here and how Becks showed up at my house, told me I was going with him, and then dared to call my bluff.

And of course being the stubborn, pigheaded, "don't you dare tell me what to do" woman that I am . . . I caved.

Fucking caved like a whipped woman, but the funny thing was that in the whole exchange with Becks on my doorstep, not once did I think of the biopsy or the pending results. Not one single time because I was so busy trying not to get lost in him.

So when he told me to go inside, change my outfit, and grab an extra pair of clothes, I didn't ask any questions. I turned and grabbed my things, and hopped into his truck to find a pile of fur and thumping tail that I couldn't help but smile at.

Yep. I wasn't fooling myself, either. When I climbed into his car, I hoped like hell that wherever the Beckstination we were going to, there would be a requirement of a lot fewer clothes and a lot more of Becks. Naked. On me. In me.

I pull myself back to the present. To the expanse of land

that holds Becks's parents' old but absolutely gorgeous farmhouse. To the barn with its horses and the brace of ducks driving his dog, Rex, crazy when they walk near him and then fly up onto a loft area, where he can't reach. I take in the field of long grass we are walking through, but mostly it's the simplicity of it all—clean air, bad cell reception, the sparkling water of the pond ahead in the distance—that I savor.

This is what I expected of Beckett Daniels the night I was at his condo and thought he didn't fit: laid back, simplistic in needs and in what impresses him. I glance over at him and question his nonchalance. The silence between us may be comfortable, but the sexual tension is so goddamn charged, I fear that if someone lit a match, the space between us would catch fire.

And then I wonder what his point is in bringing me here today, besides calling my bluff. I know that there's more to it, that he must have an ulterior motive in taking a drive to clear his head, as he so kindly explained. The small talk we made on the way here after I decided not to be angry at him anymore has been less than informative about his state of mind . . . so I'm just trying to figure out what gives here.

Because the thing that needs to give more than anything right now is the zipper of his damn shorts.

Rex comes bounding up and distracts me as Becks takes his ball and throws it ahead of us, where it gets lost in the grass. I sigh with a shake of my head, finally deciding to break the silence of our walk. "Oh, Becks, what is this between us, huh? You are so not my type." I don't mean the comment as an insult but rather just an observation, and I realize what it sounds like the minute it's out of my mouth.

I see him nod his head in acknowledgment of my comment. "Is that another one of those rules of yours?" he asks, amusement woven in his tone. I laugh aloud at the reminder of my bumbling rules, which I couldn't even think of the last time he called me on the spot.

We walk a bit more, my head trying to recollect my rules because sure as fuck I know I'm breaking about five of them right now being here with him.

"Seriously, Haddie," he says, and reaches out and takes my hand in his, our first physical connection since we left my house and my body hums anew with his touch. "What's your type? Dante?"

And the way he says Dante's name—like an insignificant and yet irritating blip on the radar—has me fighting the smirk on my lips. I keep my head down, watching my Converse move over the dusty earth beneath me, when he squeezes my hand to inform me he's waiting for an answer. A part of me wants to change the subject, make this conversation easier since it seems I just keep hurting him, but at the same time, I find I want to tell him. Maybe if I do, he'll realize he's not my type and then will back off and stop pushing for things I want with him but can't give.

"Yes. No," I tell him, and then my feet falter as I begin to explain. I stop for a moment and just look out at the vast field and trees beyond us, not sure where exactly I should go with this answer. "Shit, I usually go for the rebel. The one who has the least stability and does everything unexpected. Everything opposite of you."

He snorts a laugh and shakes his head. "Well, then you sure don't know me very well, now, do you?" I slide a glance over at him, trying to figure out if he's being serious or joking, but he cuts off the moment when he continues. "Besides, Colton is off the market."

"Well, Colton only has eyes for Rylee, so I would have never even attempted that route," I respond immediately, a little irritated at his assumption I would have made a play for Colton. "Besides, there are plenty more out there." And it feels weird to be having this conversation with him when I'm holding his hand.

"So you like getting your heart broken, then?" He tugs my hand so that I'm forced to face him. There is amusement in his smile but something a tad more intense in his eyes, and I can't seem to get a read on it.

"That just comes with the territory." I lift my eyebrows to reinforce my answer.

"Well, maybe you need to relocate and claim some new space, then." His eyes dare me now, taunt me to ask what space that might be. And damn I know where I want it to be, but I just tug my hand from his and start to wander away from him, grabbing a wildflower here and there and silently playing "He loves me. He loves me not" as I pick the petals off.

He loves me.

I hear his footsteps behind me, but I keep walking, wandering over to the shade of a tree where there is a small clearing. I sit down and prop my hands behind me. Becks steps in front of me, and I'm forced to look up at him. And of course when I do, I'm treated to the sight of his bare abs and chest—he must have taken his shirt off as he followed me—and I'd be lying to myself if I denied the fact that my mouth falls a bit lax.

I recover quickly, mad at myself for my ridiculous reaction, and avert my attention elsewhere. I mean, it's not like I haven't seen him naked before so why does just the sight of his sweat-misted bare chest make my stomach feel like it's flip-flopping?

Becks tosses his shirt down beside me and stands there for a beat while I look anywhere but at him before he sits down beside me with a loud exhale of breath. Warning bells go off in my head, and I'm not sure if it's because he's going to make me talk, or if he's going to make me want him more and then deny me, or if he's going to give me what I want and I'm not going to be able to walk away again and save the both of us.

He loves me not.

I refuse to glance over at him as he makes himself comfortable. He stretches his long legs out in front of us and reclines back on his elbows as I focus on everything around us but don't really see anything. Besides the whispering of the wind through the grass and the squawk of a bird, a comfortable silence ensconces us. And I'm more than okay with that because right now he's too damn close, and I'm strung so goddamn tight that I'd give anything to push away the words I know he's going to speak. All I want to do is take him right here in this field. Climb on top of his body and lose myself in him so that he can help me clear everything momentarily from my head.

He loves me.

"We can sit here all day, you know," he says while I remain silent, trying to figure where he's headed with this.

"Mm-hmm. It's nice. Is this why you brought me out here, to sit in an empty field and do nothing but relax?"

I keep my eyes focused ahead, but I know he's smiling because I can hear it in his voice when he speaks next. "We could be doing a whole lot more than relaxing, but that's up to you now, isn't it?"

He loves me not.

I fight the urge to whip my head his way to figure out what he's talking about. Hoping that fucking me into next week is what he's talking about. "How's that?" I ask with a whole lot of uninterest, which I really don't feel.

I hear him shift, and he moves to sit cross-legged in front of me so that I have no option but to look at him. I can't avoid him really, and hell if his proximity doesn't have my nerve endings standing on end, begging for him to touch me.

He loves me.

"Let's be completely clear on something," he says, his tongue darting out to lick his lips as he pauses to make sure that I am one hundred percent paying attention right now. And I most definitely am. "I'd really like to lay you down and take you every way possible right now." I begin to talk, to tell him I'm game, but the warning look in his eyes stops me. "Fuck you so good and hard you feel it in your dreams so that even if you try to run afterward, you can't forget me . . ."

I swear my body shudders at the challenge he issues, the wanton woman in me silently begging him to do just that.

". . . and I will." He chuckles, the sound strained with need. I watch with nonchalance as he reaches out between my legs, my eyes locked on the progress of his hands until they're hidden by the hem of my skirt. Even though I know it's coming, I still suck in a sharp breath when I feel his fingers rub ever so gently against my seam. The barrier of my panties makes the muted feeling almost more intense because it's the hint of what he can do to me that has the ache unfurling and coiling so tight, my body tenses, my back arching, my mouth dropping open.

He loves me not.

"Sweet Haddie, did you get yourself off? Did you slide your fingers right here, part yourself, and think of me?" His voice is deep and mesmerizing, a seductive sound against the whisper of nature around us. My body hums from his words, desire swelling against the stroke of his finger.

His chuckle hits my ears, but I'm lost in thought because he withdraws his fingers now that my panties are damp with my arousal. "Ah, baby, you're so ready, so desperate. I know you listened. I know you didn't make yourself come. And I want to relieve that ache for you so damn bad"—his voice trails off as he inhales a steadying breath—"but not until you talk and tell me what's going on here between us. I need answers, Haddie."

He loves me.

And of course, the riot of desire coursing through me gets doused by those words. I break my gaze from his, looking down at a ladybug that has ventured onto the hem of my skirt. It's so much easier to look there than it is to tell him I just can't do this. "Becks . . ." His name is a familiar sigh on my lips, and I try again to find the words I need. "It's complicated, and I just don't have an answer for you right now."

"Don't or can't?"

I clench my jaw at his words, cursing myself for walking into that one. I keep my eyes trained on the ladybug, uncomfortable and yet comforted by his presence all at the same time.

And I realize I have no more petals left.

Damn.

I need to pick another one to get the answer I want.

"Can't, then," he muses. "Okay, so what is it you want from me, Haddie?"

My eyes flash to his instantly, my nipples tighten, and my libido begins to hum with the silent temptation at my fingertips. "I want you to fuck me so hard, I have no choice but to remember who I am. Break me down so that I can find me again." I've never spoken more honest words before, nor had I intended to reveal so much. I know they sound just about as crass as his comment moments before, but frankly, I'm not looking for romance right now. I'm looking for exactly what I said, but now that I've spoken, an uneasiness filters in with his silence.

I hear his shocked exhale at my blatant response. Confusion flits through his eyes, and he angles his head and stares so deep within me that when I begin to avert my eyes, he brings his hands up to the sides of my face and holds it so that I have no option but to look at him.

"Uh-huh. You think you can actually say something like that to me and I'm not going to make you explain what's behind it? We'd better do some talking because you're making me hard with a comment like that. And you keep making me go back on promises I've made to myself . . . and, City, if I can't trust promises to myself, then I can't make promises to anyone else. . . ." He shifts some and adjusts himself within his shorts with a pained groan. "So either you start talking or you might just have to sit there silently while I take care of myself because fuck, woman, you're not giving me many options at this point."

Is he for real? He would really make me sit here and watch him get off rather than let me help him? He's that goddamn stubborn?

We sit in silence as I try to hide the answers in my eyes and the desire apparent in my nipples pressing through the thin fabric of my tank top. He nods his head in measured acknowledgment—of what, I'm not sure—before a ghost of a smile traces over his mouth.

"Keep those eyes of yours looking at me like that, Montgomery, and you're going to be in a whole world of hurt."

"I am?" I snort, trying to play off the fact that every part of my body is angling toward him to be touched.

"Yup, it's a bitch wanting something so bad, you're weeping," he says, his eyes flitting down to where he's dampened my panties and then back up to mine, a cocky-as-hell smirk playing over his lips.

He wants to play this game? Bring it on. "Nah, I'm a 'grab life by the balls' kinda girl . . . so if I, uh, want something," I say, repeating the same response he's giving me, eyes trailing down to his erection pressing against the seam of his shorts and then back up, "I just take what I want."

"And what is it you want?" He leans back on his hands, his arms bracing himself as he toys with me.

I work my tongue in my mouth as I fight my own smirk and the need coursing through me. "You."

"Hmm," he says. "Well, City, that there poses quite the problem because, one, I brought you here to talk. Just to talk." He pushes himself up so that he leans forward, his face dangerously, temptingly close to mine. "And, two, since I brought you out here with only that intention, I didn't bring a condom. No glove, no love." He shrugs, a victorious smirk transforming his face from arrogant to playful.

And fuck the man is gorgeous in whatever role he's playing. I sag inwardly at his statement, needing his touch like I need my next breath since he has me primed with his verbal-and-taunting foreplay. Then I realize that he could very well be playing me.

Time to call his bluff. He won't touch me without a condom? I love that he's that respectful of me, but hell if I don't want to be disrespected right now.

"That one of your rules too?" I ask with a lift of my chin and a challenge in my eyes.

"Mm-hmm."

I can see him trying to figure out where I'm going with this. See the cogs of his mind turning to why I'd be questioning a rule that's a no-brainer. I bring a hand to my throat and trail my finger slowly down between my breasts like it's a move I do every day. I watch his eyes follow, take note of his Adam's apple bobbing in response, and figure I'll go in with the coup de grâce and see if I can't make him take my own bait.

"Well, I like rules too, you know . . . and one of mine is that I take my pill regularly, get tested regularly." I wet my bottom lip and love that I see his mouth part in reaction. "Nothing like the feeling of skin on skin, right?"

His eyes flash to mine, and there's an audible sharp intake of air before he controls his response to seem blasé. "The Pill, huh?"

"Yep, the Pill and a clean bill of health. You?"

"Am I on the Pill? No." he laughs out, breaking the momentary sexual tension sparking between us like a live circuit.

"Cute. Very cute, but I was referring to your bill of health."

He angles his head and stares at me, all joking aside because this is a serious answer. "Clean as a whistle."

"Well, I don't know about whistles, but I'm sure you've got something else I can blow on." My smile is smarmy, and I love watching his eyes widen at my audacity.

"Goddamn it, Haddie," he swears under his breath. I see him angle closer into me, see his resolve weakening, his eyes scrunched and a sigh escaping, and then just as quickly, he reins it back in and pulls away from me. "Well played, well played . . . but as much as I want you to blow that something else, I've got my list of rules."

"I like a man who sticks to his principles . . . who likes to remain in control," I tease, enjoying torturing him after my damn libido has been a slave to his orders over the past week, "but I was born to break rules in order to get what I want." I tilt my head and purse my lips, staring at him, waiting for his reaction, and every part of me wants desperately for him to take my shoulders, push me back, and have his way with me.

"Well, I guess this is going to be a test of wills . . . seeing which one of us will prevail." He raises his eyebrows and leans back on his hands, making the point neither of us is going to get what he or she wants unless one of us caves.

We stare at each other for a few minutes, both of us trying to figure out how to manipulate the situation to achieve our goals when he twists his lips and nods his head. "Okay, City . . . you want sex, and I want answers, so I have a proposition." I just raise an eyebrow at him because I'm thankful he is trying to add some levity to the moment—he only calls me that nickname when we are being playful. "For every question I ask you that you refuse to answer or lie about, you have to remove a piece of clothing and vice versa. See, I've already given you a head start," he says, pointing to his shirt lying on the ground beside me. "You have a few more lies to give than I do before you're naked."

His proposition is interesting, to say the least, and I'm so focused on the fact that I have three lies until he is completely naked that I don't think everything through. Like who gets to be the judge of if I'm lying or not. All I'm thinking about is how much Becks has primed my pump and left me without release. "And what? The person who is naked first loses? What does the winner get?"

That low, seductive chuckle rumbles in his chest. "Winner gets to decide just what to do next."

Thank sweet fuck for that because this girl is ready to be taken here in this empty field. Talk about wanting the clichéd with reckless abandon. . . . If this isn't the perfectly painted picture of it, I'm not sure what is.

"You up for it?" His eyes taunt me, and his smirk goads me even though I'm already game.

"The question that needs to be asked is, are you *up for it*?" I smirk at him.

"City, you know I'm up for anything with you." He works his tongue in his cheek. "I'll even let you go first."

"I don't want you claiming I cheated now when you're naked and I'm—" I stop myself, not wanting to play my cards about what I want too quickly because if I tell him I have a strong desire to take him in my mouth and taste him, I have a feeling he'll lie on purpose. Then again, we're both in this sexually frustrated state partially because of him, so I'm not sure he'll give in that easy.

And the problem is, if I lie, I fear he'll build me to a frenzy and then walk away again to prove his goddamn point when in fact it is his point I want in me.

"I go first, huh? Don't answer that," I correct myself, realizing I almost just wasted a question on him. His grin spreads wide as he just nods his head for me to continue. "Who is Deena?"

"Deena who?," he replies like he doesn't know anyone by that name. And as much as I love the idea that he's acting like she's insignificant to him, I raise my eyebrows, wanting the answer. He sighs in resignation. "Deena is a girl I dated in high school."

I buy his response, even though I suddenly want to follow it up with another question, but he's already started to ask me something. "Look at us and our D questions. . . . Is there anything going on between you and Dante?"

I begin to lie—to tell him there's nothing—but correct myself as I count my pieces of clothing. "Dante is an ex who once upon a time I thought was the one. Until he up and disappeared one day. I have a weak spot for him, yes. Have we kissed since he's been staying with me? Yes. Do I want him back? No. Does he want more? Possibly. Do I want to sleep with him? No." And I don't know why I've laid all of that out there. Maybe I want to warn Becks away by telling him that Dante and I have a history, have kissed, but when I look at Becks, he is grinning from ear to ear.

"What?" I ask him when he just laughs.

"Well, you answered all of that for me, and I only had to use one question, so thank you. That lets me get to the important questions quicker," he says, running a hand through his hair as I curse my wordy-ass self.

He reaches out and begins to lift up the hem of my shirt, and I bat his hand away as he starts to lift it over my head. "Stop! I answered you!"

He just keeps pulling it up, and as I continue to stop him, I turn my head back to find his mouth on mine. The fight goes right out of me when the warmth of his lips and his tongue delve to touch mine softly. An unhindered moan falls around us, and I'm not sure if it's from him or me because I'm so completely mesmerized, my body completely lax and yet so very eager to respond to any request he gives me.

I come back to reality when he draws back from the kiss and pulls my shirt over my head, distraction one hundred percent effective. "You lie," he murmurs, and I'm so captivated by him right now, I don't care that my shirt's off or that he thinks I've lied because all I can focus on is his presence before me. "You want to sleep with Dante still. You just don't want to admit it. He's your past. He may be complicated, but since he's your past, he can easily help you forget whatever it is you seem to be running from just as easily as I can. And the thing is, with him, you know he's not going to be there in the morning or on the day after . . . and that's quite appealing to you, whereas you fear that with me. You love your no strings, and yet you won't cut the ties they have that hold you to whatever it is that makes you run away and remain alone."

I suck in a broken breath as he speaks with such raw honesty about the things I feel, and it scares me that he can see inside me so well. And even worse, if he sees that truth, what else is he seeing that I don't want him to? Shit just got real, real quick, and I didn't want it to.

I swallow over the lump in my throat and deny him any reaction to his commentary, hoping that will save my sanity some if I just move on. It's my turn to ask a question, and of all the things that I want to ask him, I can't get my mind off the exotic Deena. I need to know if he slept with her the other day after he left me at the farmers' market. I don't know why. If he did, was he comparing us? Was he thinking how much less complicated she is than me? I don't want to waste my question on this, but I can't pull my head elsewhere.

"Did you sleep with Deena?"

He gives me a puzzled look and then says, "No. I can't believe you'd wonder about that or waste a question on it. Don't you get she could never hold a candle to you?"

His words warm parts deep inside me that I don't want warmed, and I realize how stupid this game is immediately. How he's an open frickin' book to my volumes of closed ones.

I shift to stand up, wanting to change the topic and end this game right here, right now before he gets any closer to things I don't want him near.

"Nice try," he says, shifting us back so that I am flat on my back and he's sitting astride my waist with my hands cuffed at my sides. We seem to keep ending up in this position.

And hell if I'm going to complain.

"What's wrong, Haddie? Was that answer a little too real for you? Did you realize that *we are*, and you can't handle it once again, so you want to bolt?" He leans down and hovers over me as the truth in his words hit my ears. "Guess what. I have the only car keys. We're not going anywhere or doing anything until you give it a chance."

I stop moving beneath him, let the anger burn out when I hear the emotion in his voice. There are so many things I want to say to him, to explain to him, but the fear and its ever-constant presence are the dam preventing any deluge of truths.

"Haddie . . . ," he says, and I wonder what it is he sees right now as he looks at me. Does he see the fear—the scared little girl needing someone but afraid to get too close—or does he see the confident woman who's playing a game with his heart?

I wonder which one I'd see if I were in his shoes. Because neither one is attractive or admirable.

He leans forward and rests his forehead on mine, my eyes drifting closed with our lips barely touching. "I'm not going to make you talk. I could never force you to when whatever it is that puts the look in your eyes you have right now breaks my heart." He pauses for a beat, and I'm not sure if he does so for him or for me, but I appreciate it. It gives me time to try to clear the look from my eyes and in- flate my lungs since he just robbed them of all air. "Give us today. Forget whatever it is that's making you push me away over and over again, and give us a chance. We're good to- gether. . . . Can't you see that? Push whatever it is aside, and if after today you still want to fight against this connection we have, then I say go ahead. Walk away without your god- damn strings tied tight because I know you won't."

I don't even realize that I'm holding my breath again or that my body has gone completely lax from his words. My mind skips and homes in on the key words he's speaking, unable to fully process the generosity behind them because all I can focus on is my own desperation, which they evoke. I want this. I want a chance not to think and feel and fear, and yet I know the chance to do that will only lead to the ties I fear are already there. The ones he's already tying into double knots so I can't walk away.

I want the ability to feel, to think, to hope without the fear tingeing the edges. Even if for a day. I want to give myself this one thing, give us this even though I know how selfish it is.

He mistakes my silence for discord and continues. "Whatever this is between us is worth a shot, Haddie. You're worth it. I just want you to give me the chance to prove I'm not going to hurt you. I just wish you'd let me in to show you that I mean it."

Chapter 21

The emotion I feel is so strong that I don't think I can speak, so I try to show him. I press my lips to his as my hands roam down the strong lines of his back. I'm desperate as hell to take and sate and feel, but at the same time I want to linger and memorize every sound and taste and sensation.

"Haddie." He murmurs my name, an oath and a curse at the same time, and I steal anything else he planned on saying by slipping my tongue between his lips and taking everything I need to keep the seams holding myself together from unraveling.

"Make me feel, Becks." And this time when I ask, when I whisper it against his lips, it's not to make me forget the grief of Lexi's death but rather to own the emotions I now feel for him. The ones I can't deny anymore.

Together we begin the slow dance of undressing, removing his shorts, lifting up my skirt, and pulling down my panties because right now we both need this connection between us more than anything. I sit up and push him back, my hands on his shoulders, my lips on his. I move my hands ever so slowly so that my fingernails scrape down the firm lines of his chest until I hold his cock in my hand. And the feeling, the notion that I can make him so hard, so fast, is a powerfully intoxicating one.

He groans out as I encircle him and stroke my hand up and back over his steeled length. I drag my mouth from his, my lips tasting the salt on his skin, my nose breathing in his scent, my hands feeling him pulse and ask for more without words. I lick and nip at the flat disks of his nipples, earning me a hiss of breath and a hand fisted in my hair in response. His hand urges me farther down his body with a hurried desire while I prefer to take my time. To lick, and kiss, and tempt him with my mouth. To kill him with the slow descent so that by the time I reach the crest of his dick, the anticipation is so intense, he'll lose that stoic restraint and cry out my name like he owns it.

I slide my mouth over his infinity zone, and when my nipples scrape through the fabric of my bra over the top of his thighs, I moan at the eroticism that just heightens every single incredible sensation. I finally reach his cock and pump it once in my hand while I close the wet heat of my mouth around the crest. Becks's hips jerk in reaction and "*Fuck, Had,*" falls from his mouth, and his hand fists even tighter in my hair.

I position my body so that I'm sitting astride one of his thighs, my own sex grinding against his leg with each draw up and down of my mouth on his dick. I lick my tongue along the underside of his shaft, adding pressure there before sliding back up and circling the crest. I tease him like this a bit more, only allowing my lips to close over his head and denying the rest of his length the suction of my mouth while my own body trembles from the sensations I'm creating for myself.

His fist in my hair urges me to slide him all the way in my mouth while his other softly caresses my cheek and underside of my chin in an oddly intimate way for this carnal action. I take my time with licks, my fingers teasing his balls with scrapes of fingernails and then a gentle pulling motion down and away when they tighten up.

"Goddamn it, Had. Suck me." His voice breaks, and his hips urge up in a plea as I moan, my clit getting the perfect friction with his movement. "Fuck me with your mouth."

And his words urge me on to give him what he wants. To bring him the pleasure he deserves for always being such a generous lover with me. I place my head over him and slide him all the way into my mouth until I can feel him hit the back of my throat. And when I do, I remain still for a moment until I can't take it anymore before I slide it slowly back out, hollowing my cheeks and adding suction with the withdrawal.

I love the strangled groan my action causes and the thrill that shoots through my body at being able to give this to him, do this to him. I continue my movements, varying the pressure of my tongue, the degree of suction until his hand is urging me to go faster and faster. I give in to his demands and start working him with both my hand and my mouth, my own ache intensifying as he gets harder and larger from the increased flow of blood.

And I think he's just on the verge of coming—I'm so wrapped up in bringing him to the cusp that I don't realize he's sat up some—when he grabs at my shoulders and yanks my body up so that his lips can meet mine. The man kisses me with complete abandon and total ownership. He stakes a claim that I've already handed him, but it doesn't stop him. His tongue continues to brand me, lips bruising and hands urging my hips up and over his all the while.

One hand holds my face still so that I'm a willing victim to his barrage of mouth intercourse while his other hand lines his cock up at my wet and willing entrance. I can feel the width of his head there, ready to divide and conquer yet claim my heightened emotions with physicality as he deepens our kiss, pouring everything and then some into it. This feeling is twenty times more overwhelming than any sex I've ever had.

Letting a man claim me with his cock is one thing, but

letting Becks kiss me senseless and own my response is more moving, more intimate than anything I've ever given any man before.

He's opened me up, made me vulnerable, made me his.

He leans back and stares at me, our breaths mingling just as our hearts are. "Can you feel that, Haddie? I know you can, know there's not a chance in hell you can deny what's between us anymore. Feel this, feel me. . . . Want this, want me." Our eyes hold, and then he leans in and brushes his lips to mine in a soft and tender assault to my senses once again.

And then the moment his hands urge my hips down and he pushes his pelvis up—the moment we join our bodies— I can feel my heart tumble endlessly out of control to that deep, dark corner I can't reach, even if I stretch my muscles and fingertips as far as I can to try to grab it back. But I can't. Don't know if I could reach it if I'd want to reclaim it.

Because I've just fallen in love with Beckett Daniels.

The idea hits me as his cock bottoms out in my clenching sex, and my head falls back as I gasp.

Becks's mouth descends to my exposed neck as we both move in unison to give our bodies what we need to climb that peak that's just within reach. My teeth find my bottom lip as I lose myself in the moment, accept the feelings and sensations, and drown in the chance he wants us to take.

I moan with the movements, both the feelings they create and the touch of his hands urging me on. His mouth leaves my neck, and I find myself looking into his eyes as one of his hands moves from the side of my neck to my right breast, his thumb pulling the fabric down and grazing over my taut nipple to send shock waves through my body at the mind-numbing sensation. I cry out, urge him to continue, our eyes locked on each other's so that we can see the pupils darken and widen as we chase our pleasure.

And when it hits, when the desire skyrockets into an explosion of heat and sensation that pulls me under its addictive haze, I can't focus on anything else but letting it take me for its incredible, serendipitous ride. My body trembles, and my walls pulse around Becks as he tries to still himself so that I can feel the full impact of my climax.

"Haddie . . ." My name is a guttural groan on his lips as his hands dig tightly into my bare flesh and his hips rock into mine, emptying himself into me. His mouth finds my shoulder, his teeth pressing there as he comes, the slightly painful sensation causing my own muscles to tighten around him in an unexpected arousing response.

We sit there for a few moments, our hands lazily stroking up and down each other's backs as the sweat that mists our skin dissipates with the cool afternoon breeze sliding over us like a blanket in this outdoor haven.

After a bit he pulls away and just stares at me, the intimacy of his look so profound that I know I can no longer deny either of us the chance at what could be, regardless of whatever the future holds. He angles his head to the side and whispers ever so softly, "You're beautiful. You know that?"

And I want to laugh, want to tell him that I'm sure I must look it right now, with grass in my hair and covered in sweat and my bra half off, but there's something in the way he says the words, something in the expression on his face that stops me, moves me, undoes me . . . because I realize that he calls me beautiful as if it were my name.

Even looking like this, I'm beautiful to him.

My heart swells with so many things, I can't compartmentalize for once, so I let them take over—all of them—and own the moment for me. I reach up and frame his face in my hands and lean forward and press my lips to his, the emotion so great within me that I don't want him to see it in my eyes just yet. I'm too exposed, too vulnerable right now, so I use that to fuel my need for this innocent action with him.

He accepts the soft sigh of a kiss I offer him, and we slip into it, prolonging the intimacy between us. I shift some, and he slips from within me as his mouth leaves mine and begins a trail of kisses down the line of my neck. My body, which was so satisfied moments ago, no longer is. Fuck, the man knows how to make me lose my focus and render me thoughtless with just the touch of his lips. It's just freakishly wrong how much he affects me.

"Damn, City," he whispers to me between kisses. I can feel him beginning to harden slowly against my thigh and marvel at his recovery time but most definitely have no complaints with it.

He laughs softly, the vibration rumbles against my skin as I score my fingers up his arms, the only thing I can do coherently. He pulls back, and his laugh is more earnest, and I tilt my head down to look at him.

"Your ladybug friend has decided to beat me to the chase here," he says with amusement in his tone.

I'm unsure what he means, and so I look down just in time to see him reach a finger beneath the lace cup of the left side of my bra. He tugs it down so that the little ladybug, who's obviously preferring to be a horny toad, can escape unscathed. I'm so scattered from the sex, my tumult of emotions, his mouth, and this little distraction that I react about five seconds too late to prevent it.

And I'm such a dumb shit, angry at myself for being so lost in the damn moment that I try to cover the jagged edge of stitches sticking out beneath the steri strips before he can see it. But I'm way too late.

"Haddie?" His voice is even, but the concern and confusion lacing through it is obvious to my ears.

I shove back off him immediately—and I catch him off guard so that I'm able to escape the confines of his arms. I'm panicked and unsure what to do, so I do the only thing my mind can grasp. I grab my discarded panties and clean myself quickly before tugging my skirt down, picking up my tank top, and then striding off across the field with so many thoughts I can't think straight.

I can hear Becks behind me, swearing up a storm, as he pulls his shorts on, but I don't care. All I can think of is the question that's coming and how I'm going to answer it when he knows that scar and the stitches weren't there two weeks ago. My head swims with uncertainty, and it's prompting me to run once again, but the problem is, where in the hell am I running to? I'm in the middle of Bum-fuck Egypt, and I have no transportation.

But I don't even get a chance to contemplate what comes next because Rex is barking and circling around me in excitement, and I'm shoving my tank top over my head, and it's all tangled, and I'm flustered and frustrated.

And scared.

Scared because I just let him in, and now I'm probably going to have to shut him out. Fuck, damn, shit.

"Goddamn it! Stop, Haddie. Stop!" I can hear the plea in his voice, and I try to ignore it so that it doesn't faze me. I keep walking, keep moving to expel the frantic energy that has me doing anything but standing still. "Had! There's nowhere to go." His voice is firmer now, more resolute, and I know he's right, but I just don't want to do this right now.

But my feet falter, and the mixture of the sun and my anxiety makes me feel like my skin is on fire. I know he's closing the distance, can hear his feet crunch the ground along with his muttered curses, so I try to withdraw, prepare to disengage. Hope I can remain that way.

My arms are crossed over my chest in a protective gesture in more ways than one, and I step into the shade of a huge oak tree, head down, thoughts racing. I shrug out of his grip as his hand lands on my shoulder. It's stupid on my part, really. Like I'm actually going to escape him, but I trudge on, hoping avoidance will help in whatever context it might come.

"You can't run forever, Montgomery." His words stop me. My steps falter, and my body deflates because I know he's right, know that I've been running, but I've been doing it for so long, it seems that I don't know how not to anymore.

My back is to him. Rex sits in front of me with his tongue lolled out and his head angled up at me in anticipation, like I have a ball I'm going to throw for him. Becks's harsh breathing fills the space between us, and my heartbeat rages in my ears.

I close my eyes when I feel Becks's hands on my shoulders, steel my body for the heat of his touch and the rush of words to come out of my mouth. But nothing comes. My thoughts are so jumbled and my mind is trying so hard to figure out what to say that my mouth falls open and then closes several times before shutting again.

"Hey." The tenderness in his tone as he pulls me back against the solidity of his chest causes everything in me to feel as if it weighs a thousand pounds. And it does because the effort it is going to take to navigate this minefield is going to be unforgiving. Becks wraps his arms across my chest, cautious of my stitches, and just holds me tight. He presses a kiss to the curve of my neck and then rests his chin on my shoulder. "I'm trying not to be pushy here. I'm trying to let you have a moment to explain to me what I just saw and why you got spooked and ran . . . but you're scaring the hell out of me right now. Your silence, you running . . . all of it's scaring me."

I bite my bottom lip to stifle the quivering of my chin and to allow me a moment to fortify my voice with the confidence I don't have but need him to think I do. "The night at your place . . . ," I begin, my hands fisted and my body rigid, not wanting to accept any of his comfort right now. Needing to get through this, be strong, not break. "I woke up. Something felt pinched. I swore that I was imagining things. Spent like forever trying to prove otherwise, but I found a lump." His arms flex ever so slightly in response, and I'm grateful that he stays silent. "I freaked out. Left and went to the doctor as soon as possible, had a biopsy where they removed whatever it was. That's it." I try to add a bit of insignificance in my voice, play it off, but when I hear his unsteady inhale, I know he doesn't believe me.

I begin to pull away from him, but his arms remain steadfast in their hold. "Uh-uh," he murmurs against my shoulder, the heat of his breath hitting the fabric of my tank top and trapping it between his mouth and my skin. "Just give me a minute."

And so we stand there as he processes what he's heard, and I try to figure out where to go from here because damn it to hell, I've let him in. He's using all he has to be the can opener to peel back everything I've sealed so tight, and that scares me to death.

"What did the biopsy show?" he finally says, and the question hangs in the air like an oppressive cloud.

I swallow the truth I know deep down and aim for cautious optimism in my answer. "I don't know yet. Any day now."

He makes an incoherent sound in response, his thumb beginning to rub up and down gently in reassurance. "I'm . . . I'm having a hard time processing this, Had—"

"I know. I'm sorry. I didn't intend for anyone to know. I just . . ."

He releases me and stalks past me a few feet, his shoulders tense, and his emotion transparent in his posture. He starts to talk and stops himself, his hand gripping the back of his neck as he stares at the pond before turning back to look at me. "You didn't intend for anyone to know?" His anger surprises me. Pity, I expected, disbelief too . . . not anger. "You think that little of me? You think I'll take you in my bed but don't care about you as a person? What the fuck, Had?"

He shakes his head, his eyes boring into mine. I see his hands clench and unclench, his chest rises and falls in anger as we stand in a silent standoff. "You don't get it, do you?" The question hangs between us, and I'm not sure if I'm supposed to answer it or not, and if I am, what the hell am I not getting? Which part of everything I've done to piss him off am I not understanding right now?

He clenches his jaw and looks up to the sky momentarily as if he's asking for the universe to grant him some patience. When he looks back down, I see hurt in his eyes, and as much as I want to look away, I force myself to hold his gaze, tell myself that this look is nothing compared to what could be there if we held tight to whatever this is between us.

"I care about you, Haddie. I *more* than care about you."

"That's not possible," I tell him, immediately pushing the thought away. Uh-uh. Not possible. Caring leads to devastation, and I can't have that on my shoulders. "No strings, remember?" I spit the words off my tongue like they're acid. Defense mechanism and all that. I see the impact of my statement flicker in his eyes and chastise myself. *Crap!* How can I feel it's okay for me to feel like I'm falling for him, and yet I don't want him to have any feelings for me? But isn't a woman allowed to be a tad hypocritical when dealing with the bullshit I've had to deal with over the past year?

He walks toward me, his eyes narrowing and his mouth set in a firm line. "Fuck you and your *goddamn strings.* I may be too cynical to believe in love at first sight, Montgomery, but I believe in *the click* that happens between two people. And you can stand there all you want and lie through those sexy-as-hell lips of yours, tell me there's nothing between us . . . but there was a click," he shouts at me, jabbing his finger in his chest. *"And I believe in that click."*

His eyes glare, dare me to deny it, and I can't bring myself to look away or to refute him. The honesty in his words and the tangibility of him before me readily admitting it are just too much.

He steps closer, a ball of anger, concern, and confusion on continuous rotation. "Why . . . ," he begins, and then stops, regrouping his train of thought. "Why didn't you wake me that night? Tell me? Pick up the phone when I called and explain what was going on so that I could have been there for you? I just don't get it. . . ."

"It's not your problem." It's the easiest answer I have. I've told him more than I wanted to, more than I'd planned on, and yet I still feel lost in my decision. I'm not a half-ass kind of person, and yet that's exactly what I'm being to Becks right now. And a pitifully pathetic one at that.

"There you go again, insulting me," he says, cynicism dripping from each word. "It's not my problem, huh? You leaving in the middle of the night, scared and alone? Yeah, you're right. . . ." He nods. "I wouldn't care about that? About you? For fuck's sake, Haddie, you're not making any goddamn logical sense. . . ." He blows out a loud breath of disbelief.

"Becks . . ." Any excuses I have die a strangled death on my tongue when hurt flashes once again in his eyes. "I didn't mean it as an insult. . . ."

He groans in frustrated exasperation. "Please tell me Ry thinks you're being just as frustratingly stubborn about this as I do."

I'm not sure how exactly I give myself away, but the brief hesitancy in my movement or the hitch in my breath tells him everything. His eyes widen and his nostrils flare. "What? Un-fucking-believable! You haven't told her?" His voice rises as he walks away from me and kicks a small log on the ground so that it flies and hits against a tree, dust particles floating into the air.

I focus on those particles shining innocently against the sun's backdrop. They look so free, so light, and I'd give anything to be one of those right now.

Ashes to ashes, dust to dust.

The words flicker into my head—words as tried and true as time—but their significance right now is a bit much for me. I try to shake the images the thoughts evoke from my head and only succeed in becoming more panicked, more desperate.

"There's nothing to tell yet," I shout at him, hoping that the escalation of my voice reinforces my statement.

"Yeah, there's nothing to tell, and yet you haven't told the person you're closest to in the whole goddamn world about it. I'm sure you have some oceanfront property in Arizona you want to sell me since you seem to think I'm that fucking gullible."

His words slap at me and, God, yes, I deserve them but the anger overrides the confusion and disheartened fear. "Fuck you." My tone is low and even, a chill to it that he doesn't deserve. How dare he judge me, mock me, come at me in regards to anything with Rylee?

My friend, my business. And then I groan inwardly because he's right about it on every level, and all of a sudden it hits me that not telling her is still lying, regardless of whatever intention was behind it.

"You'd like that, wouldn't you, Montgomery?" he challenges as he steps closer, his anger vibrating off him and crashing into me. "You'd prefer to be fucked so mindless that you can't remember what lies you're keeping from whom and how many people care about you that you keep treating like crap and pushing away. What kind of game are you playing here? Let's see how alone I can be? Let's prove how stubborn I am?" He runs his hands through his hair, exasperated. "It's like you're trying to make me second-guess my feelings for you...." His words come out in a burst of heat but then trail off, and I can see the moment it all *clicks* for him. When the scattered jigsaw pieces of my sporadic and confusing actions suddenly fall into place.

Fuck me running.

Becks's head angles to the side again, and his eyes narrow. I can see him trying to process what he's just concluded. He takes another step closer into my personal space, and even though I'm outdoors with nothing around me, my feet are glued to the ground, and I feel like my back is up against a goddamn wall.

"That's it, isn't it?"

I can't speak, so I simply stare at him as my eyes burn with tears I don't want to shed. I work a swallow down my throat, and I see his eyes track me, struggling to get the words past my lips. His expression softens immediately. Within a second, his arms—the ones I don't want around me, and yet I want them so desperately at the same—are there, drawing me into him.

I tell myself to fight it, not to accept the comfort because I don't deserve it, but my body's innate reaction takes over. My hands grip in the shirt he slipped back on when he chased after me, and my face finds that spot just beneath his chin. His hand is on the back of my head holding me to him, our hearts thundering against each other's.

The world spins beneath our feet, and nature hums around us, but I feel like time stands still, and I just hold tight to Becks and to that comforting thought.

"I don't care how hard you push me, Montgomery. I'm not going anywhere," he murmurs into the crown of my head, his hands pressing me farther into him. "You don't have to do whatever this is alone."

My emotions spiral into a continual free fall with his admission. I want to tell him that this isn't anything—him, me, us, a bad diagnosis—but I'm so sick of pushing people out that for once all I want is to pull him in. My hands fist tighter into the fabric as I try to gain some kind of control of my inner turmoil, but it's useless. We stand there for a moment, both breathing each other in and trying to understand the other's reactions.

After a bit, when my fingers are relaxed on his shirt but his are still grasping me tight, I say in an even, unemotional voice that surprises even me, "Nothing has happened yet, Becks. Nothing."

He sighs, and I can feel his jaw clench. "You're scared so shitless you're running. . . . That's something. *That's more than something.*"

I accept his words, know they are the truth, but I still need to warn him away. "I don't know what it is yet, but I know that if it's what I fear, asking anyone to stand beside me, suffer as I go through it, deal with the crap that comes with it . . . the side effects, the aftereffects, the scars inside and out . . . that's something I can't ask of anyone. Ever."

His fingers dig into my shoulders as he pushes me back so that I'm forced to look into his eyes. They search mine for the remainder of the truths he knows are there but that I won't voice: life, death, losing my breasts, losing my hair, scars, infertility. I try to guard those fears, not even wanting to go there yet, not wanting to admit those to him.

"And again, I call bullshit on that. You don't get to choose the people that care about you. You don't get to make choices for others, tell them how to feel or, better yet, block them out because of what you think they'll go through." Anger starts to weave through his voice, despite the soft brush of his thumb over my cheek, a gentle reassurance against the onslaught of chastising words I hear but struggle to accept. "It's my choice, Ry's choice how we choose to deal with it . . . not yours. I just . . ." His voice trails off as he shakes his head and leans forward so that his forehead rests against mine.

"Becks, I'm just trying to do what's best for everyone."

"What's best?" He pulls back, irritation rising in him again. "God, you stubborn, fucking woman. Quit being a martyr. What's best is you letting me make my own goddamn decisions and for you to stop lying to me so that I can." He releases me and paces a few feet, energy so raw he needs to move. "What's best is you pulling your head out of your ass long enough to realize I care about you, Ry cares about you—"

"I don't want her to know." My voice is implacable as I

think of the heartache Ry's endured over the past few years and how I don't want to add to it until there is a finite answer. I don't want to add undue stress to her. "And I never lied to you. . . ."

He bites his bottom lip and grimaces. "Fuck!" he growls out to the trees above him, and then rolls his shoulders to dissipate some of the stress I see settling there. "Semantics aren't an excuse. An omission is the same as lying, Haddie, but you're missing the point entirely. It's not whether it was a lie or not. It's so damn far from that. It's you using the sex we've had to numb yourself when it should do the exact opposite. It should light your body on fire and burrow so deep under your skin that all you think about is the next time you can have me . . . because fuck if that's not what you've done to me. So I call your bluff. I'll keep calling it every fucking day until you admit you want me, that being with me does that to you too . . . but you won't, will you?" I just remain still, face impassive, body raging with emotion beneath the surface. "You'd rather stand there and tell me you prefer the numb, the void, the nothing, than admit you need me."

His eyes have their own language as we stare at each other, the power of his words bringing tears to my eyes and knocking the words from my lips. "I was just doing what I thought was best, protecting everyone from more hurt, more everything." *And I hate the numb,* I scream silently. *I hate it so fucking much that every time we touch you make me feel so alive, I realize how dead I've felt inside over the past year.*

I don't know why I don't tell him the rest. Like if I do, then I'm just sealing my fate by Murphy's fucking Law so I keep quiet.

"Really? That's all you've got for me? Next time make sure your eyes and your lips match up, City, because you're just adding insult to injury right now. Your refusal to answer is infuriating. *Need me, Haddie.* Use me as your goddamn emotional punching bag or your real one, for that matter, but fucking need me. I'm not some schmuck who's going to bolt at the first rough patch, and the fact that you still don't see that is a crock." He blows out a loud breath, jaw clenched, anger palpable. "I'm so fucking pissed, but I'm also so fucking mesmerized by you right now, and I don't know what the hell to do or say. All I know is that protecting someone from the truth is just another way of shutting them out."

My eyes snap to his, and I don't know what to say to him. There are no words to take away the fact that I hurt him, but at the same time, his plea causes my chest to constrict so that I can't help but feel the swelling of my heart. I try to justify, to apologize by explanation. "Maybe shutting someone out is my way of not forcing someone's hand to react out of duty or stick it out when the shit starts rolling downhill. Pity by association is not needed, nor is it welcome."

"By *association*?" He pulls back. "A formal way to phrase that, don't you think, considering we were *associating* in the field over there?"

I try to bite back the smirk that starts to curl up the corners of my mouth at his comment. This conversation has been so damn serious that my nervous energy grabs onto his quip, and I fire one right back without thinking. "Associating? I thought we were *clicking*."

Becks's grin spreads wide, lines around his eyes crinkling as it reaches them, and something about the way he angles his head to the side and looks at me with a combination of amusement and adoration warms parts of me that being physical with him doesn't. "Oh City, we were most definitely clicking." He laughs, full and loud, and the sound is so good to hear.

I still have my doubts, my reservations, my fear that if results are not in my favor, I'm dragging him into a bad situation, but for right now, I just want to let the feelings wash over me when I'm with him. To allow myself these moments, the calm before the storm.

And before I can finish rationalizing why I want this man, regardless of all unforeseen circumstances, Becks walks up to me and grabs me without preamble and presses his lips to mine. The kiss is teeming with such a potent combination of emotion that when our tongues meet, I can taste his anger and raw need. His mouth brands mine without apology as he takes and gives us an outlet to explain our feelings without speaking.

Because when kisses like this are involved, speaking is way the fuck overrated.

He eases away from the kiss and pulls me into his arms again, where I welcome the comfort of his body against mine. "I'm sorry for yelling at you, but irrational makes me crazy, and, baby, your line of thinking is nearing that spectrum." He sighs and kisses the top of my head. "We're not finished talking about this yet, but I think it's ridiculous to dwell on something that might not even be an issue, now or in the future. And if there is more to talk about, you will not be hiding it from me." His hands angle my head up and down so that I am forced to nod in agreement. I laugh at him, feeling lighter than I have in days. "*We are*, Haddie. You'd best get used to that."

Those two words hit my ears and ease the weight in my soul a bit, warming me. I mouth the words, *"We are,"* back to him and I catch the quick flash of a smile before his lips meet mine again.

We sink into the kiss, and he pulls back ever so slightly to reach out and pull something from my hair. "You've got leaves in your hair," he says with a smirk.

"It's the new style," I quip.

"Hm." He glances down at the ground around us, littered generously with leaves. His eyes look back up at me with a wicked gleam in them. "Well, I plan on making you look a helluva lot more stylish, then."

Chapter 22

Coffee.

The aroma calls to me like the rev of the engines on race day, jolting me awake so quickly, I grab the pillow beside me to cover my eyes from the brightness in the room. There aren't any curtains at the farmhouse, so hello, sunshine.

Thanks for that, Mom.

I grumble a curse, the morning and me not on a first-name basis today.

Well, it's probably because my eyes closed what feels like only hours ago. First there was the incredible sex with Haddie. Incredible? Who the fuck am I kidding? More like the bar was set to measure all other sex in my life.

The goddamn Macallan.

She's ruining me. Like fucking destroying me for anybody else. Deena? Who?

Then after I got drunk on her body, she curled up next to me and fell asleep. But I couldn't. I lay there for well over an hour, reliving the day: bringing her out here, sex in the field, finding her stitches, the fight that ensued, getting a helluva lot more leaves in her hair as we made up, dinner, and talking by the fire followed by foreplay there, which led to the bar being set.

Despite how incredible the day was, my mind kept drifting back to those test results she hadn't gotten back yet. To the feelings she's stirred up inside me and how the possibilities of what those results could hold might affect her when she's already running scared as it is.

Her body was so warm, so damn tempting, I let it soothe the concern burdening me, and finally fell asleep as dawn bled into the night.

Coffee.

The scent and soft humming I hear pull me from my thoughts. Ones I don't want to have, but damn if Haddie hasn't burrowed under my skin, made me want more than I should. Made me think thoughts that would make my mom jump for joy.

Thoughts veer toward wondering if Colton's newfound one-pussy-is-good-enough-to-commit-to-for-life theory holds any relevance for me.

And that's saying a hell of a lot.

My morning wood is flying full staff, and with the scent of coffee leading my nose and my libido literally pointing the way to the one person who can satisfy both my needs, I push up out of bed and shuffle toward the kitchen.

As I make my way down the hall, I come up with the perfect idea of where to take her on the way home. She needs a day where she doesn't have to worry, preoccupied enough that she doesn't have time to think about the unknown that I know rules her minute to minute.

I'm feeling on top of the world when I round the corner to the kitchen. It's when I see her, though, that I feel like the bottom drops out.

Damn.

Just damn.

She's sitting on the window seat, back against the wall,

knees against her chest, and a cup of coffee in her hands on top of them. Her face is angled toward the vast view of the farm spread before her. The sun streams in the window and lights up the gold of her hair in a halo-type effect. She has on my T-shirt and I'm unsure what else since it drapes down and covers her hips, blocking the view I really want to see. She has a soft smile on her face as she watches Rex outside snap his jaws fruitlessly at the flies buzzing overheard and just out of reach.

There is something about her right now that looks so pure, so fragile, when she is usually anything but, that pulls at me. I blame it on the sunlight at first, convince myself it's the combination of her relaxed and wearing my T-shirt that makes my dick ache. Makes the thought *She looks like an angel* flicker through my groggy mind.

But hell if I'm not staggered by the sight.

I desperately want her to look at me, want to see what her eyes would say, but can't find it in me to break the moment. For her or for me. Because I'm too busy trying to figure out why I feel so fucked-up all of a sudden.

I was a man looking for coffee and maybe some morning dessert of sweet Haddie, and now I'm speechless, and I know there's no turning back for me.

As soon as she shifts in her seat, she sees me, but she's not startled like I'd expect. A slow smile spreads across those perfect lips when her eyes meet mine. From a distance, they look like they're glistening with tears, and for the first time in for-fucking-ever, I can't move. I just stand there and stare at her, speaking only through our visual connection. As much as I need to look away so she can't read what's in my eyes, I can't because I realize it's not the bottom dropping out at all.

Nope. Not in the least.

It's my heart bottoming out as it tumbles and falls.

Well . . . *fuck*.

Shouldn't I be freaked that the woman in front of me just

stole my breath and made me feel different from any way I've ever felt before? Rational thought says we've been seeing each other such a short time that the grapple hook I just felt dig into my heart can't be for real. Besides, the Cupid-and-arrow routine is bullshit.

But *the click*? Now the click is sure as fuck real. And hell if it wasn't just as deafening as a clap of thunder.

I already feel like she's struck me with lightning, so the sound of thunder is par for the course.

"Good morning." Her voice pulls me from my thoughts. "Coffee's ready."

Coffee.

Yes.

That will help clear my head and hopefully loosen my tongue, which is suddenly tied because I fear that this self-revelation will change everything.

"Are you positive?"

She asks me the question with a look of curious caution in her eyes. I can tell that she wants the opportunity I've just laid out before her but fears it all at the same time. And I get the range of emotions, but I also know that giving her the chance to be in control of something will help her, ground her, make her feel less like everything in her life is spiraling out of control.

"Do you trust me?"

She laughs low and rich with a suggestive smirk and a sparkle in her eye. "After what I just let you do to me, you're going to ask me if I trust you?"

Goddamn.

It's only been a few hours, but her comment has visuals of our prebreakfast sexcapade coming back in full HD color. I don't think I'll ever be able to eat another Thanksgiving dinner on that kitchen table without thinking of eating sweet Haddie out. Facedown, ass up, hands ordered to stay gripped on the edge or I'd stop the flick of my tongue on her clit. Her body writhing, her mouth moaning, and that sweeter-than-sin taste of hers hitting my tongue as she bucked beneath my grip on her hips as she came with a scream of my name.

And then she said a single word, *More.*

I meet her eyes as we exit the truck, and I know she's thinking the same thing right now. How I pulled her to the edge of the table, then slammed into that tight, pulsing pussy of hers as she was still riding out her orgasm. And holy fucking hell. *Just incredible.* The feel of her, skin on skin, is just something I don't think I can ever contemplate doing without now.

My dick hardens at the thought again, how taking my time never crossed my mind because I was only thinking about the endgame this time around, knowing she'd already got hers. The visual of pounding into her from behind hits me again, wetting my thumb and pushing it against her tight rim of resisting muscles. How she squirmed beneath my touch, her mouth crying out, "Yes. God, yes, Becks. Do it. I'll come." Her words the only consent I needed to push my thumb into her perfect fucking ass and mimic the movement of my dick in her pussy.

I close my eyes behind my sunglasses for a second, reliving the sound of her scream as she came so hard, her legs gave out, her every muscle tightening around my thumb and cock until I couldn't hold back any longer and lost myself to her as well.

My God. Just when I thought she couldn't top the night before, she went and raised the bar again.

If it gets much higher, I'm going to wish I was a damn pole-vaulter.

"Becks?"

Her voice pulls me from the pistons trying to spark in my mind because hell if she's not the only fuel I need to fire up my engine right now.

"Hmm." The hum deep in my throat makes clear to her

just what I'm thinking about. "You bring up this morning, and I might just think I need to do it again."

"Is that a promise?" she asks with a flash of a wicked grin as she saunters to the back of my truck, where the tailgate is down. She quirks an eyebrow at me as she bends over and leans her chest on it, her body bent at the waist, her ass sticking out, tempting me like no fucking tomorrow.

"Christ, baby, I don't think you want to play with this fire." I walk slowly toward her, wanting to take what she's offering, except I know just around the corner are a few of the crew, waiting for us to get started.

She wiggles her ass at me as I come up behind her and trail a finger up and down the seam of her jeans shorts. I hear her suck in her breath, see her hips still before she presses backward into my hand. I withdraw my touch and step back—I'd take her right here, right now, but I'm not really ready to let any of the guys see her like this, give them real-life visuals to go along with the thoughts I know they're going to be thinking when they meet her face-to-face.

She turns around when I step back, and angles her head at me. "You know what they say about playing with fire, right?" She leans into me and taunts my lips with hers. The fucking sugar to try to sweeten me up.

Damn tease.

"You get burned?" I answer, eyebrows raised, trying to figure out where she's headed with this because I sure as hell know this isn't the answer she's looking for. My answer's typical and Haddie's is anything but typical.

"Hmm." She hums against my lips. "Yes, but that just means you need to get your hose wet to put out the flame." She brushes her body up against mine again, and hell, if she does that one more time, this whole idea at the track is going to get thrown out the damn window so I can go play firefighter.

Because this hose sure as fuck is getting wet again.

"I like the sound of that," I murmur before I slip my

tongue between her teasing lips, a three-alarm fire already lit within.

"Hey, Daniels! We doing this, or you going to pussyfoot around all day, wasting our time?" Smitty calls to my back, his voice echoing off the concrete walls of the infield near pit row.

Seriously? He always has the worst damn timing.

I raise my hand in the air, middle finger brandishing my hello wave to him. His laugh carries over to where we stand. "Maybe later, dear, but right now we've got the car primed and prepped, so get your ass over here."

"Coming," I yell back to him, my eyes locked on Haddie's.

"Promise," she whispers to me with an impish gleam in her eyes and a little wiggle of her body so that her tits rub against me one last time before she steps back.

I can't help but grin even wider because how fucking lucky am I to be standing here with a woman who would make a quip like that? Twisting an innocent response into a dirty thought. Talk about one hell of a turn-on.

And hell if I'm one to break a promise.

Or a rule.

We hold each other's gaze a moment longer, and I love seeing her eyes full of feistiness when so much of the time we've spent together they've been conflicted, guarded, sad. I don't know what it's going to take, but I want to keep that look there permanently.

"No worries there, sweet Haddie," I tell her as we turn hand in hand and head toward the pits. "I'll make that fire of yours rage and then use my hose to put it out in a blaze of glory. It would be my pleasure."

Little does she know I'm talking about a helluva lot more than just sex.

Chapter 23

I can't keep myself from smiling, and it feels normal for the first time in forever. I don't know how Becks knew his idea would help, but somehow I feel revived again.

Who would have thought strapping on a helmet, getting behind the wheel of an old stock car, and zooming around the track would be so invigorating? And it wasn't just the adrenaline that refreshed me. It was the ability to control my destiny.

I mean I know I was going only a quarter of the speed Colton goes when he flies around the track, but I didn't care. The notion that how fast I go, if I hit the wall or not, I could stay out there all day long if I wanted to, except for stopping for gas, let me feel like I was in control of my own life.

And the moment my mind started to wander, I'd push the gas pedal a little harder, go a little faster so that I had to concentrate on living and not on dying.

What a concept.

Becks walks me up the sidewalk to the front door, his hand in mine, and I realize I'm not ready to let him go just yet. I mean, this morning when he found me looking out the window, the tears in my eyes were from a potent mixture of the fear of tomorrows mixed with the comforting knowledge that I am trying to let him in . . . for today at least. I had one foot planted firmly and one foot out the door, waiting for the first sign it was time to bail.

And now? Now I feel like one foot is still firmly rooted while the other is in the air, suspended, as my heart urges me to plant it down permanently beside its partner.

And all in a span of forty-eight hours.

What is he doing to me?

If I didn't know any better, I'd say I'm cockstruck by him, but that's just not possible. Hell yes, his bedroom prowess is fine as fuck, but there's something more here—and as much as it scares me, it's also really alluring. It holds promise for possibilities that just might be on the horizon.

But what the hell do I know? Tomorrow I could be hit by a Mack Truck, as Rylee so nicely suggested.

Or be diagnosed with cancer.

I shrug the thought away. It has no place in the here and now after the incredible past thirty-some-odd hours with Becks.

Oh my God. I actually know the hours, have figured them out subconsciously. I really am cockstruck. *Fuck me.* Hmm— yes, please, but I force myself to pull my mind from its comfortable place in the gutter and focus on how this just isn't possible.

As much as I like my alphas, I always make sure that the sex is so stellar that even though they think they are in control, I can reduce them to whimpers if I hold out on sex to get what I want. And now look at me. Standing here next to Beckett Daniels—Mr. Slow and Steady—and I'm cockstruck, dick-whipped, legs-spread-wide-served-up-on-a-platter, whatever way you want to say it.

Did the fat lady sing?

And before I can scour the neighborhood to see where she's hiding, Becks tugs on my hand and pulls me into him as we near the front door. I lean against the solidity of his chest as he wraps his arms around me. Then I close my eyes and absorb the comfort of his nearness because we are light-years away from where we were yesterday morning when we were in this exact same position bristling with sexual tension.

The funny thing is that we've all but devoured each other, and yet I feel that want and need ten times stronger now.

He presses a kiss to the top of my head as we hold each other tight. "Thanks for going with me to the farmhouse." The timbre of his words vibrates from his lips on the crown of my head down through my chest pressed against his, leaving me to feel like he's a part of me somehow.

"For going?" I tease. "I believe I wasn't given an option since you were so intent on calling my bluff."

"Hmm . . . but it was so much fun mounting that bluff and coming down off of it, now, wasn't it?"

My body reacts viscerally to his words, a contented sigh on my lips. He can prove it to me right now—once again—if he wants to because hell if my body pressed up against his isn't already spiraling into the oblivious free fall of desire that only he holds the parachute to.

"Wanna come in?"

He laughs, his hand running up and down the length of my spine. "As much as I'd love to, I can't."

Unexpectedly I feel rejected, as if I haven't gotten my fill of him yet. "You have something better to do than me?" I pull back from him, my lips in full pout as I look up at him and bat my lashes.

"Not in the least." He smiles softly and leans forward to press a soft sigh of a kiss against them. "You're cute when you pout, but coming in would break my rules, and you know how much I hate to do that."

Him and his frickin' rules. "Rules? Which rules would those be?" *Tell me, Becks, so I can break them.*

His mouth widens into a full blown megawatt grin as he shakes his head. "Well, it would break two of them . . . the pinkie-toe rule and the first-date rule."

"Come again?"

"Oh, you can guarantee that," he replies before I realize what I've said. I just roll my eyes at him.

"The pinkie-toe rule?" I reiterate.

"Yeah, if I come in, I'm going to want to bang you on every piece of furniture in your house just like you do your pinkie toe. It's an inevitable thing that's just going to happen." He raises his eyebrows as I laugh at him. "I don't want to do that because, one, by the looks of the bike in the driveway your way-too-present and way-too-male roommate is home. As much as I'd love him to hear you screaming my name, I don't want to share a single part of you with him, and even if it's by sound . . . it's not going to happen. I don't share. *Anything*."

Although I'm laughing at his ridiculous pinkie-toe rule, the possessive tone of the rest of his words and the look in his eyes—amused dominance—are quite a turn-on.

"And, two," he continues as I study him, "breaking rule number one would lead to breaking rule number two, no sleeping together on the first date."

"First date?" I sputter, my head shaking back and forth as I try to understand him.

"Yes. First time I've come to your house and picked you up and taken you somewhere." He shrugs. "Call me old-fashioned, but *first date*."

I snort out a laugh and then try to stifle it. "Well, it seems you already broke that rule—yesterday, last night, this morning. Just in case you've forgotten, and then if you did, I'd be more than insulted." I lean in and whisper, "We've already slept together."

"Oh, I assure you I didn't forget, but this is the first time I get to walk you to the front door and kiss you good night. That's an important first, and I'm not going to overshadow the importance of that kiss because you're so busy thinking about how hard I'm going to fuck you up against the front door once we get inside."

I have a hard time swallowing after that statement. He's telling me he's not going to come in, and then he says something like that? "Wall sex, huh?" I try to play off the allure of the idea.

He fights the smile on his lips and almost wins, but his eyes give away his burgeoning desire. "Yep. Wall sex is highly underrated," he says matter-of-factly as he takes a step toward me. I move away only to realize my back is against said front door.

"Why's that?" I breathe out, his proximity and the topic of conversation beginning to make my heart quicken.

He steps in again so that my body is pressed against his with nowhere to retreat. "Because," he says, bringing his hands up to frame my face so that I have no option but to look at those mesmerizing eyes of his, "when you're pushed against the door with your legs wrapped around my hips, your body weight makes it so that you take me as deep as you possibly can." He makes a humming sound of appreciation in his throat that mimics how I feel right now, desperate for the feeling he just described. My lips part to beg him, but I keep my dignity—for how much longer, I'm not sure.

With his eyes fastened to mine, he runs his hands down my shoulders, along my rib cage and stops right at my hips so his fingers can grip me there. My breath hitches as I wait for him to lift me up and press me against the door, oblivious to the fact that we are outside and that's not going to happen.

His fingers grip a bit tighter as he lowers his face oh so slowly to mine. That mouth of his, which I want to do so many things to me, brushes gently against my lips when he pins me to the door. And rather than the desperation I feel, Becks keeps the kiss so tender, so reverent that we sink into it so gently, I become lost in him.

He lifts me gently, my legs wrapping around his waist instinctively, but our lips never leave each other's, and the eroticism of our connection is not lost on me. Our bodies fit together, his erection against the V of my thighs almost as perfect a fit as our lips.

Even as my desire swelters to unfathomable heights, the kiss remains slow, measured, meaningful, with our fingers tangling in each other's hair. It softly ends, a pleading protest falling from my now swollen lips as he pulls back to look in my eyes.

"Good night kisses are my favorite," he murmurs, and damn, I can see why he favors them, especially when they're like that. Knock the breath from your lungs, turn your knees to jelly, and overwhelm your mind so thoroughly, you can't think a straight thought. His hands are back on my hips as he holds me, lowering me to the ground, my mind so shaken that I momentarily forget about my suspended state.

He angles his head, his eyes swimming with so many things that I'm too scared to look too closely. "Good night, City."

He takes a step back, and I want to cry in protest, but all I utter is " 'Night." He looks at me for a beat longer, with a ghost of a smile before he turns and starts to walk down the path.

"Hey," I call to him, my scattered wits slowly returning now that there is distance between our bodies. He turns and narrows his brows at me. "Do you have a three-day rule too?"

"Three days? You'll just have to wait and see now, won't you?" A lopsided smirk curls up his lips. "I never give away my secrets." He goes to turn to walk away but stops and faces me. "Hey, Montgomery? The question you should be asking me is if the three-day rule I have is for a phone call or for the wall sex."

And with that, he grants me a lightning-quick grin before turning and walking away, his laugh floating over to where I stand, thighs clenched and head shaking as he leaves me once again, a woman already wanting more.

Damn you, Beckett Daniels.

I watch him pull out of the driveway, knowing the ache in my chest is only going to get worse as I fall farther and farther down the rabbit hole.

When his car is gone from sight, I open the front door, shut it, and then sag against it in a state of complete exhaustion that feels oh so good. And then I laugh to myself when I realize this very position is exactly where I hope Becks plans to meet me three days from now.

Wall sex.

Damn.

Chapter 24

throw my purse on the counter and rest my hip against it, thoroughly exhausted. I've yet to recover the sleep I lost from my night spent with Becks out in Ojai or the late-night-into-early-morning phone calls we've had the past few days. More time spent getting to know each other. Not that I minded because not sleeping with Becks is such a damn good way to lose sleep. Besides, I've been busy humoring him and abiding by his ludicrous and completely back-assward rules. But as ridiculous as they are, they are actually kind of sweet too.

And since we've been talking every night, obviously the three-day rule did not apply to phone calls. I can only hope it means tonight I get the push-up-against-the-door wall sex he'd hinted at.

Like the sooner, the better.

Becks has built the anticipation so handily that waiting to get up to my bedroom is not an option.

I grab a drink and head out to the backyard per my usual end-of-day routine, the last rays of the sun calling to me before the night claims them for itself. I sit down in my favored chaise and bring my lemonade up to my lips. My thoughts drift to my time with Maddie this afternoon and how she was so cheerful and genuinely happy and how my heart felt so much better leaving her this time.

I know the grief will always be there for her, a constant, but at the same time, I'm starting to see pieces of the little girl she was a year ago before this nightmare we're never going to wake from happened. And those glimpses tell me there's the possibility of so many more just around the corner.

I process a couple random thoughts about work and the last Scandalous party coming up in the next few days. I'm more than satisfied with my job for them and know the message I received earlier this morning about how the higher-ups were raving about the job I've been doing boosted my confidence at the possibility of landing them as a client going into this last event.

And then of course my mind wanders to Becks. I don't even try to fight the smile that graces my lips at the thought of him and everything he's come to mean to me in such a short amount of time. I mean, if someone would have told me that I'd be falling in love with a man this quickly, I'd have told them they were crazy. But I rationalize and justify that we've been friends for more than a year so the transition to *falling for each other* is not as drastic as it seems.

And hell it feels so damn good. Butterflies in the stomach when my phone rings, staying up all hours of the night on the phone, talking about anything and nothing, just mesmerized by each other's voices. It's early yet, I know, and as good as it feels, I'm trying to pace myself, trying to take stock of everything because the fear is still there, still clawing at my psyche. Making its presence known with each thought, with every action so that I second-guess myself, but I'm trying desperately hard to ignore it. Push it down. Keep it at bay.

I close my eyes and lift my face to the sun, settling into the feeling when my phone rings beside me. I fumble for it, keeping my eyes closed, expecting it to be Becks since it's getting close to his quitting time, and I'm quietly hoping I get to see him tonight. It's been a few days and that just feels like forever right now when you're in that getting-to-know-you stage.

"Hello?" The smile is on my face, my ears anticipating the timbre and cadence of his voice, which calls to me on so many levels.

"Ms. Montgomery, please."

The disembodied monotone of the voice shocks me. "This is she," I respond, half of me wanting to look at the screen and see who is calling and the other half that has my anxiety ratcheting tells me I'll find out soon enough. But I already know.

"Hi, Ms. Montgomery. This is Dr. Blakely. How are you doing today?"

The forced cheer in her voice causes the hair on my arms to stand on end. "That depends on what you're going to tell me." My voice is a mere whisper over the line.

"Well, I'd like you to come in and have a chat with me."

The saliva leaves my mouth, and my heart thunders in my ears. I'd like to think the sound prevents me from hearing properly, but I know better than that. I know that good news is given over the phone when test results are all clear, and meetings are scheduled when the results are bad. And regardless of how pleasant Dr. Blakely's tone is, I can hear it in her voice, can hear the same quality to it as when she spoke to Lexi about her prognosis before shipping her off to the reconstruction specialist and the oncologist.

"Can't you just tell me over the phone?" I ask, hoping against hope.

"I think it would be best if you came in so we could talk."

And I know. Right now I know, but I'm still reaching.

"I can come in whenever it fits your schedule," I tell her, thinking if she puts if off a week or two, I just might be wrong, that the results are nothing to worry about. I'm playing mind games with myself, I know, but I don't care.

"How about tomorrow afternoon? I have some colleagues stopping by in the morning to meet with me in regard to your file, and so I'd like to speak with you after, if that's okay? Say three o'clock?"

And the mind games are useless now. *Tomorrow* screams urgent. *Tomorrow* tells me cancer.

Tomorrow says *Fuck you*, Haddie.

I force a swallow down my throat, working to find the words I need to respond. "Okay." I'm surprised she hears me, my voice is barely audible. I drop the phone and sit there, staring at the sky.

I have cancer. She may not have said the word, but she didn't have to.

My glass slips from my hand and falls to the ground. I watch the lemonade spill onto the grass and then slowly seep into the earth. Disappear. Gone forever.

Ring around a rosie.

I wonder if it's cold down there—beneath the surface of the dirt—when they bury your body.

A pocket full of posies.

I fixate on the thought. Wonder if Lexi is cold.

Ashes, ashes, we all fall down.

I close my eyes, unwilling to accept and not wanting to believe that fate has come knocking on my door. So I shut down, welcome the numbness, the disengagement I know is happening from my complete lack of tears and my inability to play the mind games needed to help me deal with the phone call.

I'll cope tomorrow. Right now I just want to shut the world out.

Time passes. I hear car doors slam as neighbors come home from work. I hear mothers calling their kids inside for dinner. The night fades and eats up any sign of light until it's completely smothered. Street lights flicker to life.

And yet I sit here. Not wanting to move. Not caring if I

ever do because that means tomorrow is closer, and I don't want tomorrow to come.

My phone rings and alerts me to texts but it sits on the table where I dropped it, and I don't have enough energy to pick it up, even if I wanted to. Which I don't.

I'm so cold, despite the warm night air. My soul is chilled, and my thoughts are frozen, obsessed with replaying the doctor's words over and over in my head.

"Hey." The voice from behind me startles me, despite my having known somehow he would find me. I squeeze my eyes shut, expecting the onslaught of emotion to come, to overwhelm, to break me down, and yet nothing does. Abso-fucking-lutely nothing. Feelings, emotions, reactions are so dull, so nonexistent, I should be scared, but I'm not. I wait for the butterflies, for the ache in my heart and the tingle between my thighs at the voice that riles them up, but they're not there.

Because I feel nothing.

"Your car was in the driveway. I kept calling your cell, and you didn't answer, but I heard it ringing back here, so I came in through the gate," he explains, his voice becoming louder as he nears me.

I look straight ahead and murmur incoherently at him as his footsteps continue to grow closer. Once his body is be-side mine, it takes everything I have to scrape together some semblance of a smile and force my head to angle up to meet his. "Hey."

He sees it immediately. I know he can see the emotions warring within me, but he recovers quickly, eyebrows drawn together as he studies me. "Everything okay?" he asks as he lowers himself to the chaise, his hip pushing my legs over so he has room.

Am I okay? Ha. I want to laugh at the question. "Hmm," I say in response.

He reaches out and cups the side of my face, his thumb

rubbing over my cheek in that way that usually makes me melt, but I remain unresponsive in every way. "Everything okay with Maddie?" I nod my head, knowing he's searching for a reason for my silence. "Did the doctor call? Any news?"

I can hear the concern tingeing the edges of the question, and it's truth-or-dare time for me: lie to protect him or tell him the truth and test the promises he made at the farm. I teeter on that fine edge of my moral compass, but then my split-second decision is one I think I made the moment I received the call.

"No, not yet. She called to tell me something's held up at the lab, but in relooking at my scans, she's not too worried." The lies roll off my tongue just as easily as the relief they cause makes his posture sag.

I'm going to hell. I just lied to Becks. I'm going to hell, and I deserve it. Every damn lick of fire against my flesh, I deserve.

Then the panic hits me. I shift to place my hands under my thighs so that he can't see them tremor with the adrenaline coursing through my system. My mind spins in an eddy of fucked-up thoughts, and as each one whips out of the whirlpool and hits my conscience, I feel worse with each passing second.

I should confess, make things right. I know I should, but the words don't come off my tongue because images of Lexi and Danny and Maddie hop on the eddy, collide with every truth I should reveal, and knock them down.

"Haddie?" I'm brought back to the present when Becks says my name again, and I try to focus on him through the tears that don't even well, but that burn like hell. Hmpf, like hell—that's rather fitting and deserving.

"I . . ." I don't know where to go with this conversation, which path to take to gain some distance so I can process everything without the pressure of what it will do to everyone else. I think of the heavy knowledge so apparent in

Lexi's lively eyes. Her awareness of what she was leaving behind for us to deal with.

I have three options now: Hurt him so badly that I push him away and gain some distance, fess up to the lie and ask for some space, or beg him to make me feel to see if it's even possible or if I'm already dead inside.

I stare at him, his blue eyes radiating concern as he grants me patience to figure out the words I need to say. And I'm not ready to talk yet.

I reach out without thought and pull his mouth to mine, desperation emanating off me, causing it to crash into him and take hold. If I'm going to Hell, I might as well get a piece of Heaven first. And fuck yes, this makes me the most selfish woman on the face of the earth, but I can't make a decision yet, can't voice my feelings yet, so I give into the greed and take.

Within seconds of our mouths clashing together, between a shocked gasp from Becks and his rush to take what I'm offering, I already have my hands on his zipper and am pulling his thickening cock from his trousers.

"Had—what—wait—are—"

"Shh. No talking, just fucking, okay? It's day three." I retrieve the excuse, hoping he'll just go with it and not question me any further.

I feel the hesitancy in his lips, his mind trying to scramble and catch up to how he's already hard and ready in my hand. Our mouths remain savage on each other's, teeth scrape, tug, and I suck on his tongue, earning me a strangled groan that lets me know he's ready for what I'm striving for: complete mental obliteration.

I shift my positioning and slide off the chaise, leaning over not to break the connection. His hands meet mine as we both work at the buttons on my shorts, shoving them with my panties down to the ground so that I can step out of them. Now free of his undressing job, his hand finds its way back between my thighs, parting my folds, testing my readiness, but I dance backward from the V of his thighs before he can find his purchase.

I don't deserve this consideration from him, don't deserve anything from him since I'm giving him nothing in return. I turn abruptly around so that I straddle his legs where he sits on the edge of the lounger, my back to his front. I can't bring myself to watch him as I do this—use him—and he sure as hell doesn't need to see the tears that threaten to fill my eyes with each passing second.

I reach down between my legs, and Becks sucks in a breath as I grip his erection in my hand and position it at my entrance. I rub the crest back and forth a couple times over my seam to wet it and then, without giving him a moment to ready himself, slam my hips down hard and fast, sheathing him in one slick movement.

His groan fills the night air around us, our bodies shrouded from the view of neighbors by the night sky and overhanging tree branches. I don't even give him a moment to sink into the sensation before I am on the move. I'm not fully ready for him, so my muscles stretch and skin burns at the friction as my body catches up to my running thoughts and urges.

But that makes me *feel*. It means I'm not completely numb. As fucked-up as it is, I welcome the pain as a punishment for the lie and for what I ultimately know I'm going to do.

I slide up and down Becks's cock at a fervent pace, never giving him a moment to think or a chance to resist. I need to control this right now, him right now, because I can't control anything else, and that fear is eating me alive right alongside the guilt. So I own him, own the moment, all the while hating myself.

I bring him to his orgasm at a rapid speed, the friction and vigor helping him light the fuse for his detonation. He comes with such violence, I can hear it in his cry, feel it in the muscles of his thighs locking tight and how his fingers dig into my hips.

"Holy shit," he says when he's finally caught his breath. He wraps his arms around me and presses his forehead against the line of my spine as he comes down from his orgasmic haze. "What in the hell was that?" His tone is one of shocked satisfaction, and I bite my lower lip to hold back the sob that catches in my throat.

"I think you should go now." The evenness to my tone scares me. I feel his body jolt from my words. His chest, which was heaving against my back, stills, and the evidence from our union starts to seep out of me.

"What?"

I give him credit for remaining calm but almost wish he'd be angry because that's easier to hold on to, to feed off of.

"You mind telling me what the fuck this is all about?"

I rise from his lap and collect my shorts and panties from the ground where they sit beside my empty lemonade glass. I use my underwear to clean myself up and then toss them to him to use without meeting his eyes. I notice them land on the chaise beside him without him so much as reaching for them.

"Suit yourself," I mutter as I pull my shorts up, my motions on autopilot once again. "You can see yourself out," I say as I start walking toward the house.

Within a flash, I'm being spun around to face the wrath of Becks. He tries to talk, but every word gets overlapped by the one before it as confusion wins the war over his emotions. "I'm lost here," he finally gets out, his expression matching his words. "Do you mind telling me what the fuck is going on here? I'm a patient man, but hell if you're not testing that right now with whatever game you're playing."

Our eyes remain locked, except the darkness around us allows me to keep the secrets hidden so that he can't see the truths I'm protecting. "No game, Becks." I shake my head and clear my throat to try to gain some conviction in my tone to reinforce the mistruth. "I think we're moving way too fast, and I don't really need this added stress in my life right now."

"Come again?" His voice rises as he takes a step closer, jaw tensing and head shaking. "Did you not just ride me? That sure as hell isn't the action of a woman trying to distance herself."

"Think of it as a parting gift." I instantly regret the flippant comment when I see him wince in reaction. The escalator to hell is only getting faster right now as I pile lie upon lie, hurt upon hurt.

"A parting gift?" He emits a sliver of a laugh laced with derision. "I'm trying really hard right now to make sense of this, how we went from orgasm to mindfuck, and I'm drawing a blank." I clench my fists to combat the hurt in his eyes piercing my heart. "Did I do something wrong? Is there something you're not telling me? Did Dante finally wear you down? What?"

And with that comment, Becks unknowingly opens the gates of Hell for me to walk through. I grab on and run with it, own it as if it were the truth. Anything to push him away right now, give me time to think. It's so much easier to hurt him this way than it would be with all of the crap that cancer brings with it.

He asked me for a day at the farm. One day just to let him show me how good we could be together. I gave him that day and then some. But now I can't give him anymore with all of this hanging over my head. God, yes, it has been so good, but he doesn't deserve to deal with this disease. Hell, I don't deserve to. It's just so much easier to cut ties now than to drag him behind me with ropes of obligation binding us together.

"Yes." My voice breaks with the single word. I clear my throat. "Yes, Dante and I had a heart-to-heart earlier today. We're going to work things out. You know he's more my type than you are, so it shouldn't surprise you that I choose him."

The expression on Becks's face reflects a man who's gone nine rounds in the ring as my words punch him. I can see him try to process what I've just said, see him try to acknowledge it, but the acceptance never comes.

Our eyes don't waver from each other's as he steps forward and raises both hands to frame my face so that I'm unable to look away. "I don't know what the hell is going on, Montgomery. I have no fucking clue. You want space? Fine, I'll give you space, but don't for one second think I'm buying the fact that you choose that douche bag over me." He exhales a broken breath as he figures out the rest of what he wants to say. My heart thunders in my ears, and my own breath is just as uneven as his but for the opposite reason. "I'm going to leave right now. I'm going to walk out that door and give you some time to figure out whatever the shit is in your head, but I don't want it mistaken for a single second that I'm walking away from you." He squeezes his eyes shut momentarily before opening them back up and the clarity in them has me feeling like he's seeing into my soul. "I don't walk away from the people I love without a fight, and damn it to hell, Haddie Montgomery, you'd better prepare for that fight because I'm in love with you."

My mouth drops open from his unexpected confession, and I can't even try to wrap my head around it because Becks's lips are on mine, clearly driven by the emotion of his statement. It's a short but holy-mother-of-hell kiss that leaves me breathless when he drags his mouth from mine.

And when we separate, he doesn't meet my eyes. He steps back and turns on his heel without another word, and walks into the house, slamming the front door behind him, the sound so loud, I hear it where I remain rooted in disbelieving shock.

The chills come, my body trembles with the truth just laid at my feet, and my heart tears in two from hurting him and letting him walk away without making a concerted effort to fight for him.

I know I have a bigger fight ahead of me. A fight I don't want to drag someone else through.

Holy fuck.

He loves me. The damn wildflower was right after all.

I'm not sure how long I sit out in the cocooning darkness and silence of the night, using the still to quiet the self-inflicted riot of emotions in my head before I shove myself up and move inside. I go through the motions of washing my glass, straightening up. I'm bending over, putting a bowl away in the lower cabinets when Dante's voice startles me.

"Fuck me, Haddie. You can't tempt a man like this and expect him to walk away without a taste. Or a fight."

I scramble to stand up and shut the cabinet, my mind registering Dante's words but thinking that Becks could be saying them just as easily to me. I flash my eyes up to find him leaning against the wall, his shirt off, a beer in one hand, and irritated disgust evident in his expression. The comebacks are firing through my brain, but I hold them back, trying to keep from fueling the temper I know he has when he drinks.

And a drunk Dante is an unpredictable Dante. This I know from experience, so I remain silent.

"So nice of you to finally come inside after your little *fuck* in the backyard," he says, sarcasm dripping from his slurred words. "It seems to me you're really walking on the wild side these days, babe."

"Dante." I nod my head, my voice even, and stand to full height when I finally speak to him.

"Dante," he mimics me with a laugh that's anything but warm. "Really, babe? Gonna be all frigid with me when an hour ago you were being fucked in the backyard by *that guy*?" He walks toward me in an unsteady swagger, judgment in his eyes. "What happened to the wild child I used to know? The 'throw caution to the wind, willing to screw

anytime and anywhere' girl I dated? The one I matched dare for dare?" He stops, takes a sip, and chuckles. "You're too good to settle, Haddie. A three-minute fuck in the backyard with that asshole tells me you are most definitely settling."

"Fuck you." The words are out of my mouth without a thought. How dare he come at me, telling me I'm settling when all I can think about is Becks: what I just did to him, how I hurt him, and the confession he left me with?

... you'd better prepare for that fight because I'm in love with you ...

The pain is sharp and lingering, and then it registers that Dante was here when Becks and I were outside.

I was so wrapped up in everything that I never even thought about him coming home. All I could think about was pushing it all away, losing myself, and not once did I think about Dante. Being home. Having a spectator.

Fuck a duck.

My eyes flash up to his, and he sees that I realize I had an audience when I was outside. "Yep." He nods his head. "I came home in the middle of the action. Sorry, but no man is going to pass up watching a porno going on in his backyard." He takes a step closer to me as my anger bristles from the invasion of my privacy.

Yes, I had sex outside, but it was in my backyard, and the only line of sight we were in was from my own house. If it was in any other capacity, I might actually be turned on from the idea of being watched, but Dante's disdainful approach is making me ill at ease. I curse myself for my carelessness.

"Don't worry. I didn't watch for long. Just enough to remind me how fucking hot you are ..." My teeth grit when he chuckles again. "Fuck, babe, you gave me a stellar visual. Do you have any clue how fucking hard that made me? A man's gotta get off, and, God," he groans as his free hand cups his crotch and adjusts himself, "I could really use the help since you're standing there like a goddamn vacant motel room waiting to get occupied."

Is he fucking serious? I may be overwhelmed with everything, but I'm not stupid enough to fall for this. And as much as I hate his comment, I also welcome the fire it sparks inside of me.

Hell if I'm not looking for a good fight right now. Anything to occupy my mind and push away everything from the day.

Bring it on.

"Sorry, but this isn't the Sleazy 8 Motel you're used to. I don't rent my room by the hour."

"Oh, now, there you go, insulting me when you know damn fucking well that I last much more than an hour when I'm renting your room out." He winks at me with a lopsided grin as he enters the kitchen and pulls another beer from the refrigerator. The hiss of the top coming off fills the silence between us.

"No vacancy. Not now. Not ever." I quirk an eyebrow at him, knowing damn well our playful banter has the possibility of turning ugly real quick when it comes to Dante.

His grin is slow and arrogant, eyebrows raised, eyes taunting me. "Mm-mm-mm. We'll just have to see about that," he says, taking another step closer and concentrating on what to say next. "He doesn't deserve you, Had. He isn't what you need. Look how fast he bailed after he fucked you . . . or I should say, you fucked him. Man, you ride a mean cock." He winks at me as he reaches down to adjust himself, and I watch him, study him, to try to see if he's joking here or if asshole-I've-been-drinking Dante is about to make an appearance.

He lifts his beer to his lips and downs it in one long swallow, all the while his eyes remain on me. He sets the bottle down with force, the sound echoing through the room, before he closes the final space between us so that he's standing well inside my personal space.

Warning bells ring softly in the back of my head, but I shake them off. I've been here with Dante before, know I can handle him. Nothing a swift knee to the crotch to prove a point can't fix since he's most likely drunk enough that his reflexes are delayed.

"Well, I'm glad I could provide this evening's entertainment for you," I say, trying to defuse the situation. And then I say to myself, "Fuck it." He most definitely was an asshole for watching us, for taunting me over it. "It's interesting, though, that you're so full of criticism, and yet you hid inside, instead of coming out and proving just how much better you are than Becks. You tell me I'm not the same girl you used to know, but I'm thinking you're not the same guy, either." I love watching the irritation settle over his features as he tries not to react to my goading. "It's called growing up, in case you haven't reached that phase yet."

I take a step to the right, but his hand flashes out and grips my upper arm. He steps into me, his alcohol-laced breath hitting the side of my cheek as I stare straight ahead instead of turning my head to meet his eyes.

"You have no business being with him." He grates the words out.

"Well, here's where you realize that I don't give a flying fuck what you think. It's none of your goddamn business how I live my life and what I'm doing. You lost that right when you walked out, leaving me high and dry. I thought we'd already established this fact, no?"

"It's not my business, but it's everyone else's in the neighborhood's who can hear you making him come in your backyard? C'mon, Had, I deserve better than that." He presses his body up against mine, but unlike with Becks, I feel absolutely nothing.

"Let go." I snap the words out, liking the predicament less and less by the moment. I try to shrug out of his grasp and find myself pushed against the wall with some force.

"Uh-uh," he grunts from the motion, his face closing in

on mine again until his mouth is at my ear and his body is flanking mine. "Since you seem to be handing it out like it's free, I might as well get my piece of your pie."

Warning bells sound louder now, and I'm trying hard to keep the panic from reaching my eyes. But I've got my wits about me enough to know that I'm alone in my house with a man who can clearly overpower me, so as much as I want to make my move right now, I need to make sure I time it perfectly. The unease I feel tickling at the base of my neck tells me I might only get one shot at this.

"Have another beer and keep dreaming and it might happen in like . . . hmm . . . *never*." I laugh at the words, trying to portray confidence that I don't really have. I ignore his last comment, not wanting to get into any discussion about what he wants from me with our bodies pressed against each other's.

"Oh, sweet Haddie," he murmurs, causing my breath to hitch at Becks's pet name for me. "What? It's okay for him to call you that but not me?" He reaches up to trail a finger down my cheek. I fight the shiver of revulsion that courses through me from his unwanted and intrinsically intimate touch. "C'mon . . . let's quit dancing around this—you leading me on, turning me on, kissing me, then pushing me away. I mean, shit, I've always appreciated a chick that's hard to get, but it's not like I haven't had you before, right? So why the game, babe? Because I'm done playing it and ready to take what I came here for."

His comment confuses me, until the myriad feelings inside me collide with one another, until they vaguely start to make sense to me. Startled, I drop my head back and meet his eyes for the first time when the realization hits me. Am I that fucking dumb? Have I been so preoccupied with Becks and then the test and the biopsy results that I didn't see it all along? And then add to that that the few times Dante and I kissed I was unknowingly fanning the flames of his reason for coming back here: to get back together with me.

If he had shown up like this months ago, I probably would have brushed his mistakes under the rug and given him a second chance. But now—now there's Becks. And whatever it is we are, I know it feels like it has the potential to be a hell of a lot stronger than what Dante and I were.

The sound of Dante sucking in his breath pulls me back to the present, where the expectant look on his face tells me he's dead serious.

There will be no taking of anything from me unless it's my fist in his face.

"Dante, I think it's time for you to leave." My pulse begins to pound in my ears now as he stares at me, jaw clenched, eyes boring into mine, and the muscles of his shoulders and neck rigid with tension. I watch indecision flicker through them as I try to keep my breath even and body language nondefensive.

"Just like that, huh?" The derision lacing his voice is almost tangible. "I think it's only fair that I get a fighting chance. You've fucked him. Now, you'll fuck me, and then you can make an educated decision as to who makes you come harder. Simple as that."

I struggle with the right words to tell him he's high as a kite if he thinks I'm having sex with him. Even if I'd wanted to, the oh so romantic way he just *informed* me I was going to fuck him would have had me locking down my crotch like a bank vault.

"You've got another think coming if you think that fancy line's going to work on me, Teller." I try to keep my warning light, joking, but I let him know I'm not game with his plan.

He laughs low and soft again, and there's just enough edge to it that my throat constricts as I try to swallow. "I think you misunderstand me. I'm not asking you to fuck me. I'm telling you you're going to. No one turns me down, least of all you. . . ." His voice trails off as he digs his fingers a bit tighter on my arms and leans in so his lips brush over my ear. My nerves are invigorated by his words, my eyes flickering over the room, looking at the dish on the table a few feet from me where my cell sits, beside a vase and my keys. "I've been more than patient as you've led me on, teased me, taunted me, all the while getting off with him. Well, now it's my turn to have my say."

"Well, if this is your way of *having your say*, you're going about it all wrong, Dante. Thanks, but no, thanks."

My well of emotions has run empty, and so I meet him stare for stare, refuse to back down because fuck if I'm going to let him push me around. He can take the first flight to hell before I'd willingly hop into bed with him.

His hand on my arm flexes as he attempts to deal with the rejection. He goes to speak and then stops, does it again, and then before I can react, his mouth is on mine.

I don't even let the shock register before I'm shoving against him, my knee coming up and making contact. He grunts when I connect, his lips off mine as he doubles over in pain, the sound of his misery filling the house. I think I hear *son of a bitch* or maybe him calling me a bitch. I don't know, and I don't care because that pull of Dante Teller that's always been irrefutable to me is no more.

All I see now is a manipulative prick who didn't have the balls just to come out and tell me he wanted me back. And then went about trying to prove his point in completely the wrong way. Force? Is he fucking kidding me? Who is this man?

Being a badass is one thing. Being an asshole is another.

I rush to the table and grab the phone, my fingers dialing without thought. "Please leave Dante or I'm pushing SEND right now on nine-one-one."

He looks up at me, face red, teeth clenched, but disbelief still in his bloodshot eyes. I know he's had run-ins with the law before, and this is the last thing he'd want. I step forward and pick his keys up from the hall table and take my house key off the ring before throwing them at him. They hit his shoulder and fall to the ground as he keeps groaning.

"Get out!" I scream at him as the adrenaline starts to fire now that I'm away from him and can physically react to the threats he threw at me.

He grabs his keys with one hand, his other still on his crotch. It takes a minute, but he hobbles to the front door and fumbles with the handle for a moment before opening it up.

"I'll have your shit on the porch later tonight for you to collect."

As he walks out, I hear my name as a murmur on his lips, and his tone sounds almost apologetic. A little too fucking late for that. I know he cares about me, know we had something once, but anything there could have been, he just killed by trying to force himself on me, and I think he knows it.

His lack of a fight tells me.

He tries to straighten up, his eyes meeting mine, and I see the apology there, but I don't say another word as I slam the door shut and flip the dead bolt. The minute it's closed, I sag with my back against the door, my body shaking so badly, I slide down until I'm sitting on the floor.

I sit there for some time, so many emotions ebbing and flowing that by the time I bring myself to get up, I'm spent emotionally and physically. I drop the phone from my hand and realize that my other is unknowingly and out of habit examining the breast opposite it.

It always comes back to this. No matter how perfect or how imperfect the person or the situation in my life, at the end of the day, the fate I'm waiting to be dealt is still there, hanging over my head.

Chapter 25

"Had, I'm here. Now are you going to tell me what's going on?" Rylee pulls her sunglasses from her eyes and angles herself so that she can face me. "Something's up with all the cryptic answers you gave me on where we're going, why you need me here."

I look at my oldest friend and know I need the support and levelheadedness she'll bring me. "I need you not to be upset with me because I'm already being eaten by guilt for hiding this from you . . . but just know I had the best intentions for why I didn't tell you." I watch the emotions flicker over her face and am reminded of Becks last night, her reaction similar to his in so many ways that I swallow down the double dose of guilt the sight brings me.

I can see her mind working, can tell she's withholding the questions fleeting through her eyes, and appreciate her biting her tongue and keeping her need-to-plan-everything-the-hell-out ass quiet. She nods her head at me and says, "Okay." Her eyebrows narrow as she reaches out and squeezes my hand. "You know I'll hold your hand through anything, even negative blood test results," she says, infusing her positivity into a situation she misunderstands.

"Thank you . . ." My voice trails off, and it's all I can say because if I lead her on any further, then I'm just being more of an asshole than I already have been. I have enough on my conscience, and I don't need to weigh it down any more. "But this is more than a negative blood test result."

Her body visibly jars from the suggestion in my comment, fingers squeezing my hand, a gasp of air inhaled. "Had . . . ?"

"I found a lump, Ry." My voice is so soft, it's barely audible, but I know she hears me because she nods her head for me to continue. "I had it biopsied a few days before you got back—"

"Why didn't you tell me?" I can tell she's hurt I didn't confide in her but also love that she doesn't address it because she knows this is much bigger than that.

I lower my head and fight the tears that threaten from disappointing her before I answer. "I know you're mad at me, but I couldn't tell you. I couldn't bring myself to make you sad when you deserve all the happiness in the world. I mean, you'd just come back from your honeymoon. I wasn't going to hit you with this."

Her eyes well with tears as she accepts the apology I haven't managed to put into words. "So you had the biopsy . . . ," she says, turning the focus back on me. "Now, why are we here? Do you know something already or—"

"No. Nothing. Results." I'm reduced to one-word answers as the reality of what's about to happen hits me. It's almost as if telling Rylee has made this all real.

Because she's my person.

We stare out the windows of the car for a moment in silence, watching the world around us move on while we think in slow motion. She squeezes my hand one more time and then opens the car door, leading the way, my nerves humming louder with each step we take.

The waiting room is empty, and yet we still speak in hushed voices about nothing important. Eventually we fall silent, busying ourselves by repeatedly checking social media on our phones. And even though I don't want him to, the only reason I keep checking is to see if Becks has messaged me. And how screwed-up is it that after the things I said last night, I'm just not sure whether I'm happy or sad about his lack of contact.

We're called back after about fifteen minutes and ushered into an office space, where we take a seat across the desk from Dr. Blakely. I make introductions between her and Rylee, and all the while a voice is screaming in my head, *You hold my fate in your hands.*

After the niceties are over, Dr. Blakely folds her hands on her desk and looks at me, a soft yet strained smile gracing her lips but not easing the gravity in her expression. I know Rylee notices it too because she reaches over and links her fingers with mine.

"As you know, when we biopsied the lump, there was a possibility of it coming back cancerous."

I grip Ry's hand tightly because what's coming next may make or break me. My ears buzz with noise, and my every nerve is on edge, waiting for the doctor to continue.

"The results came back, Haddie, and I'm sorry to have to tell you that we did find the tumor to be malignant."

I freeze—my heart, my hope, my breath—as my world comes crashing down around me. Fragments of my life, my possibilities, my future shatter as they hit the bottom of my empty emotional well, lost to the darkness I can't see through. The buzzing grows so loud that I see her lips moving but can't hear her over it. My chest constricts, the pain of drawing in a breath so goddamn difficult, I convince myself it has to be from the parasitic cancer eating at my breasts, invading my lungs, and holding them hostage too. My thoughts spiral out of control. Everything I thought I knew now seems foreign, unknown, scary as hell.

It's the lone sob that escapes from Rylee that snaps me back to the present. My tunnel vision zooms onto the sound even though I can't tear my eyes from Dr. Blakely. Her lips have stopped moving, the concern for me evident in the tears that glisten in her eyes as she allows me to digest what she's just told me.

I'm not sure who is holding on tighter, Rylee or myself, but I hear the scrape of her chair and then feel her fighting out of my death grip. I release her hand reluctantly, only to feel her arm go immediately around my shoulders and pull me against the shuddering of her chest.

I clench my jaw, tell myself to let go, to embrace the numbing cold that feels like it's beginning to seep into my bones. I rein it in—everything that I can—and lock it away so that I can deal with it at another time.

The time being *never*, but lying to myself is just par for the course right now, and frankly I might not be around to suffer the repercussions of my lies, so who the fuck cares?

As I look back at Dr. Blakely, my voice is loaded with emotion I can't seem to feel. "Can you please go back and start over because I kind of stopped processing after the word *malignant*?"

She nods her head, glancing over to Rylee in a silent thank-you for her support, before bringing her eyes back to mine. "The pathology reports came back showing cancerous cells, and those reports in conjunction with the scans we did lead us to diagnose you with stage two."

"We?" Rylee interjects with the question that's on my tongue, but I can't seem to get over the disbelief.

"Yes, my colleagues and I," she says. I catch Dr. Blakely glance at Rylee and give her an appreciative smile before meeting my eyes again. "I actually was having a meeting with them about another case and asked them to review yours, as well."

I stare at her, mouth agape, eyes vacant. I feel like a deer in the headlights, but the difference is, I'm not sure if I want to move out of the way or get taken down in one fell swoop. I blink my eyelids, and it feels like they are scraping over sand as I try to process this all and come up empty.

And I find that strange, considering my mind knew this; family medical history predicted this. But it's one thing to feel it and think it, and a whole different thing to hear it stated as fact, have doctors meeting about you — or your file, rather, because your contaminated body isn't there.

"So, what was the consensus?" Rylee again, her voice strong as she plays the role of patient counselor, which she does every day of her life in her job, except this time it's for her best friend instead of one of the abused little boys she's responsible for.

"We believe we need to act fast. Looking at your family history, the cancer your sister and mother experienced was aggressive in all facets, so we want to make sure to hit this head-on and knock it dead without giving it a fighting chance." I want to believe the conviction in her voice, the competency behind her diagnosis that we can knock it dead but have a hard time mustering up the enthusiasm to match it.

I zone out as she goes on about further lumpectomies followed by chemo and then radiation courses to force a response and then hopefully remission. I listen to time frames of treatment, and my head spins, thinking it's not possible because I have a few more days before I can secure the Scandalous deal. Then my mind wanders to the health insurance plan I was luckily able to secure a few months ago to cover myself and any new hires I add on.

I keep half an ear on the conversation, knowing they are talking about my body, my life, and yet I can't connect, can't believe that I'm about to go through what I helped Lexi through. The brutality of it, the complete obliteration, the devastation of it.

And then I think of my parents. Oh, God, my parents. Having to tell them, scare them, watch them suffer through this for a fourth time in their lives, my mom blaming herself all over again as she did with Lex. How she carries her death on her shoulders as if it were her fault. I fist my hands so tight that my nails break the skin, the sting welcome because I'm actually feeling something again instead of this droning buzz holding my body hostage.

I selfishly think of my body. My body, which will soon look like Frankenstein's monster's body, jagged pieces sewn together to make a whole. I know it's vain, but the horrid images of Lex's scars on my body that flash through my mind knock me back a step farther than I already have been.

And yet Rylee and Dr. Blakely keep talking about the logistics, the scheduling of it all, and then I think of Maddie, and it nearly breaks me. When the sob catches in my throat, both of them turn suddenly to look at me, and my decision has been made.

Screw the lumpectomies.

I want to live.

"I want a double mastectomy."

I watch the approval flicker through Dr. Blakely's eyes as Ry's hand squeezes my forearm. "While this was going to be my next suggestion and the best course of action, I must advise you and make you aware—"

"I'm aware that my breasts are going to kill me if I keep them. I want them gone." I make the assertion with more confidence than I actually feel, but my courage makes up for the difference because I'm scared so fucking shitless that my voice should be wavering with nerves instead of the tiny break it had. "Nothing helped my sister, but I want the fighting chance . . . so I want them gone as soon as possible. I need drastic. Lexi was gone in six months. Six months. I have a life I want to live. Things I need to do, and I can't do them in six months because I haven't even planned them yet, so . . ." My voice trails off as all of the things I've ever wanted to do flicker like a slide show through my head. The tears come now, a wave of hope trying to ride the rampant storm of emotions waging inside of me. "I haven't even planned them yet," I tell them both again through the broken sobs.

I'm focused on the sky above us. The clouds float there so nicely, form a set of shapes, and then float some more to change to a different one. Wouldn't it be so easy to be like that—change, shift, adjust—without so much as a thought of the next storm about to roll in threatening to decimate you.

Rylee allows me the silence to think, and I use it to listen to birds chirping and the leaves of the trees all around us rustling in the breeze. This section of the park is vacant at this time of day, and I'm so thankful that she knew I couldn't face reality just yet.

She sighs, and I hear the sniffle she tries to disguise as she turns her head away from me where we lie flat on our backs on the grassy hill, looking up at the sky.

"I have to tell my parents," I whisper, barely breaking the silence.

"We'll go there next. I'll go with you, okay?"

I murmur in agreement. I'm thankful she offered because I know she'll be able to be the voice of reason when hell breaks loose.

"We have three weeks before the surgery and then two weeks after that before chemo starts." I appreciate her matter-of-fact tone, her businesslike efficient approach to my treatment schedule makes it seem like it's not happening to me. "We'll figure out a schedule in the next week or two so that between your parents and me and Becks and whoever else wants in, you have all the help you need after—"

"No." I can feel her body startle in awareness next to me at my outburst.

"No, what?" The caution in her voice tells me that she fears what I'm going to say next.

"I don't want anyone to know besides my parents . . . and you . . ." My words trail off as my thoughts wander.

"Okay." She draws the word out, confusion lacing her tone. "I'm not following you here, Had, but you've been through a lot today, so I'm just going to go with the flow until it settles in and you realize what an idiot you sound like."

I don't take the bait she's using to draw a reaction from me. She knows I have a volatile temper, knows I usually react without thinking, and since I'm not reacting at all, it's scaring her. This is the best and worst part about having a friend who's so close to you. You know what to expect from them, and they know what to do to get a reaction out of you.

But right now I'm still so numb, I don't react.

"Okay," she repeats again in the same exact way that's starting to annoy the hell out of me. "So then it'll just be your parents, me, and Becks that—"

"Becks isn't to know." The words come out with conviction—the first real thing I've said since walking into Dr. Blakcly's office—even though my head and heart are at odds with the decision that I thought about numerous times during my sleepless night. I close my eyes and chase away my visual of the drifting clouds in order to let the guilt in, but it just falls by the wayside in favor of the fear. My fears are all valid now.

"What do you mean, Becks doesn't need to know?"

Because he said he loves me. My head screams the words, but my lips remain sealed, etching the path of lies so deep, that I don't think I'll ever be able to climb out of the groove.

I hear her body shift to a seated position and can feel the heat of her glare daring me to open my eyes, but I just keep her waiting. Instead I silently reiterate all my reasons, which I went over last night. The same ones that I had initially stood by, but I'd let falter when I allowed new emotions to get in the way. To cloud my judgment.

I can't bring Becks into this. I can't ask him to step into

my ticking time bomb of a life and hope the timer doesn't detonate prematurely, bringing both him and me down in different but equally devastating ways.

And then I think how arrogant that is of me. To assume I'd be the one in his life. That we're soul mates.

But for some reason, I just know. It's that goddamn click.

Besides, I won't have the time or emotion to invest in a romantic relationship when my thoughts are going to be selfishly on myself and trying to survive. That's not a fair situation to put someone in even if he tells me to let him make the decision for himself.

I can't let him fall in love with me as I have with him. Hearts may heal with time, but accepting someone's love when you've experienced the brutality of this illness first-hand yourself is the ultimate act of selfishness.

And I may be self-centered at times, only think about me, but this is one time in my life when I am thinking one hundred percent about others. About Becks and that smile that reaches his eyes and the gentleness of his touch and that solid-gold heart of his that some woman—some healthy woman—deserves to have. One who will love him without the sky falling down around them.

I realize that I've opened my eyes and they're scouring the grass for some reason, focused there instead of looking at Rylee, and then it hits me. I'm looking for a dandelion, a sign from my sister that things are going to be okay. But I can't find a single one.

And as silly as it seems, that reinforces my decision.

But how do I tell Rylee all of this? I know what she'll say. She'll tell me I'm crazy. That I need to stay positive, that my mom beat this beast. That I'm only hurting both of us by shutting Becks out when I need more people in my corner than ever before. She'll add insult to injury and try to use peer pressure to make me open the doors and let the world in when all I want to do is shut everyone out and hide in the dark for a while.

So I lie to my best friend. Buy some time. Derail her tirade of stubbornness.

"For now. Please?" I open my eyes again and meet her confused look. "I just need some time to accept all of this, deal with this before I can bring someone else—lots of someone elses—into this situation. I don't want the assessing looks of pity, the constant phone calls where people talk in circles because they're too chickenshit just to come out and ask my prognosis, or the unexpected knocks on the doors with another foil-covered Pyrex dish as if a frickin' casserole will cure me."

Rylee nods, and yet I know she still doesn't get it. But it's not her decision to understand. And frankly I'm sick of having to explain myself. My schizophrenic emotions return with a vengeance. Grief giving way to anger, anger turning into disbelief, disbelief somersaulting into a feeling of welcome isolation.

I can't keep track of them anymore, and I really don't care to.

I shove up off the ground, needing to move, to embrace the rage I have but still can't feel. I try to calm myself and focus on what I can feel: the tightness in my chest because I need to cry but can't seem to urge the tears to come.

I want to tell her that my body's already broken but just know she'll arch her eyebrows and give me that "you've gotta give me something better than that, Montgomery" look she has mastered to perfection over the near decade we've been friends.

"Remember that goulash crap the neighbor across the street brought after Lex's . . ." Her words trail off before she says *funeral* but the memory of that awful food has the corners of my mouth tilting up in a smile.

"The stuff that looked like dog food?" I turn to look at her.

"It smelled like it too." Her nose crinkles up, and I don't know what it is, but the laughter bubbles up. The first sounds of it fall from my mouth and hit my ears, sounding so strange against the tumult in my head.

But I can't stop it.

I can hear the hysteria, can hear the anxiety weaving there, and yet I still laugh loud and deep, the breeze carrying it away and into the distance.

When I look up, Rylee is laughing too, but hers is physically contradicted with tears sliding down her cheeks as her eyes hold steadfast on mine.

Thoughts flicker as I laugh. Fear festers up, and I shove it away momentarily because I need this moment—the sky, the breeze, my best friend. Something to hold on to, to pull back up when I need it on the dark days that I know will be coming. The ones that will try to steal my soul and blind my light.

But this moment gives me the clarity that I'm gonna fight like hell.

I'm gonna fight like a girl: lipstick on, hair done, and attitude in place.

Because shit, I've got hearts to break still and heels to wear.

Hearts and heels.

Hearts and heels.

Damn. I'm scared. Petrified.

Trying so hard to keep my grip on reality.

So fearful of the unknown.

Chapter 26

Emotionless, I stare at myself in the mirror. I take in my swollen eyes and the dark circles beneath them, noting the disbelief still in their hollow reflection. I can still hear my mother's shriek from earlier when I told her, as well as see the stunned look on my dad's face, followed by his gritted jaw and sudden departure so he could go break down in his bedroom over not being able to protect the only woman left in his life still untouched by the monster that has decimated his family.

I shake off those painful recollections and begin tugging my clothes off, suddenly desperate to take a shower and scrub every single part of today from my body. My mom's perfume lingers on my skin. The perfume that shouldn't be there because I shouldn't have seen her today.

So I welcome the scalding water as I scrub and cleanse, even though I know I can't wash *this* away. I tell myself I need to call Rylee later and apologize for being rude and brash rather than appreciative and gracious for all that she's done for me. I know she understands why, but it still doesn't make it right.

I climb from the shower and grab a towel, which I twist around my hair and on my head. I grab a second, so emotionally drained I'm not thinking straight, and start to dry off and cross into my bedroom to grab my robe on my bed. As I near it, I look up and catch sight of my naked body in the mirror hanging on the wall beside my dresser.

I freeze. Then I walk toward it, completely lost in my thoughts and drowning in the fear from earlier today. I can't take my eyes off my breasts in the reflection.

They're pert and full with pink nipples. I stare at them and wonder how something that looks so harmless can hold so much power over me? I wonder how something that can bring pleasure, can nourish a baby, can also steal my life so easily.

Then I begin to wonder what I'll look like when they are gone. Will I look like a patchwork quilt of scars? Will they be able to salvage my nipples so that I don't have to have fake ones tattooed on so that I can pretend to look normal? What will be physically left of this major feature that expresses my gender, my sexuality?

I won't even have my hair to help with that ... so I'll be a bald, flat-chested person with only makeup on my soon-to-be-bloated face to denote that I'm a female.

The thought staggers me. Suffocates both my thoughts and my breathing.

I like to think that I'm not a vain person, but everybody is in a sense. Is this God's way of punishing me for always being pretty? For never going through that gawky stage as a teenager when every other girl was gangly and awkward and I was svelte and desired by the boys? The things I have always taken for granted, always been so comfortable with are going to be taken from me, and while I never thought I'd really care, all of a sudden I'm terrified of what I'm going to look like and how people will perceive me.

The tears that I've kept hostage all day finally erupt into a maelstrom of sobs. I drop the towel as I bring my hands to my boobs and cup them, feeling the weight, the smoothness of the skin, their roundness. I've had them my whole life, and yet I don't think I've ever thought to memorize everything about them. Such a weird thought.

I tell myself through the exploding grief that when I get through this, I'll have them reconstructed. That while I think my natural breasts are pretty close to perfect now, when I'm sixty, they'd be saggy and flat, so I'm lucky because the new boobs I'll get will remain perky and full well into my nursing home days. Rationalization at its finest.

And then I start to laugh through the tears as I recall a Shel Silverstein poem I read to Maddie the other night. One about how a little boy shaved his head because he hated his wavy hair only to find out his hair was straight and it was his head that was wavy.

I don't know why the thought is so funny to me now, but I can't stop laughing as I look at the mirror and wonder what I'll find beneath my hair. Tears fall as fast as the laughter from my lips until the sound dies but I continue to cry.

I stare again through my tear-blurred vision, my hair wet and stringy—my towel having fallen from my head during my laughter-sob fest—and my body still pink from the scalding water of the shower. This is the same body I've looked at for the last twenty-eight years, and yet I know that in the coming weeks it will no longer seem like or look like mine.

I close my eyes, not wanting to focus anymore on what will never be the same. I crawl onto my bed and beneath my covers, trying to find some kind of solace, but I don't think it's an emotion one can hope for when facing a cancer diagnosis.

Next I lose myself to my thoughts, suddenly questioning my knee-jerk decision this afternoon at Dr. Blakely's office. Should I opt for a single mastectomy and save my other breast? Keep a piece of myself?

That's stupid. The remaining breast would just be a continually ticking time bomb. I made the right decision. I tell myself that over and over as the tears slide silently down my cheeks and wet the pillow beneath me.

But the doubt still niggles its way into my psyche.

I know what to do to reinforce my decision. I reach to the edge of the bed and grab my cell. Within moments my voice mail is activated, and Lexi's voice is filling my ears.

Time is precious. Waste it wisely.

"Give me strength, Lex," I whisper into the silence.

I realize how much I don't want to be alone right now. I know it's the loneliness talking, but I miss the sounds of Dante moving about in the kitchen downstairs. I reluctantly admitted to Rylee what had happened with him and why he's gone merely because I didn't want to lie to her again but knew she'd be worried that I was alone.

Shockingly she gave in to my need for solitude after I explained that with her knack for planning, I knew after the surgery I'd probably never be left alone. And I needed as much time to myself right now as I can get. But lying here with only my thoughts screaming through the silence, I wish I would have accepted Ry's offer to spent the night and snuggle up with me.

But I didn't.

So I replay the voice mail again.

And again.

Because I know if I keep the phone replaying the message, it will prevent me from dialing Becks.

I miss him. Desperately. I'm doing the right thing because if I feel like this after such a short time, it makes me realize just how he'd feel if he went through all of this with me and then was left alone in the end.

Fucking brutal.

Exhaustion starts to win the battle over my internal thoughts. My finger hitting the repeat command every two minutes and thirteen seconds as the voice mail ends to start it anew.

I begin to drift off to sleep.

I don't walk away from the people I love without a fight, and damn it to hell, Haddie Montgomery, you'd better prepare for that fight because I'm in love with you.

The words flicker through my mind, and I'm so tired and worn-out from the day that I vaguely wonder if I'm remembering or if my finger actually dialed his number and I'm hearing him say them to me.

Regardless, I succumb to the pull of slumber, my last waking thoughts focused on Becks conquering my heart rather than the cancer invading my body.

Chapter 27

BECKS

The engine revs down the backstretch, the computer in front of me reporting all of the gauges in the car that I usually study and scrutinize religiously.

But not today.

Today the constantly fluctuating numbers don't register at all. I see them, I record them, but where they usually reflect specific issues with the car, today they don't trigger to life anything in my brain.

"We good?" Colton's disembodied voice comes through my headset, and I realize I didn't even check what I was supposed to, so I can't answer him. I don't have a clue.

I'd love to say, *Yeah, we're good*, but this is my best friend's life in a car that will fly close to if not over two hundred miles per hour. I can't bullshit him, even though the thought crosses my mind.

"Sorry, Wood," I tell him, calling him the nickname someone on the race team gave him years ago. "Got distracted with something. Wasn't able to track the numbers." I ignore the glances from the crew when they hear my explanation over their headsets. They saw me sitting at the computer. No distraction occurred whatsoever. "Give me a sec, and I can pull them up, make sure they're within range."

"Feels like they are," Colton says, his voice strained from the force as he enters turn three. "Ass end's not sliding anymore on the top side. Feels like the guys fixed it with that last adjustment."

"Good," I tell him as I scramble to study the numbers and make sure his assessment is in fact correct.

Fuck if Haddie's not gotten to me—goddamn voodooed me—but hell if I can tell Colton that. Explain to him I'm so distracted by a woman who keeps pushing me away that I can't focus on my fucking job. Yeah. Cuz that's professionalism at its finest.

"*Good?* That's all you've got for me?" The car accelerates out of turn one, his voice vibrating with the pressure against his body. "Why don't you work on pulling your head out of your ass and doing your fucking job, huh?"

I bite the knee-jerk reaction on my tongue to tell him to go to hell. I deserve the shit he just gave me after blowing our meeting yesterday with Penzoil because I was too distracted.

"Numbers are within range." I tell him as my eyes glance over the last gauge readings. "We're all set."

There's silence on the radio, and I know he knows I'm off my game right now. He won't ask why because hell, we're guys and don't get all touchy-feely, and shit, but I never fuck up with sponsors. And I fucked up with Penzoil without a doubt.

The silence hangs there, the sound of the engine all I hear on the open mic as I wait to see if he's going to push my buttons here or if he'll rake me over the coals in private.

It's one or the other. Colton's not the type of guy to let something like this go. Not because I fucked up, but because as much as he'll never admit it, he cares. The stubborn bastard.

"Good. I'm taking her for another twenty. Balls out," he

finally says. And I know it's his way of saying, *You paying attention now?*

The car's dialed, and for him to run full throttle is something he knows I hate. Runs the risk of fucking up its perfect state. He's goading me into reaction, and fuck him, I've got enough shit to deal with, I don't need him on my back too.

"Have fun," I tell him, noticing Smitty down the line whip his head over to look at me when my typical arguing with Colton over unnecessary risks doesn't come.

Fuck. It must be pretty obvious, I don't have my shit together.

Colton's only response is a deep rev of the engine, which to me says, *Fuck you.* I start packing my shit up as my mind absently notes the turns one through four as he hits them from the pitch of the engine alone.

I debate sticking around for him to get out of the car and dealing with the ration of shit I know he's gonna give me but figure it's not worth it. I'm pissed and moody and going to blows with my best friend isn't something I want to tempt.

Although, fuck, is it tempting.

Maybe I just want to get a reaction out of someone since it seems like I can't get shit out of Haddie.

Zip. Zero. Zilch.

Anger, accusations, indifference . . . anything would be better than the silence.

It's been five days since I went to her house and found her in the backyard. I can still see the look in her eyes, feel the desperate hunger in her touch. But riding next to that is the rejection on her tongue and the sting in her words.

And then she got me so goddamn flustered that I told her I loved her. Fucking loved her. Something I hadn't even fully admitted to myself because thinking you feel it is one thing, but saying it aloud—putting it out into the universe—you can't take that shit back. And then what did she do in return?

Nothing.

Not a goddamn thing.

Not a single *Becks wait* or *Don't go.* Not a *Wow this is too fast* or *Are you fucking crazy?* She gave me nothing but guarded eyes and complete withdrawal.

I shove the hurt back down. Push away the unanswered phone calls and unread texts, the numerous times I've driven past her house to see if she's home, and the time I spent pounding on her door last night because her car was in the driveway. My pleas for her to open up, to talk to me, tell me she's okay, that she hates me, really chooses Dante. Something. Anything. This suspended state of limbo fucking sucks.

The woman's reduced me to a needy son of a bitch, and I hate it.

My thoughts are racing faster than Colton around the track right now, and I just need to quiet my head for a bit. I shove up out of my seat, ignoring the looks I get from the rest of the guys in the view box, and grab my keys. I glance down at my cell and pretend I'm reading a text as I make my way to the door. "Tell Wood something came up, and I have to bail. I'll call him later."

I don't wait for a response because I need to pull a Haddie.

Lose myself for a bit so that I feel a whole lot less.

Fuck.

Listening to what my damn heart is saying is new for me. And it's a goddamn muscle, so why am I hoping that it can give me some answers?

Muscles may not be able to make sense of something, but hell if they can't ache with pain when they're used and abused

And she sure as fuck did just that.

So why do I still want her?

Fucking love.

*   *   *

The music is bluesy, the lighting on the dark side, and the beer ice-cold as it slides down my throat. The best part about being in my favorite pub besides being left the fuck alone is that all I have to do is raise my chin to Vivian, and she brings me another round without a single word.

It may be her first week on the job and we've just met, but Viv's my new best friend for that alone.

The texts have finally stopped after two hours of constant pestering. But not a single one is from the person I want.

I'm enjoying feeling sorry for myself, wallowing in a damn ocean of barley and hops with a few odd shots thrown in here and there. My lips are numb, my head is quiet—spinning but still quiet—and I still don't have a fucking clue how she could choose him over me.

"More her type, my ass," I mutter to myself, thinking of the last thing she said to me. Sweet fuck. I can blame my drunk mind on why I don't understand, but the haze isn't strong enough to forget that I'm drinking because I can't make sense of it sober, either.

I raise my chin to Vivian again. Might as well add to the clutter of glasses lined up on my table.

I lean back in the booth I've commandeered at the back of Sully's Pub and cross my legs, which are stretched out on the bench. I run through the possible scenarios in my head, trying to figure how we went from sleepless nights and that look in her eyes when I left her after the trip to Ojai to here.

I mean, fuck, it was hard not to go to the last Scandalous event a few nights back. Took everything I had to not go sit in a dark corner of the club and watch her, make sure she's okay. Just see her—because damn, I miss her—but then that would be stalkerish.

I refrained by drinking a six-pack and watching the game.

I thank Vivian when the bottle slides onto the table in front of me and consider calling Rylee. It's a stupid fucking move on my part, but what other choices do I have at this point? It's gotta be the alcohol pussifying my thoughts.

But damn, the alcohol just might have a point.

Then I realize that as much as I want to know what the hell Haddie is thinking, I also want to ask Rylee if she's gotten the test results back yet. I know it's nothing, but there's that tiny bit of worry that's still unsettling. And since Haddie won't communicate with me in any way, shape, or form, I decide to ask Rylee.

My God, that's pathetic.

Wait. I can't ask Rylee about test results because she doesn't even know about Haddie's damn biopsy in the first place. There goes that plan.

I close my eyes, welcoming the off-kilter spin of my world right now because if life's not going to make sense, you might as well do it drunk, right?

"Gonna drink yourself into a good mood or what?"

I snap my head forward at the sound of Colton's voice and immediately look over to where Vivian stands. She scrunches up her face and mouths the words *I'm sorry* as she points the blame at Miller, the bartender who knows Colton and me as frequent customers.

Fuck. When did he get on shift? I thought I had lucked out with a new waitress and old Earl, who couldn't care less what I was doing over here by myself.

I ignore Colton and close my eyes again, putting my head back to the same position against the back of the booth.

I hear Colton chuckle and then plop down across from me in the booth. It takes only seconds before I hear the clink of another bottle on the table and a polite thank-you as he's served.

And I wait for it—the ration of shit—but he doesn't say a word. So I sit with my eyes closed until the suspense of what in the hell he's doing is so consuming that I have to look. I crack my eyes open and angle my head over to find him sitting there the same as me but he's staring at his beer bottle, peeling the label.

"Hey," he says with a lift of his chin, and then goes back to his label without even meeting my eyes.

"Hey," I respond, trying to accept his nonchalance when he's usually a get-straight-to-the-point kind of guy.

"Watcha drinking?" he asks after a bit, pointing to the empty glasses gathered in the middle of the table.

"Scotch."

"Scotch?"

"Macallan," I add.

"Good shit," he says with an appreciative hum.

"That it is," I sigh out, paying attention to the label on my own beer now. "Tastes like Heaven—smooth, addictive—but hell if it doesn't pack a punch."

"Why do I get the feeling we're not talking about alcohol here?"

My eyes lift to meet the intensity in his. I see concern and compassion there and want to talk about it at the same time as I want to avoid discussing it.

About Haddie.

And even stronger than my need to spew my guts is my wanting to ask him about her. Chicks talk about shit like this—guys don't—so maybe Haddie talked to Rylee. Told her about why she's pushing me away, that I confessed my love like a jackass.

God, this is so fucking frustrating.

"Sorry about Penzoil."

Colton's head startles with the whiplash of switching gears. "It happens," he says, and I know I've had a lot to drink, but I'm not processing this laid-back guy responding to me very well. I feel like he's holding back, walking on eggshells, and avoiding pushing me when that's usually the norm.

Might as well just add a bit more discord to the eddy of confusion already whirling on the broken merry-go-round in my head.

"Nah. I fucked up. It's on me. Got a lot on my plate."

"You okay? Your parents and Walk okay?"

"Yeah, they're cool. . . . Sorry. All's good in the hood." His genuine concern for my family has me immediately apologizing for the second time in mere seconds. I tilt the bottle to my lips, the flavor not even registering anymore because the potent taste of rejection is stronger. We sit there in comfortable silence before I finally confess, "It's the *goddamn Macallan*."

It's all I give him, yet he nods his head before taking a swallow of his beer. "You don't brown-bag Macallan, Daniels."

"I'm aware of that," I tell him, glad he caught the correlation between Haddie and the Scotch. "Can't enjoy it—brown bag or not—if someone else is swigging from your bottle."

He blows out a breath and slouches back in his seat with a shake of his head. "Dude, that's rough." His eyes glance up to read mine. "She blew you off?"

"In so many words."

"I'd ask if you understand why, but by the empty bottles on the table and the mere fact that she's a chick, I'd say the answer is a big, fat, fucking no." I don't fight the smile that pulls at my lips. "I told you dude, *estrogen vortex*. No use in even trying to figure it out."

"Truth." I tip my beer toward him and fall silent for a minute, the bottle in my hand easier to look at than Colton as the confession forms on my tongue. "It's all your fault, you know."

He chokes out a laugh, his face scrunched up as he tries to figure out just what in the hell I'm talking about. "This is gonna be good," he says, clapping his hands together and rubbing them back and forth. "Lay it on me, brother. Can't wait to hear your fucked-up logic."

I glare at him. "You started all this shit. We—you and I—were perfectly fine—single and ready to mingle—and then you had to go and get struck by the almighty voodoo."

His laugh is loud and draws attention from other patrons beginning to fill up the bar. "Struck? More like knocked me on my ass. Dude . . . I'm sorry. . . . Wait. No, I'm not." He slaps his hand on the table. "I'm not going to apologize because when it happens to you, you'll get it. All of it. The barebacking, being okay with someone holding your balls in their hands, the . . ." Colton's head snaps up to mine as the puzzle pieces fall into place. His eyes widen as the smirk starts to play at the corners of his mouth. "No fucking way . . ."

"Viv?" I look away from him immediately and search for my new best friend and her constant supply of mind-numbing gifts.

"For the love of all things holy . . . you didn't . . . you're not . . . you fucking are, aren't you?" he finally sputters out. And just what I need: Now Donavan knows I've been voodooed.

Let the shit storm begin.

I refuse to look up at him, don't want him to see the misery in my eyes now that it's unofficially out on the table. Fuck. Here comes the ribbing I deserve but sure as hell don't need. Viv might as well double up the next round because I think I'm gonna need it.

"Nah . . ." Denial is my only option.

"Sweet Jesus, dude. I go on my honeymoon, you bang the maid of honor, and then you tie your dick in knots over her—"

"At least you acknowledge it's long enough to tie in a knot." I shrug, the beer sliding down so nice, and it feels like I can breathe a bit now that I'm no longer lying to my best friend.

He snorts out a laugh. "In your dreams, dude. Have another."

"Fuck off. And thank you. I believe I will have another." I lean my head back against the booth again and sigh, wanting to say more but not sure how much ammo I want to give him because I sure as hell don't need to take any more shit right now from anyone.

"Good. I'm buying. That way I can get you good and drunk."

"I believe I'm already on my way there," I admit. He murmurs his consent, and I force my eyes open so the room stops spinning behind my eyelids. And so I don't see that image of her standing there, mouth telling me to go but eyes begging me to stay. "I just . . . It doesn't make sense. . . . I . . . *Fuck!*"

"That about sums it up."

I appreciate his silence after the comment as I try to grasp the shifting thoughts in my head. "With Ry . . . did you . . . were you . . ."

"Confused constantly? My dick begging for more, but my head saying back the fuck up?" The quiet amusement in his voice tells me he gets it, understands where my head's at right now.

"Basically." I scrub my hands over my face. "This is so messed-up."

"Yep. And if I wasn't feeling your pain, I'd be laughing at you too." I glare at him. "You, pussy perplexed? It's just too fucking comical for words."

"Fuck off."

"Thank you. I believe I will be getting just that later tonight while you're here crying in your beer. It's easier all around if you just admit the Haddie Hex is in full effect." I roll my eyes at him but stop when he clinks the neck of his beer against mine. "Voodoo, bro. Don't knock it till you try it."

"Ha. Now you're all for it when a year ago you fought it every step of the way."

"Fought it until I realized a voodoo pussy is a grown man's Lucky Charms."

Why the hell is he talking about cereal? "Come again?"

His flashes me a grin. *"Magically delicious."*

I don't even fight the laugh that falls from my mouth. Colton Donavan at his finest. "You are so fucked in the head."

"And your point is . . . ?"

"My point is . . . you're right. About all of it."

His laugh fades as his eyes meet mine over his bottle of beer. "Life hasn't been easy for her this past year." His statement is completely matter-of-fact, and as much as I know he's right, it still fucking sucks. All of this.

"True"—I bob my head in agreement, synapses trying to fire through the alcohol-induced haze—"but I just don't get it. Why tell me there's something between us and then tell me she'd rather have someone else?"

"And you *believe her* about the someone else?"

I look at Colton and try to process the look he's giving me. His eyes are apologizing, telling me something. . . . Vague hints of what it might be float in the far-off distance, but I can't seem to pull them close enough to comprehend. "Her words were about as clear as fucking Crisco."

Colton laughs at my pain and the fact that Crisco is anything but clear. Sounded good, anyway.

"Fuck! All I know is that she said she was working things out with Dante, wanted to give it another shot."

"The roommate, the ex-boyfriend?" The startled look on his face rivals how I feel. "Well, all I know is that she's going through a lot of shit right now and—"

"What shit?" I immediately recall the look Colton was giving me moments ago. What was he apologizing for? For the fact that Haddie is blowing me off or because he knows something I don't? "Colton—"

"Well, well, well, if it isn't wonder boy himself." The voice off to my right snaps my mind from Colton and ignites my temper like a blowtorch lighting a candle.

"The ex?" Colton's voice is low and even as he asks me the question. His eyes tell me to calm the fuck down but his posture says, *Fuck off, Dante. Game on.*

"Dante." I nod my head without even looking at him, knowing if I do that urge I had earlier to push someone else around will come back tenfold. I glance over to Colton and see him checking Dante out, his hand sliding up to the neck of the empty beer bottle in his hand, *just in case*.

Gotta love a friend who's willing to break a longneck for you to have your back.

"Why are you over here crying in your beer? Is it cuz you fucked the fight out of our little filly?"

Now that comment has me raising my eyes to meet Dante's. The warning I flash is met with a matching dare from him. Who the fuck does this guy think he is, and what the hell is he talking about?

Doesn't matter. None of it matters except he just disrespected her, and that's all I need to know.

You don't disrespect women. *Ever*. Whether you're sleeping with them or not.

"Leave it," the king of hot tempers warns from his place across from me in the booth.

"I've got this," I tell Colton as the adrenaline begins to surge through me, my mind fixating on the asshole and how he deserves everything that's coming to him if he keeps this shit up.

Dante's laugh mocks me. "Apparently you don't *got this*." I'm already sliding out of the booth when he makes the comment. "You might want to brush up on your skills because when I was with Haddie the other night, she sure as hell couldn't get enough. *More* I believe was her word of choice."

My mind flashes back to Haddie on the kitchen table at the farmhouse, telling me, *More*, and my synapses don't need to fire because I don't even need to think.

I just react.

I collide with Dante, moving at full force. I don't even bother throwing a punch, don't even think about it because I want the fucker on the ground. And he's solid, but so am

I, when I connect. Our momentum forces us into the table behind him.

Glass breaking and shouts from afar barely register as we fall to the ground cussing at each other. He gets in the first punch as we scramble for positioning, and I feel the connection, hear the whoosh of air as it escapes my lungs from the kidney punch but don't feel a goddamn thing. I'm so amped up from the past week that my churning emotions manifest in the impact of my fist as I gain top position.

The connection of my fist against his gut feels like a small weight is lifted from my shoulders. And fuck does it feel good.

He lands one.

I land one.

He cusses me out in between our fists flying. I don't even hear what he's saying because all I think is *Keep opening your mouth and give me access to knock those perfect teeth of yours out.*

But the feeling of impact as I land a punch is fleeting because my mind keeps fixating on the fact that he was with Haddie the other night. That she asked him for more when she hasn't asked me for anything but to leave.

I see red. Can't see anything else because my mind is so preoccupied with Haddie, with the idea that this asshole touched her.

It's Colton's harsh call of my name that breaks through my hypnotic fog of anger. It's his hands I fight off as they try to pull me away from Dante. And I struggle against him, even when I come to my senses and realize that Dante is securely pinned beneath me, face splattered with the same blood staining my knuckles.

"Goddamn it, Becks! Get off him." Colton's strong enough that his arms wrapped around my shoulders prevent me from continuing. "They're gonna call the cops if you don't break it up."

I grunt in agreement, my breath too labored and my head too filled with rage to answer him. I'd take the cuffs in an instant if it meant that Dante was properly put in his place.

"You sure?" he asks me, and I nod before he releases his hold on my arms.

And God strike me dead for lying to my best friend, but the minute he lets my arms go, my fist connects with Dante's jaw again. The sound of my knuckles hitting him ricochets through my head in a satisfying crunch.

"Fuckin' A, Becks!" Colton's arms are back around me, and this time I struggle even harder, wanting to finish the job. He's successful in pulling me off Dante, and even as I struggle with Colton, I can still see Dante sitting up, using his torn shirt to wipe some blood from the corner of his mouth. "Calm down."

"Let me go!" I argue, ready to lay one on Colton too if need be to get him to release me.

"Goddamn it, quit fighting me, will ya? They're calling the cops, dude." He yanks me up and backward, and I struggle away from him now that I'm on my feet and Dante's retreated. "Christ! Calm the fuck down."

"I'm gonna kill the son of a bitch." I'm so wrapped up inside my own head right now, so deafened by the buzzing anger, that I don't even hear him.

"Killing him's not going to get rid of her cancer, dude."

But I sure as fuck hear that.

I feel like everything stops—then there's the quick intake of air as Colton realizes what he's just told me—but my head doesn't want to believe it.

"What did you just say?" The quiet disbelief in my voice is no rival for the rage vibrating through me. I turn my body now to face my oldest friend. I recognize the apology in his eyes, see acknowledgment of the deceit in his body language, and I'm fucking floored. *"You knew?"*

"Becks." It's that soothing tone that I hate.

"You knew?" I ask again, my voice escalating as I take a step toward him, hands fisted, jaw clenched.

"She doesn't want anyone to know. No one." He emphasizes the last words so I can hear that he was torn over keeping it from me, but my rational mind isn't listening.

My irrational side sure as fuck is, though.

"So that was a slip?" I shout at him as I take another step closer. "You only told me—let it slip—to calm me the fuck down?"

He laughs softly, glancing at the space between us and then back at me. "*Calm* is not quite the word I'd use about you right now." He takes a step forward as I grit my teeth because being angry at him means I don't have to process what he's just told me.

Haddie has cancer.

"You want to take a shot at me too, Becks?" He goads me, sacrificing himself so I don't fly off the handle and take it all out on someone else. He lifts his chin and taps at it. "Right here, fucker. Dare you. But I bet your ass it's not going to do a goddamn thing to help Haddie."

"Make me feel better, though." I grumble the words at him, anger still riding high but the *oh fuck* aspect starting to take over.

Colton judges me for a minute as I stand there stunned, fists loosening, mind scrambling to grasp the magnitude of what he's just told me.

Trying to understand how Had's feeling. Why she doesn't want me to know? The fear she's facing alone.

My friend approaches me, defense in his posture but sympathy in his eyes. He puts a hand on my shoulder and directs me toward the booth and then pushes me to sit down. "You didn't tell me." I say again, the only concept I'm choosing to grasp right now.

He blows out a loud sigh as he sits across from me and motions to Viv with his hand to come near. "I know—it fucking blows—and I'm sorry, but, dude, I'm married now. I promised Ry. I was put in a fuck-all spot between you and her."

"And she is the one sucking your dick. I get it." I say the words, knowing they're crass and not caring because I'm still amped up on adrenaline.

"Let me know when your mouth is done running and using up all your energy so I can kick your ass for talking about Rylee like that." The warning is delivered loud and clear. "It seems to me you still have some fight left in you. I promise you I have a harder left than that fucker does," he says, lifting his chin toward the other side of the bar, where Dante is nursing his bloody nose, the bouncer at his side, coaxing him out the door.

"Sorry. . . . This whole thing blows. . . . I'm just . . ." Colton nods his head at me in acknowledgment, forgiveness laced with the guilt that's eating at him reflected in his eyes. And it makes me feel a tad better to see it there. Like teeny tiny. I grab my right wrist with my left hand and flex it. The fucker hurts like a bitch from punching Dante.

"Fuck." He blows the word out, making it sound exactly how I feel.

"What can I get you, boys?" Viv's back and in front of us, trying to act like everything is normal—like the melee never happened—and I just hang my head, drowning in my own thoughts, too occupied to be embarrassed.

"Macallan neat," Colton says, my shoulders tensing at the significance of his request.

"One shot for each of you, handsome?"

"Two glasses, one bottle, please. And a bag of ice for his hand."

Both Viv and I raise our heads and look at Colton, her for the tip she might be getting and me because I don't want to sit here and drink. I want Colton to drive me to Haddie's. Like ten fucking minutes ago.

"That's pretty pricey for—"

"Not a problem. Thanks," Colton says with a flash of his "public" smile as he dismisses her.

"Thanks, Wood, but I don't want to drink anymore. I need you to bring me to see Haddie." I start to stand, and Colton is up just as fast, his hand on my shoulder pushing me back down, before I can even get steady.

"No can do, brother." He gives my shoulder an extra shove before he sits back down. "First off, you're drunk. Not a smart move to show up at her house right now. Alcohol makes you say shit, man . . . like profess your love when the last thing she wants to hear out of your mouth now is that you love her, . . . She'd think it's out of pity, . . ."

I keep staring at the table as Viv slides two glasses in front of us. She starts to pour, and Colton tells her thanks but takes the bottle and pours them himself so that we have privacy.

He slides the bag of ice over to me, but I just look at it. I deserve the pain in my hand. Haddie has cancer. Her hurt's going to be a whole lot worse. I wish a simple bag of ice could fix it for her.

". . . you telling her that means you're only doing it because she's sick. Not because you really feel that way."

I wince at the word *sick* and then blow out a breath, knowing he's right . . . that the last thing she needs is me drunk and blubbering all over her. But, Christ, all I want to do right now is see her, touch her, talk to her.

He pushes the glass in my hand and wraps my fingers around it when I don't respond. But if I don't drink, then I sober up faster, and get to see her that much sooner.

"I already told her." The words come out in a whisper as I stare at the Macallan in my glass. I don't even realize I've said the words until Colton sputters beside me.

"Fuck me, dude. I think we're going to need another bottle of this shit." He taps his glass against mine. "Bottoms up."

I'm on autopilot as I swallow the Scotch. It's a shame to

waste it on me right now. I don't appreciate the taste or how damn smooth it is because all I keep thinking about is Haddie.

The neck of the bottle clinks as Colton refills our glasses. "Breathe, brother," he tells me, my fingers gripping the glass so hard, I'm surprised it doesn't shatter in my hand.

"What am I . . . how am . . ." I blow out a breath in frustration because I can't process the thoughts whipping through my mind fast enough.

"Ry's with her. She seems to be dealing, you know. She's a tough chick, Daniels."

"Yeah, but fuck . . ." I can't even speak in complete sentences. I toss back the second pour of the Macallan. This time the burn's a little less, and the warmth's a little more.

"I know, Becks." It's all he can really say, and I appreciate the fact he's not bullshitting me, telling me she's going to be okay, telling me I'm a stupid fucker for going and falling for her.

My eyes burn just as much as my throat right now. So many questions I want—no need—to ask her, and the one in the forefront is like a ghost that keeps slipping through my fingers. The alcohol dims my logic enough to figure out what the hell my subconscious is trying to tell me, but my mind isn't grasping it.

"She kicked Dante out last week."

Well, fuck. That works. I can't think straight enough to figure it out. The question is just out of reach.

"She's not with him?"

"Nah . . . kicked him out. He either was just fucking with you because he's jealous or he really tried to get in her pants and she gave him the boot . . . and if that's the case, I should have added a fist to his face too."

Relief rushes through me. And then confusion followed by anger again. She's all alone? What the fuck? Shit's being thrown at me so fast right now, I'm having a hard time coming to terms with any of it.

And then it hits me like a goddamn bulldozer. *She knew.* She fucking knew that night. She was pushing me away, trying to protect me, choosing for me. Just like I told her not to.

Well, fuck that.

I shove up out of the booth again. My vision goes black, and the whole room pulls me into its tumultuous tornado of darkness and stars.

"Woah. Easy. Easy."

I hear Colton's voice. Feel his hands on me, but I can't focus. The seat's beneath my knees again, and my stomach lurches into my throat momentarily until I can swallow the bile and the gallon of alcohol back down.

"I need to see her," I plead with him. Because even though I'm so shit-faced I can't stand, my stubborn stupidity keeps hitting me in the face over and over. How could I not have seen right through her and what she said to me? How could I have been such an idiot?

"I know you do but not till the morning. You're sleeping with me tonight," he chuckles, trying to lighten the mood.

"When hell freezes over." I mutter, but just maybe it has because, holy shit, Haddie really is sick.

"I think it already has, dude."

I snap my head up as fast as I can without making the earth tumble and fall around me again. "What?"

He clinks his glass against mine and throws back the swallow of amber liquid. "You love her? What the fuck is up with that? I got you were dipping your wick, but now you want a permanent place to burn your candle?" He shakes his head and laughs before resting it back on the booth behind him.

I can't help the laugh that falls from my lips, grateful for his random humor right now. "Candle?"

"Mm-hmm." He's buzzed enough now that he doesn't continue the train of thought. Instead we fall back in silence, our eyes closed, heads fuzzy, and glasses empty. "Got quarter of a bottle left. We finish it off, get Sammy to drive us back to my place," he says, referring to his bodyguard and sometime driver. "We'll sleep it off, you'll get a clearer head, and then you go see her tomorrow and fight like fuck to prove you want to be a part of her life. Sick or not sick."

I choke back the emotion clogging my throat, stunned by my best friend's ability to know this is what I need to hear when he's never been good with emotions or relationships.

And from just hearing the word *sick* out loud in reference to Haddie.

"Yeah." The word is barely a sound as it passes past my lips.

"She's gonna beat this, Daniels."

Images of Lexi flash through my head from the pictures I've seen in Haddie's house—the only way I'll never know her. And I can't help but acknowledge the fear creeping in that that could be all I'll have left one day of Haddie.

I'm immediately pissed at myself for even thinking it. Furious that for one moment I thought she's not going to fight the fight so she can walk the walk afterward. But fuck if I'm not scared, even with liquid courage flowing through my veins like it's my own blood.

"She has to be."

Chapter 28

I left Rylee with just a note saying, *"I need to think,"* after she spent the night with me like old times. Too many bottles of wine, too many trips down memory lane, and so many laughs our ribs ached and cheeks hurt.

And it felt good that Ry was just Ry with me. Not looking out of the corner of her eye to stare at me with that pitying look I hate or to make sure that I wasn't going to keel over and die.

Hence the reason I've kept my diagnosis from everyone.

I'm good with my decision—glad I've decided to keep it on the down low to just Rylee and my parents—but hell if my heart's not hurting right now.

I was doing good. At least I thought I was. I was so busy thinking about surgery next week that I was pushing away all thoughts of Becks. And his parting words to me.

Those words were earth shifting to me, but I'd also noticed his attempts seemed to fade with each day. Hell yes, I'd back off after the rejection time and again if I were him, but at the same time I needed it there. His annoying texts, continuous phone calls, drive-bys past the house when he didn't know I was home because I'd parked in the garage. It all reassured me. So the fact that the attempts had faded after day five had proved to me that his words were bullshit.

If he didn't keep trying after five days, he sure as hell wasn't going to stick around for months of chemotherapy and radiation. The proof's in the pudding.

It wasn't until last night that I realized subconsciously I was testing him. Waiting him out. Making him prove the love he had professed to me.

I thought he'd given up, that his words were bullshit, until I got the text last night and the voice mail. And then it just blew my carefully constructed false front to smithereens. I sit in my car remembering it, resting my forehead on my hands overlapped on the steering wheel.

Maybe it was the mass quantities of wine. Maybe it was having Ry sleeping in her old bedroom again. Maybe it was the emotional overload of everything about to happen. Whatever it was, when I read the text, a small thrill went through me, tearing through my resolve, which was already hanging on by a thread.

Huh. Thread. Strings. Can't get the hell away from ties when it comes to Beckett Daniels.

All the text said was: **I'm calling you in two minutes. You don't have to pick up. But please listen to the voice mail. B.**

Something was different to me with his text this time. I'm not sure if it was because of me or because of something in his tone, but it had my fingers itching to answer when my phone started ringing a minute later. Instead I fisted my hands and waited it out until the minute the phone alerted there was a new message.

When I heard his voice, my heart squeezed with ache and loss. "Had . . . I don't know if you're just deleting my messages or actually hearing them, but I want you to hear this one. I want you to listen to my voice, hear the determination in it. . . . Nothing's changed. You're worth the goddamn fight. *Gloves are on*. I'll go every damn round with you to prove it. All you've got to do is step back in the ring with me. You've already knocked me out, but I'm still fighting. Take the chance. Bell's about to ring."

I think I listened to it over and over, tears sliding down my face as I wanted to pick up the phone and call him back but was so scared to do it, to invite him in. My gloves are on for a different type of fight, so how can I have the strength to go at it with him too?

I fought my subconscious telling me that I didn't have to put the gloves on if I just opened the door and let him in. Then I wondered if the slight slur in his speech meant he was just bullshitting me and was drunk and lonely. And after that, I sat in bed contemplating whether he knew . . . if Colton had told him.

Sleep came in short bouts because every dream was filled with him, or about him, so that I'd wake up longing to hear his voice again, feel his touch, see his smile. I was so exhausted and restless by six that I got up, left Ry a note, and came here to be close to the one person who understands this more than anyone.

It's so peaceful here, so beautiful, and a tad cold, so I lean back in my seat, which I've reclined, and close my eyes for a moment, allowing the serenity of being near her to pull me under.

The noise of the trash truck in the distance pulls me from sleep. I startle awake when I come to, immediately realizing where I am and that the sun is higher in the sky. Next I move my seat back upright, take a sip of water from the bottle in my console, and check my phone, which I'd set to silent as it rested in the console.

I note the missed calls from Rylee and a few from Becks and squeeze my eyes shut, throwing my phone onto the passenger seat. I have to talk to her first. Sort my shit out so that I can figure out where to go from here. That sudden fluttery feeling returns to my chest as I climb out of the car and start walking across the green grass dotted with stone markers.

Guilt mixed with sadness weighs heavy with each step. I haven't been here since my diagnosis. My head's been screwed-up enough that I feel guilty that I haven't been here to tell Lexi that I let her down. That I have cancer now too.

I don't want her to worry. I know it's silly because this is just a place when technically her spirit is all around me, so I know she already knows, but at the same time, I feel guilt nonetheless.

I smile softly when I reach her spot beneath the large oak tree, the branches giving her special spot shade and prolonging the life of flowers here from the harsh California sun. "Hey, sis," I tell her as I lower myself to the ground, running my finger over the engraving of her name, before leaning my back against the tombstone like I used to sit for hours those first few months after she died.

I swear I hear her voice, can feel her when I'm here. And I know it's all in my head, but I don't care. It's all I have left, and so it's enough for me. At least I tell myself it is.

I talk to her for a bit, filling her in on miscellaneous things, telling her little things about Maddie that a mom would want to know, stalling telling her about the diagnosis. I inform her that the Scandalous event went flawlessly, and our company has officially secured its first huge client. Ridiculous really that when the admission of my diagnosis is finally off my chest and no lightning bolt strikes me dead, I sigh in relief.

I explain to her through my tears that I'm going to keep it from Maddie as long as possible. Protect her from the memories and the devastation. I tell her how Mom and Dad are handling it, the charm on mom's necklace getting constant use as it's worked back and forth on the chain.

And then I fall silent again, wanting to tell her the rest, but I know the minute it's out of my mouth I'm going to realize just how stupid I've been. Testing him, pushing him away, making decisions for him that he should get to make for himself.

I rearrange the flowers in their urns, buying time, and even that sounds ludicrous because it's not like she's going anywhere. A cool breeze floats across the cemetery, and I settle cross-legged facing her marker, hands picking at the grass and separating the blades mindlessly.

"I met someone, Lex," I finally say in a whisper. "You might have even heard me mention him before. His name is Becks." I laugh, knowing she would because it's so cliché to fall for the best man. "Yeah, the one with the nice ass from the Las Vegas trip." I explain to her about the wedding night and the constant push and pull between us since then. About his confession that he loves me and my lie to protect him.

"I can't ask him to go through this with me, Lex." The tears start again as I think of how brutal this will be, going at it alone. It's not what I really want, but I know it's for the best in the end. "He's thirty-two. He should be out at clubs and meeting hot women and living his life, not stuck with a woman with scars instead of tits. Having to hold me up so I can puke because I'm so weak and sick from the chemo. He deserves a woman who has the time to take care of him, not a bald, bloated, boobless woman who is so tired from being sick, she doesn't want to go out."

I push the tears off my face. Knowing my words are so true but so desperately wanting to be selfish and ask him to stick it out. Deal with all the crap because I'm so damn worth it. But I can't. He may be in the ring, but I'm just not sure if I can force him to fight for something that's going to devastate him.

"I know what I'm doing is right, Lex. If you could see what you leaving has done to Danny ... it's ..." I squeeze my eyes, trying to shut out the images of him broken and crying so hard, he couldn't speak. Of him looking like a zombie to the point my parents took Maddie for a bit so that he could get himself together enough not to scare her. And then I realize I don't want to push the thoughts away. I need to remember them, use them as a steadfast reminder of why I can't drag Becks into this.

Why he can't know that I'm in love with him too.

Hell yes, I'd step into the ring with him, would love him to fight beside me.

"I love him," I whisper into the silence. "And I'm scared to death." The sobs rack my body as I finally say the two things I've been holding in, have been ignoring over the past two weeks. And there's something about saying a hard truth aloud that makes it both more real and more cathartic. Almost like even if it's just me in a cemetery, I still can't take the acknowledgment back.

"Give me a sign, Lex. Please give me something to tell me that you're listening. That I don't need to be scared because your wings up there are shielding me from the worst of it. I need to know you're by my side."

"She is by your side." His voice startles me. Scares the hell out of me really, and I know a part of it's because I thought I was alone, but the other part is I wonder how much he's heard. "Every second of every day, she's by your side."

I'm wiping the tears off my face with my shirt as I turn around to face Danny. He's standing behind me, his hands shoved deep in his jeans' pockets and his head angled to meet my gaze. "Until she had Maddie, you were the one she took care of. The one she thought of before herself. We used to fight about it, actually. How she'd think of you before she'd think of me."

I push myself up from my seat, my right foot numb from sitting for so long. I know I look like a mess, but I don't care because Danny's words captivate me. Something about Lex that I never knew. Something to hold tight to when I thought there'd never be anything new again.

"I'm sorry," I whisper but all the while a little part of me smiles at how lucky I was to have that connection to my sister.

"Don't be," he says, taking a step toward me and then looking at her grave for a moment. "That's one of the things I loved about her. Her commitment to her family, to you. I knew that when we had kids, she'd be fiercely protective and incredible with them because of the way she was with you."

I bite my lip to prevent more tears from falling and know already that I'm going to fail miserably. I step beside Danny, my posture echoing his as we both stare at the dates on the stone marker, which reinforce that Lex is never coming back.

"You didn't tell me." The hurt woven into his voice squeezes my heart. I reach over and put his hand in mine and keep it there as I try to explain why I didn't tell him about my diagnosis. "Your mom told me last night when she dropped Maddie off. She needed to talk to someone besides your dad about it and didn't realize that I didn't know yet. . . . I'm so sorry. Had. . . . I don't even know what to—"

"There's nothing to say," I tell him. "It is what it is. They caught it early. Hopefully, that will help." I say the words but don't feel any truth behind them. I feel like a broken record on repeat because there is no conviction in my voice. He just nods his head and squeezes my hand, the silence that was comforting now filled with unease. "It's all so raw still . . . Lex being gone. I thought maybe if I waited to tell you until after the surgery, I'd have better news. It would dredge up less of *everything* for you. I don't know." I shake my head and exhale loudly. "I don't know anything right now, Danny. I'm sorry I didn't tell you, but I was just trying to do what I thought was best for you."

"You don't get to make those decisions, Haddie. For me. For anyone. *That's my choice*. That's their choice. You're not God, so stop playing everyone's cards for them. You're robbing us and yourself of possibilities because of it." He falls silent, which only serves to emphasize his words as he turns to face me. When I lift my eyes to meet his, I see a different man before me. Yes, I see the grief still weighing heavily, but I also see a quiet resolve that hasn't been there before. He stares at me for a moment before just barely shaking his head and then pulling me into him and wrapping his arms around me.

At first I just stand there, the numbness I choose to feel dictating my immobility. His words are soaking into my psyche, a verbal backhand to my way of thinking. And I know he's right. Every single word. So when the guilt and shame and acknowledgment over what I've done to Becks, done to him, hit me like that Mack Truck Rylee warned me about, everything I've held in comes bubbling up.

I start to move, start to feel again. I wrap my arms around him and cling there, tears escalating in strength and volume as the house of cards I've built to protect my heart comes tumbling down. Danny holds me as I get it all out, quiet murmurs of support being said but nothing else besides that until all that's left in me is hitching, tearless sounds.

He keeps his arms around me for a moment longer before we separate, both of us wiping away tears. He steps forward and kisses his fingers before he runs them over her etched name.

"I miss her so much, Had. Every single moment of every goddamn day." He falls silent as he reins in the tears before continuing. "Every day I think she's going to walk through that front door, that I'll hear her bitch that I left my shoes in the way, hear her laugh as I tell her about my day, watch the love in her eyes as she holds Maddie . . . every damn day. . . ." His voice fades off.

His words tear into me and reawaken a sadness that somehow was untapped somewhere, and before I can think, the question is off my tongue. "Do you ever wish you'd never met her?" His head snaps up, the shock and anger in his eyes has me scrambling to explain myself. "I mean, was loving her worth the risk? If you hadn't met her, then you'd never have had to go through all of this. You'd never have had to watch her die, be alone. . . ."

Danny hangs his head for a moment before looking back toward her marker. "I don't regret for a single day any moment I spent with her—good, bad, and ugly." He looks up to meet my eyes. "She was my everything, Haddie. And, God . . . fuck, it broke me, watching her suffer, watching her die. . . . Look at me. I'm still broken," he says, holding his hands out to his sides, "but I wouldn't give up a single second I had with her because even though the end was brutal, do you have any idea how much of her light she left me to hold on to?" A ghost of a smile spreads across his face, and somehow it reaches his eyes for the first time since she died. "She gave me hope and laughter. She gave me love so strong, I'll always feel it, feel her. She gave me a lifetime of memories in the few years we had together . . . and most important, she gave me Maddie."

And the way he says that, with astonished gratitude, has a soft smile spreading on my lips too.

"Would I give anything to have her here? Give up everything I own so that she could watch Maddie grow up and so she could sit in a rocker on the porch and grow old with me? Without a fucking doubt, I would . . . but you know what? We lived every moment together like it was our last, even before she got sick. We used to always say *no regrets.* How little did we know what that motto would come to mean for us. . . ." His voice trails off.

He runs a hand through his hair as he takes a few steps away from me and then stops. "You asked me if it was worth the risk," he says before turning back around to look at me. "I miss her. I lost her . . . but look at all that I would have missed, never experienced, if I'd never opened myself up. Is fate cruel? Hell yes, it is. Would I have rather not have loved her so I didn't feel this constant grief? Never. She was worth it . . . every fucking risk. . . . She was worth every single one." And even though there are tears glistening in his eyes, his voice has never sounded more resolute.

We stare at each other for a moment before he mutters that he needs a moment to compose himself. He starts to walk away, and I tell him to stay. I'll wander so he can have some time with Lex.

I walk carefully through the cemetery and come to an unoccupied grassy patch up on a hill overlooking the rest of it. I lower myself to the grass and prop myself back on my hands, raise my face to the sun, and enjoy the warmth of it drying my tears. Danny's words strike a chord in me, my heart so happy that my sister was able to experience that kind of love in her short life. And then I start to think of Becks, and I begin to wonder if I'm robbing us of a chance at that.

Could he be the one? Could we have a love like that? I have no clue, but Danny's right. Who am I to try to control fate for us? Hell yes, the fear is still there and the desire to push him away to protect him, but at the same time, I feel that tiny thrill of possibility.

A dandelion catches the corner of my eye, and the sob chokes in my throat. Memories light up my mind, and I can't help but think of this as a sign that Lex is hearing me, understanding me, rooting for me.

I lean over to pick the dandelion up and hold it up in front of my face, staring at the plethora of seeds tempting me to blow them into the wind. I close my eyes, the first tear slipping over, but this tear is a combination of acceptance, sorrow, and relief.

"I wish I may, I wish I might, have this wish I wish tonight," I say, repeating our dandelion duo mantra. "I wish for *time* so I can make a thousand more wishes on my own."

Then I close my eyes and blow as hard as I can. I open them to watch the seeds take flight and dance across the breeze. And I can't help but waste one of those wishes right now as I wish to be one of them, free and in flight without a worry.

"Time is precious, Haddie," Danny says off to my right as I continue to watch the dandelion seeds.

"Waste it wisely," I finish Lex's motto for him.

And I've already wasted too much of it.

Chapter 29

BECKS

The percussion section in my head has finally quieted down some as I sit on the balcony. I'm slowly fading into recovery sleep, feet propped up on the railing, and a bottle of water in my hand.

My mind whirls a million miles an hour, after spending the better part of the morning on my laptop doing Google searches on mastectomies and what to expect as the caregiver when helping someone going through chemo and radiation.

Scary fucking shit.

Basically kill you to try to cure you.

You'd think modern medicine would have a better solution than this, but I guess you take the tried-and-true route until you need to take a different one. Stick to what works and all that.

And it'd better work. No ifs, ands, or buts.

Now I just need to see her. Hold her. Tell her face-to-face the gloves are on, and I'm waiting in the ring.

Then the first of many waiting games will begin.

After she apologized for not telling me, Ry promised to

call the minute she heard from her. She said she thought Haddie was visiting Lexi and already had her brother-in-law on the way to see if she was at the cemetery and to make sure she was okay.

I put the cap back on the water bottle and lower my hat over my eyes. My phone alerts me to a text—probably the hundredth of the day between Ry, Colton, and myself—so I don't have any expectations when I lift it up to look at the screen. But when I do, the gas is knocked from my tank.

Meet me in the ring?

The smile spreads wide on my face, the response giving me so much more than the simple request it reads as. I tell myself to calm the fuck down, that we've been here before, and that if she gets spooked, she'll run again.

But that doesn't stop the surge of relief that comes.

I scramble to respond, pissed when the doorbell rings because answering this text is ten times more important. "Come in," I yell, head down and focused on texting her back.

Rex lifts his head to look toward the door, and I'm just about to hit SEND when I look up and drop the phone with a loud clatter on the table.

Haddie stands in the doorway of the patio, shorts, tank top, sweatshirt tied around her waist, but it's when I come to her feet that I'm knocked off my stride.

Damn.

She's wearing a pair of pink flip-flops.

I shove away my mom's stupid-ass dream about the shoes—she's just being crazy, after all—but I can't help the lingering notion that this was meant to be. That my mom just might be right. I draw my eyes up from Haddie's feet to take in her hair pulled back in a clip, cheeks flushed, and eyes red and swollen from crying.

She looks like she's been to Hell and back, but I've never thought her more beautiful than right now.

Her eyes hold mine. So many emotions are in her gaze,

but the ones I see and hold on to like a green flag on race day are the hope, the acceptance, the resolve that's there.

I rise from my chair, not wanting to take my eyes off her for a single second, taking in everything about her, and make my way to her, heart pounding, smile widening.

I hope she feels this—whatever this is between us—because I feel like every single part of me wants to prove to her—right here, right now—how much I love her. How much I'm going to be there for her.

When I get close to her, my feet falter as I notice the story in her eyes—I can see it clear as day now—and I just hope she lets me help write its happily ever after.

Chapter 30

Becks walks toward me, the muscles of his bare torso bunching with each step, a cautious smile on his face, and every part of me knows this is the right decision. That I want him, need him beside me. That he's good for me.

My bottom lip trembles as he closes the distance, shame taking the lead among my emotions for causing all of this trouble when it didn't need to be there. I control the urge to step toward him; I want to let him make the first move, see if now that he knows what an absolute mess I am, he still wants me.

But once he gets within a few feet, he stops, and I can see him try to pull back to allow me to set the pace. His eyes reflect relief, hope, love . . . but I can also see him try to guard his emotions, hold them in. We stand here, and I tell myself that I did this to us so it's his first step to make, but after a few moments with everything I want so damn close, my resolve flies out the window.

Within seconds I'm in his arms, and I'm not sure which one of us made the move, and I really don't care because it feels so damn good. "I'm so sorry," falls from my mouth over and over again as he squeezes me so tight, I can't breathe except to repeat my apologies.

He just keeps repeating for me to "Shh, baby" over and over until he pulls back and frames my face with his hands and presses a kiss to my lips in between our repeated phrases. Tears are coursing down my cheeks, and I don't care because all I care about is his mouth on mine, his arms around me, my name on his lips.

He looks at me, his eyes asking before his mouth does. "Haddie?" *Are you sure? Can I do this with you? You ready to fight with me beside you?* Every single question is there in the way he says my name.

I nod my head to him, leaning forward to kiss him to reinforce my response. His heart is thundering against mine, his hands a welcome comfort against my tearstained cheeks as I press my tongue between his lips. I moan when our tongues touch and begin to dance that slow seductive reconnection.

I know it's only been a week, but I feel like it's been forever.

My hands move over his bare torso, hungry and fearful all at once. My mind is still hoping he doesn't reject me, despite his kiss, his touch, his continuous murmurs of encouragement telling me otherwise. My teeth pull and scrape against his bottom lip and he gives me a groan of satisfaction that encourages me to keep going.

"Haddie," he pants as he tries to stop kissing me but continues doing it nonetheless.

"Mm-hmm?" My hands slip behind the waistband of his board shorts and squeeze the swell above his ass.

"Had," he groans, "we need to talk."

I still my hands, my lips against his, and pull back so that I can look into his eyes. I slide my hands up his torso, earning me a hiss of his breath until they frame his face. "Yes, we do need to talk. And I'll talk all night with you . . . answer every question, apologize seven ways from Sunday," I tell him, leaning forward and pressing my lips to his, "but right now I want you, Beckett."

I can see the skepticism flicker through his eyes, the immediate doubt that we're back where we started on day one. I rein in my need—to feel for the right reasons for the first time in what seems like forever rather than to use it to chase away the pain—and realize that I might be making the decision to step into the ring, but it's not fair to keep him continually against the ropes.

He's right.

As much as I want to cement our connection with the physical desire between us, we need to talk. I groan when I step back from the warmth of his body and exhale a shaky breath. I stare at the hollow of his throat for a second, suddenly nervous to speak with him because now this is all real.

"You're right," I finally say, my voice soft and heart pounding. I look up to him and meet his eyes. "You deserve some explanations." Tears pool in my eyes because as much as I know I want this, I never thought how I was going to explain myself without sounding like a damn idiot.

"Come here," he says, putting his hands on my hips and pulling me into him so that I'm back against the firmness of his body. "I just want to hold you for a minute, okay? Just give me this because right now you don't need to explain shit except for why you're never going to do this to us again."

And I choke on the sob because my mind immediately goes there—to the poison in my body and how I might not have a choice whether I do or don't hurt us again. But he said *us*, which allows me to quiet my head and snuggle a little farther into his comforting warmth.

He sighs when he catches what he said and how I took it, and squeezes me a little tighter to emphasize his words. "Not now, Haddie. Don't think about it now. There are going to be plenty of moments, plenty of days where the cancer is going to get between you and me, but don't let it ruin this moment. Because right now, you're just this heart-breakingly gorgeous woman full of fire and spunk, and I'm this mild mannered guy who's missed the hell out of you. You're not sick, and I'm not healthy. . . . *We just are.*"

His words wind their way into my soul, take hold of my heart and start tying double knots in the ropes he's looped there that connect me back to him. And for the first time, fear doesn't fuel anything because he's right: We have to live in this moment, appreciate this moment, just he and I.

City and Country.

The longer we stand there wrapped around each other, the easier it is to believe that we can do this. That I can let him in wholeheartedly and trust that he'll make the best decisions for himself.

Regardless, I still feel that it's important to make sure he's well-informed so that he knows what he's getting into.

"Becks, can we talk?"

He chuckles, the sound a welcome reverberation against my chest. "Now you're starting to sound like me."

"Funny . . ."

He pulls me with him toward the patio furniture protected from the sun under a trellis. He doesn't release me but rather keeps his arm around me and guides me to sit on the couch so that I'm cradled in his lap, my back against the arm of it and my legs lying across his thighs. He looks at me, eyes narrowing, the ghost of a lopsided smirk tugging up one corner of his mouth.

"Hi," he says, and I can't help the smile that spreads across my lips, my stomach fluttering with anticipation from feeling such a different type of emotion than I have over the past few weeks.

"Hi."

He leans forward and presses one of his signature Beckett kisses to my lips. The most innocent brush of lips, but it leaves you feeling like he's just opened you, stolen a piece of your heart, and is never going to give it back. And that's a good thing because he doesn't need to steal bits and pieces of it anymore. . . . No, I'm ready to hand it over wholeheartedly.

"I have a few things I need to say—explanations, apologies—so I'd appreciate it if you let me say them, okay?"

He nods his head to me and leans back some before licking his lips and raising his eyebrows to tell me that the floor is mine.

Or rather the ring.

"I watched Lexi die. Day by day, breath by breath. And when I wasn't watching her, I was busy watching Danny fall apart. We were all devastated when she died, but he lost himself for a while. And then there's Maddie and everything she's gone through...." My voice fades off as I try to get a grip on my emotions so that I can get through this without breaking down because I really need Becks not to just listen to me, but to really hear me.

He runs a hand up and down my bare leg, my concentration so fierce to keep it all together that I don't even realize he's doing it until I feel the ache unfurl in my center. I welcome the feeling but know I can't sate it until I finish this.

I'm trying to turn over a new leaf. Talk, then action; reason, then lust.

"So after Lex died, of course, the worry turned to me in my family. I'd already thought about it, already knew deep down, somehow that I had the same fate." He starts to shake his head and correct me, but I stop him by bringing my finger to his lips. "Not the dying part, but the breast cancer part. It all weighed heavy on me, stole me from myself really. Then one night after I picked the broken pieces of Danny off his living room floor, knowing he'd never really be whole again, I swore I'd never do that to someone. I'd never let anyone get close enough to me so that when I eventually got sick, they'd have to suffer like Danny did. I vowed to protect the people I cared about, the people who had choices to avoid being in that situation ... to never let someone love me...." The first tear falls over and slides down my cheek.

"Haddie." My name is a sigh on his lips as he reaches up and wipes the tear away before I shake my head for him to leave it. He can't touch me or I'll fall apart, and I can't fall apart yet. I need to finish this before I can break. Then I can use him—*use us*—to help fortify myself so we can move forward.

"I know, but it made perfect sense to me. *And then you happened.*" I look at him and see so many things that I never expected, most of which are the parts of me I'd lost with Lexi's death. "I don't know how to explain what . . . how you . . ."

"You don't need to because I feel the same." He scrunches his head down so that his eyes are even with mine.

"No, I do need to," I explain, finding my words again. "You told me you loved me, and I stood there and shoved you away. I hurt you on purpose, and that has eaten at me. All I wanted to do was to call you and tell you I was sorry, that I didn't mean what I said, but I was trying to protect you from this." I put my hands out in front of my chest, my eyes closing momentarily while I try to figure out how else to emphasize how sorry I am.

"Had." His hands are back on my face, directing it up so that I have no choice but to meet his eyes. "I told you I was in it for the fight. I wasn't going anywhere. I still am and always will be."

He leans forward and kisses my forehead as we both accept the moment, the possible future, the definite fight we have ahead of us.

"But aren't you worried that you're going to be with this girl who's going to be a hot mess . . . who's going to lose her hair, possibly be infertile, be sick all the time from chemo or radiation . . . who might not make it?" My voice breaks. My words sound so hollow, so foreign as I try to disengage myself from those truths that I hate to say but need to clarify nonetheless.

"Montgomery." I'm so in my own head momentarily that it takes the third or fourth attempt for me to hear him. Startled, my eyes flash back up to him. "I say this with all of the courtesy in the world . . . *but shut the hell up*. I don't want to hear—"

"I know, but it's reality and reality is—"

His hand goes playfully over my mouth so that the rest of my sentence sounds like a muffled garble. "Uh-uh. This is where you stay quiet, and I get to talk. Understood?" I hear the teasing in his tone but also hear the authority.

I nod my head as he blows out a breath and runs his free hand through his hair before setting it back down on my bare thigh. "You don't get it, do you?" He smiles softly and angles his head to stare at me, his thumb rubbing circles absently on my leg. "That first night . . . hell, you asked for no strings, but I knew if I had you, I'd only want more. Then I tried tying those damn strings any way I could, but you severed them just as quickly as I knotted them." He shakes his head for a moment before meeting my eyes with a vivid clarity in his gaze. "You're that once-in-a-lifetime type of woman, Haddie."

"What are you talking about?"

"You're the goddamn priceless Macallan."

I scrunch up my nose and look at him. Then our conversation from my doorstep weeks ago comes back to finally make sense of his words. The sincerity in his tone strikes me next, and his conviction has my chest constricting with the emotion I feel for him.

"Well, at least I'm a good one," I say, earning a smile from him.

"The best." He nods his head with a murmured appreciation. "I wouldn't care if you were a Two Buck Chuck bottle . . . I'll pick you every time, Haddie. Scars, inability to have kids, bald, sick, emotional . . . you're beautiful to me. Every single way. I'll still pick you every goddamn time." His eyes bore into mine. They dance with the same emotion his tone reflects. "There's just always been something about you that I can't resist. . . ."

Tears flood my eyes—and the overwhelming acceptance he's just given me is undeserved but gives me the courage to start taping up the boxing gloves for the fight of my life.

With him in my corner.

And it's funny. All along I've told him no strings—pushed him away the minute they even started to intertwine—so I never realized how liberating it would be when I willingly tied them myself.

I start to become comfortable with the idea, accept it, and something he said at the farmhouse hits me.

"It's the click."

"Yes, the click," he says with a soft chuckle. "But you know what? The click's irrelevant now. The click was our initial connection. Now? Now it's the clanking."

"Clanking?" What in the hell is he talking about?

"Yep. It's the sound the chains are making as I wrap them around your heart and shut the damn lock." He flashes a cocky grin at me that does ridiculous things to my insides. "Screw the strings. They can be cut. I'm using chains to tie us together because it takes a hell of a lot more to break those."

I try to mask the girlie sigh that wants to fall from my lips in giddiness. "That sounds kind of kinky." I raise my eyebrows at him, my heart full and the coil of desire only increasing.

A slow smile spreads across his lips. "They sound a little unforgiving, but damn, City, we just might have to try that out. It kind of turns me on."

I lean forward and kiss him. *"Promise?"* I whisper, my lips moving against his.

"I'll promise you whatever you want as long as you tell me you're not going to push me away again." The playfulness in his eyes fades to solemnity. I can tell I've hurt him and hate myself for it.

I reach out and smooth a hand over his chest and up to the line of his jaw. "I'm not going to promise I'm not going to push, Becks, because I'm going to get scared. Hell, I'm already scared about what's going to come ... but I promise that I'm not going to run. I'm not going to shut you out. Because *we are*," I tell him. He gives a devastating smile. I lean forward and taste his temptation and lose myself for a moment in it.

I rest my forehead against his, my last confession burning on my tongue. "I've used sex for so long to make me feel so I can forget, and I don't want to do that anymore," my lips whisper against his as I lay all my cards on the table. I can feel the heat of his breath, smell the scent of his cologne as I wait to make sure he hears my words. "You've changed that for me. My gloves are on, Becks, but they're for the one battle I've yet to fight.... There's no need to wear them with you. ..." I press another kiss to his lips and move my hands to the base of his neck so that my hands can play idly in his hair. "I know how I feel about you, and now it's time to show you. Let me make love to you."

I hear his quick intake of breath, his body tensing in momentary restraint before I feel his lips spread into a smile against mine.

"You don't have to ask twice," he laughs, and in a swift motion, his hands have lifted my tank top over my head.

The minute it clears my face, I have only a moment to see the fire in his eyes before his lips are on mine. I drown in the intensity of the kiss, his complete dominance of my senses as he uses his mouth to own each and every sound he coaxes from me while his hands skim over the bare flesh of my back.

They graze across my rib cage to my chest, and I can't help but freeze when he cups both of my breasts. Cold, hard reality pulls me from the eroticism of the moment and the hot sex that's in my near future. "Becks ..."

He brings his lips to my ear, where his heated breath warms my skin. "You are so fucking beautiful, Haddie Montgomery, with or without these." He flicks his thumbs over my hard nipples, causing me to gasp from the sensation. "These do not make you the woman I love. Not in the least. *You got that?*"

He presses a soft kiss to the space just below my ear as the emotion and meaning behind his words hit me like a one-two combo punch. My eyes well with tears but I don't have a chance to comprehend anything else because Becks closes his mouth over one of my nipples and sucks.

Emotions mix with sensations and tackle me from every angle as I move my hips to try to relieve the ache he's adding to with his alternating sucks and scrapes of teeth. "Sweet, sweet Haddie," he murmurs to me, followed by a satisfied grown in the back of his throat.

He takes his time enjoying my breasts, all the while removing my shorts, his clothes, and I'm so taken by his thoroughness and adept skill that it rather shocks me to find that he's also repositioned me. My ass hangs half off the couch, my shoulders against the back of it, and my legs are spread wide.

He begins to kiss his way down my abdomen as I feel the featherlight touch of his fingertips skimming from my knee up the inside line of my thigh. Soft and gentle. Thorough and attentive.

So damn addictive.

I exhale when his fingers brush over my sex, a teasing taunt that causes me to tilt my hips and physically ask for more. He chuckles softly, his fingers parting me at the same time he blows softly on my clit. "Becks . . ."

"Mm. I want to taste you," he murmurs a second before I watch him lower and then feel his mouth on my bared flesh. And it's not like I'm not watching him do it, but the warmth of his mouth still shocks me, makes me tense up.

His fingers slide back and forth once, then twice, before he tucks them into me. I'm wet instantly, my body so primed for him as he begins to slide his fingers in and out of me at the same time his tongue laves my external center of nerves.

I weave my fingers in his hair, a gentle way to tell him when the sensations are just too much. And when I tug on his hair, he just laughs softly, the vibration of it an added element to his ministrations as he completely ignores my request.

He looks up at me, eyes hungry with a carnal sensuality. "You said you wanted to feel for the right reasons . . . so sit back, do anything but shut up—hell, scream if you want—and let me make you feel to remember . . . not to forget."

He presses a kiss to the top of my sex before using his tongue to part me as he slides back down. This time, though, his fingers pull out to part me so that his tongue can plunge in, driving my need to levels that render me senseless.

Soon the ragged cry falls from my mouth, and I push my hips toward his mouth and my head falls back against the couch while I absorb the seduction of his tongue. I force myself to open my eyes so that I can watch him manipulate me, own me . . . love me.

And there is something so raw and real in the moment his eyes raise to meet mine, my taste on his tongue and my body at his mercy, that I begin to tremble as the first strains of my orgasm begin to pulse through me.

"Oh God!" I cry out when it hits me full force, lost to him and the moment because this may be a physical release, but it's also the emotional offering of my heart. My body slowly liquefies as the spasms abate, Becks still groaning with desire as he tastes my pleasure.

I swear I hear him say, "That's one," but I'm so lost to the world beyond that using energy to respond is nearly impossible.

I let my head fall back, eyes closed, muscles still riding the orgasmic aftershocks. His mouth leaves the V of my thighs, and the cool breeze is a slight shock when it hits my swollen flesh. His body brushes against my thighs, and then I feel his smooth crest positioned perfectly at my entrance.

"Look at me, Haddie." His words pull me from my

pleasure-induced coma. The mixture of authority and compassion in his voice tugs my insides in every direction imaginable, giving me a glimpse of what I've always gravitated toward and what I now find incredibly sexy.

Only Becks could pull this mix off.

The only thought I can manage before he pushes his way into me at an achingly slow pace is what a lucky, lucky woman I am to have found him.

And not to have lost him.

Our eyes lock while we both succumb to the slow, sweet burn of pleasure as he bottoms all the way out. He stills, his hips flexing in a show of restraint from driving in me at the thunderous rhythm his eyes tell me he's dying for. And that little movement of his hips seems like nothing, but it causes his dick to press against the exact place I need to feel it.

My breath hitches, and my fingernails dig into my own thighs when mindless pleasure takes hold as he slowly pulls out, every single nerve paid perfect attention from the pace he sets. I look down to where we are joined, the head of his cock buried inside me, but the remainder glistens with my arousal. He begins to slide back in, the hotter-than-hell image of him becoming part of me in all ways possible is the only thing I can focus on.

I'm lost to the thought and the sight until I look up and meet his eyes. He's inches from my face, so I can't mistake the emotion swimming in the aqua pools in front of me: love, desire, need, want.

And the last one solidifies everything I feel for him and then some: It's *awe*.

My heart swells, and a smile spreads on my lips as I lean up to kiss him. The action earns me a rough growl since my whole body tenses with the motion, causing my muscles to tighten around him.

Our restraint snaps.

Desire consumes us as he yanks my torso forward so he can tackle my mouth with his tongue. I taste my own arousal on his lips, and that mixed with the increasing tempo of his hips' cadence causes the tingle of sensation to turn into an earthquake of aching need.

My hands begin to roam, demanding more with scoring fingernails and bruising holds as his mouth brands my body and his dick dominates every sensation I have. The onslaught is so intense, so riddled with passion and urgency, that as my body begins to tighten around him, I lose myself completely.

I can't concentrate anymore. I have to remind myself to breathe, tell my thighs not to squeeze him out as they press against his torso from the building pressure. My lips fall lax, my ability to kiss him lost from the inundation of experiencing so much at once. I'm unable to do anything . . . anything that is but *feel*.

I look up at him, my slow and steady, to find him anything but that. His eyes blaze into mine, demanding that I give him everything of myself right now. The look alone makes my mouth go dry—the glimpse of my bad boy coming through momentarily. He reaches down and digs his fingers into the flesh at my hips to tilt them and alter the sensation.

And all of it—the look in his eyes, the ownership in his touch, the breath he's stolen from me, and his heart that he's given me—pushes me over the edge. My body explodes into a sea of liquid fire that leaves every part of me burned with Becks's indelible mark.

He pulls me forward, fitting himself to me skin to skin so that he can piston his hips harder, faster, drawing out my orgasm while igniting his. He buries his face in the curve of my neck as he calls my name over and over in a matching rhythm to his thrusts. He rocks us, our bodies tangled up in each other's and our hearts getting used to the weight of the chain and lock settling there for good.

My heart is thundering so loud in my ears that I almost miss the words he says, but there's no mistaking them once my mind processes them. My muscles freeze momentarily, the tears stinging my eyes a complement to the soft smile on my lips. I squeeze my arms around him a bit tighter, my soul sighing in contentment before I lean back and meet his eyes.

I need him to see me when I say it for the first time.

"I love you too, Beckett."

Chapter 31

" I had tons of fun today. I'll see you when I get back from my trip, okay?" I cringe at the lie, hoping Maddie can't hear the guilt in my voice. At first she's quiet on the other end of the line, my body rocking as I wait for her to call me on the carpet. "You have a blast at your slumber party tonight, okay?"

"I will. It's going to be sooo much fun!" She giggles, and the sound warms my heart because she's taking baby steps to normalcy. And I fear if she finds out I'm sick, it'll knock her back some. "Fly safe with angels. And call me lots if you can! Love you, Haddie Maddie."

"I will," I say, thinking of the only angel I need looking out for me. "Love you more, Maddie Haddie."

"Hearts and heels."

I catch the sob that threatens with her comment and fortunately am able to suppress it. "Hearts and heels, baby girl."

The phone clicks, and I gasp out when I remove the hand I'm holding over my mouth. I slide down the wall, my phone clattering to the ground beside me as I fight the range of emotions that are on constant recycle today.

I hate lying to Maddie, even if I'm doing it with her best interests in mind. But it still sucks telling her I'm going on a business trip tomorrow when in fact I'm going in for surgery. I don't want her scared or worried. I want her to be the little girl slowly healing, learning to live again without her mommy.

It was Becks's idea to tell her I was going on a trip. He had asked to tag along on our girl day last week of Chuck E. Cheese's, pedicures, new strappy sandal shoe shopping, and ice cream on the boardwalk. When Maddie had asked why Nana had to take her to her Girl Scout's meeting next week, I drew a blank. My mind was so busy focusing on all the details of the Scandalous deal I'd just signed and how I was going to manage it while going through treatment that she caught me off guard.

And that was when Becks stepped up and informed her he was taking me on a trip to spoil me. Maddie had been so excited at the prospect of me flying on an airplane that the topic had dominated the rest of the conversation.

I sigh and lean my head back, settling into my last few moments of solitude before Becks comes over. I close my eyes and enjoy the smile that comes so easily at the thought of him. He's provided humor during the tedious hours waiting between pre-op blood work, endless scans, and other appointments. He's held me while I cried on the few nights when the fear settled in before sexing me up so damn good that I'm so tired I don't even have the strength to summon the emotion again.

And he's shared his mom's homemade chocolate chip cookies with me.

Now, that's serious.

My smile spreads wider now, my body warming at the thought of him, heart swelling and psyche so glad I let him in the ring because I'm so lucky to have him with me for this fight.

I love him.

The thought still stuns me . . . how easy it is to feel it, to accept it, when I did nothing but push it away.

And it's so much easier to focus on that these last couple days than it is my surgery tomorrow. I'm handling it well—the freak-outs far and few between—but the fear is still there, the worry a constant presence.

Becks calls them my shadow—fear and worry—and he's even made a game of it to try to make me laugh and ease my mind. Anytime we're outside where my shadow is present, he positions himself so that he steps on it. At first I thought he was crazy, but then we started making a game of it: two crazy people walking erratically down Santa Monica pier in some weird competition, screeching and laughing every time he'd try to stomp and I'd evade him at the last minute. I was well in the lead of the stomp-to-nonstomp ratio when we reached the end of the pier.

Then Becks grabbed my arm, pulled me into him, and caught my lips with his. It was a kiss that rivaled no other with the sun above us, the sounds of the amusement park around us, and the taste of saltwater taffy on his tongue. And when he started laughing, his lips breaking from mine, I looked at him to figure out what exactly was so funny. He just quirked an eyebrow and looked down to where he was standing on my shadow.

Stomping out fear and worry thoroughly with his tennis shoes.

"I win," he said, flashing me a devilish grin.

I shiver in delight, remembering how great it was to lose to Beckett Daniels. Who can argue with a man who takes you home to have a romantic dinner of McDonald's hamburgers on a checkered blanket on the balcony? Handy thing that blanket turned out to be when he decided to have his way with me after we played truth or dare staring at the stars in the sky. The best part of the night besides the obvious was that he promised next time I'd get his mom's homemade lasagna.

He must really love me.

I smile at the thought, and when I pull my head from the

memory, I realize that my hand is worrying the charm on my new necklace back and forth. The necklace that appears to be interlinking chains with a heart-shaped padlock for a charm. The one I received two days ago with a card that said *Clank, clank*.

I guess I'm just like my mom after all, worrying my charm over my chain, but *my shadow* has been stomped out by Becks, so all I have left to cling to, besides hope, is this— my love and all of the people who love me.

As I begin to laugh into the empty silence of my house, I realize that for so long I feared how lonely Lexi must have felt facing this battle. It was her body against this terrible disease . . . but after these past two weeks, after letting Becks in so he can love me, I realize that she was anything but alone. She had an army of supporters who loved her dearly, just as I could if I let people know—and the thought comforts me to no end.

First the surgery and then telling people. Baby steps.

I've found peace for the first time in a long while with my sister's death. Maybe it's Becks's presence, maybe it's tomorrow's surgery—I don't know—but I do know that there is a sense of calm now within the painful tumult in my soul that had been missing.

I hang my head down and just let the laughter come freely.

"Now, that's the best sound in the world."

I lift my head up to find Becks leaning against the door-jamb of my bedroom, jeans on and a shirt unbuttoned at the collar and with the cuffs rolled up. I don't think I'll ever get used to the sight of him standing so comfortably in my bed-room, nor will it ever get old. And I'm so used to my relaxed and casual man that I forget how stunning he looks when he's out of his beloved board shorts. Although I quite like the lack of shirt that often accompanies the shorts, this look also gets my motor running. I scrape my eyes at a leisurely pace up his body and take in that disarming smile of his before meeting his eyes.

"I forgot how nice you clean up, Country." My smile widens as he steps forward and squats down on his haunches in front of me.

"And there's no chance in hell I could forget how beautiful you are."

"Smooth, Mr. Daniels, very smooth."

He leans forward and presses a soft kiss to my lips in a move that awakens the other five percent of my body that his presence alone didn't spark to life. I slide my tongue between his lips and bring my hands up to the base of his neck when he drops to his knees to deepen the kiss.

"Hmm," he hums in protest as he drags his lips from mine. "I'd love to continue this, but we have somewhere we need to be right now."

I shake my head and meet his eyes, confusion flooding through me. This is my last night before surgery, and we'd agreed to spend it snuggling together, eating junk food before my midnight cutoff time and then staying up to talk before leaving for the hospital.

"I thought we'd agreed—"

"We did," he says with a smirk before pressing a kiss to my forehead and then standing up. He reaches a hand out to me to help me stand. "But I lied. Stand up, pretty lady. You've got twenty minutes to get ready so that we're not late." I look up at him, our hands clasped and hearts joined, and I see so much more than a handsome man.

I see my future.

He pulls me up off the ground. I lean in for a kiss and am handily turned so that he can swat me on the backside. "No funny stuff, Montgomery. There's plenty of time for that later. Hurry that fine ass of yours up, *Your Highness*. Your chariot awaits you."

I roll my eyes and snort at the regal tone he uses. "I'm the furthest thing from a princess you'll find," I say as I walk toward my closet, our hands remaining in each other's until our arms stretch so far, they slip apart.

"I beg to differ," he says, his eyes following me like he doesn't want to take them off me.

"Well, then, that makes you my knight in shining armor." I raise an eyebrow at him, knowing he'll argue immediately.

His mouth curls up at one corner, and he laughs. "Wanna see my sword?"

"Only if you know how to use it, sir."

"Oh, I like the sound of that"—he raises his eyebrows at me—"and we both know I can use it."

I can't help laughing as I cross the distance and press a kiss against his lips, way too happy for a girl who's going in tomorrow for a mastectomy. But Lex's parting words echo in my ears.

Time is precious. Waste it wisely.

And I waste very little as I get dressed, not wanting the night to slip away too quickly since tomorrow is D-day. I'm not sure what he's up to, but I'm secretly excited. As much as we'd agreed tonight was going to be low-key, a part of me is grateful that whatever Becks is doing, he's trying to make my last night as a *whole me* special somehow.

Just as he's tried to make every moment of the entire past few weeks count.

Or maybe I'm wrong. Is Becks really making things special just because of what's happening tomorrow or is this just how Becks is in a relationship? Either way, I'm the lucky one on the receiving end of it.

When I'm finished, I go into the family room to find it empty and him nowhere in sight. "Becks?" I call, but there's no answer.

I look in the kitchen and then turn the corner when the fading dusk through the open front door catches my eye. I walk toward it, curious what the heck is going on. When I step through it, my hand flies to my mouth to cover a gasp that can't be muffled.

I have to do a double take to make sure of what I'm seeing is real.

Yep. Sure is.

Becks is standing beside a carriage, complete with horses and a coachman, a grin plastered on his face. "Your carriage awaits."

I notice neighbors out on their lawns, admiring the sight as I walk toward him—more than flustered—trying to process what in the hell he's doing. "What are you . . ." My words trail off as one of the horses neighs.

"If you're going to fight the fight, City, you need to arrive in style." I can see the pride in his eyes over thinking this up, and I immediately melt at his thoughtfulness.

"Princesses don't wear boxing gloves," I tease him as I take his outstretched hand, still in awe.

Becks tugs on my hand and pulls me into him so that our bodies connect. "This princess does." He presses a soft kiss to my lips. "Hearts and heels, Montgomery. Hearts and heels."

"Where are you taking me?"

"Wouldn't you like to know?" Becks taunts before brushing another teasing kiss on my lips like he's been giving me here and there. I'm snuggled up next to him, his arm pulling me in close, as we cruise under an entirely different horsepower from what we're used to.

The occasional silence between us is comfortable as we both get lost in our thoughts about tomorrow. My curiosity is also in major overdrive, considering my hospital bag sits in front of us, telling me we're not returning home, but at the same time where we are going is unknown. Becks knows the suspense is killing me, and he's quite enjoying watching me squirm.

The sky fades to black as we travel, passengers in nearby cars staring as they pass us, but I don't notice the fast-paced Los Angeles world because I'm so busy noticing the man at my side.

Because this girl's learned that slow and steady is most definitely the way to go.

"We're here!" he announces unexpectedly as the carriage turns into the driveway of an unassuming business park. I glance around at the empty office buildings complete with industrial roll-up garage on one side and a small front office with an entry door right next to it.

"Becks?"

"No questions," he says with a raise of his eyebrows and a devilish grin on his face. "Let's go."

Chapter 32

I narrow my eyes at Becks's back as he rattles the key in the door, unlocking the dead bolt of the tinted glass door at the office side of one of the buildings.

"Are you starting a new company?" I attempt a guess for the twentieth time in the past three minutes.

"Will you shush and be patient?" Becks drops his hands, leaving the keys in the lock, and turns to take my face in both of them before pressing a chaste kiss to my lips, which does the job easy enough.

I just bite my bottom lip and nod my head to try to hold back the next guess, which is already on my tongue.

Becks turns back to the door, and the click of the lock sliding open breaks through the night around us. The only other sound is the clicking of hooves as the horses shuffle their antsy feet. He ushers me into the darkened office, his hand placed on the small of my back to urge me forward. We clear another doorway when all of a sudden I'm hit with a tsunami of sound and fluorescent lights.

"Happy boob voyage!" The room of people erupts in a chorus as I stumble backward into Becks, staggered from the sheer shock of the surprise. It takes a second for me to process the scene in front of me.

We are in some sort of warehouse where blow-up inflatables are skirting the perimeter of the space—huge slides and bounce houses—and one in particular that sits in the middle of the room makes me laugh and shake my head. It's a huge blow-up boxing ring, complete with oversized inflatable gloves—in *pink*.

I laugh—my cheeks hurting from smiling so wide—but it's once I finish looking at the large scale of the room that I'm able to focus on the details. My heart swells so full of love that even though Becks's feet stamped my shadow out, it full on evaporates when I see everything in front of me.

Everyone that I could want to send me off is here: my parents, Rylee and Colton, Danny sans Maddie, Rylee's parents, Lexi's friends, colleagues from PRX, old college pals. . . . I'm stunned speechless at the sheer number of people standing here, all cheering and clapping at such an oxymoron of a party.

And all of them are wearing a bra somewhere, somehow on their person. Men have tie-dye bras on their heads, wrapped around their arms. Women have them over their clothing on their chest or wrapped around their waists so that the cups attempt to cover their butts.

I scan the crowd, unable to move as I take them all in, and then I meet Rylee's eyes. Hers are full of tears as she stands there completely motionless amidst everyone else moving about. We step toward each other instantly and pull each other into a hug. We cling to each other, words spoken through actions and understood from the pure test of time between us.

"I was so worried you'd be angry at me for telling everyone," she murmurs in my ears as we rock each other back and forth, "but I couldn't let you think you were doing this alone."

I pull back and look at my best friend, *my go-to girl*, and with tears filling my eyes, the smile comes so easily that I know this was meant to be. "Do you think I could ever be mad at you?" I bring my hands up to frame her face and wipe her tears away with my thumbs. "You'd never do something to hurt me."

I pull her into me for one more quick squeeze and swipe away my own tears, unexpectedly completely okay with this party because it's like a switch has been flipped in me all of a sudden. Between Becks over these past two weeks and Rylee and all of this love and support, I realize I feel like the old me again.

I finally got her back just when I need her the most.

"Now, quit crying." I tell her, "It's time to kiss these ta-tas good-bye in serious style!"

I hear her laugh as I release her only to be turned around by hands on my shoulders so that I face Colton. I burst out laughing when I find her tattooed bad boy with a lacy pink-and-black bra wrapped around his biceps.

"Colton! I think I want to keep that bra for when I get me some new tits," I say as he wraps me in his arms for a big bear hug.

The timbre of his chuckle fills my ear. "Sorry, Had, but Ry promised me she'll be wearing this later tonight. You get through this, and you and Ry are going on one hell of a shopping spree for bras, okay?"

I laugh at him as he releases me, but it fades off when I meet the intensity in his green eyes. "You've got this, Montgomery. And we've got you, okay?"

I clear the lump in my throat, the ever-stoic Colton Donavan showing just a tad of emotion to someone other than his wife. The notion touches me deeply, and I squeeze his biceps and mouth, *Thank you*, as I'm spun around in another direction.

I land squarely in the arms of my mother, who pulls me in and squeezes me so tight, I can't breathe, and my tears have nowhere else to go but to leak from my eyes. "I love you so much, my Haddie," she whispers through her own tears. "We're going to beat this. No question."

I nod my head, unable to speak from the emotion clogging my throat. We stare at each other for a moment when she looks down and notices my new necklace. "Wow, so beautiful," she says to me, and I can't help the smile that pulls at the corners of my mouth as I think of Lex and our jokes about Mom's damn necklaces.

For the next thirty minutes, I feel like I'm on a constant spin cycle, being pulled from one pair of arms and well-wishes to the next. My dad, then Danny, and so on.

My cheeks hurt from smiling, and my heart overflows with the love and support surrounding me. Love and support I thought I could do without but now realize how much I need it.

I hug an old friend from PRX when I turn around and come face-to-face with Becks, his arm around the shoulder of an older woman. When she looks up, there is no mistaking the resemblance between mother and son.

She's beautiful, with hair the same color as him, tall in stature and graceful in her movements. When Becks nods my way, she turns her face so her eyes meet mine, and the smile that spreads on her lips is so full of warmth and welcoming that the nerves I'd normally have meeting his family are nonexistent.

"Mrs. Daniels?" I ask, holding my hand out.

"Oh shush," she says, stepping forward and pulling me into her arms. "I do hugs, so get used to it." She squeezes me tight and keeps her hands on my shoulders when she steps back. "So nice to meet you, Haddie. She's so beautiful, Beckett," she says, looking over to her son with an approving smile, which makes him roll his eyes and me laugh at his discomfort.

"Nice to meet you too. Sorry it's in this fashion."

"Nonsense. It's Trisha, and don't you go apologizing to me!" She furrows her brow just like Becks does, and it warms my heart. "I'll let you go, but I wanted to come meet this girl my Becks here was telling me I had to make lasagna for. I know if he's sharing it, he must really like you." She pulls me in tight and hugs me again, her mouth close to my ear when she speaks. "It's okay to use my boy when you need strength. His back won't break if you do, but his heart just might break if you don't."

She presses a kiss to my cheek as she steps back again, her hands sliding down my arms to grab my hands. She squeezes them as I accept the advice she's just given me and realize how true it is.

"My Becks here is a good man. . . . I'm all for him ruining your lipstick, but if he ruins your mascara, you need to come let his mom know so I can put him back in his place."

"Oh, Jesus, mother!" Becks barks out, cheeks flushing, and it's rather adorable.

My grin spreads from ear to ear as I look at Trisha, her eyebrows raised to make sure that I've heard her request. I nod my head. "I will." I laugh out.

"Now, go be with your friends. My boy is going to walk me out because I just wanted to meet the girl I'm making dinner for once you feel up to it. So nice to meet you."

"You too."

Trisha starts to walk away, Becks already beginning to scold her, when she stops and turns to look at me. "You wouldn't happen to have a pair of pink flip-flops, would you?"

I look at her for a moment, my forehead scrunched up in confusion since she's thrown me for a loop. "Yes, several. Why?"

Trisha's grin spreads to megawatt proportions as Becks swears again. "Perfect. I just knew it!" she exclaims as he walks her toward the door. I can hear her voice chattering away excitedly the whole way there.

What the heck was that all about?

I turn around and take in the whole scene. My friends, my family, all of them are here to support me, and I feel truly blessed. I wander over to the table of food, only slightly aware that I have only so many hours left I can eat before my presurgery food cutoff time.

I grab an appetizer from the table, making small talk with everyone, and accept a cocktail when it's placed in my hand. When in Rome, right? I reach the end of the table and the laughter starts again when I see the cake. It's the torso of a woman, with a matching bra and panty set, but it's what's written on the abdomen of frosting that cracks me up. "Save your bumps, check for lumps."

"Funny, right?" Becks's voice is in my ear as his arms slide around my waist and pull me back into him.

I close my eyes and accept his warmth and the calm that comes with his touch. "Thank you," I whisper into the crook of his neck, my eyes squeezed close as I accept the risk he took throwing this party tonight.

"Well, Rylee helped a lot, so she deserves most of the credit, but we figured you were worth it," he teases, pressing a kiss to my temple.

"A lot worth it!" Rylee's voice is to my left. I turn, still in Becks's arms, to face her and belt out a laugh to find her with a trayful of shot glasses filled to the hilt with amber liquid. "If this toast was needed at any time in our lives, it's tonight," she says with a gleam in her eye, referring to our salute, which has stuck with us through college parties, bad boyfriends, and all the things life has thrown at us.

I step out of Becks's arms and help her place the tray on the table so nothing spills. When I turn to hand one to Becks, I notice that almost everyone in the room around us is double-fisting full shot glasses like the ones on the tray. I guess I was too absorbed in my boob voyage cake to notice.

Ry grabs a glass and hands me one. "You ready?"

I grin with a nod to her. "Ready as I'll ever be." And the look she gives me tells me that she knows I mean more than just slinging back shots.

"Okay, everyone! On the count of three. For my best friend, my sister from another mister . . . time to make cancer your bitch." The crowd around us hoots and hollers, me included as we all raise our first shot glass in the air. "One, two, three . . ."

"One for luck and one for courage!" The entire room erupts into a synchronized toast before falling silent as they toss back the first and then the second shot. Cheers erupt, followed by people swearing as the burn hits their throats.

And hell yes, it burns . . . but it also feels so good right now. All of this, all of them, because it means I'm alive. The thought causes more than my throat to burn as I blink back the tears that sting my eyes now as the entirety of the moment hits me.

I fall silent as I take it all in, my eyes watching everyone I love around me, and I don't realize I've zoned out until Becks removes the empty shot glasses from my hands. "Sorry," I tell him, startled at how lost in thought I was.

And I think he can see the emotion that's running rampant within me because he steps up and brushes a soft kiss to my lips. "I think it's time to step into the ring, Ms. Montgomery," he murmurs, trying to break me from my funk by turning our bodies toward the inflatable boxing ring. "You need to get a little practice in. . . . Hit me with your best shot."

"You're on, Country."

"I'm sure I can find one of those sexy ring girl outfits somewhere you can put on."

I punch him in the shoulder at the comment and shake my head.

"You're gonna have to hit me harder than that. You fight like a girl."

"*Exactly*. Let's hope so."

I hug Rylee for the bazillionth time, assure her I'll see her in the morning . . . well, later today, when I wake up from surgery, and shoo her and Colton out of the door of the warehouse.

I blow a breath out to collect myself and watch as Colton opens the door of the Range Rover for her before sliding in himself. Sammy puts the car in gear, and I follow the taillights out of the parking lot, empty at this god-awful hour of three in the morning.

I'm exhausted. Emotionally fulfilled but absolutely exhausted.

And I realize maybe this is exactly what Becks wanted. For me to be so tired that I couldn't worry about what's going to happen three hours from now because I was so busy being inundated with love.

How did he know this is exactly what I needed when I didn't even know it myself?

I shake my head, not sure how I deserve this man after everything I put him through, but resolved that whatever comes next, I'm not giving him up without a fight.

"You've got a nasty right hook, you know. . . ." His voice startles me. I didn't realize that Becks had walked into the office. I thought he was still gathering all of the cards and gifts that friends had brought.

He flicks the switch, bathing the office into darkness as I turn toward him. He steps into the room, a light from the warehouse at his back causing shadows to fall on his face, and I can't help but be brought back to a few weeks ago: He looked exactly the same the night of Rylee and Colton's wedding.

And look where that got us.

I just stare at him, so many words running through my mind but none of them is quite right to express the sheer emotion that I feel for him. I thought the cancer diagnosis was going to rock my world, and it did—but not nearly as much as the man before me has.

"You tired?" he asks when I don't respond to his comment.

"Yeah, but I'm just taking it all in. I can't put into words what tonight meant to me. I didn't think I wanted anyone to know, and yet the love I felt . . . I'm just speechless, so thank you."

He closes the few feet between us and reaches out to move a strand of hair off my face. "You know I'd do anything for you, right?"

The promise in his words and the look I can see in his shadowed eyes reinforces everything I feel about him. I lean forward and press my lips to his, the taste of him pushing back thoughts of where we're headed next because right now it's just Becks and I.

His hands slide up my torso, nerves humming to life from his touch, despite the fatigue. They move over to cup my breasts, causing bittersweet tears to sting my eyes as he leans down and brushes a reverent kiss on each of them through my shirt.

When he lifts his eyes back up to mine, I can see the emotion glistening there, can feel his love palpable and real as it reverberates in the space between us. "Sweet Haddie," he murmurs as he leans forward to brush those devastating lips of his against mine again, "I love you."

Every part of my being sighs at the words he doesn't need to say because he shows me so handily those feelings in everything he does for me. "I love you too." And when he leans back and looks in my eyes, I know he sees it reflected back at him.

He pulls me into his arms and just holds me tight. I memorize everything about him right now: the feeling of safety, the sense that everything is going to be okay. The little things I can hold on to later when I'm doubting my decisions for putting him through this. And then my mind recalls a lost promise.

"Hey, Country?"

"Mm-hmm?" he murmurs into the crown of my head.

"You said you'd do anything for me, right?"

"Yes," he answers, drawing the word out as he tries to figure out where I'm going with this.

I look up at him, sure there's a devilish smirk on my face. "You never fulfilled a certain three-day rule, you know."

He raises his eyebrows at me, working his tongue in his cheek. "Which one might that be?" He feigns innocence.

"Well, you did call me, so . . ." I trail my finger down the bare skin at his throat, my teeth working my bottom lip and my body on high alert as it waits in anticipation for what I know he won't deny me.

He looks over my shoulder at the wall behind me, his playful grin flashing his intent. "If you insist . . ." he groans at the same time he reaches out to me. Our hands and bodies collide in a frenzy of removing clothes and roaming mouths and unsated need.

"We have to be at the hospital soon," he murmurs as he lifts me up so that my legs are around his hips and my back is against the wall.

"Time is precious, Daniels. Waste it wisely."

Epilogue

1 year later

It's the same dream I've had on and off over the past year. I know it's a dream, but I can never seem to shake it or the harsh reality it throws in my face like a bucket of ice water.

The cemetery is quiet despite the sound of her calling to me, pleading to be found. I search endlessly, trying to find her, but know I'm not going to. Unless you count my warm fingertips against her name etched in cold granite, just like the love she scored into my heart.

It's an odd place, so peaceful yet so very cruel to rip away the ones you love. For her to be here this young after suffering so horribly is something I can't think about much. She fought the fight no doubt, but that right hook of hers just wasn't strong enough in the end.

I'm starting to run now, knowing she needs me to find her before it's too late. Just one more touch, one more glance, one last kiss, before she disappears forever. This is my favorite and most hated part of the dream because I want her to be there and I don't want her to. Such a no-win situation.

Fuck the person who said to love and lose is better than to not love at all.

How cruel is it to still love and know you'll never see them again except for in dreams.

I see her blond hair blowing in the breeze on the other side of the tree where she always sits to wait for me. Our one last rendezvous, touch, kiss . . . memory. I reach out to touch that golden hair of hers and—

Rex's bark pulls me from the dream just at the best part when I get to touch her. I groan out a curse, my body physically shaking from the realness of the reverie. No matter how many times I have it, the dream still rocks me to the core and causes me to think about what-ifs and what-could-have-beens.

My heart's pounding still as I squeeze my eyes shut to guard them from the blinding sun and my damn mother and her no-blinds-at-the-farmhouse policy. I reach out to the space beside me, and when I find it empty, I sit up immediately.

It's one thing to have the dream and believe the whole time I'm in its confines that it's real, but it's another to wake up and the immediate reminder how it's not real isn't in her spot. When I can't physically reach out and touch her to reaffirm that she's here and whole, the riot of emotions the dream causes doesn't fade as quickly.

I scrub my hands over my face, trying to scrape the dream from my memory. The constant reminder of how goddamn lucky I am. I shove up out of the bed, my mind wondering if my plans for later today are what's dredged the dream back up when I haven't had it for several weeks.

On my way to the hallway, I slide open the top dresser drawer and feel in there to make sure it's safe and sound. My hand connects with the sharp edges of the square container, and I breathe a bit easier, all the while my nerves hum.

I make my way into the bathroom, take care of business, and brush my teeth before shuffling down the hallway toward the first indulgence I plan on having this morning, coffee.

There will be many more indulgences today but of the noncaffeine variety.

I turn the corner into the kitchen and déjà vu of our first time here hits me. So many things have changed over the past year, but at the same time, so much has stayed the same.

She still steals my breath with her courage, her fiery spirit, her unyielding love, her beauty inside and out.

Haddie stands at the window, her athletic body, thinner now as she tries to gain back the muscle she's lost with treatment, haloed by the morning sunlight. Her hair is short, the regrowth finally long enough to be cut and styled for the first time last week. She was so excited by the fact, but I watch as her fingers play absently with it at the nape of her neck and know she's still unsure, regardless of how sexy she is, rocking the pixie cut.

I remember her laughter as I told her that, lucky me, I get to take a new woman to bed with me every couple months as the hairstyles change. I'll say anything to ease the lines of worry from her face.

The thought makes me smile as I watch her. We've been to hell and back in this past year—gone through more things than any new relationship should ever be tested with—but look at us. . . . We're stronger than ever.

She finally stopped pushing.

And started accepting I was in it for the long haul.

"Good morning," I murmur, my voice catching in my throat as the dream comes flooding back to me. She turns slowly to face me, tears streaming down her face in silence, cell phone clutched in her hand.

My heart drops through my stomach as my eyes flicker back and forth, hoping against hope what I fear isn't true. I brought her out here so that she'd be occupied instead of sitting at home and fretting endlessly about the results of the latest scans and tests. The typical four- to five-day wait being the hardest thing to endure in this whole process.

For her and me.

It's brutal, watching the one you love hope and try to remain positive after enduring rounds of chemo and now radiation to get their hopes dashed and spirit crushed when they're told the cancer is still there, still eating away at them bit by bit, day by day. It may have shrunk or not advanced, but it's still there.

It's hard to fight the uphill battle with renewed vigor each time you have to start it over.

I move to her, tears burning the back of my throat and my chest physically hurting as I watch her sob, so overwhelmed by emotion that she can't speak. I pull her smaller frame into my arms, careful not to squeeze her too hard against my chest since she's still sore from the first procedure she had last week to prepare her for possible reconstructive surgery.

"Becks." She says my name, but I just keep shushing her, trying to soothe her and accept the resignation that we're going to have to start the cycle all over again. Lose the hair she's just grown back.

"Becks!" The way she says my name this time pulls me from my thoughts and I look down as she leans back.

I take in the tears streaming down her face, but then I notice the smile spreading over those lips of hers. I force a swallow down my throat, afraid to hope that smile means what I think it means. My heart pounds and my head shakes back and forth as she nods her head up and down, answering the question in my eyes.

"Are you serious?"

Her smile is so wide now, the laughter bubbles up and the sound consumes me, overrides all of the fear and worry—her shadow I've carried on my shoulders over the past year—and tells them they have no place here anymore.

"It's gone," she says, her body vibrating with excitement, with life, with a future. "The scans are clear."

I hear a whoop and don't even realize it's my own voice as I lift her up gently and whirl her around in excitement. Then I try to process everything as I press my lips to hers over and over and find that I can't.

I can only focus on one thing right now, and that is how much I love and admire this woman in front of me. How I can't live without her.

We just went a full twelve rounds and finally got the knockout.

She starts giggling as I proceed to kiss her over and over, the only way I can speak right now after the heart attack I almost had, thinking the results were the opposite.

She pushes me away, trying to speak. "I just got the call before you came out. . . . I was processing it all. I couldn't speak. I'm sorry for scaring you."

"Oh, baby," I tell her, framing her face and lacing it with kisses, the taste of salt on my tongue from our tears of joy a welcome change.

And then my mind clicks.

"Hold on. I'll be right back!" I tell her as I bolt from the kitchen.

HADDIE

Disbelief owns my battered body right now, but it's the most welcome feeling in the world. I'm grateful for Becks giving me a moment so that I can try to process the unbelievable. So I can grasp that I beat this.

Holy fucking shit!

The adrenaline hits, and even though Rex is still barking outside to come in, I'm trembling so much, I lean against the wall and slide down to the floor.

I close my eyes momentarily, seeing Lexi's face when I

do, and I silently thank her for helping me. My dandelion sister, who used to blow wishes into the wind and hope one day one would come back for her.

Mine just came back. I got the more time I asked for.

My mind switches gears to try to remember more details of the doctor's call but don't remember much after *all clear* and *no evidence of disease remains*. I pinch the skin on my thighs, hoping it's not a dream because if it is, I don't want to wake up from it.

I need to call my parents and Rylee and Danny, but my hands are having trouble hitting the screen from their trembling. I'm trying again—my mind going five thousand miles an hour—when Becks returns.

I let my phone drop in my lap as I try to brush the tears from my face, knowing it's going to do no good. *I earned these tears.* When I glance up to him standing in front of me, he has this look on his face, eyes intense and full of love, that makes my breath falter.

"What?" I ask him, suddenly self-conscious under his scrutiny of my short hair and bandaged chest so that I start to cross my arms over it.

"Uh-uh," he says as he lowers himself to the ground beside me and takes my hands in his so that I can't cover myself up. "Don't you dare cover up that beautiful body of yours."

I roll my eyes and get that lift of his eyebrows in reprimand, which causes me to smirk. He leans forward and brushes a soft kiss to my lips before settling on the floor next to me. He blows out a breath before nodding his head in complete acceptance—of what, I have no idea.

"Today I had planned for your family and Ry and Colton to head on out here and have a barbecue. I had grand plans of entertainment and fun to keep your mind occupied and free of *the shadow*." I smile at him and his thoughtfulness. He's so damn good to me. "I had plans for a bonfire down by the pond. Friends, family . . . surround you with love so that I could do something. . . . I had it all planned perfectly." He looks down at our joined hands and laughs softly. "But as we've both learned over the past year, sometimes fate has different plans for us."

I snort at the truth in that statement. At how cancer tested me. At how HaLex should have failed with my preoccupation with my treatment, but how instead Danny stepped forward and offered to help, and now it's thriving and in demand. At how I broke my own rules and tied those strings I didn't want into double knots around the heart of the man in front of me.

"That's so sweet of you. We can still have them over, have a celebration instead," I tell him, mistaking his fixation on our joined hands as one of disappointment.

He slowly lifts his eyes to meet mine, and that soft smile on his lips owns my heart like I never could have imagined before. "What's the one thing we've learned through all of this?" he asks me.

"That cancer sucks ass."

He throws his head back and laughs loudly, the sound so welcome to my ears when he's been so worried himself over the scans. "Well, that's true, but that wasn't what I was going for."

"Um . . . that wall sex is definitely hot." I say, my fingers walking their way up his bare chest, my thoughts turning to how I want to be festive with Becks.

"You are incorrigible!" he says, grabbing my wrists and holding them in his grip, humor in his voice and his pants beginning to tent. *At least I know it's a possibility.* "But very right again. And maybe if you can be serious for a second, we can have some very hot wall sex in a few minutes." He raises an eyebrow at me and mixes it with that cocksure smirk of his, and I know he's just thrown down a challenge that I will willingly accept.

"So I answer the question right, I get wall sex?" He nods,

causing my libido to stir to life and my mind to scatter, trying to figure out what the answer could be.

"Hm. Let's see. . . . You like rules."

"And you like to break them, you smart-ass."

"I need help, Mr. Daniels, because you mentioned wall sex, and now all I can think about is you pinning me over there"—I point to the wall behind him—"and you sliding your rock-hard—"

"You're distracting me." He laughs as he leans forward and presses another kiss to my lips, his tongue lingering with mine for just a moment before he leans back, the gravity in his eyes again. "What's the one rule we've lived by this whole year? Our motto?"

I angle my head to look at him and wonder how Lex's motto that we've adopted as ours holds any relevance when it seems we have all the time in the world now.

"Time is precious. Waste it wisely," I tell him, a ghost of a smile on my lips at how that advice in the voice mail she left me—that I still listen to—has come full circle in this moment.

"Exactly," Becks murmurs. "If that's our motto, then we need to wise up here. . . . I don't want to waste another precious moment without you as mine, Haddie Montgomery."

I begin to tell him he already has me when it hits me. My hands begin to tremble again, but this time for a very different reason. I watch as he reaches into his pants pocket and produces a black box, which I never even noticed because I was so stunned at my good news. I suck in a breath, his words and the sight causing my mind to leap ahead to what he's about to do.

And I'm not sure where I want to look more: at the box as it's opened or at his eyes as he asks me. I look up because I'm only going to get one chance to catch this moment—this look in his eyes—and I'll have forever to look at the ring on my finger.

I laugh nervously, realizing he'd better be asking me to marry him because I just mentally agreed.

"We've been to hell and back, and I love you more for every single step of that journey. I only hope you feel half of what I feel when you look at me, when you love me, or when you laugh with me. The world stops for me—time stands still—when I put my arms around you. I love that feeling, and I love that I've only ever felt that way with you. I want to be the first thing you touch in the morning and the last thing you taste at night before you dream. I want to spend the rest of my life with you, Had. . . . I want to stop wasting that precious time. Will you marry me?"

I launch myself at Becks with a shriek, our bodies colliding and falling backward as I rain kisses all over his face, repeating how much I love him again and again. Somewhere in my barrage of expressed love, he manages to hold my hand still enough to slide the oval-shaped diamond solitaire onto my ring finger.

"Is that a yes?" he laughs out as I straddle his hips and lean down to kiss him again, my lips on his. Smile, kiss, smile, repeat cycle.

"Yes!" I cry out at him, my heart so full of love and the future that all I can think about is that this gorgeous, caring, wonderful, sexy man beneath me really wants feisty, tell-it-like-it-is me to be his.

My city to his country.

I lean forward and press my lips to his again, slipping my tongue between them, my hips grinding against his out of pure physical response. He groans at the sensation, and I start laughing.

Wall sex *is* hot.

But just-got-engaged-sex-on-the-kitchen-floor is even better.

Why waste time maneuvering to the wall? It's a precious thing after all.

You saw how they fell in love.
Now see how Becks and Haddie first met.
Turn the page for a bonus scene!

The bass of the club's music hits hard as I scan the nearly naked women surrounding us—every single one of them ripe for the picking. A bat of fake lashes. An accidental lean over the bar, tits on display, and painted lips offering up what is literally and figuratively on the table.

So why am I not finding some hot piece, offering to take her up to our room? Shit, I could use a little release after the stress of a long week.

It's Wood's fault. That's my go-to answer. *It's always his fault.* And hell if I'll tell my best friend he was right when he said, "She's got a hot friend."

Hot friend, *my ass*. Haddie Montgomery's more like molten fucking lava.

I sweep my eyes across the crowded dance floor and try to move past her, but it's no goddamn use. *Don't kid yourself, Daniels. You've been looking at her all night.* I toss back the rest of my drink, but my damn eyes remain fixed as she throws her arms up in the air and swivels her hips. Those long, shapely legs move to the beat, and hell if I can't get the thought of them and those sexy-as-fuck heels wrapped around me somehow, someway, out of my damn head.

I avert my gaze, try to distract myself with one of the

many easy targets in the club, but no one else calls to every part of me like Haddie does. And of course my eyes shift back to the floor just in time to see her dress sneak up some. Every toned inch of those thighs is on display as she grinds her hips to the beat. I groan. And I don't even care that I do, because hell if a sane, red-blooded American male would look away from that perfection.

"Hey," I hear to my right as Colton's hand, which is holding my fresh drink, bumps against my arm.

"Thanks," I say, forcing myself to pull my eyes from the sight of her and focus on the man who's like a second brother to me. But when I meet his eyes, they're studying me, amusement mixed with confusion. *Here we go again.* I hate when Colton gets this damn look. "What? What the fuck is that look for?"

"Seriously? You have the two-point-five look on your face, dude," he says, taking a sip of his beer and shaking his head as if he's ashamed.

"Two point five?" I sputter, completely shocked that he of all people would say that after the revelation he dropped on me earlier. The one where he admitted that he, the man who's the king of condoms, is sliding skin on skin with his girlfriend, Rylee. Taking that giant leap of trust for the first time ever to bareback with a woman. The confession still staggers me even after more than a few cocktails.

And he's accusing me of the two-point-five look? I don't think he has any room to throw stones in the fucking glass house he built. "Two point five?" I repeat. "This coming from the barebacking cowboy himself? *Whatever.* You have no idea what you're talking about. Have another."

"Which one is she?" he asks, slinging an arm over my shoulder and pointing toward the dance floor.

"No one," I say, trying to deflect him. "Just a whole lot of flesh on display, and fuck if it's not something to look at while I get nice and drunk. I've got an asshole for a boss, so this buzz," I say with a laugh when he tightens his arm around my neck in a headlock for my dig at him, "and that woman over there are—"

"Hot damn!" he says, catching my slip of the tongue. And hell if I wouldn't want to be slipping my tongue into her, but shit if I didn't just give ammunition to the king of antagonization to start making his own digs in retaliation. He slaps my back harder than necessary. "I knew just by the sappy-ass look on your face you were looking at some woman on the floor, imagining wedded bliss, and the two-point-five kids you're going to have with her."

"Shut up, dude. You are so far from—"

"So which one is she?" he goads, and I know he's only just getting started. He'll keep at it until I give him something to be smug about.

I look back out to the floor with him scrutinizing my every damn move—trying to figure out which woman has caught the eye of a picky son of a bitch like me. And when I look, a part of me is relieved that Haddie and her best friend, Colton's date, Rylee, are no longer on the dance floor . . . and then another part of me is pissed because I sure as hell was enjoying the show.

"Hot blonde, red dress, two o'clock?" Colton asks, drawing my eyes to the woman on the floor, shaking her shit like she should be on a pole. She's definitely hot, all the right curves in all the right places, but nah, not my thing. Owning your sexuality is one thing, but putting it on display? I'll pass.

I look over at Colton and roll my eyes. "Seriously?"

"With those moves?" he says, eyes flicking back out to her. *"Damn."*

"Dude, I'm all for moves like that in bed," I say, causing him to snort out that laugh of his that makes me smile, regardless of the mood I'm in, "but if I want to screw a mannequin, I'll go to Macy's. Besides, isn't eating out of plastic hazardous to your health? BPA or some shit like that?"

He throws his head back and laughs while I take a long

drink of my Merit Rum and Coke. And of course I feel bad for talking shit about the unsuspecting woman.

"BPA sounds like an STD to me, but fuck, dude, live on the wild side." He bumps my shoulder with his. "One taste won't kill you."

"This coming from Mr. Discriminating himself? I assure you, it most definitely is not all the same."

"Yeah, you got me there." He shivers in mock disgust, and I can't help but laugh. He looks back out toward the dance area and nods his chin toward where Red Dress is still bumping and grinding. "Not even just for the night?"

"Nah, you know me. Not my thing."

I hear their laughter float over the music before I see them, grateful for the interruption. I lean my elbow on the railing and turn to watch them walk up, pretending not to care. Colton turns too when he hears Rylee, so I'm able to watch their approach without him noticing. I take in Haddie's more than handful-sized tits, which bounce a bit with that walk of hers. The combination of blond hair against her tanned skin begs me to run my eyes down the length of her svelte figure. When my gaze makes its way back up, her mouth is spread wide in a grin, and fuck if I don't want something else spread wide on her with me in between them. I get lost in the thought, and when I refocus, she is staring right back at me, lips pursed, eyes curious.

"Yes?" Those chocolate-colored eyes of hers hold mine. Tempt me. Dare me. Question me.

"Sorry." I shake my head, a sheepish smile in place. "I was just thinking." *Smooth, Becks.* Brilliant response to why you were staring at her like you want to eat her for dinner. Shit, might as well be breakfast since I'm sure it'd be an all-night affair, with her body sure as hell being the main course.

"Thinking?" She asks as she reaches out and takes my drink from my hand and tips it up to me, silently asking if it's okay. I nod my head, and she lifts it to her lips, taking a sip before handing it back to me. "Thanks. Don't you know, Country, that you're in a club, in Vegas of all places, so thinking's not allowed?" She sidles up next to me, her body brushing against mine and snapping my every nerve to attention.

"Country?" Where the hell did that nickname come from?

"Yeah," she says with a smirk before shaking her head to get her hair out of her face. "Laid-back. Polite. Good guy. Slow and steady wins the race." She raises her eyebrows, challenging me to argue with her assessment.

And fuck if she's not right, so why am I sensing that *Country* is a bad thing for her? And why the hell do I care? "Nothing's wrong with slow and steady," I tell her, enjoying how she angles her head to the side and just watches me. "A man shouldn't be faulted for drawing things out just to make sure the endgame is that much sweeter."

And I feel like I've scored a touchdown when I see her eyes widen, take note of the quick intake of breath. Interesting. Playing field seems to be wide-open. Good thing I'm a patient man because this woman most definitely does not sit on the sidelines.

"Sweet is good," she leans in and says in my ear, her words a whisper, "but some girls like a little spice added in." She leans back and flashes me a smart-ass grin, tossing the ball back in my court. Goddamn if it's not hot that her comebacks are as witty as her tits are perfect.

"City, I assure you I have talents that can't be put on a résumé." I take a drink and raise an eyebrow, failing miserably to hide my smirk, "Besides, it's not the sugar or the spice that matters but rather the man who's mixing it."

We stare at each other for a moment in a silent standoff, as we try to figure out what the other is saying. Is there interest here? Would it be worth it? Damn, who cares? Because she most definitely would be one helluva wild ride.

A slow, knowing smirk curls up one corner of her mouth.

The music changes and becomes more seductive as she shakes her head ever so subtly. *"City?"* she asks, and then runs her tongue over her top lip as her eyes taunt me.

My mind goes blank as I focus on her mouth. Shit, I need to play this safe. For all I know, this is just how she is with everyone, a little flirty and a whole lot of fun. After all, it can't get more complicated than going after the best friend of my best friend's girl.

I look out at the floor again, bodies grinding, connections being made even if only for the night, before I look back at Haddie, her eyebrows raised and her body so on fire that my dick begs to fly full staff. It's probably just me. And the alcohol. And the influence of the club around me.

It's probably nothing.

But then again, *damn.*

Just damn.

I can't resist. If I can't reach out and touch, I might as well leave a mark with my words. Let her think about how a laid back country boy might not be such a bad thing after all. "Yeah, City," I repeat. "Classy, nonstop, and always wanting to be in the thick of it all." I take a drink, my eyes locked on hers while she watches, contemplating what I've said.

"The thick of it, huh?" She takes my drink from my hand again and smirks as she sucks ever so slowly from the straw.

And once again, my eyes are drawn to those lip-glossed lips of hers and notice how they are drawing on my straw. *So that's why they put straws in men's drinks.* I have a whole new appreciation for those annoying little fuckers now. I watch her tongue play with it momentarily and realize that part of the reason she's so damn sexy is because she's not purposely trying to be.

Something catches her eye, and I follow her head as she turns to watch Colton lead Rylee up the stairs toward the mezzanine. At least I don't have to worry about him sticking his nose in where it doesn't belong now. When I look back toward Haddie, she's moved toward me, her face closer to mine. I can smell the scent of the alcohol from my drink on her breath, and hell if I can understand why that makes me want her that much more.

"Yep. Always wanting to be in the middle of the action," I say, lifting the straw out of my drink and taking a sip.

Haddie twists her lips until the smirk breaks its way through. "Action's always good. Being in the middle of it's even better." She arches an eyebrow at me as I try to figure out what her next words are going to be but remain silent. It's time to let her wonder what I'm thinking for a change. I hold her gaze, the swirling lights overhead changing color and reflecting in her blond hair. "And I think I'm wanting some right now."

I force a swallow, those taunting yet innocent words of hers causing a visceral reaction that I try to ignore. "What kind of action are you looking for?" There. Let her figure out if I'm flirting or if that's just how I am, because I can't tell shit with her. And fuck, I can always figure everyone out. So what's so different about her?

She doesn't answer. Instead, she turns and looks over her shoulder. "You coming?"

And fuck . . . there are so many ways my mind answers that question that I groan. I swallow over the ache that our flirting and her damn, fine ass in perfect view creates. "You know what they say?"

"What?" she asks, stopping momentarily, "Every good man's place is behind a woman?"

I chuckle. That most definitely was not where I was going with this conversation, but there she goes again, wanting me to take the bait. "The only reason for a man to be behind a woman is because he's checking out her very fine ass." And hell if that's not the truth right now.

She licks her lips and I have a hard time looking away from her tongue as it darts out and then back in. "Haven't had any complaints so far, Country," she says with a shake of her head, her hair swaying all the way down her back. "And ... uh ... there are many more places I'd prefer a man to be," she says with a wink before turning and walking into the crowd, without even checking to see if I'm following.

Yeah, on top of you. Or under. Or . . . Shit, my mind reels with the possibilities.

She may think I'm slow and steady but hell if I'm stupid.

Time to dance.

sigh as I pull open the door, wanting to melt into the cool air-conditioning of the Fine Arts offices. The southern California heat mixed with the second week of school has really done a number on me. I'm tired from a late night hanging out with Layla—my fault but still aggravating nonetheless—and having to deal with some dipshit undergrads in my teaching assistant session I just came from isn't helping matters.

I don't mind if a student doesn't get something. I have no problem helping them so that they do. But when the students are too busy chasing skirts and worrying about who the Trojans take on this weekend to listen, it's not my problem they received bad marks on their first pop quiz.

And it's not helping my mood that I need to get laid something fierce. There's nothing worse than a woman in need of a good orgasm.

Or two.

Or three.

I drop my backpack on the counter with a shake of my head and a mental note to rectify the situation with the first willing candidate who meets my discriminating standards. Then again I'm on the verge of being desperate enough, I might throw them out the window for the right mistake.

I start rifling through the bazillion pieces of paper stuffed in my mailbox—such is the life of a graduate student in the Cinematic Arts. Shit, save a tree people. Use e-mail. I start filtering through them, tossing almost all of them into the recycle bin. I automatically toss the ones about elective seminars without even reading them because at the beginning of a semester the last thing I have time for is something that does nothing to further help me write my thesis.

"Quinlan! Just the person I wanted to see!"

As I turn around to face my graduate adviser, the smile comes naturally to my face since I'm one of the select few fortunate enough to be under her tutelage. "Hi, Dr. Stevens." She gives me a stern look, which causes me to laugh at the formality of my greeting, so I cave to her oft-repeated request and correct myself. "Hi, Carla."

"Better." She laughs the word out. "Now I'm not looking for my husband when you say that," she says, referring to her spouse, who is a cardiologist.

I nod my head in agreement. "Why do I have the feeling that I'm not going to like the fact that you wanted to see me?"

Please, God, don't let her ask me to add something else to my already overflowing plate of obligations, deadlines, and drafts I need to write.

"I'm kind of in a jam and I need your help." She scrunches up her nose like she knows I'm not going to be too happy with what she's going to say next. "Like, 'I'll give you a three-week extension on your first draft due date' kind of help."

I worry my bottom lip between my teeth and know that no matter what she asks, I'll say yes. She's my mentor, for God's sake. Anything not to disappoint her. "Okay?" I draw the word out into a question, fearful and curious all at the same time.

"Well, Dr. Elliot has a seminar under his department that is starting . . ." She looks down at her watch and winces. "Well, it started about five minutes ago, actually. Anyway, he's asked if I can help him. His TA, Cali, was supposed to do it, but she had a last-minute schedule change to accommodate one of her professors . . . and all of his other teaching assistants have classes right now. . . ."

I bite back the urge to make a smart-ass comment about how Cali's conflict is the need to flirt ridiculously with the professor she has the hots for, university protocol be damned. Instead I look at Carla and blow out an audible breath, sure that my expression reflects my displeasure.

I'm usually on top of all of the department's goings-on, but my last-minute trip to the Sonoma race to watch Colton mixed with playing bestie to Layla's unexpected breakup and the usual first-month-of-school discord has left me in the dark about course specifics. It had better be a damn good class if I'm going to have to be stuck sitting through it.

"You know I'm agreeing to this because I'm already behind on my draft and need those weeks, right?"

"Exactly!" She smirks. "I don't have that PhD behind my name because I'm unintelligent."

"That's low." I just shake my head and smirk as I reach over to grab my bag. "So give me the details."

"You're a lifesaver!" She reaches out and pats my shoulder before handing me a folder full of papers. "So the seminar is on sex, drugs, and rock and roll, in a manner of speaking." She quirks her eyebrows up, eyes asking if I'm okay with that.

Like I have a choice. I can just imagine some stiff professor giving a seminar about something so completely foreign to him. Now I'm going to have to waste my time mollycoddling someone when I have so many other things that would be a better use of my time. Sounds like a real *barn burner*.

"Who's teaching it?" I ask, my tone reflecting the cynicism I feel over the contradiction between teacher and subject.

"A guest lecturer. I forget his name, but he's a big deal in rock and roll." She rolls her eyes. Her musical taste includes only classical music and jazz. "Oh and he's cute," she says with a smile, and then she cuts me off before I can ask her any more details. "Now, shoo. He's probably mangling the sound system as we speak. Microphone on upside down or something. Class is in the GFA building, room sixty-nine."

Mentally I roll my eyes at the room number, thinking how something else that number represents is a much better way to occupy my time than listening to a monotone oration.

I shake my head one more time and sling my bag over my shoulder. "Thank you, Quinlan," she says in a saccharine-sweet tone that makes me laugh.

"Just so you know, I'm cursing you right now," I say over my shoulder as I open the door and begin the journey across campus.

I'm winded, hotter than hell, and cussing out Carla even more by the time I reach the closed door of the lecture hall. I pull open the door and step into the mini-reception-type area. The doors to the actual theater of seating are open, so I hear laughter from the students inside when I walk in.

Two coeds exit the bathroom on the other side of the atrium, both way overdressed for students attending a lecture, and one is applying lipstick while the other is giggling uncontrollably. They walk past me, and I hear hushed comments about how they "just had to see for themselves" if he's as hot in person and "damn security for kicking them out" before they push through the doors I've just entered

My curiosity is now definitely piqued. Who the hell is the guest lecturer if there is security here?

Maybe it's one of Dad's friends. Stranger things have happened.

"So you see, it was the Grammys. . . . It's not like you can say no to him when he just won album of the year and asks you to hang out. Little did I know," the male voice says in a low tenor that's almost a contradiction: smooth like velvet but with a rasp that pulls at my libido and makes me think of bedroom murmurs and hot sex, "that I'd go with him and walk into a private club where everything is laid out like candy—drugs, women, record producers. He turned and looked at me and said, 'Welcome to Hollywood, son.' Shit, I looked at Vince here and thought, Is this what I have to do to make it here? Play this game. Or can I do this the old-fashioned way? And I don't mean sleep my way to the top, either."

The room erupts into laughter with a few whistles as I clear the doorway. I recognize him immediately. He may be on the stage at a distance, but his face, his presence, is unmistakable. I've seen it gracing tabloids, TMZ, *Rolling Stone*—you name it, and he's been on it.

He's Hawkin Play, front man and lead singer of the highly popular rock band Bent.

And according to his most recent press, a man on a path to drug-fueled destruction. So that exaggeration most likely means he was caught in possession of some drugs.

Why in the hell is he here, then?

I walk farther into the auditorium and falter at the top of the steps because just as my ears are attuned to his voice, my body reacts immediately to the overpowering sight of him.

And I sure as hell don't want it to.

I tell myself it's just because I need some action. That my battery-operated boyfriend is getting old and the visceral reaction of my racing pulse or the catch in my breath is just from my dry spell. Well, not really a complete dry spell, per se, but rather a lack of toe-curling, mind-numbing, knock-you-on-your-ass sex, which I'm not able to find lately.

Don't even think about it. He may be hot, but shit, I grew up with Colton, the ultimate player, so this girl knows what a player sounds and acts like. And from everything I've seen splashed across headlines and social media, Hawkin plays the part to perfection.

But the notion that just like the drug rumors blasted across the magazines, him seeming like a player could be manufactured just as easily lingers in my subconscious. I stare at him again as the class laughs, his ease in front of a large crowd completely obvious, and I immediately wonder if I had a chance with him if I'd take it.

My head says to stop thinking thoughts like that, things that are never going to happen, while my body is telling my legs to *open wide*.

I force myself away from thinking such ludicrous thoughts and focus instead on finding an open seat in the room packed full of coeds. I begin walking slowly down the aisles, glancing back and forth to try to find an open seat, but there's not a single one to be found.

I glance forward to see a beefy guy walking toward me with an irritated expression on his face. It immediately hits me that I have nothing to prove I should be in this class, no paper, nothing to show to the security that appears to be bearing down on me that I'm not a fan girl and have a legitimate reason for attending the lecture. Well, maybe they'll kick me out and then he won't have a TA for the day.

Just one less class I'll have to sit through.

He approaches me and reaches out a very muscular arm toward me. "Course paperwork?" he asks in a hushed whisper, trying to not disrupt whatever Mr. Rock Star at the front of the class is babbling on and on about.

I take in a deep breath, trying to figure how I'm going to play this. What I really want to do and what I know is right are two different things, so I suck it up and take the higher road.

Reluctantly.

"I don't have anything," I whisper back. "But I'm the TA for the course."

"Sure you are." He chuckles with a roll of his eyes. "TA doesn't stand for 'tits and ass,' honey."

I clench my jaw, reining in my frustration as we begin to draw the attention of those around us. "I just came from the department offices. I don't have—"

"Is there a problem, Axe?" his liquid sex of a voice booms across the room, causing all of the heads in the room to whip over toward us on the stairway.

Axe, I presume, turns his body to look back at Hawkin, which opens up his line of sight to see me.

"No problem," Axe says, and before he can say anything else, Hawke speaks again.

"So nice of you to show up on time." Sarcasm drips from his voice, and my eyes snap up to meet his despite the distance between us.

And I swear I hate everything about myself right now because I feel a jolt to my system and a quick bang of lust between my thighs as our eyes connect, and that slow "I'm a God. You Can Bow Before Me" smile slowly curls up one side of his mouth.

And damn it to hell if that doesn't make him look even sexier.

But good looks sure as hell don't make him any less of an asshole.

My own lips pull into a tight, scowling grimace, thoughts firing, but the damn words don't come because I'm still momentarily frozen by whatever just ricocheted between us.

"Well, at least you're quiet, huh? Not one to disrupt unless you count arguing with Axe on the stairs."

How did I know he was going to be a prick? "I wasn't arguing. I'm not a—"

"Look," he says, cutting me off. "There's one seat left, and it's right here." He points to a front row seat right in front of the lectern when a man hurriedly stands and vacates it. I watch the occupant stroll to the side of the room and turn to lean his back against the wall, arms crossed, grin wide, as all the while he shakes his head at Hawkin like they have a private joke between them.

He seems vaguely familiar but I don't get a chance to figure it out because Hawkin speaks to me again. "C'mon now. I don't bite. . . . Right, guys?" he says to the rest of the lecture hall, and the audience erupts in a cacophony of hoots and hollers, egging me on to go take the seat.

I also hear a few offers from the females that they'll take the seat if I don't.

I'm sure they would. Particularly a seat that's astride his hips if my hunch is right.

"Please, take your time. We like waiting." His voice floats through the room but grates on my nerves.

I grit my teeth as I move reluctantly, my anger escalating with each step I descend toward the front of the room. As much as I don't want to be here dealing with the likes of a cocky asshole like him, my graduate career does have requirements, and I really don't think pissing off what I have a feeling will be one of the most popular lecturers of the year is the brightest idea.

But hell if I don't want to tell him to kiss my ass with that smart mouth of his while I stride up the steps toward the exit and flip him the bird instead.

But my degree is more important, so I swallow my pride and my anger, even though I'd much rather verbalize it as I reach the front row. I keep my eyes fastened to the honey color of his gaze, refusing to let him think he's gotten the upper hand, despite me following his directive and taking the seat he so *graciously* offered.

I reach the seat and stop before I sit down and stand my ground, my eyebrows arched and eyes telling him everything my lips can't. He meets them challenge for challenge while all the while those lips of his smirk and taunt me.

I force my eyes to remain forward, not to wander and take in the whole of him because I don't want to see how sexy-hot he is face-to-face; don't want to notice his cologne, which is a mixture of fresh air and outdoors; don't want to feel my cheeks flush because I know my nipples just hardened and I'm quite sure they're more than obvious through the thin layer of my bra's lace and my T-shirt's cotton.

After a moment, when I know I have no point I can really make in front of several hundred students, I lower my eyes and take my seat. But instead of continuing on right away, he stands in front of me a few seconds more, making sure I know who has won this ridiculous little show of control between us.

And of course as he stands in front of me with his hips right at my eye level, I can't help the two thoughts colliding: the one of him being in control with the one of just how well his worn denim jeans are filled out behind that button fly of his.

I immediately chastise myself. Tell myself that it's my sex-deprived brain—well, more like other deprived body parts—that is directing my thoughts like a nympho's. And that alone fuels my dislike of Hawkin even more because I should be focused on being pissed off at him rather than wondering about how he performs in *other ways* . . . off the stage.

LOVE
ROMANCE
NOVELS?

For news on all your favorite romance authors,
sneak peeks into the newest releases, book
giveaways, and much more—

"Like" Love Always on Facebook!
f LoveAlwaysBooks